LOW
LAKE

A gripping crime mystery full of dark secrets

GRETTA
MULROONEY

JOFFE
BOOKS

Published 2018 by Joffe Books, London.

www.joffebooks.com

© Gretta Mulrooney

ISBN 978-1-78931-006-1

For Anthea.

PROLOGUE

Two Years Ago

It was a lovely spot, calm and peaceful. The lake water stirred with a hint of evening breeze and the little boat rocked gently by the jetty. In the clear sky, the moon hung full and creamy. It looked close enough to touch. It was like a scene in a painting. She found herself humming a childhood rhyme.

I see the moon
And the moon sees me.
God bless the moon
And God bless me.

The trees were tall and heavy with leaves. There were so many greens in the English countryside, so many subtle shades. London had its pockets of green, but they were always dusty and tired-looking from exhaust fumes. Especially now, in summer.

This was the real thing. You couldn't hear any traffic, or even planes overhead. Money might not buy you love or happiness but it certainly bought peace and quiet.

Privacy, too. You could listen to your own thoughts, hear the birds settling for the night, see the stars appearing.

She hadn't meant to lose her temper. Where had that flash of anger come from? It happened sometimes, like a firework igniting in her head. She shouldn't have had a drink and a joint at lunchtime — the combination often made her aggressive. She'd been looking forward to this evening so much, and she didn't want to spoil things. Life was changing, improving. New horizons were opening.

She'd known enough nights that were bitter, dark and miserable. This one was full of promise.

She felt warm and serene now, and full of anticipation. She was aware of her own breathing and the scents of the evening. The grass was soft and springy underfoot. An owl hooted, a haunting, faraway call. A lamp shone golden through the window of the summerhouse. She had a sense of euphoria, a delicious lightness in her limbs. For a brief moment, she relaxed into the feeling, enjoying it. Then she dug her nails into her palms. She knew what was coming. She turned to alert her companion, but when she opened her mouth no sound came out.

Lights were sparking on the lake — red, orange and pale blue, like a jagged rainbow reflected on the water. They were beautiful and terrible. A warning.

They were the last lights she saw before she staggered forwards.

The cool water welcomed her in, endless dark swooped down and her eyes closed forever.

CHAPTER 1

The young woman was lying face down in the water. She wore jeans and a red vest, printed with the slogan ARCHAEOLOGISTS DO IT IN TRENCHES.

The sun lit her in a faint lemony glow, and her long, slender body, just covered by the water, twisted slightly. Her black hair flowed outwards, like water weed. Her image had been decorated with a frame of pink hearts and silver stars. Her name was Kim Woodville and she had drowned two years ago. Tyrone Swift studied the photo and handed the phone back to Jack North.

'How did you come by this?'

'Ben Ramsay, my cousin, took it. He found Kim. He added those hearts and stars. Typical of Ben — he's a bit childish. I'm the only person he shared the photo with. Nobody else knows about it. Ben watches loads of crime series on TV and he thought he should capture the scene.'

'It's a strange thing to do.' Though Swift knew people used their phones on all kinds of occasions nowadays. When he'd attended the funeral of Thomas Maddox, a young man who had died during his last investigation, he'd been disconcerted to see a couple of Thomas's friends taking photos of the coffin.

'I know. That's why I told Ben not to tell anyone else he took it. I thought the police might object. Ben's sort of . . . well, different. Immature. He can act oddly. I feel peculiar about showing it to you but I thought it might help you. I've kept it because it makes me feel that in some way I'm sharing Kim's last moments. I was hundreds of miles away from her at the time. Sometimes I look at it and try to comfort her. Stupid, I know.'

People tried to console themselves over a death in all kinds of ways. Swift supposed that North's murmurings to a photo were no different to visiting a grave and placing flowers or mementos. He'd known families of victims who'd created little shrines, gone on pilgrimages, raised money for good causes. All of these things helped to heal the heart. Or at least, stop it hurting so much.

North was gazing at the photo, his eyes moist. His flatmate, Bella Reynolds, had emailed Swift at his website, *swiftinvestigations.com*, a couple of days previously:

Hallo Ty,

Remember me from uni? Hope so! Long time no see/hear. I read that you're a private investigator now. I'm flat-sharing with a guy called Jack North and he'd like to talk to you about looking into something. It would be good to catch up too. Could you contact me? I live in Strawberry Hill these days.

Hope all is well with you. Where do the years go?

Talk soon, Bella.

Bella Reynolds. Long bright copper curly hair flowing from a centre parting, freckles, light brown skin, a gurgling laugh. Very tactile. He recalled her telling him that she got her unusual mixture of red hair and skin colour from her Scottish mother and Trinidadian father. He and Bella had been at Warwick University together, although she'd been a year below him. They'd met in the student union bar and had had a brief liaison one autumn term. He'd been drinking too much at the time, troubled by life and carried away by easy access to cheap alcohol. Those months were hazy. He'd liked Bella's passion and the way she shook her hair back when she danced, but once they staggered out of bed they couldn't find much to talk about. The relationship had fizzled out over the Christmas break. He couldn't recall what she'd been studying. He did remember that she'd been keen on a disgusting cocktail called Brain Haemorrhage. It was so called because it contained Irish cream in peach schnapps that curdled and floated in the glass, resembling brains. The memory made him shudder.

Swift had come to the flat in Strawberry Hill to find out what Jack North wanted. When North walked into the living room, Swift thought a child had entered — a child dressed in chinos and a suit jacket. Then he realised that the man had dwarfism. After a while Bella had come in to join them, carrying coffee. She sat beside North on the sofa, plumping a cushion. She looked almost unchanged from the woman Swift had known at Warwick, except that her hair was now a short halo of soft curls and her teeth were startlingly white. Jack North's red hair was almost exactly the same shade as Bella's.

Bella touched North's head, then her own. 'We're a matching pair of Belisha beacons.'

Swift laughed. 'You'd be useful in the dark.'

Bella poured coffee and handed one to him. 'You went into the Met on their graduate entry scheme, didn't you?'

'That's right. After that I worked with Interpol and then I decided to set up my own investigation agency.'

'I looked you up because I knew you'd joined the police. That's when I saw that you do private investigations now, so I showed your website to Jack.'

'I had a look at the kinds of things you investigate.' North was quietly spoken, measuring the words. 'I thought you might be able to help. I've been worrying about it and thinking about taking some action. I'd have done something sooner but I had health problems and had to have treatment. Then I got to know Bella and she encouraged me to contact you.'

Swift nodded. 'Okay. Tell me what's on your mind.'

'It's murder. Unsolved murder.' Bella's eyes shone. Some people found murder exciting, and she was clearly one of those.

North shook his head. 'Well, we don't know that, Bel. That's what I *think*.'

'Oh yes. True.' She sounded disappointed.

North picked up his coffee and ran a hand through his hair. 'It's about how Kim died. She was only twenty. She actually died of drowning in the lake where she lived. She had an epileptic fit while she was in the water. Kim was like a sister to me and I've always thought it was appalling that she died like that. She was there all night, alone. Ben found her early the next morning. At first, the family thought that Kim must have had a seizure, fallen in the water, lost consciousness and drowned. But then the police said that she had two bruises on her upper arms, as if someone had held her from behind. Problem was, there was some uncertainty about exactly how old the bruises were. Then they found her ex-boyfriend Pete Hussain's watch near the lake and questioned him a couple of times. A witness came forward, saying that he'd heard Hussain there the night Kim died. They arrested him and we thought we knew what had happened. But then the whole thing fell apart. The police had to drop the case and let him go.'

'Do you know why?'

'I know some of the details. A guy called Cliff Bailey came forward and said he had heard Kim arguing with Hussain by the lake on the night she died. He told the police that she was shouting at Hussain, calling him a bullshitter. He claimed he saw her through the trees and heard Hussain saying something back, although he couldn't remember what. It was about ten thirty. There's a public footpath by the boundary near the lake and Bailey was walking home from the pub. But then Bailey started wobbling, changing his story. Said he couldn't be sure it was Hussain's voice. Turns out he and Hussain once had a fistfight, so maybe he had a grudge to pursue. A little while after that, he was diagnosed with a brain tumour. He died a year later. Then the police managed to lose Hussain's watch, so that evidence had gone.'

'Why would Hussain have wanted to harm Kim?'

'They had a volatile relationship. He'd hit her in public once, and had been seen. He acknowledged that he'd bruised her sometimes. She'd finished with him, told him to get lost. He'd been on his own the night she died so nobody could verify his whereabouts, and he said he'd dropped his watch when he'd been by the lake with Kim on another occasion.'

Swift frowned. 'It sounds as if the evidence against him wasn't that robust. If Hussain didn't harm Kim, maybe she did drown accidentally.'

'I'm not saying that isn't *how* she died. It's the *why*. Why was she in the lake? Kim was terrified of water. She never, ever went in the lake on her own. She usually had warning of an epileptic seizure. Not everyone does, but Kim used to get what she described as red-hot pins and needles in her arms and legs and she'd want to scream. She'd have known to try and get help or make herself as safe as possible. She certainly wouldn't have gone near the water.' North was twisting his fingers together, seeming increasingly upset as he talked. He appeared to be an emotional, sensitive man.

'Presumably Kim's epilepsy and fear of water weren't a secret?'

'She'd grown up locally, so people would have known,' North said.

'And with Hussain out of the picture, there was no evidence of foul play?'

'No. But there must have been. I just know it. She must have died in absolute terror.' North looked at Bella, who patted his shoulder.

'Kim was frightened of water because her mother once tried to drown her,' Bella said, again with a certain relish. 'Tell Ty about that.'

'Yes, it happened when Kim was little. I think she was around three years old. Her mother was high on drugs and tried to drown her in the bath. Luckily, a neighbour walked in and stopped her. The fear went back to that. Can you imagine? She'd escaped it once, yet that's how she died. It's so cruel. So unfair. Sometimes she told me she thought she could remember it — someone's shadow over her, their hair falling down, laughter and her face under water. She said she could remember panic but most of all a huge, looming shadow. She'd never have a bath, always a shower, and even then she would keep the water to a trickle and stand with her back to it.' He rubbed his eyes, and swallowed hard. 'Actually, it was even more complicated than that. Kim feared water but she also had a morbid interest in it. She'd sit by the lake and gaze into it. She was fascinated by stories about ships sinking, or planes or helicopters ditching in the sea. She knew all about the *Titanic*. I remember once she cut out a piece from the newspaper about a guy who'd survived for months in a life raft in the Pacific after his yacht capsized. She carried it around for ages. I think she liked to read stories about survival, how you could defy the power of water. Once, in order to overcome her fear, she tried to learn to swim, but she couldn't stay in the pool. That's what she was like, Kim. Courageous. Faced things. But after the swimming lessons failed, she never again went into water of any depth. She wouldn't go near the lake unless one of us was with her and then only to hover at the edge. There was a little island in the middle of the lake and a boat you could row over there, but Kim would never get in the boat. And she would never go in the lake at night. Never.'

Recollecting it all was making North agitated. His eyes glistened with unshed tears. Bella looked at him with concern.

'Take your time,' Swift said. 'It's hard, remembering these sorts of things.'

'Yes, go easy on yourself,' Bella added.

North nodded. 'I had good times with Kim. Happy memories. She was a real character and such a laugh. We were very close, even though she was younger than I was, and I miss her. I feel I owe it to her to try and find out what happened.'

'Were you and Kim related?'

'Not blood relatives, no. But we thought of each other as sister and brother and we said we were the family we'd choose if we could. As I said, we were close.'

'Where was Kim living?' Swift asked.

'Tell him about Low Lake, Jack,' Bella urged, topping up their coffees.

North took a sip from his mug. 'Yes, okay. Low Lake. It's where Kim lived with my cousin and his family. It's a big old place about fifteen miles from Banbury, in Oxfordshire. The family setup at Low Lake wasn't exactly straightforward. Jakob Ramsay was my first cousin. He and his wife, Gill, gave Kim a home. They took Kim in when her mother was arrested after trying to drown her. Kim's father, Gill's brother, was dead by then. It came out that her mother had abused her in other ways too. She was a drug addict. She was sent to prison for what she did to Kim, as well as for dealing — a long sentence. Kim was an only child so Gill offered to give her a home. Gill and Jakob already had two children of their own and two from Jakob's previous marriage. Kim was a strange mixture. She could be high octane, a bit in your face, but then for long periods she would be withdrawn and quiet. She had a short fuse. She pushed boundaries and she sometimes caused disruption in the family. She was upset about something before she died and excited too. She told me in an email that she'd had a falling-out with Gill but there was something else bothering her as well. She said she'd finished with Pete Hussain and she'd met new people, and it was obviously giving her a buzz. I felt bad after she died. I should have made more effort to find out what was wrong.'

'Did she often fall out with Gill?' Swift asked.

'That's the thing. No. It was unusual. She didn't say what it was about. I asked Gill after she died but she didn't want to talk about it, said it was nothing important, water under the bridge.'

'Did you live near the family?'

'About twenty miles away,' North said, 'on the outskirts of Oxford. I used to go there a fair bit in the summer when I was young because they had the lake to swim in and big grounds to hang out in. After I went to university in Liverpool I didn't get much time to visit.'

Swift looked at him. 'Do the family at Low Lake know that you're considering this investigation?'

'Jack wanted to talk to you first, and get an idea if it's something you'd look at,' Bella said.

North nodded. 'I think Gill will be okay about it. Like everyone else, she believes what the coroner said at the inquest — Kim must have been by the lake because it was a hot night and she started fitting and fell in the water. The lake shelves away into deeper water very quickly. It's quite sunken, hence the name. Kim often hung out in the summerhouse by the lake and sometimes she slept there. She used to say she must have gypsy blood because she didn't like being confined in a house. She liked to move around. When it was warm enough she often slept outside, in a little tent she had or sometimes just in a sleeping bag under a tree. But she wouldn't have gone in the lake on her own, not even to cool off, and especially when she didn't feel well. I just know that it wasn't an accident.'

Bella excused herself and went to see to something in the kitchen. North's phone rang. He said he was on call and would have to answer.

Swift sat and mulled over what he had heard. Kim Woodville's death was tragic, but young adults often took risks or made rash decisions that ended badly. Then again, she had been troubled and there was the possibility that she had rowed with someone. Swift hadn't taken on any major work for months, living on savings and income from Cedric Sheridan, the friend who rented the top flat in his house. After several complex, fraught cases he had needed a break. He'd spent a couple of weeks in Connemara, visiting relatives he hadn't seen for years and staying in the cottage where he had spent his childhood holidays. He had reminisced with aunts and cousins, eating his own weight in home-baked soda bread and rowing every day on Lough Corrib. He had also been occupied with his baby daughter, Branna, helping Ruth, her mother, with childcare. He had needed and enjoyed the sabbatical but now he was ready for work and his bank balance could do with an injection of cash.

North put away his phone. 'I'm sorry, I have to go to the surgery. I'm a vet and there's an emergency. Bella knows quite a lot, she can fill you in a bit more if you can hang on.'

'Just before you go, if Pete Hussain wasn't responsible for what happened to Kim, do you have any ideas about who might have been?' Swift asked.

'No, none. Like I said, she could be antsy with people but I don't think it was enough to make anyone want to harm her.' North lifted a rucksack and paused in the doorway. 'Maybe it was Hussain after all. If Kim had met someone else, he might have been jealous and angry. Maybe he shouldn't have got off.'

Jack called goodbye to Bella, who had switched on music in the kitchen — Beyoncé singing 'Silent Treatment.' Swift stretched his long frame in a comfortable armchair and looked around. The flat was in a modern block but the living room was decorated in a rustic style, with pine cabinets, an oak bureau, deep chairs upholstered in bottle-green corduroy and wallpaper and curtains in a fern pattern. Swift thought he could have been in a country farmhouse.

'So, how long has it been?' Bella asked, standing in the doorway holding a wooden spoon. She had donned an apron featuring a Banksy print of a girl with a red balloon.

'Years. Don't make me count.'

'Oh gosh, that makes me feel ancient. You look the same. Bit of silver here, that's all.' She touched her temple.

Swift smiled. 'You too. Apart from the short hair.'

'I got it cut for a charity challenge at work and decided I liked it.'

'What do you do?'

'I'm an auctioneer and valuer. I specialise in eighteenth-century European china and paintings. I love it. I get to travel, live in the past and deal with beautiful objects. Every day is different and I never know when something rare will turn up, often after someone has cleared out an attic. Last week I was in Vienna, selling a beautiful pair of Sèvres vases to a collector.' She glanced at her watch. 'That will be a late one now for Jack. We were going to eat in together for once. Would you like to share a bowl of cassoulet with me? There's plenty and it's better than eating alone. We could gossip about back in the day.'

He accepted and followed her to the handsome kitchen, which was fitted with an Aga stove, acres of pine, a slatted square farmhouse table, scrubbed and restored, and a flagstone floor. Bunches of dried herbs hung from the ceiling, completing the impression that they were deep in the country. The food was hearty and delicious and accompanied by crusty bread and a mellow red wine.

'Is this flat yours?'

'Yes, I bought it about eight years ago. Glad I managed to get into the market. My parents coughed up the deposit.'

'How do you know Jack?'

'I was looking for someone to rent a room to and a friend who works in veterinary supplies suggested him. We met up and liked each other. People say we look a bit alike because of the red hair and I suppose there is a superficial resemblance. I do realise that I'm probably a bit of a Kim replacement. I'm fine with that.'

Swift smiled. 'The thought had occurred to me.'

She nodded, tearing a piece of bread. 'Jack was living on his own in a tiny studio flat. I think he was pretty lonely. He doesn't have much confidence socially and he hardly goes out. That doesn't matter to me because I'm gregarious, so I'm rarely at home, but I do feel for him at times. He's a young man, he should be mixing more. Of course, his size can make social contacts awkward. He immerses himself in his work with small animals and does lots of extra hours. He's a great guy to share with — neat, considerate and so sweet. He even leaves the toilet seat down! He's quite nervy and shy and I'm an extrovert so we sort of find a balance. We rub along really well.'

While they ate, Bella told him that Low Lake was an early Georgian house, built in 1716 by the Gayton family. They hung onto it until the 1950s, when the last childless family member died. A film star bought it then but hardly lived in it. He rented it out, letting it deteriorate until the Ramsays pitched up in the late nineties.

'It has huge grounds. I understand that Gill Ramsay's aunt Sadie put up a lot of the money to buy it and do it up. She's a wealthy widow. She lives there with the family and I gather that she's the cause of quite a lot of friction. Not an easy woman. I wouldn't like to get on the wrong side of her. She never liked Kim and they used to have big arguments.'

13

Swift got the impression that Bella was much taken with the drama of the family. 'You've been there?'

'Just once, to dinner. Jack had told me so much about them and I was dying to take a look, so he cadged me an invite. It's an impressive place. Gill wears multi-coloured floaty skirts and shawls and comes over all earth mother. I think she sees herself as an Angelina Jolie type figure, gathering children to her bosom. The kind of woman who breastfeeds until the kids are toddlers. Jakob's first wife was Sri Lankan so it's a bit like the United Nations at the dinner table. An interesting setup there. Jakob had an affair and Gill threw him out, but then he moved back in. He lived in a flat in a converted stable block adjacent to the house and they had an uneasy truce. Then he died about six years back. Heart attack.'

Swift leaned forward. 'Now I'm intrigued. Were the Ramsay and North families close?'

'Not particularly. Jack spent time at Low Lake in the school holidays, but I don't think there was much mingling otherwise. Jakob's mum was Belgian but his dad was from Oxford. They've always maintained links.'

'Did you ever meet Kim?'

She shook her head. 'No. I met Jack a while after Kim died, so I've only heard about her. Did he show you the strange photo with her looking like Ophelia?'

'You know about that? Jack said only he and Ben knew.'

Bella shrugged. 'I've seen Jack glued to his phone sometimes, and one day I caught a glimpse of a photo. It was soon after he moved in. So I looked at his phone when he was in the shower. To be honest, I thought he might be looking at porn. There are lots of things I can accept but porn isn't one of them and I wouldn't want a guy who was addicted to it under the same roof. That would have been a deal-breaker. There was no porn, thank goodness, but I saw that Ben had sent him that photo of Kim. Typical Ben behaviour, from what I know. I've never mentioned it. I know how much Jack misses Kim, so best not to go there.'

Swift had been engaged to be married once but now he was in his late thirties and had lived alone for some time. He wondered if he could manage the intimacy of sharing again. The thought of someone scrutinising his phone when his back was turned made him deeply uneasy.

Bella finished her last mouthful of food. 'Listen, when you look into this, you'll find that not everyone liked Kim as much as Jack did. He was devoted to her, I know. He's soft-hearted and trusting. Kim obviously liked him a lot and she was supportive and understanding. He's always had to take medication and his dwarfism has caused some physical problems. He had to have quite a lot of dental surgery as a child. So I think they had plenty in common in terms of life's challenges. But I gather that she could be difficult and temperamental. Jack rarely saw that side of her. But then, Jack's an easy person to like and he never posed any threat to Kim. He's uncritical to a ridiculous degree, maybe even a little naïve.'

'Are you saying she took advantage of him?'

Bella stacked their plates. 'I didn't know her, so I can't say. I don't have that impression. I think he adored her, yet he wasn't part of her daily life. It's easy to be kind to someone you only see occasionally and who is devoted to you, don't you think? I wouldn't say that to Jack, you understand. It would be treading on his memories. I think that a successful friendship depends on leaving certain veils in place.'

Swift thought that the cocktail-downing dance-floor diva had matured into a warm, level-headed, compassionate woman and just the kind of friend Jack North needed. She brought out a selection of cheeses and biscuits and made coffee. They talked on about their years at Warwick, swapping notes on people they had known and kept in touch with and some they had lost track of.

Bella threw back her head and laughed, and he speared a chunk of Stilton, smiling. 'When I saw your email, your laugh was one of the first things I remembered about you,' he said.

'I get it from my dad. I call it my Trinidad chuckle. He laughs right from the belly.' She sipped coffee, blowing on it. 'You've mellowed. Back at Warwick, I thought you were a dish but a bit intense and solemn. It was kind of attractive but alarming. You've still got that serious look but you smile more.'

He smiled now. 'I had a lot of growing up to do. The intensity hid anxiety and grief. Ruth, my ex, is a psychologist. She suggested it was due to my mother dying when I was fifteen and she explained that it can take years to recover from that kind of shock. Looking back, she's right. That's why I was drinking too much then as well.'

'You used to talk about your mum sometimes when you were drunk. You sort of leaked tears. I felt so sorry for you but I didn't know how to handle it. It made me awkward around you because I'm close to my mum — she lived just up the road in Rugby, but I felt I couldn't talk about her. I think that's why I was kind of relieved when we drifted apart.'

'Did I talk about my mother to you? I don't remember that.' That nineteen-year-old callow and troubled young man seemed far away, a stranger almost.

'In bed, in the small hours, when you were pissed and half asleep. You missed her terribly. You used to describe how she worked in the garden in the summer and how proud she was of her fruit trees and strawberry beds. When Jack talks about Kim, it reminds me of you back then. The same raw grief. I've been lucky. I've never experienced a bereavement of someone close, not yet. Tell you what, I found a photo of us looking bleary in the student bar. I can't remember who took it, but after I contacted you I had a look for it.'

16

She slid open a drawer in the table and handed him a photo. The two of them holding drinks, sitting at one of the battered metal tables in the student union. He was unshaven, his hair bushy and tangled, in a scruffy denim jacket over a grey T-shirt. His eyes were glazed from however many pints he'd had. Bella was wearing a patched blue waistcoat, a shirt with frilly sleeves, layers of plastic beads around her neck and lots of dark eye makeup. She had both hands on his shoulder, with her chin resting on them.

'Look at us, so young and uncreased,' he said. 'Well, apart from the clothes — they're pretty wrinkled. Look at me, practising my soulful look. Sorry, Bella. You were probably expecting tenderness and sweet nothings from a lover. I must have been a self-indulgent pain. I moderate my drinking these days. I learned that alcohol can make me maudlin.'

'No worries. The sex was lovely so, you know . . . So, an ex? Are you married now? Attached? I don't see any rings.'

'I was engaged to Ruth but it didn't work out. I was wrapped up in my work with Interpol, spending time in Lyon, and she met someone else and married him. We have a daughter together, Branna. We didn't plan her, but now that she's here we wouldn't be without her. I was seeing someone a while ago but she was murdered.'

'Wow! That's horrible! How did she die?'

'She was strangled by a guy who'd been paid to harass me. Her name was Kris Jelen — she was Polish. She was a talented tailor and ran her own business.' He had a momentary flashback to the night he found Kris in her flat, lying on the floor amongst scattered cloth and sewing equipment. He closed his eyes for a moment. He still carried a heavy burden of guilt about Kris's death. When he opened his eyes, Bella was gazing at him softly and he looked away. 'Now I'm seeing Nora, Nora Morrow. She's from Dublin but she's been in London for a while. She's in the Met. And you?'

'I was about to get married but he called it off the night before the wedding.'

'Ouch.'

'Yes, very ouch. We seemed well suited until we started to make definite plans. He said he was feeling trapped and confused. I was in pieces, of course, and it took me ages to recover. But looking back, I reckon it would never have worked out. Then he married a couple of years later and they've got kids. I suppose he just needed the right person to trap him. I'm still looking for Mr Right — if he exists. I've done internet dating and met quite a few weirdos. You wouldn't believe some of the blokes I've spent an evening with. Have you got any single, presentable, hetero male friends who aren't weighed down with baggage and maintenance payments?'

He thought that if Bella knew more about his daughter and the complex webs in his life, she'd rate him as a serious baggage carrier. 'I'll have a think. No one comes to mind immediately.'

'Well, do your best. I'd like to have a kid and my biological clock's ticking. Thirty-seven and counting . . .'

He left after a second coffee. As she showed him to the door, Bella grew serious.

'I hope you can find out what happened with Kim. Jack was so fond of her. He says she always accepted him for who he was, she treated him the same as everyone else. He hasn't always met that in life, not even in his own family. He has nightmares sometimes, about drowning or about Kim being in the lake and trying to get out. He's told me he wakes up in a cold sweat, shivering. I hear him in the early hours, going to the kitchen to pour a whisky.'

'It's a horrible way to die, however it came about. We'll see. Good to catch up with you, Bella. I've never met a person with dwarfism before and I'm curious. How does Jack describe himself? I hope you don't mind me asking.'

She smiled. 'Not at all. It's better if people ask. Jack uses "little person" because he thinks it's accurate. He doesn't mind "dwarf" but "midget" is offensive. I think one of his other cousins at Low Lake used to tease him and call him that, but he doesn't like talking about it.' She kissed his cheek. 'It's good to see you again. Let's not lose touch.'

On the way to the station, Swift had a text from Ruth.

Sorry about last minute request but could you have Branna Thursday morning? I've been asked to step in for someone who's gone off sick.

Ruth now lectured in psychology, and she had been rebuilding a career in London. It was important to her to be as available and responsive as possible. He would look after Branna but it would mean heading out to Hendon, where Ruth was renting a poky flat. He texted back, confirming arrangements.

He sat on the rocking train recalling Bella on the dance floor, gyrating madly to 'Who Let The Dogs Out,' her beads jangling. The memory made him smile. Her simple joy in life had brought him out of himself. Poor woman, lumbered with his youthful tendency to morose, alcohol-fuelled introspection. He'd got the better part of the bargain. Still, at least she'd enjoyed the sex.

She shouldn't have cut her hair, he thought. It had been glorious.

* * *

The noise from upstairs was deafening, competing with construction work next door. Oliver Sheridan's heavy tread shook the ceiling. He was banging doors, screaming and ranting at his father. It wasn't the first time this had happened. He had once bruised his father's arm when he'd worked himself into a rage. He had been going strong for a good ten minutes. Swift could hear him clearly from his

19

living room. He had been exercising prior to going for a row on the river but he stopped mid-stretch and stood in the centre of the room, ready to intervene.

'Shut up, you old bastard! What if I did use your credit card? You never give me anything so I took something for myself.'

Another inaudible reply from his father, Cedric.

'Oh shut the fuck up! You gave your bloody car away to that interfering know-it-all downstairs. How come you didn't offer it to me? I'm your son, I should have had first refusal. Just because he sucks up to you and runs little errands. Mister good cop. Golden boy.'

Swift was just about to head upstairs when there was a crash, then silence. Then Oliver's voice, still loud but frightened now.

'Dad, Dad! Come on, Dad! Christ, come on, Dad!'

Swift took the stairs two at a time. Cedric was sprawled on his side on the living-room floor, Oliver kneeling beside him, shaking him by the shoulder.

'What happened?'

'He . . . he just sort of froze and turned a funny colour. Then he swayed and fell. What is it?'

'Call an ambulance. Hurry!'

Swift pushed him out of the way and knelt beside Cedric. His face was purple. Swift couldn't detect any breathing but there was a faint pulse. He turned him onto his back, gently tilted his head and lifted his chin. He started CPR, alternating between two rescue breaths and thirty chest compressions. He had been taught CPR during his first months at police training college, but this was only the second time he had performed it on a real person. He hoped he was remembering correctly. Cedric was wearing one of his gaily patterned shirts, sky blue with random dark cherry dots. His familiar, dear face was drained of colour. Swift worked on, counting and breathing, sweat and tears blinding him, until the ambulance arrived. A paramedic held him gently by the shoulders.

'I'm Gemma. It's all right. Come on now, it's all right. We'll take over now.'

He got up and moved away. Oliver was standing hunched by the wall, biting his lip. He was square and stolid, densely boned. Swift stood in front of him and looked down at his sweat-streaked cowardly face. As usual, there was a faint scent of mildew about him. Not for the first time, he wondered how a fine and generous man like Cedric could have produced such a nasty son.

'You've done this, you bastard,' Swift said to him. 'I hope you can live with yourself.'

'I didn't do anything! I didn't touch him! He was old. Stuff happens to old people. Don't try to blame me.'

Swift couldn't bear to look at him. He turned back to his friend and heard Oliver run for the stairs. Gemma had attached a defibrillator to Cedric's chest. After two shocks, she nodded to her colleague, who covered him with a blanket. Gemma looked at Swift.

'He's hanging on. We have to get him to hospital. You did the right thing. You did your best. Are you his next of kin?'

'No, his friend. His next of kin has just run away. I'll come with him.'

He sat in the ambulance, watching as Gemma placed an oxygen mask over Cedric's face. Her colleague radioed the hospital, advising of a cardiac arrest. Swift reached over and touched Cedric's hand, willing him to hold on. Traffic was heavy and the ambulance siren roared into life.

'Will he be okay?' Swift asked. He knew it was an impossible question.

Gemma smiled at him. 'You did well by him. I can't say if he'll be okay. The cardiac team at the hospital will be able to tell you more. Have you been friends a long time?'

'A long time. Since I was a child.' Cedric had been a close friend of Swift's great aunt Lily. When Lily left Swift her Victorian terraced house in Hammersmith, he had also inherited Cedric as a sitting tenant.

At the hospital, Swift gave the nursing staff details about Cedric and then waited for a couple of hours in a tiny, airless room, drinking lukewarm coffee and pacing. He rang Milo, one of Cedric's closest friends, to tell him what had happened.

'I'm having a couple of days in Bournemouth but I'll come back straight away,' Milo said, sounding frightened. 'That bastard Oliver. I've always said he'd worry Cedric to death.'

'He hasn't yet. Keep hoping. I'll give you any news as soon as I have it.'

Eventually, a doctor found Swift. 'Mr Sheridan is still critical but we've stabilised him. I'm afraid you can't see him yet. I believe you're a friend of his?'

'Yes. A close friend. He lives in my house.'

'We've tried to contact his son but we can't reach him.'

'They have a difficult relationship.' As far as Swift was concerned, the main difficulty was that Cedric kept making excuses for Oliver and allowed his son to visit him, despite his abusive behaviour.

The doctor looked as if he'd heard this before. 'Well, we'll keep trying. You can wait if you want but I suggest you go home and phone us in a couple of hours.'

'What are his chances?'

'He is responding. It's very hard to say at this stage. He is in his eighties and this is a huge trauma for the body. He's a fighter, though.'

Swift went home to Hammersmith. He was supposed to meet Nora Morrow that evening but he texted her, telling her what had happened. She replied within minutes.

So sorry to hear that. Will ring you later x

At home, he went straight up to Cedric's flat. The kitchen was still filled with the savoury aroma of the soup Cedric had made that morning. They had planned to have lunch together after his row on the river. He stirred the thick mass of vegetables. Cedric was always liberal with smoked paprika and the broth was a rich dark red. Sometimes he added a dollop of sour cream to the soup bowls with a sprinkling of parsley on top. He was a man who took care, who liked the small touches that lifted life. A man who liked to give pleasure to his friends.

Swift bowed his head, overcome by sadness and pain.

CHAPTER 2

Jack North was doodling busily on a notepad as they talked over coffee in Swift's basement office.

'Handy, having an office in your house,' North observed.

'Certainly keeps the business overheads down. Apologies for any noise from next door. My new neighbour's a trumpet player and he's having a soundproof loft conversion to practise in. It will benefit me in the end but there's some crashing and banging while it's in progress.' As if to prove his point, a few hollow thuds sounded through the walls.

Swift glanced around, thinking yet again that the office needed a lick of paint. Since Lily died, he had made few alterations to any of the décor in the house. A decisive man by nature, it was the one thing he procrastinated over. No doubt Ruth would interpret this as holding on to memories. Lily and his mother had been close and he had turned to his great aunt for solace after her death. Lily had used the basement for her work as a chiropractor and there was still a chipped hand basin in one corner of the room. The sun was bright and angled through the window, mercilessly exposing the wear and tear of time. He thought of how he judged people by their environment when he visited their homes and reckoned that a visitor to his might well think: *stuck in a time warp.* Possibly, that was exactly what was going through Jack North's mind. Swift realised how dingy the cream paintwork had become and decided it was time to freshen up the room and deal with the damp patch under the window.

He looked down at North's doodle and thought he could make out a lion's face. On his own, without Bella, North seemed tongue-tied and shy. Bella obviously oiled the social wheels for him. It occurred to Swift that Kim Woodville might have had a similar personality to Bella: outgoing, assertive. People often seemed to be attracted to the same types of friends and partners. Was that true of Ruth, and Nora, whom he was seeing now? As far as he could see, they had little in common except a keen intelligence. He watched North's deft, sure strokes with his pen.

'Take me back to when you first met Kim,' Swift suggested.

'Right. Let's see. She must have been about seven, so she'd already been at Low Lake a while. It was Jakob's birthday and my parents called in, taking me with them. That was the first time I'd been there. My dad was in the RAF so we moved around a lot before we settled in Oxford. I was impressed by how big the house was. It seemed very grand. The noise and bustle impressed me too. I'm an only child so I spent a lot of time on my own. I wasn't used to a busy family. When we arrived, Kim was doing handstands in the drive. She ran up to us and started talking to me, and we just hit it off straight away. She seemed older than seven. She had this direct way of speaking, quite bold, I suppose. Other children often just stared at me or didn't know what to say. Or they patronised me, following their parents' example. I had few friends, because of moving around so much but also because of being a dwarf. When you have dwarfism, you get used to what I call the sliding glance. I've been on the receiving end of quite a few jibes and sneers. Kim didn't blink, she just asked if I could do handstands and when I said no she said she'd teach me.'

He had finished the lion and started on an abstract pattern. Swift sipped his coffee. He caught a glimpse of himself in the mirror opposite. His black curly hair was looking wilder than usual and he couldn't remember if he'd combed it that morning. His cousin Mary called it his raggle-taggle gipsy look, but Nora told him she liked the windblown, weathered style. She said it made him look like a Connemara fisherman.

His thoughts drifted to Cedric, white and frail in his high hospital bed, with drips and tubes snaking from his body. He'd rung the hospital early in the morning, to be told that Cedric had improved a little. Milo was already with him and Swift was going to visit once he had finished with Jack North. North seemed absorbed in his drawing and he realised that he would have to keep prompting him or they would be there all day.

'So after that you became a regular visitor at Low Lake?'

'That's right. Aunty Gill was very generous and said I should visit whenever I wanted. The more kids, the merrier, as far as she was concerned. It was a bit of a paradise for children — huge grounds with a woodland area and of course the lake, where you could swim. And the island in the lake had a terrific treehouse. We spent hours roaming around and acting out adventures. There were always snacks in the summerhouse — fruit and juice and homemade flapjacks. An old-fashioned childhood, I suppose. A bit like a storybook. I used to stay some weekends and school holidays. I know that it must have rained sometimes but in my memory, it was always sunny. Happy days.' He sighed and finished his coffee.

'It sounds idyllic.' Too much so, Swift thought. Perhaps his career had made him jaundiced, but there was usually a fly in the ointment and all this endless enchantment sounded like a children's story. North seemed a timid romantic at heart and he had been a lonely child. An impressionable combination. Bella had indicated a more complicated setup.

'When did you find out about Kim's epilepsy?'

'She told me very soon after I met her. That struck me too. She was upfront about her illness, talked about it freely and described how it felt. She said it was like a clingy friend you didn't want but who wouldn't go away and you were stuck with them for life. That was when I realised that you didn't have to be ashamed of who you were, that you could stick your chin out to the world. Not that I've ever quite managed to copy Kim in that way. She had what are called tonic-clonic seizures. They're severe. I saw her having one once. We were eating breakfast. Suddenly she screamed and went all stiff and then her arms and legs started twitching. She slid to the floor and lost consciousness. Gill stayed very calm. She put a cushion under Kim's head. The thing Kim hated most about her epilepsy was that she wet herself sometimes when she had a seizure. Valery, Gill's daughter, used that against her now and again, called her piss pants whenever they had an argument. And they argued a lot.' He tapped his drawing. 'I remember one summer, Kim and I spent hours in the summerhouse writing a book about a girl with epilepsy and a boy with dwarfism. They were siblings. We called them Suki and Jordan. They were brave and had all kinds of mad adventures. Kim did most of the writing and I illustrated it. I wish I still had it.'

'Did Kim hang on to it?' Swift asked.

North shook his head. 'We'd left it in the summerhouse. Valery got hold of it and tore it into little pieces in front of us. Kim went for her and they were punching each other until Steve turned up and separated them. I remember Kim split Valery's lip. She was strong and muscular, and a better fighter.'

'Did Kim get into trouble for that?'

'I expect Gill told them both off and gave them a lecture about channelling anger appropriately. I'm fond of Gill but she's a bit of a bore when she starts sermonising, and I don't think her homilies ever had much effect.'

'I need to get a picture of the Ramsays and any other family members. How many people lived at Low Lake?'

North turned to a clean page and sketched a family tree as he spoke. He seemed more at ease when he was drawing.

'So, there was Gill and her husband Jakob, until he died. They had two children, Steve and Valery. Then there were Will and Ben, Jakob's sons from his previous marriage. His first wife died of cancer. Sadie Stanley, Gill's aunt, lived there and Adela, Jakob's cousin, was there for a while.'

'And who was still living there when Kim died?'

'Gill, Sadie, Adela, Valery, Ben and Steve. Valery and Ben still live there. I'm not sure where Adela is now. Will joined the army at sixteen and never came back. Steve has a place in London now and does cars up for a living and trades them. He used to have a workshop in the stable block near the house before he moved out. I think he still keeps some valuable old cars in there.'

Swift nodded. 'So, two adult children still living at home.'

'Aunty Gill would have liked it if all the children had stayed. She said she always longed to keep her family around her. Kim called her a smother mother. Valery and Kim were the same age. Valery works in her mum's business, teaching home crafts. Ben's been in and out of different jobs, sort of floats about. I'm not sure what he does nowadays. He was diagnosed with ADHD when he was a child. Spends a lot of his time watching films and taking naps.'

'Bella told me that Gill and Jakob had a semi-detached arrangement.'

'That's right. He lived in a flat in a converted stable. He had an affair and Gill found out. He went off to live with this other woman but it didn't last and he moved back. Kim took the piss out of the situation between Gill and Jakob. She said they communicated by leaving each other notes. She reckoned that Jakob only stayed around because Gill and her aunt controlled the money and owned the house. Kim said he'd come a cropper by having the affair and he'd been neutered.'

'Can I keep the family diagram? It would be helpful, since it's a complex structure.'

'Of course, yes. I phoned Aunty Gill about you. She seemed a bit put out so I went to see her last weekend and we talked it through. She was worried that I was going to cause a lot of distress for no reason.'

'She has a point. If I don't find anything indicating that Kim's death wasn't accidental, I'll still have trodden on toes in the process.'

'Well, I do realise that. In the end, Gill said that it's okay with her if you go there, as long as you don't upset anyone.'

Swift pocketed the diagram without comment. If Kim Woodville had been killed, someone was going to be upset. 'I understand from Bella that Mrs Stanley and Kim didn't get on?'

'That's true. Sadie Stanley is a domineering person and she always seemed to resent Kim. She thought Gill was taking on too much by offering her a home. Kim was very quick-witted and she used to wind Sadie up. In fact, I don't think Sadie ever had much time for children in general but it suited her to live there.'

'Last time we met, you said that Kim could be disruptive.'

'She was strong-willed. A bit wild at times, I suppose. She used to shoplift in the village sometimes. Just small stuff — sweets, toys, things like that. I don't think she ever got caught but she showed me her stash now and again. She hid it in the hollow of a tree near the summerhouse.'

'Did Gill know about the shoplifting?' Swift asked.

'I don't think so. Kim never seemed to get into any trouble over it. The other thing about her was that she didn't like being told what to do. I liked that about her but some people found it rude. Sadie was always criticising her, and Kim would give as good as she got. She used to have real ding-dongs with Valery too. They never hit it off. The biggest rows always seemed to be at mealtimes. I remember Kim once threw a baked potato at Sadie and it hit her in the chest. I think Ben used to egg Kim on sometimes. They had a similar sense of humour.'

'And what happened about the flying potato?'

'Aunty Gill took Kim away and made her have "time out" in her room. She probably climbed out of the window and went off to the summerhouse. She usually did what Gill told her, or pretended to. She sort of skirted around her. She knew she'd probably have ended up in care if it wasn't for Gill, but she said Gill made her feel claustrophobic. Gill knew she often exited the house via the window but never commented. Actually, I suppose they engaged in a kind of mutual avoidance.'

'How do you mean?'

'Well . . . Gill would come over as all mumsy and protective, but sometimes I thought she looked a bit wary of Kim. As if Kim might be a ticking time bomb.' North laughed. 'Gill often wears crocheted shawls that she makes herself and Kim used to say that if you got caught up in one of them you'd be trapped like a bug in a spider's web and never escape.'

'And Jakob? Did Kim get on with him?'

'She said he was okay, but then he left the children to Gill most of the time. He had a job in an export business in London and always worked long hours. I don't think he earned much. He'd come home with comics or magazines for the kids and pat them on the head. I always found my cousin Jakob a colourless kind of man. When I wasn't there, I could never remember what he looked like.' North leaned back in his chair, his eyes misty. 'Oh, I miss Kim so much. We never rowed or fell out. We used to laugh like drains. She was a terrific mimic. She used to imitate the way Sadie Stanley twisted her mouth and patted her hair before she uttered her catch phrase, "Well, all I can say is that in my day, we used to . . ." It was usually something to do with children's manners. I still can't believe Kim's gone. I've felt very alone since she died. That might seem odd because I hadn't seen her for a while before she drowned. Once I went to university in Liverpool we chatted by email, but it's not the same as seeing someone. But she was, you know, always there to talk to. I see or hear funny things and I want to tell her but she's gone.'

Swift looked down at the family tree. Kim and Jack North hadn't been blood relations. North was staring wistfully into the distance. Swift decided to chance the question. 'Were you and Kim ever lovers?'

A fiery blush rushed up North's neck. He shifted in his seat and nodded. 'I've never told anyone.'

'Okay. I'm not going to say anything. You're my client.'

'We made love just once, in the summerhouse. It was cosy in there, with a sofa and little lamps. And it was private, away from the house, amongst the trees. You could pull the blinds down and shut the world out. Kim was seventeen. I was twenty-two and still a virgin. Sad or what?' He gave an embarrassed shrug. 'We were chatting. I was doing my degree then and Kim asked if I had any girlfriends. I said I could never work up the courage to approach women at uni. It was getting me down. I was struggling in my life because of it. Kim said I needed a bit of practice and she kissed me and, well, it just went from there. It was easy, friendly, uncomplicated. We laughed afterwards and Kim had me in stitches, imagining the scene if Sadie Stanley had found us. Kim helped me a lot that night. I got some confidence, had one or two girlfriends afterwards. Nothing that lasted, though. So, you know, Kim was special to me for lots of reasons.'

Swift thought that many men and women, himself included, had a soft spot for the person they had lost their virginity with. 'Was Kim a virgin?'

'No. She'd started seeing Pete Hussain by then. He lived in London but he used to visit Great Howe, the village nearby. They'd have bust-ups, then get back together. She said he didn't like being told where to get off.'

'Did she seem frightened of him?'

'No. But then Kim rarely showed fear, except where water was concerned. She didn't talk that much about Pete, just that he was her bad medicine. She knew he wasn't good for her but she kept going back for another taste. I remember she said that he suited her because he had his demons and so did she. I met Pete once, one Christmas when I was down from university. Very handsome but not that bright. Not as intelligent as Kim. I didn't like him but I could see why women would. That combination of good looks and a dangerous edge. He and Kim teased each other a lot. Combative teasing, bordering on quarrelling. It made me uncomfortable.' North leaned forward, rolling his pen between his fingers. 'I do want to stress to you that Kim would never have gone in that lake. Valery once pushed her in and she stayed on her own for days afterwards, and wouldn't go anywhere near the lake for weeks. She refused to travel on ferries or to go by sea. When the family went on holiday, she missed out on all the sea and river trips and when they were on a beach, she stayed well back from the water. I don't know what happened that night, but I know it was something bad.'

'Did you ever hear Kim express suicidal feelings?' Swift asked.

'Absolutely not. Kim was a positive person.'

32

'But you hadn't seen much of her around the time she died. Something might have happened that you didn't know about. You said she had something on her mind.'

'I'm sure she would have told me if anything was troubling her that badly. But I feel guilty that I didn't ask further. I should have rung her, found out what was up. But I'd joined a vet's practice in Liverpool for the summer holiday as an intern. I was busy and wrapped up in the challenge. I wanted it to go well.' He tapped his phone. 'Here, this is the email she sent not long before she died. I assumed the problem was something to do with her love life or her plans for the future.'

Hi there little Jacko,

Hope u ok. Swotting away as usual, I xpect. Hope the internship/free labour goes well.

Had a big row with Gill last night. God, she can be a drag.

Told Pete to get stuffed. Had enough of him. Relief!

Tell u what, life gets complicated sometimes. Lots going on. I've met someone and it's strange. And I've sort of met someone else too, in a weird and amazing way. It's a bit of a thrill. I've a knotty problem to work out. Knots and more knots. Tricky.

Big luv xx

'Did you show this to the police?'

'I forwarded it to them. They acknowledged getting it, and that was it. I phoned them as well, about Kim's fear of water. I got the impression they thought I was a nuisance.'

Swift handed the phone back. North scrolled through, and then held it out again to Swift. 'Look, this is Kim as I prefer to remember her. Alive.'

It was a short video of Kim, taken amongst trees with a lake in the background. She stood with her thumbs hooked into the belt of her jeans. Tall, with long, wavy black hair, a strong face with a full mouth, and thick, dark brows. Her face had character. She did a few moonwalk moves, laughing. She looked as if she had been a vibrant young woman before she was reduced to a sodden corpse.

Swift handed the phone back. 'What was Kim doing with herself before she died?'

'She was working part time at a local museum in Great Howe. She was very friendly with the family who ran it, the Dunbars. Elaine Dunbar was an archaeologist and Kim had developed an interest in the subject. She volunteered at a local archaeological dig that Elaine headed up, at the site of a Roman villa. She wanted to study archaeology but she needed to get some exams under her belt. She was bright but she struggled with the discipline of essays and research. Gill had homeschooled the children and Kim reckoned that she'd missed out because of that. She said they did a lot of busy work instead of proper lessons.'

'And if she *was* arguing with someone the night she died, you have no idea who that might have been?'

North pulled at an earlobe. 'The only people I ever heard Kim argue with in any serious way were Mrs Stanley and Valery. I've racked my brains about Kim's death. I just can't think of anything more I can tell you.'

'Did Kim use social media?'

'She wasn't that keen on it. She said a lot of weirdos hung about on it. She had a Facebook page. Two in fact — one personal, and the other for her archaeological work. That's called KimDigger. I think they're still live. I don't think she used Twitter or Instagram.'

'I'll take a look. You know, Jack, unless I discover differently, there's no evidence that Kim's death was suspicious. Did anyone benefit from her death?'

'You mean financially?'

'Yes, or in any other way.'

North shook his head. 'Unless someone thought they'd got rid of a problem. That would be a benefit.'

'You might have a point. We'll see. I'll be in touch. Can you forward me the photo and video of Kim and the email she sent you?'

'Sure. Here they are.'

North sent them, swung down from his chair and made his way to the door. He walked stiff-legged, with a rolling gait. As he went up the stairs to ground level clutching the iron railings, a couple of teenagers passing by glanced and sniggered. One made an inaudible comment. Swift grimaced. North's loyalty to Kim and his fondness for her was understandable. If you had an appearance that singled you out, complete acceptance was a powerful draw. They had shared the burden of major life challenges. He wondered what it must have been like for the other children in the family when Kim arrived in their midst, an outspoken, damaged girl. It sounded as if Valery hadn't been too pleased. He folded the family diagram and tucked it in his pocket, locked up and set off along the Thames Path to catch a bus to the hospital.

* * *

A nurse informed him that Cedric was due to have a pacemaker fitted the following day, to regulate his heartbeat. Cedric was sleeping in a small ward, propped up with pillows. His skin was pale, his eyelids blueish and his hair lay flat against his scalp. Swift sat beside him, thinking how illness and confinement in hospital took you away from the world and reduced you.

It was hot in the ward. He took off his jacket, rolled up his shirtsleeves and looked up press reports about Kim Woodville's death. There were a couple of brief mentions in the local papers. The fullest was in a Banbury weekly.

Promising Student's Tragic Death

Kim Woodville, twenty years old, drowned in a lake earlier this week.

A family member found her at her home at Low Lake, near Great Howe. Police are investigating and it is not yet known if the death was suspicious. None of Kim's family was available for comment.

The landlord of The Green Man pub in Great Howe commented that Kim suffered with epilepsy and this might have contributed to her death. Kim was a keen volunteer at a local archaeological dig at Frynfold and worked at the Bickmore Museum in Great Howe. Dr Elaine Dunbar, the project director at the Roman villa excavations, told us that she was deeply shocked by the news. She said that Kim was an excellent and talented student who showed great promise and will be a loss to the community.

A London man is helping police with their enquiries.

Cedric stirred, murmured, and opened his eyes. 'Ty, dear boy. How good to see you.'

'Hallo, Cedric. Even better to see you.'

Cedric inched up on the pillows. 'What day is it?'

'Thursday.'

'I keeled over, didn't I?'

'That's right. Your heart.'

'Did I turn the soup off?'

'All taken care of.'

He had asked Swift the same questions the previous day. A doctor had explained that people could experience confusion and memory loss after a cardiac arrest.

Cedric raised both hands, his thin fingers fluttering. 'Yes, the soup. Did you eat the soup?'

'I had some of it. I've frozen the rest for when you get home.'

'Enough paprika?'

'Just right.'

'Good, good. This is all very inconvenient. I had a busy week planned. I feel so tired. It's exhausting, being in hospital. They never leave you alone.'

'It's not a place for rest.' He wondered if Cedric remembered Oliver's visit and the row. Cedric hadn't mentioned it. 'Can I get you anything?'

'No, dear boy. I'm okay. Milo brought in a big bag of goodies. I gave most of them away. Don't tell him, will you?'

'I won't. I see he brought you your pyjamas.'

Cedric yawned and shifted in his bed. He was wearing bright red pyjamas with thin stripes in green and yellow. The vivid colours emphasised his pallor.

'They're opening me up tomorrow. Fitting a pacemaker to keep me ticking correctly.'

'That's good. I think you can bypass the scanners at airports when you have a pacemaker.'

Cedric smiled. 'I don't think I'm going to be travelling anywhere too soon. Oliver hasn't been near me,' he added quietly.

'Hasn't he? Maybe that's for the best.'

Cedric looked at him. 'Maybe. What happened to me wasn't his fault you know, Ty. It was just one of those things. I'm a bit of a creaking gate at my age. I don't want him blaming himself.'

Swift thought that was unlikely. He loved Cedric for his kindness and generosity but wished he could be more clear-sighted about his son. Cedric's eyelids were drooping, so he kissed his hand and said he'd be back tomorrow. Cedric gave a tired smile and a tiny wave.

Outside, the late afternoon had turned drizzly. The gloomy sky was thick with fat clouds waiting to burst. It was almost four and Swift felt lethargic after the enervating heat of the hospital. He would have liked to take his boat out on the river but conditions weren't promising. He knew just the place to idle away the dregs of the day. He caught a bus to Hyde Park and walked fast through Mayfair towards Soho. He stopped for a few minutes by a café courtyard to listen to a woman in a silvery dress singing an operatic aria. Her voice soared and swooped over the street clamour. He pulled up his collar, shook rain from his hair and carried on to Soho, to a three-storey shop that sold a huge selection of crime and pulp fiction and played sixties music. He went down into the musty basement, remembering to duck through the low door — at six foot three, he'd lost count of the times he'd cracked his head on it. He browsed for a while and bought a coffee and a ginger biscuit.

He sat in a deep wingback chair that accommodated his long legs, crossed his ankles and looked up Kim Woodville on Facebook. Her main page had a photo of her head, an unpleasant image of her pulling her eyes into slits and poking her tongue out. The entries stopped a couple of months before her death. He looked through the posts, which were infrequent, with no ongoing conversations. They were mainly shares from websites called Midnight You, Inner Enemy, Get It Off Your Chest and Nuts&Proud. He read some.

Be cautious when you hear gossip about a girl. It often comes from a sad guy she's jilted or some bitch who's jealous.

I can tell myself I'm lovely and worthwhile. You can do one. Suck it up.

I don't care if anyone likes me. Most of you lying scumbags don't like yourselves.

Note to self: fortune favours the brave.

Last week I stepped in some dog turd. Then I looked again and saw it was my life.

The world is full of users and losers. I might as well be a user, top of the dung heap.

I've never been to the USA but I've been in some fucking states.

Hey, I might be a wreck but I haven't been wrecked.

What doesn't kill you turns you into a screwed up mental case.

This last share had one comment, from Valery Ramsay: *you said it, #1 bitch.* He thought the photo that Kim had chosen to head the page was significant, although he was unsure if she was deliberately undermining herself. He flicked into Valery Ramsay's page. Her photo showed a heavily made-up, sulky-looking young woman, pouting for the selfie and wearing a low-cut T-shirt that exposed cleavage.

The posts on Kim's page seemed eerie and sad, full of defensive anger, posturing and questioning. He turned to the page for KimDigger. It was headed by a picture of a beautiful jewelled clasp, gleaming with ruby and sapphire stones. The posts there were more frequent, with some likes and comments from other archaeology enthusiasts. A different person might have written them.

Rotten weather at Frynfold today but found a coin and glass beads, probably from Germany. Exhilarating! Dying for a hot bath.

Aching leg muscles. No finds today. Just mud and more mud. Bring it on! Love it.

I've just finished setting up a new exhibition about Roman farming at the Bickmore Museum. Come and see and don't forget to make a donation.

Archaeology is sexy, dontchaknow. Found a wooden and leather phallus, about eight inches long. Elaine says it's probably a sex toy. Ooh! Naughty people living at Frynfold back in the day.

Come to Elaine's talk at the museum next Friday on Roman food. Found evidence of an apiary yesterday so they definitely had honey at Frynfold. Sweetened my day.

Dig deep and deeper still. It's not what you find, it's what you find out.

This young woman sounded more confident, upbeat. KimDigger had found a meaning and purpose in life that had eluded Kim Woodville. Swift knew people who went to work to forget their troubles. He had often done so himself. He wondered if that was what it had been like for Kim, if when she was digging in the earth, absorbed and engaged, she forgot herself.

He put his phone away and sat in the cosy warmth, reading *Man in the Shadows* and listening to Simon and Garfunkel while the rain washed the streets.

* * *

Swift was appreciating that a fifteen-month-old who had just started walking was dynamite. His experience of children was limited, but he was learning fast. His daughter was a determined character with a short fuse. He captured Branna as she was about to pull a lamp from a table. She gave him that stony look she used when she had been thwarted. She had hearing loss and Swift turned her to face him as he spoke and signed, *Don't touch. That's dangerous.* Her new hearing aids were daffodil yellow and decorated with kittens. She pulled away from him, rocking unsteadily on her feet and saying something in her own babble.

'I know you understand me. Come on, do the sign for *don't touch.* Indulge your father. Please?' He smiled, signing *don't touch* again.

She pursed her lips, gazed at him then laughed and signed, shaking her head, swinging her hands apart, then pushing her right hand forwards.

'Well done, Branna! Terrific girl! Oh, I think I hear Mummy.' He made the sign for *mummy* and Branna started lurching towards the door.

Ruth put down a bulging briefcase and cuddled her daughter. She was letting her hair grow and it was skimming her shoulders. Branna liked to weave her fingers through it and then give it a hard tug.

'Have you two had a good time?' she asked.

'We have. We had a long walk by the river and then we went to the club and inspected my boat. Branna sat in it and tried it out for size. After that, we weeded Cedric's flowerbeds. Well, I weeded and Branna tried to eat rose petals. She knows the sign for *rose* now.'

'How is Cedric?'

'He's doing okay. He was disoriented for a couple of days but he says things are making sense now. He had a pacemaker fitted successfully. He's sitting up and chatting to Milo.'

He sat on Ruth's sofa in her tiny living room while she put Branna in her high chair and gave her a banana. Ruth looked much better these days. She had suffered badly with postnatal depression and become painfully thin. Now her skin glowed again and she had put on some weight. He watched her stretch, saying that she'd had some keen students that morning. He checked himself out, content that he no longer felt the old aching loss whenever he saw her. He could appreciate her beauty now without his heart twisting. But there were still times when he wished things could have worked out differently.

He and Ruth had a chequered history. They had been planning to marry when she left him for Emlyn Taylor, a barrister. She had married her new man speedily and moved to Brighton. After a few years, Taylor had developed a severe and rapid form of MS and Ruth had turned to Swift for help. Branna had been conceived on the one occasion when they slept together. She had been born prematurely, and then hearing loss had been detected. Taylor's MS caused him to have unpredictable outbursts and angry rages. When he discovered that Ruth had been seeing Swift, he had conducted a vicious campaign against him through a petty criminal who had caused the death of Kris Jelen, Swift's lover. Taylor was charged with assisting a crime and had been disbarred. Ruth had stayed with her husband despite his behaviour, feeling that she should be loyal. But her own health deteriorated, and she had left him the previous year, unable to deal with the stress and unwilling to expose Branna to his volatility any longer. Taylor's mother was now looking after him in the house in Brighton. Ruth had stayed temporarily with Swift, and then rented a one-bedroom flat in Hendon while she re-established her career. She rarely mentioned her husband and Swift didn't ask about him. The last time he'd seen the man, he'd told him that he would have no further contact with Branna.

It had taken Swift a long time and many hours of conflict and pain to get over Ruth. Sometimes he felt like a man who had sustained a bad injury and had at last been able to throw away the crutches.

'The good news is I've been offered a permanent part-time contract at the college, starting after Christmas,' Ruth told him. 'It's so good to be back in the swing of things. Now I just need to get childcare sorted.'

'That's great news, Ruth. You're turning a corner. And by the way, Branna's wearing most of that banana.'

'Oh God, look at her!'

Ruth fetched a flannel and wiped her daughter's face and hands. Then she lifted her from her high chair and blew loudly into the soft skin of her neck. Branna squealed in delight.

'Daddy says you can sign *rose*, that beautiful scented flower,' Ruth said. 'Such a clever girl. Can you do the sign for me? Can you sign *rose*?'

Branna looked at her father. He put his forefinger and thumb together, nodding. She copied him and drew her fingers clumsily in front of her nose. They both applauded her and she clapped herself, then yawned and rubbed her eyes.

'Let me just get her down for a nap,' Ruth said, 'then we can have a coffee. How can one small person occupy so much time and energy?' She paused at the door. 'I'm not sure I've said this properly before. Thanks, Ty, for holding the fort last year while I was depressed and distracted. You got Branna started early on signing and I realise now how crucial that was.'

She had gone before he could respond. He listened to Ruth and Branna chatting as Ruth changed her and put her in her cot. Once Ruth had left her husband and regained her health, she had become determined that Branna's hearing loss wouldn't hold her back. Since Ruth moved back to London they had both been working on sign language with Branna, agreeing which words to introduce each week. It was good to operate together as a team with their daughter.

While they were drinking coffee, he took out his phone.

'Can I pick your professional brain about something?'

'You can try. It feels a bit rusty these days but I'm happy to give it an airing.'

'I'm looking into a case of a young woman who drowned a couple of years ago.' He explained about Kim's childhood, her epilepsy and Jack North's concerns. 'I looked at Kim's two Facebook pages. They're very different. I'd like to hear what you make of her from them.'

Ruth looked through the two pages, sipping her coffee. She sat back. 'How old was Kim when she died?'

'Twenty.'

'I'd have thought that the first page, Kim Woodville, belonged to a younger girl, early to mid-teens. The kind of stuff she's channelling isn't that uncommon with adolescents. It's a bit mawkish as well as crude. There's a lot of confusion, questioning and self-doubt. Aggression, too. She's trying to work things out, define her life. She's representing it with other people's thoughts and sayings rather than expressing herself openly. It's a safer way of communicating, very popular with teens on social media. Plenty of older adults do that too, of course, particularly with political views. There's disgust and pride about herself and wariness about other people. She's talking herself down before anyone else can, but at the same time indicating she can defend and look after herself. That's not surprising, given her early history. When something traumatic happens to you as a child, it tends to define you for the rest of your life. She's trying to bolster herself, too, trying to say that she can take the world on.' She scrolled again on the screen. 'The photo is interesting. Quite aggressive. Maybe "take me as I am" or "see how ugly I can be" or even "I won't conform to stereotypes." A complex young woman. Sad, too.'

'I thought the KimDigger page could almost have been a different person.'

'Yes, although the voice is still infused with a kind of yearning. She's more comfortable as KimDigger. The photo of a beautiful artefact contrasts with her ugly self-image on her home page. Archaeology gives her a role, status, validation of who she is. A preferred identity.'

Branna let out a loud wail, clearly deciding that today's nap would be brief. Ruth went to fetch her, declaring that there was no rest for the wicked. Swift checked his phone and saw that he had an email from Nora, arranging to meet him at the cinema that evening. He replied, saying that the tickets would be at the box office. He spotted a blob of pulped banana on the carpet and scraped it off. At last his personal life was turning a corner. He felt a small, quiet ripple of hope.

CHAPTER 3

Autumn was advancing stealthily, with mustard, orange and russet leaves drifting through the air. It was a quiet, windless day. Swift was approaching Low Lake, driving parallel to a high stone wall covered in dark green ivy. He turned sharp right through tall pillars onto a gravel driveway, which curved through lawns filled with shrubs. Several redbrick garages were tucked away just to the left of the pillars. A man was cutting the grass, perched on a heavy-duty sit-on mower and a woman was weeding and raking the gravel. He pulled up in front of a substantial double-fronted three-storey Georgian house with scaffolding at one side. It was symmetrical and, like the garages, built in brick. Three steps flanked by low stone walls led to the front door, which had a small wrought iron balustrade above it. The door was wide and panelled, with a fan light in yellow and green glass.

A skinny elderly woman answered his ring. She stood in the doorway, cradling a bunch of freshly cut flowers. She had a canvas belt holding gardening tools around her waist. Her salt-and-pepper hair was in two long plaits, which she had twisted around either side of her head and secured with a large metal claw clip on the top. A wartime, austerity look. In keeping with the hairstyle, she was wearing a printed 1940s tea dress, blue with yellow and white daisies. It was bunched around her middle under the belt, the hem dipping at one side. She had thick dark down along her top lip and bloodshot eyes that glared at him.

'Yes?' she said curtly.

'I have an appointment to see Gill Ramsay. My name's Tyrone Swift. Are you Mrs Stanley?'

She stared as if he had insulted her. 'Wait there.'

She shut the door. He stood on the step, feeling like an unwanted salesman. The minutes ticked by. Someone was at the top of the scaffolding, working on a chimney. There were clanging sounds, accompanied by tinny music and the cheery babbling of a DJ from a radio. Swift watched the mower making striped patterns on the lawn. He was about to press the bell again when another woman pulled the door back. She was tall, well built and wearing a fringed yellow, green and blue woollen shawl.

'Come in. I'm Gill. This way.'

She strode ahead, her long panelled skirt flapping. He followed her down a wide hallway, through double oak doors into a sitting room.

'Do have a pew. There's coffee coming.' She threw herself back on a velvet sofa, drew her crocheted shawl around her and linked her fingers through the holes. Her skirt was busily patterned in shades of aubergine and pink, with clusters of tiny roses, lilies and ivy, and paired with a pink and dark green corduroy shirt. Her hair was the same greyish mix and texture as Mrs Stanley's but shoulder-length, with a fringe.

'Thanks for seeing me,' he said.

'I can give you half an hour. Then I have a class.'

'Do you teach?'

'I run workshops here, in one of the old stables. Screen printing, crocheting, patchwork and découpage. They're very popular. I have to turn people away sometimes. There's such a demand, I do YouTube tutorials as well.'

The workshops explained the indigo stains on her long fingers. She had an easy, honey-toned voice that glided over the words. Her large eyes were shiny and crinkling with crow's feet at the corners.

'Jack North said he's spoken to you about employing me to look into Kim Woodville's death.'

She shook her head, pursing her mouth. 'Jack should have counselling to get over his grief. That would be a wiser way to spend his money. I know how much he loved Kim but he's being foolish. I don't really want to discuss it but I will, for Jack's sake.'

'Jack has told me about the police enquiry, Pete Hussain and Cliff Bailey. Can you tell me about the morning Kim was found?'

'If I must. It was all very confusing and harrowing. I'd just come home from hospital the previous day. I'd had a knee operation and I was still feeling groggy. I heard the terrible news through a fog of painkillers. Valery came into my bedroom to tell me. Steve, one of my sons, dealt with the police and he went to identify Kim's body. I wasn't fully mobile for weeks because an infection developed and really set me back. I was in a wheelchair for Kim's funeral.'

'You've never had any doubts about how Kim died?'

'Obviously we all had a lot to come to terms with, especially after Pete Hussain was released. I had no idea that Pete had been physically harming Kim. Then there was that Bailey man, muddling everything. I know it's terribly sad because he was only fifty-eight and he was suffering with a brain tumour, but what he said about Kim arguing with someone threw everything into confusion. It was a bewildering time. The police never established that anyone else had been with Kim that night. In the end, we had to accept that it had been a dreadful accident.'

'I understand that Kim had had a seizure.'

'That's right. Kim was very much a law unto herself, you know. She didn't always take her epilepsy medication as she should, even though she knew the risks. Sometimes she said she'd mislaid it and we had to get another prescription. I suspected that she disposed of it in a kind of denial. She had a severe form of epilepsy, what used to be called "grand mal." It came on after her mother tried to drown her but I believe it ran in her mother's family, as these things often do. She had complex feelings about it. Sometimes she spoke about it as if it was something to be proud of and at other times, she said it blighted her life. We had regular discussions about it but she took little notice of me. The autopsy showed that she'd missed her medication for several days before she died and we couldn't find it when the police asked about it. It's important to take anticonvulsant drugs regularly, and missing it meant the chance of a seizure was high. Young adults are often conflicted about taking medication, you know, especially long-term drugs. It's a kind of rejection of the illness. A form of anger and perhaps a type of self-harm.'

She had a patronising, didactic manner. She seemed very sure of herself. She had folded her arms, and her shawl had slipped down her shoulders. Her large bosom strained against her shirt and he could see a portion of her solid-looking bra where a button gaped.

'Jack says that Kim would never have gone in the lake on her own.'

'Yes, yes, I know. He repeated that endlessly, and that she would have known a seizure was coming on. He badgered everyone about it, including the police. He even mentioned it to people at her funeral. Highly inappropriate. But the night she died was close and humid and it's possible that the lack of medication skewed her judgement. It's also possible not to have warning signs of a seizure, even if you do usually. The pattern can alter unexpectedly, especially if the person is stressed or if medication isn't consistent. You'll appreciate that having parented Kim I knew more about her epilepsy than Jack did. You know, the coroner had no doubts. Neither did the police in the end. The inquest reached a decision of accidental death.'

'So I understand. Did the police talk to all the family?'

'All of us except Will, who was in the army, stationed in Belize. He's still there. They were in and out of here for over a week, checking everything, traipsing around the lake, taking photos. They literally left no stone unturned, and yet in the end they managed to make a mess of their enquiry. You know about them losing evidence?'

'Yes, Jack told me.'

'Well, it's all in the past now. That's why I think Jack is wasting his money and your time.'

'Maybe Jack is using me as a way of working out his grief. Maybe I can put his mind at rest.'

'Maybe. Frankly, I wish he would have more sense but I felt I had to accept his decision, given his need. I'd just be grateful if you could do whatever you have to do as quickly as possible and with no fuss. It opens it all up again for us, you know, and unlike Jack, we've managed to move on. We will always remember and cherish Kim but we've put the tragedy behind us.' She gave him a soulful look but the words sounded hollow.

'I appreciate that.'

The door flew open, banging against the wall. A fair-haired, heavy-hipped girl in straining white jeans came in carrying a tray, which she plonked down on a small table.

'This is my daughter, Valery,' Gill said. 'You've spilt some coffee there, Val. Do wipe it up, darling.'

Valery swiped the puddle of coffee with the sleeve of her sweatshirt. Swift thought she was the sourest looking young woman he'd ever met. Sucking lemons didn't even come close. Her Facebook photo flattered her. She had pasty skin and narrow shoulders, which she hunched in as she sat beside her mother, combing her fingers through her straggling hair. It was coloured in two layers at the ends, an inch of dark green above bright pink. He wondered how it was done and remembered seeing women in the hairdresser with layers of what looked like baking foil wrapped in their hair.

'You've come here because of Jack?' she asked him. She had a gruff voice that sounded as if it was trapped in the back of her throat.

'That's right. I'm checking Kim's death.'

'The midget's wasting your time and his money,' she said. She turned to her mother. 'I've set up the materials and the tables for the découpage workshop. There's been one cancellation, but I explained she'd have to pay at such short notice and she didn't argue.'

'Thanks, darling. That means we can get started immediately.' Her mother beamed at her.

'Did you and Kim get on, Valery?' Swift's coffee was so strong he almost gagged. A shadow of a grin crossed Valery's face and he wondered if she had made it that way on purpose.

'Not really.' She shrugged. She was sucking a mint and now and again poked it through her lips on the tip of her tongue. He thought it was odd behaviour for a woman in her twenties.

'Sibling rivalry. Chalk and cheese,' Gill said to Swift. 'You know how it is in families. There's often lots of emotions at play, especially when personalities are so different.'

'No, I'm an only child so I've no experience of that. And Kim and Valery were cousins, not siblings.'

Valery flashed him a look he couldn't read. Mainly animosity, he thought.

'You liked playing tennis with Kim, didn't you, darling? And cricket. You both liked that,' Gill said to her daughter in a warm, indulgent voice, smoothing her hair back.

Valery jerked her head away. 'Maybe. Sometimes. Seems a long time ago.'

'Did Kim seem upset or worried about anything in the days before she died?'

Valery shrugged again and played with her shirt cuff. Her mother crossed her legs and sipped coffee.

'It was warm weather,' said Gill, 'and Kim had been sleeping in the summerhouse or her tent for at least a week. She loved being outdoors. Her mother was abusive, you know, and one of the things she did was lock Kim in her room and leave her for hours, so Kim sought the sky, open spaces and the winds. She loved that old song, "Don't Fence Me In." We played it at her funeral. I was in hospital for six days before she died. She didn't bother to visit me but that didn't surprise me. She hated doctors. She'd had many medical appointments over the years at various clinics. Some doctors had been stern and disapproving with her about missing her medication. As you can imagine, that didn't go down well with Kim. I remember that she was terribly rude to one consultant, grabbed her file from his desk, threw it at him and ran out.'

Valery gave a loud, exaggerated yawn and patted her mouth, rolling her eyes. 'Drama queen central,' she muttered.

Her mother carried on, scarcely missing a beat. 'I did glimpse Kim just after I came home after my surgery. I told her my operation had been successful. She seemed fine. She was working and the rest of the family hadn't seen much of her, except for some mealtimes.'

Valery played a little tattoo on her knees and crunched her mint. 'This is all *so* immensely riveting, I'd love to stay and reminisce. Talk about the good old times with Kim — *not*. But I'm afraid I have to vanish. I've got to feed my rabbits.' She got up abruptly and left the room, banging the door closed.

There was a silence. 'Valery suffers with dreadful PMT and heavy periods,' Gill told him. 'I do feel for her. It makes her so moody and emotional. She's struggled since early puberty and sometimes she gets terribly depressed over it. She has to have an operation for fibroids soon because she bleeds for so long. It makes relationships with men very challenging for her. Physical and psychological health are deeply entwined, especially in women. Her brothers don't always understand that and give her a hard time.'

Swift thought that Valery would be able to hold her own and that Gill was being indiscreet about her daughter's personal problems. Revealing them to a male visitor was a bit indelicate. Gill had spoken with great intensity about Kim's epilepsy and her daughter's condition. It was as if she found satisfaction in illness. Then again, maybe Valery liked her health problems being paraded.

'Does Valery work with you?'

'That's right. We run all the workshops as a joint enterprise and Val manages the bookings. We make a good mother and daughter team. Val shows me how to do the YouTube material.'

He hoped Valery was more polite and polished with paying customers. There was a bright banality about Gill Ramsay. He wondered if she was a woman who chose not to see what might cause her discomfort.

'Is Kim's mother still in prison?'

'No, she was released on licence about eight years ago. I was informed. Given that she had tried to drown Kim, one of the conditions of her licence was that she made no contact with her. Kim always said she didn't want to have anything to do with her mother and I'd advised the authorities of that. I told Kim that her mother was out of prison. I thought she should know that.'

'How did she respond?'

53

'She said very little. She rarely talked about her mother. It was a closed subject. That was her way of dealing with what had happened.'

Or Gill's way of not dealing with it, he thought. 'You said that Kim seemed fine before she died, but she told Jack that she'd fallen out with you. He said that was unusual.'

'You see, this is the kind of thing Jack is picking over. Opening up things from the past that are better left there.'

'It would help if you'd tell me.'

She rubbed her forehead and gave an impatient shrug. 'Jack idolised Kim because she took to him for some reason. Whenever he visited, they were inseparable. I suppose she felt she could look after him, protect him in some way because of his dwarfism. He was here intermittently, and there were aspects of Kim he was unaware of. She could be underhand and quite calculating.' Gill fingered a seam in her skirt. 'Well, if you must know, Kim used to steal. It started when she was around nine years old. Small things over the years, bits of jewellery, and cash now and again. It's not uncommon in young people who have had a troubled start in life. They're stealing love, you understand.'

'Yes. I do know something about the reasons children steal.'

'Well, good. She mainly stole from me, the caregiver. We'd spoken about it a number of times and she always blew up at me. Sometimes she denied it, other times she returned the bracelet or ring she'd taken. A couple of weeks before she died, I noticed that two hundred pounds had gone from my float in the workshop. I keep some cash handy because people want to buy materials. I spoke to Kim, she refused to admit she'd taken it and things became heated. I decided to leave it as I couldn't get anywhere with her. I made sure I locked the cash box in a cupboard after that.'

'Someone else might have taken the money.'

She shook her head. 'I knew it was Kim. She had a certain look when she'd been caught out. Almost like a kind of excitement. Look, no one else knew about the theft. I never told anyone, so I'd rather you keep it to yourself. It was petty and I don't want Kim's memory tarnished.'

Swift nodded briefly. 'I don't think Jack was as naïve about Kim as you think. He told me that she used to shoplift in Great Howe and hide the goods near the lake.'

Gill raised an eyebrow. 'I was never aware of that. I can't comment.'

'But it does sound as if her behaviour was often challenging,' he said.

She folded her hands together. 'Having children is a challenge. Do you have children?'

'I have a baby daughter. I understand that it's a huge responsibility, but satisfying as well. Just before she died, Kim told Jack that she'd met two new people and things were tricky. It's not clear what she meant. Any ideas about that?'

Gill shook her head. 'No, none. Kim spent a good deal of time in Great Howe. Maybe she'd met people there. She was a complicated girl and young people are usually struggling with things in their lives. She hadn't mentioned anything.'

'It must have been difficult, introducing Kim into your family, given what she'd gone through. It was brave of you to offer her a home.'

Gill plaited the fringes of her shawl. 'Kim needed stability and kindness. As her aunt, it was the least I could do for her. My brother Malcolm was highly intelligent, but unstable. He started taking drugs at school and continued at college in London, where he moved on to stronger substances. Then he got involved with Kim's mother, who was a dealer. She dragged him right down — to the gutter, you could say. He dropped out of his degree course and they lived in squalor, on handouts and benefits. Paula,

Kim's mother, was only eighteen when she gave birth. She was an inadequate, needy person. I went to the disgusting basement in Tottenham where they lived to try and persuade Malcolm to leave, but he refused. He looked like a skeleton. There were cockroaches in the kitchen. Kim was tiny, running around in dirty clothes and a filthy nappy. My brother died of an aneurism soon after that. Paula found him dead in bed and, well, after his funeral we had no more contact until she was arrested. Kim had no one else so I stepped in. I've always thought that giving unconditional love and nurture is the greatest blessing in life. A calling, if you like. I think of it almost as a vocation. We all have to use our talents to the full, don't you think?'

He remembered Bella's comment about Gill. She seemed to fancy herself as a cross between Angelina Jolie and Mother Teresa. Swift could see why Kim wouldn't have confided in her. 'Of course we should use our talents if we can. But Kim must have posed you some difficulties, having had such a rocky start in life.'

'Oh yes. But difficulties are what make us, aren't they? They test our mettle. Kim did have a troubled start in life but she responded well to a caring, reliable environment. We all worked with her, you see. Most children respond to steady and encouraging love, fondness and kindness. I'm not saying she wasn't hard work at times. Kim was, well, a free spirit you could say. She always had trouble sleeping and she said she slept better outside, under the stars. In allowing her that freedom, I helped her to grow and set her own boundaries.' She nodded at her own words.

Her pretentious opinions were starting to irritate him. 'Jack indicated that Mrs Stanley and Kim didn't, er, share many fond moments.'

A slight frown and a small sigh. 'Oh dear, that was a real personality clash. My aunt has old-fashioned, strict views about children. But you see, that's part of growing to maturity, learning how to navigate these difficulties. That's how children learn to cope with the world.'

By throwing potatoes across the dinner table, Swift thought. 'Jack mentioned that Kim was close to someone called Elaine Dunbar, an archaeologist.'

'Kim became interested in archaeology after watching the Indiana Jones films. I suppose Hollywood can have a beneficial impact sometimes. She loved to watch *Time Team*. She met Elaine Dunbar at the museum in Great Howe. Elaine's family own the place. Elaine runs the excavations at a Roman site. There'd been some excitement about a find there not long before. Kim started helping out at the museum, then had a part-time job at the excavations. I couldn't say if Kim and Elaine were close. I don't really know the Dunbars.'

She spoke in an offhand tone and Swift wondered if she hadn't liked Kim breaking away from the closed family circle.

'What can you tell me about Pete Hussain?'

'Very little, except that he had a reputation for being troublesome. I remember reading in the local magazine that he disrupted the village carnival by throwing bangers under one of the floats. I never met him. I rarely visit Great Howe. My work keeps me here and it's a large property to run and take care of. I did advise Kim that she might want to choose more wisely but she clammed up when I broached the subject.'

'It didn't worry you that she was seeing someone who was known to be aggressive?'

She blushed slightly. 'Kim was very private about her personal life, and she flared up if she thought I was prying. She was an adult, after all. I respected that, you see. You must give young people space. I always told the children I wanted them to see me as a best friend as well as a mother.' She smiled, looking self-satisfied.

Swift didn't think he would get much more from Gill Ramsay for now, apart from more of her hazy and irritating philosophy of parenting. He found her complacent, and her presence was strangely draining.

'I would like to talk to everyone who was here around the time Kim died.'

'Let's see.' She counted on her fingers. 'My aunt Sadie, Valery and Ben.'

'What about your other son, Steve, and your husband's cousin, Adela?'

'Steve was away at a car rally in Northamptonshire. He hurried back as soon as he heard the news. I think he arrived a couple of hours after Kim's body was found. Adela was in Banbury. Steve lives in London now. He has a girlfriend there, and he wanted to build up his motor business.' She sighed heavily, as if this was a great sorrow to her.

'I would like to come back to follow up. I'll call and arrange a time with you. Would it be okay if I take a walk in the grounds and to the lake now?' he asked.

'Of course. I have to get to work but Ben is around today. I'll ask him to give you your bearings, if you'd like to wait here.'

She tied the ends of her shawl together and glided away. There was a vase of fiery red dahlias near the door and she caressed their heads lightly as she passed.

After she left, Swift sat for a moment taking in his surroundings. Then he stood and moved around the large, handsome room. It was painted in cream and lime, with two walls papered in a pattern busy with insects and butterflies. The floorboards had been painted white with knots, grooves and scuffmarks left on show. There was a round pine table covered by a circle of thin glass decorated with layers of random post-it notes, postcards and sheets of stamps. He leaned over it, examining the display. Presumably this was the sort of stuff done in the workshops. The postcards were scenic, some very old in sepia. Some were Victorian, showing women posing provocatively in chemises. Others were gaudy, of the saucy seaside variety, in which fat women were being ogled by thin, bespectacled men. Shelves in an alcove by the table were covered in flowery découpage and filled with coloured bottles, vases, shells, ceramic fruit, silver plated stiletto shoes, glass beads and small pictures of men in Regency costume with splatters of red and pink paint covering their faces.

There was a loud rap on the front window. Swift saw a young man eating a hot dog, beckoning to him. Outside, a radio on the roof was turned up high and the man was singing along, snapping his fingers.

'Are you Ben?'

'Ben's my name, trouble's my game,' he replied in a bad American accent. He licked bright yellow mustard from his bread roll and held out a hand. 'Put it there, dude.'

'Hi, I'm Tyrone Swift.'

'I know. I googled you when I heard you were coming. I read all about your work. Exciting! You've found missing people and solved murder cases. Impressive sleuthing, dude! Do you tote a gat?'

Swift smiled. 'I don't own a gun. I don't have a trilby. I have got an old trench coat in the back of the wardrobe though. It was my dad's.'

Ben laughed loudly and snapped his fingers. 'Cool, dude. Real cool!'

'That's me. Could you show me the way to the lake?'

'Sure thang. Hey, poor old Kim was the lady in the lake, right? That makes you Philip Marlowe.'

'I'm not sure I can match Marlowe's style. Have you read any Raymond Chandler?'

'Sure. All of his stuff. And Dashiell Hammett. I love all those films, all those tough guys. Big shoulders, big personalities, trouble shooting, fistfights, and smooching dames. *An RKO Radio Picture!*'

Swift shook his head. 'You're doomed to disappointment with me then.'

Ben put his hands on his hips and looked Swift up and down. 'You're tall and muscly, check. Kinda serious-looking and I reckon you can handle yourself, check. That'll do for now. Hey, have you ever been attacked while you were investigating?'

'Let's see.' Swift counted off on his fingers. 'I was stabbed in the thigh when I worked for Interpol, I've been hit over the head a couple of times, I was knifed in the arm a while back and I've been punched in the face and kicked in the kidneys. Will that do?'

'Wow! That's cool, dude!'

'You think? It was terrifying and I get bad dreams.'

Looking excited, Ben led the way across the lawn, gesturing at three adjacent stone buildings. With a snigger, he said that one was where his mum and Valery messed about with sticky-back plastic, one was where his brother Steve kept some cars and the last one on the right was where his dad used to live, 'sent into exile for bad behaviour.' They followed a track through dense shrubs, onto a hedged path. Moss-covered statues of classical figures, some looking the worse for wear, were dotted about. A woman in a toga had lost her nose and an archer poised with a bow had a cracked left foot.

Ben talked nonstop, about detective, science fiction, spy and action films, Quentin Tarantino, Steven Seagal, Charlie Sheen, Jason Statham, Bond, *Star Wars*, *Mission Impossible* and *Game of Thrones*. Clearly, he liked to immerse himself in fantasy worlds. He talked about how he had tried and failed to join the police, how he got sacked from the DIY store because he had fallen asleep in the staffroom and about his current job in a shoe shop in Great Howe.

'Amazing how many people come in to try shoes on with great big holes in their socks. I have to look at all those horrible toenails!'

He was a good-looking young man. His eyes were striking, wide, with amber flecks that seemed to glow in the light. His hair was thick and wavy and grew low on his brow, a dark toffee colour, and his honey-toned skin was clear and glowing. He had wide, full lips. He was well-built, his hands capable-looking. And his mouth never stopped moving. He scarcely drew breath as they headed through woodland to a good-sized lake with a dilapidated jetty and a handsome four-seater clinker rowing boat, painted dark green and white. A small wooden summerhouse stood nearby. In the middle of the lake, Swift could see an island with a treehouse on it.

'So, do you think I'd have made a good cop?' Ben demanded. 'I mean, did they miss out on a good thing?'

'Frankly, no. You've got verbal diarrhoea. You have to do more listening than talking to be a good cop. You have to have good recall and the ability to knit strands of information together.'

Ben nodded and looked sheepish. 'Straight from the hip. I do talk a lot. Always have. I try not to but it just happens. And my memory's crap. But hey, dude, I should waste you for dissing me like that!' He crouched and pointed a pretend gun with both hands, arms straight.

It was beginning to give Swift a headache. 'Ben, could you stop the fake accent and the gumshoe stuff? It's very wearing.'

Ben scuffed the ground. 'Okay, I know. I go on. Everyone tells me. My brain gets fizzy, like a firework. Spins round and round like a Catherine wheel.'

Swift laughed. Ben was an exhausting but likeable man. 'If you really want to help a private detective, tell me about Kim on our way around the lake. How old were you when she came to live here?'

'Let's see.' He counted on his fingers. 'I was eleven.'

That made him in his mid-twenties now. He seemed much younger. Valery, too, seemed immature for her age. Swift wondered if Gill encouraged this, keeping them dependent. 'Jack North said you got on with Kim.'

'We were okay, me and Kim. We kind of understood each other. She said that when she had a seizure, it felt like her brain was fizzing so she sort of knew what I meant.

When she didn't want company, I left her alone. She could be a bit frightening when she was in a bad mood. She always stood up for me when Aunt Sadie started in.' He sniggered and did a Hitler salute. 'Kim called her SS. You know, as in Nazi.'

'So she didn't get on with Sadie Stanley,' Swift stated.

'Aunt Sadie doesn't get on with anyone. She's always criticising us all.'

'So why does she live here?'

Ben rubbed thumb and fingers together. 'She put a load of dosh towards buying the house, so it's her right to live here. She's got the biggest bedroom. Dad was always skint and Mum only makes a small profit from her home crafts. Sadie reckons the place would fall apart if it wasn't for her money. Kim said she makes a career out of having her hopes disappointed, so living here is her vocation in life.'

'Kim sounds like a quick-witted woman.'

'She was. She was brainy and sharp. She could work stuff out, sort of hit the nail on the head about things. SS could never get the better of her.'

'Was Kim happy here?'

'I reckon, yeah. Well, she never said she wasn't. She was moody, though. She'd tell you to piss off, snap at you. Except Jack. She liked him best. Probably because she didn't have to put up with him all the time.'

'How about the rest of the family? Did she get on with them?'

'Valery hated her. Don't ask me why. A girl thing, I suppose. Val's always been a spiteful cow. Always moaning about her ovaries. Who wants to know? I remember once she shouted at Kim that it was a shame her mother hadn't managed to drown her. Will never took much notice of her. Steve had some arguments with her, mainly about using his car. Kim sometimes made fun of Mum and Dad. Not to their faces, though. She said she knew which side her bread was buttered.'

'I guess most children have fun at their parents' expense.'

Ben shrugged. 'Suppose.'

'How did Kim respond to Valery?'

'I reckon Valery got to her but Kim hardly ever showed it. Most of the time she was good at keeping people at arm's length. You couldn't tell what she was thinking. That used to annoy Valery even more.' Ben laughed. It was clear whose side he had taken.

'What about Adela?'

'She lived here for a while. She was okay with Kim, although she didn't agree with Mum letting her camp out at night. They used to argue about it. Kim had a tent or else she used to sleep in the summerhouse. She had a little Primus stove and she'd bring food from the house and cook it for herself. She kind of came and went, taking whatever she wanted. She got on Adela's nerves when she borrowed her stuff without asking. Adela said she needed to be reined in, should behave like the rest of the family. Then Mum would go on about Kim being *a wounded spirit*.' He clasped his hands over his heart and rolled his eyes.

'Do you see much of Steve? I gather he was away when Kim died, and got back the morning you found her.'

'Yeah, he's car mad, always off at shows and auctions. I rang him that morning to tell him to come home. I've only seen him once since he moved to London, when he came for a day last New Year. Mum keeps on at him to visit more often and bring his girlfriend but it doesn't happen. The day he moved out, he was the happiest I've ever seen him. He says he's doing well with his motors. I keep hinting he might invite me to the big city, but he always says he's busy.'

'Did you know Pete Hussain?'

Ben snapped his fingers. 'Big bad Pete! I knew Kim hung around with him. He was mean. Used to come here from London being the big "I am," throwing his weight around with the country bumpkins. He did a bit of drug dealing. Some of it hard stuff, I reckon. He had a fight with a guy I worked with in the DIY shop, gave him a black eye. I always steered clear of him. I don't like pubs or drunks, they frighten me. My dad always used to tell me, "Run, don't fight." Kim never talked much about Pete. I knew she used to see him in the summerhouse sometimes. They'd play music and drink cider, smoke dope. I found a used condom in there once and chucked it in the lake. Yuk.'

So many things that Kim didn't talk about. Swift wondered if Ben had been an occasional voyeur on those nights in the summerhouse. 'Did your mother know about Pete meeting Kim there?'

'Mum? Shouldn't think so. She hardly ever comes down here. And Kim could ice you out if you got too personal.'

'What did you think when Pete was arrested?'

'Dunno really. He could be rough. Maybe they did argue and he lost it. Maybe he didn't mean Kim to drown. But then the police cocked it up, didn't they?'

They had circumnavigated the lake and from a point where it curved, Swift had a good view of the treehouse.

'That's a fine-looking structure.'

'Mum bought it and had it put up years ago. We call the island Ape Island. I got the name from *The Simpsons*.'

'But Kim never went there.'

'No way. She wouldn't cross water. Valery liked that. She used to say it was one place Kim hadn't spoiled. The rest of us used it loads. We'd hang out there in all weathers. Sometimes we had sleepovers there. I still do. It was our place, just for us kids. Our parents never went there.'

Swift could never resist the lure of water and a boat. 'I've never been in a treehouse. Could we row over and take a look?'

'Sure. Can you row?'

'It's my favourite activity. Let's go.'

CHAPTER 4

Ben was a messy rower, all splashing and mistiming, but at least the effort stopped him talking. It was lovely on the lake, the day mild and calm. As they pushed the boat out, Swift could see that the lake shelved suddenly down, the water darkening. As they drew near, the island looked like a small jungle, bordered by rushes and covered in ferns, dark green ivy and several tall hornbeam trees. Up close, the treehouse at its centre was substantial and impressive, octagonal and built on stilts with a sturdy ladder for access and a veranda running around the circumference. It had proper windows with a branch design around the frames and a front door with *Ramsay* written on it. The sun had broken through the clouds. The damp earth on the edge of the island smelled of lush ferns and vegetation.

They pulled the boat up onto the shingle and climbed the ladder. Inside the treehouse were nests of mud-spattered, rainbow-coloured floor cushions, shelves cluttered with books, toys, bottled water, fruit juices and biscuits and a stack of sleeping bags and pillows. A flight of model aeroplanes hung from the ceiling. Leaves and clods of earth were strewn across the floor. Two striped canvas hammocks, suspended from hooks, swung gently in the breeze. Ben seized a packet of biscuits and climbed into a hammock. Swift got into the other and accepted a custard cream. They munched and rocked. Outside, birds chattered and tree branches rustled. Ape Island was a haven. Swift hated to break the peace but he was here to seek information.

'How was Kim before she died? Did you notice anything different about her?'

'She was out a lot. There was one day when she was sitting in the summerhouse looking at her laptop and she seemed to get sort of excited. Like something was giving her a buzz.'

'When was that?'

'Must have been a couple of months before she died.'

'Any idea what she was looking at on her laptop?'

'No. She closed it sharpish when she saw me coming. I said she looked happy and she told me to mind my own business. We couldn't find her laptop after she died.'

'Jack said you found Kim's body. What time was that?'

'Just gone seven in the morning.'

'What were you doing down at the lake so early?'

'I'd slept here for the night. I always sleep here on a Wednesday, don't ask me why. Just a thing. Helps to break up the week. I'd come down about eight the night before. I always wake up early and I was rowing back over for breakfast. That's when I saw her, face down in the water.'

'And you didn't hear anything during the night?'

'Nope. I was asleep by ten and I always sleep like a log.'

'You took a photo of Kim in the water. Jack showed me.'

Ben nodded eagerly. 'In case they needed evidence. But then Jack told me it was a bit off. I often get stuff wrong. I took it while I was waiting for the police. They told me to stay where I was and not move around or let anyone else come down to the lake. I knew that anyway, about not contaminating the scene. Mum was in bed after her op so when I phoned the house I got Sadie. I phoned Steve and then I just sat on the grass and watched Kim. There was a breeze so now and again her body moved with the water. I kept thinking she might roll over and open her eyes but that was daft. Aunt Sadie calls me a barmpot.'

'What's that?'

'It's a northern saying. She grew up in Yorkshire. It means an idiot.'

'Pretty rude.'

'That's what she's like. She says she tells it like it is.' Ben didn't seem upset by his aunt's insult. He was humming, his ankles crossed, and crunching his fourth biscuit.

Swift lay, watching branches of hornbeam shifting and creaking. The treehouse faced west, and now the sun was sliding down the sky, tinting it a faded rose. Small flies were dancing in the dusk and a 'V' of birds made their way across the horizon. Kim seemed to have carved her own path in the Ramsay family. She sounded waspish and edgy, difficult to get on with.

Ben had fallen asleep, his mouth open, and his head lolled to one side. Swift slid out of his hammock and looked at the drawings and posters covering the walls. They provided a chronology of the Ramsay children's presence in the treehouse. The posters featured Disney films, *Star Wars* and Tolkien characters, a couple of boy bands and stars from *Game of Thrones*. The drawings ranged from pictures of pirates, witches and spacecraft to more mature sketches — a couple of self-portraits of a thin-faced boy initialled SR, views of the lake from the treehouse and a coloured cartoonish one of the Ramsay family sitting at a round dinner table. It was well executed and sharply observed. Each person had a labelled balloon drawn over his or her head. Gill Ramsay's said QUEEN

BEE, Valery's POOR ME, Sadie Stanley's ACID AUNTY, Ben's ZZZZZ, the thin-faced boy's GIVE ME A BREAK, Kim's CUCKOO IN THE NEST, an older man, presumably Jakob, WHATEVER, and a man wearing army fatigues, who must be Will, ESCAPE TUNNEL. The chicken sitting on a serving dish in the middle of the table had a long knife stabbed through it, dripping blood, and bore the balloon HAPPY FAMILIES. Tacked at the end of the pictures was one made in a different, less able hand. A jagged pencil drawing of a huge pair of hands holding a young child under a bath full of water. The child had a clownish, sad grimace on its face and bubbles coming from its nose and mouth. The drawing's viciousness troubled him.

Swift turned his attention to the shelves of well-thumbed books and comics. The Harry Potter series was there, as well as Roald Dahl, CS Lewis and stories about dragons and vampires with lurid covers. There was a stack of games on the lowest shelf: Twister, Ludo, Snakes and Ladders, Tiddlywinks, Connect Four and Risk, which he and his cousin Mary used to play endlessly in their early teens. He pulled the box out to remind himself of the territory cards and saw a medication pack squashed behind it. He teased it out and read the pharmacy label.

Ms K Woodville. Levetiracetam 750 mg. Take one daily. 1/7/2015.

The half-empty blister pack inside held oblong tablets. Swift knelt on the floor, turning the tablets over, and then slipped them into his pocket. Kim had died on 15 July. She never came to the treehouse. Someone else must have hidden her medication so that even if she had wanted to take it on the day she died, she wouldn't have been able to find it.

Ben's phone pinged and he sat up, yawning and brushing crumbs from his jumper. 'Mum. Reminding me I have to do my laundry. She gives me tasks to do on my days off work to keep me focused.'

'Do you always do what your mum tells you?'

Ben laughed. 'Sometimes I go AWOL. I know she means well and I'm a hopeless case, but she can get on my nerves. I do just enough to keep her sweet. Kim showed me how. She said you have to manage your parents without them knowing you're doing it.'

'You don't fancy moving away from home?'

'Nah. I like it here. It's comfortable. What would I do without Ape Island?'

'Who drew the family portrait on the wall here?'

'Steve did that one day when he was pissed off. Good, isn't it?'

'It's revealing, doesn't take any prisoners. Just as well your parents never came here. And this one of the drowning child?'

'Val did that. Nasty, right? She's a right cow sometimes. Takes after Sadie.'

'Very nasty. Did the police ever look in here when they were investigating Kim's death?'

'Don't think so. Kim never came here, did she? So there was no reason.'

Swift offered to row back, not wanting to watch Ben's flailing arms. He could feel the medication pack in his pocket, wedged against his thigh. Ben visited Ape Island frequently and had found Kim's body. The photo he had taken could be read as a warped desire to maintain a connection to her or her death. He really ought to be considered a possible suspect, but Swift couldn't see him in such a light. He was transparent and apparently lacking in guile.

'Do you know why anyone would want to harm Kim?' Swift asked as they crossed back over.

The late afternoon sun was low, illuminating Ben's face. He trailed his fingers in the water and flicked them, creating spray. 'Not really, although she reckoned Larry Barton would have liked to strangle her after what happened to Nadia.'

'Who's Nadia?'

'Larry's daughter. Was, not is.'

'Go on.'

'Nadia and Kim were good mates. One day they went to London to celebrate Kim's birthday. Kim persuaded Nadia to have a henna tattoo done at a place in Shoreditch. She had some kind of allergic reaction, really severe. Anna something.'

'Anaphylactic shock.'

Ben snapped his fingers. 'That's it. Nadia collapsed in London about an hour after the tattoo was done. She was rushed to hospital and died before her dad got there.'

'When was this?'

'Kim's eighteenth. The shit really hit the fan. Mr Barton's a widower and Nadia was his only child so, you know, crap for him. He blamed Kim. Came round here after the funeral, raging. Mum had to calm him down.'

'Kim must have been terribly upset.'

'She went very quiet for a while. Hid away, really. She wouldn't talk about it. So, listen, do you want me to help with the investigation? I'm on the inside, I'd be a good informer. It would be cool.'

He looked so eager that Swift thought he had better throw him a line. 'Just let me know if you think of anything that might be relevant. Particularly anyone Kim might have been having problems with. That would be helpful.' Ben smiled, happy to be given a task, although Swift suspected he'd forget about it as soon as something else caught his attention.

When they'd moored the boat, Swift asked him where Kim's body had been. He pointed to a spot in the water to the right of the jetty and about half a metre in. Then he said he'd be on the case day and night and shot away to do his laundry.

Swift took a look in the summerhouse. It consisted of a single room, with plain whitewashed walls. There was a slatted bench to sit on below hooks and shelves holding towels, towelling robes, bottles of water, mosquito candles and a dozen or so granola bars in bright purple wrapping. A long sofa covered in a patchwork quilt was set against another wall — the scene of Jack North's happy surrendering of his virginity and the place where Kim had frequently camped out.

He walked back to his car in the fading daylight. The woods were silent apart from the occasional rustling of falling leaves or late conkers. Mrs Stanley was at the front of the house, hacking at bushes with a pair of shears and throwing the cuttings into a large garden sack. Swift nodded to her.

'Can I have a word with you about Kim Woodville?'

'Maybe. Not today. I'm busy, sorting all this out. I don't know why I pay those gardeners, they don't do a proper job. You can't get any decent help these days. It's all take the money and run.' She had a turned-down mouth and patches of pinkish skin on her narrow face and over her beaky nose.

Swift nodded. 'Another time then.'

'Maybe. *If* I have the time and inclination. I don't jump when people click their fingers, so if that's what you were thinking, you're very much mistaken.' She gave a little humourless laugh, as if she had uttered a witticism, turned her back on him and carried on chopping away.

Just as he reached the car, he heard her call out, 'Mind you, I wasn't surprised at what happened to Kim. Bad blood will out. She spelled trouble from the day she came here. A disaster waiting to happen, she was. Mark my words, I always said she'd come to no good and I was right.' He ignored her and headed down the drive.

Out on the road to London a chilly wind whipped up and the sky turned misty. Huge crinkled leaves landed on the windscreen and blew away. When he was halfway back, his phone rang. It was from Oxfordshire police. He had left a message, requesting a call back.

He switched to hands free and listened.

71

'DS Josh Houghton here. You were asking about Kim Woodville's death.'

'Thanks for getting back to me. As I said, I'm taking a look at what happened and I understand you were involved at the time.' Swift explained about Jack North.

Houghton had a flat Midlands accent and an easygoing manner to accompany it. 'I remember North. Bloody nuisance he made of himself. He phoned me at the time and sent a long email. Very excitable. The inquest was clear. Kim Woodville had a massive seizure, fell in the water and drowned. People with epilepsy can drown in the bath.'

'What about Pete Hussain?'

'That was a balls-up. I don't know if he had anything to do with it. My DI at the time was recently promoted and new to the patch. He got overzealous because he'd never dealt with a drowning before. Then he didn't secure the evidence properly so he got suspended, ended up in a disciplinary.'

This was more than he had expected. Houghton seemed pleased at his cocky DI's downfall and happy to pick over it. 'You're talking about the watch?' Swift asked.

'Correct. We found it in the bushes by the summerhouse. A guy Hussain worked with said he'd told him he'd lost it earlier in the year. Said he was pissed off because his mum had given it to him. We know Hussain used to meet Kim by the lake so it could add up. Then we lost the bloody thing anyway. Hussain had the cheek to send a letter of complaint afterwards.'

'Jack North mentioned bruising.'

'There was bruising on her upper arms. She'd been gripped from behind. Hussain acknowledged that he used to get a bit hands on with Kim. He said he'd last seen her earlier in July and that they'd had a slanging match but no sex. He maintained he couldn't recall gripping her upper arms then, but on the other hand he couldn't rule it out. He said she liked a bit of restraint when they were fighting or having sex. Then the pathologist couldn't date the bruising any more exactly than to within the month before Kim's death. So that was going nowhere.'

'Do you remember where Hussain said he was the night Kim died?'

'Home alone. He finished work at nine, said he was knackered and went straight home. He was renting a room in a flat in Bow and no one else was in. Hang about — I'm just looking over the case notes. Yeah, time of death was between ten thirty and midnight, so he could have got to Low Lake but only just. He was driving an old banger at the time and I reckon it would have seized up if he'd gone over fifty.'

'What about the other members of the Ramsay family?'

'As I recall, two of them were away. Gill Ramsay was laid up after an operation. The others were around that night so I suppose one of them could have popped down to the lake and chucked Kim in. But there was no evidence to suggest that and none of them were suspects. No one was, except Hussain.'

'What about Kim's phone and her computer?'

'Her phone was on a bench in the summerhouse. We checked the data on it. There was nothing unusual. She'd sent no emails in the weeks before she died. There were some to Jack North in the months before. There was one text to Pete Hussain from the end of June, telling him to stay away from her. He hadn't replied and he acknowledged that he'd ignored it. Said he saw her once more, when they had the row. She'd made a few calls, and they were to the museum where she worked or to home. Her last call had been that afternoon, to the house, to say that she wouldn't be back for dinner. Sadie Stanley took the call. Only thing we couldn't find was her laptop. It was missing and it never turned up.'

'Isn't that a bit unusual? You'd expect most young people to be busy with emails and texts.'

'I thought that too at first but then her family said she didn't use social media that much. She was an unusual young woman in many ways and that was one of them.'

'What about the fact that Kim would never go near water, into that lake on her own?'

'So? She was known to be a bit foolhardy and unruly. She missed her medication. Messed about with it, from what her aunt told me. And she wouldn't have known what she was doing once a seizure started. She'd managed to cause awful trouble for another girl who died, you know.'

'Nadia Barton?'

'That's it. Persuading her to have a tattoo. I know her dad, Larry. We're in the pub quiz team. Poor chap's never recovered. Never will. He's a shadow of himself now, that man.'

'It was hardly Kim's fault. Nadia had an unexpected allergic reaction. That kind of random accident can happen.'

'Well, if she'd never persuaded Nadia to have it done, that girl would be alive now. Nadia was easily led, too influenced by Kim. Her dad didn't like her mixing with that family, said they're all oddballs, but young people won't be told.'

'What about this row Kim was supposed to have had by the lake the night she died?'

Houghton gave a dry laugh. 'What about it? Bloke called Cliff Bailey thought he heard something. But he was getting so he forgot his own name and the way home. And he hated Hussain. They'd got into an argument one night and Hussain had given him a swollen nose. Everyone knew Cliff was starting to behave oddly and it turned out he had a brain tumour. If my DI hadn't been the eager new kid on the block and had listened to me, he'd never have taken a statement from Cliff without getting a doctor to see him first. So that put us on the back foot. Bailey was an unreliable witness and we couldn't find that anyone had been by the lake with Kim.'

'So you don't think Hussain just got lucky and got away with it?'

'It's possible but with no reliable evidence . . . We found his DNA in the summerhouse but that added up because he used to meet Kim in there. He's a lowlife drug dealer and caused trouble in the area, but I never rated him as dangerous in that way. Although that aggressive type can suddenly lose control, I've seen it happen. We didn't do everything by the book but the evidence didn't hold up. Listen, that girl Kim was a wild one. Camping out under trees, roaming around at night, sleeping in that summerhouse with no lock on the door, boozing heavily. Very risky behaviour. I wouldn't let my daughter carry on like that, especially if she had a serious health condition. That aunt of hers seemed to have no clue about what she was getting up to. But that's the Ramsay family for you. Hippy-dippy. Very *alternative*. Have you met Gill?'

'Yes. She seemed to fancy herself as the family guru.'

Houghton laughed. 'That sums her up.'

'Well, thanks for your help, it's been useful.'

Swift ended the call. Houghton had made a fair point about Gill Ramsay — she'd been markedly hands off with Kim. Swift still hadn't worked out why. It was the first he'd heard of Kim drinking heavily. Yet another version of her.

It was seven thirty and he was hungry. Often, on an evening like this, he might have wandered to his local pub, the Silver Mermaid, met Cedric and had a meal, a bottle of wine and a game of dominoes. At home, there would be no laughter from upstairs, no riffs of jazz drifting down, no aromas of jam bubbling or casseroles cooking. *Oh, Cedric,* he thought. *Come home soon, old friend.*

* * *

Nora threw him a banana and chose a yellowy-green apple for herself. They had pulled in by the riverbank just below Richmond, near the stone obelisks that marked the meridian line. There was an abundance of dock leaves, cow parsley, marsh marigolds and nettles growing near the foreshore. The sun was gentle, the mulchy scent of autumn in the air.

'Elizabeth the First died near here, didn't she?' Nora asked.

'I think so. There used to be a palace here and I guess a queen would have died in one of those.'

'Lucky old her, popping off in her bed and not being beheaded or cut to pieces on a battlefield.'

Nora munched happily and stretched. She was a detective inspector in the Met and he had first encountered her when he was looking for a missing woman. They had failed to act on a mutual attraction and then life, including Swift's ongoing involvement with Ruth, had got in the way. He had been seeing Nora now for a couple of months and so far, so terrific. She was as keen a rower as him and a strong one, although she rarely found enough time to come on the river. She was devoted to her job and ambitious. He knew she often put in extra hours.

She leaned an ankle on his knee, closing her eyes. 'Bliss, sheer bliss.'

'My company, of course.'

She opened one eye. 'The river.'

It was wonderful that she shared this passion with him. He had started rowing after his mother died, using it as a way to free his mind for a while from grief and cares. When his father promptly remarried a colleague called Joyce and provided him with an unwanted stepmother, he had decamped frequently to Lily's house, and the river was on the doorstep. He had taken his boat out daily, seeking relief in the mesmerising repetition, the sheer hard work, the concentration needed to read the tide and the wind. He had found solace in the way the light changed on the water and the rhythm of the oars.

'The Thames has kept me sane over the years,' he said.

She nodded. 'The movement and the water. Good harmony.'

He was discovering things about her. She was direct, sometimes to the point of bluntness. She used the word 'fierce' a lot, meaning very. She didn't want children, saying that she'd never had any maternal urge. According to her they were okay in small doses, as long as you could hand them back. She liked watching snooker, and said that the slow pace calmed her. She had a quick temper that abated as fast as it flared. She was still a little raw about having been dumped by Alistair, her previous partner, who had decided that a job in New York was preferable to her. She liked to check out property for sale. She had a small but handsome flat in Herne Hill and said it suited her, yet she constantly scrolled her way through the For Sale websites. Swift called it 'property porn.' Nora said it was just a bit of harmless fun and she liked snooping on other people's lives. 'OMG, look at that hideous wallpaper!' she would cry, or, 'How can anyone have their bathroom photographed with the loo seat up? Must be a fierce manky man living there.'

Swift was more concerned about the child aspect. He didn't want more children, that was no problem, but there was Branna. Nora had met her a couple of times and seemed to be fine with her. She had learned some sign language to use with her and appeared to like her company. It was just that after about half an hour, Nora started glancing at her watch and looking mildly bored. Still, it was early days. He gave her a bottle of water and they watched the Saturday afternoon comings and goings at a nearby pub.

'Talking of movement,' she said, 'I'm picking up my new car on Tuesday.'

'Thought you swore you'd never have one in London because of the crazy traffic?'

'I know, but it'll be handy and I've never had a brand-new one before. We'll go for a jaunt in it somewhere, so I can get the feel of it. Maybe down to the coast?'

'Sounds good. Once I know when Cedric's coming home, I can plan more.'

'How is he?'

'Improving slowly. His pacemaker's working as it should and he's having physio. He's still very tired but his memory is better. They hope he can come home next week. Milo has pretty much moved into the hospital. He brings in takeaways and snoozes in a chair by Cedric's bed.'

'Any sign of Oliver?'

'No. I left a message on his voicemail, telling him where his father is, but no response. Cedric doesn't mention him now.'

'Oliver's a tosspot. He'll turn up sooner or later. That type always does. He doesn't deserve a lovely dad like Cedric.' Nora went on to tell him about a murder investigation she was working on and asked how he was doing with Kim and the Ramsays.

'Kim Woodville had something on her mind. If I can find out what that was, I'll make progress. She seems to have been excited as well as struggling with something. It seems odd that her laptop was missing after she died, yet her phone was found. It could all add up to something or nothing. Young adults often like a bit of drama. But maybe someone did force her into the lake and watched her drown. She hated water and wouldn't have gone in willingly.'

'If she started having a fit on land, then it might not have been too difficult to steer her into the lake,' Nora said.

He nodded. 'Especially if the bruises on her upper arms were from that night. Someone could have held her from behind and forced her forwards. Once she started having a tonic-clonic seizure, she'd have been confused and not in control. If that's what happened, it would have been fairly easy to do. A man or a woman could have done it. Her cousin Valery seems to have hated her. I'm talking to her next week.'

'You think she hid Kim's medication because it was her plan to cause her death? Seems a bit far-fetched.'

He shrugged. 'I'm not discounting the idea.'

'Well . . . Girl hatred. Strong stuff. Tell you something for nothing, Ty, girls at their worst are much more devious and scheming than boys. I was a nightmare teenager. My poor mother. I barely spoke to her for a year. I loathed her intensely because I had spots and puppy fat and I felt she didn't understand. I just blanked her. She used to ask me what she'd done wrong but I'd never tell her. I'm ashamed now, thinking of it. Boys are as transparent as glass in comparison to girls.'

'And do they stay that way? Am I?'

She smiled. 'Ah well, you're a special case.'

'That's not an answer.'

'Can't show all my cards.' She leaned forward and kissed him. She smelled of toasted nuts and crisp apple. Like apple crumble. 'Tell me a bit more about this vigorous stepmother of yours. Joyce reminds me of one of my friend's mothers. I see you squirming when you're around her.'

'I suppose the problem is me, not her. She means well and I do feel a responsibility for her but she's just too much. She taught in the same school as my father and he married her within a year of my mother dying. There was this overwhelming, nosy woman moving my mum's things around and redecorating, trying to find out my interests and what I liked to eat. I didn't want a stepmother. And then my father died within a couple of years of marrying her, leaving me with her. I resented her and I still do. I do my best to avoid her but she seems impervious to my evasions. Immature of me, I know.'

'Does she have other children?'

He shook his head. 'No.'

Nora pursed her lips. 'Maybe Joyce reads you better than you realise. She sounds like the maternal sort. Maybe she's just very fond of you because you're the only child she'll ever have. She hangs on in there because she loved your dad and knows that you never really get over losing your mother when you're young. She must feel a responsibility towards you. It must be hard, being a stepmother. The lines are blurred and when it comes down to it, you're always a replacement. There's always the shadow of the biological mother behind you.'

He knew there was truth in Nora's words and that he resisted it. He just didn't want to deal with it. 'Maybe,' he said, 'but I don't need step-mothering, and Joyce and I have nothing in common except an uneasy truce. There *is* a time when I like Joyce very much, though.'

'When's that?'

'When she's away for a month or more on one of her far-flung cruises with no phone signal or Wi-Fi. Yes, I'm very fond of Joyce when she's on the South Atlantic or exploring the Siberian coast. I think of her warmly then.'

'You're a horror.'

'Agreed. Shall we get on?'

She threw him a shrewd look, and lifted her oars. They rowed on, past Kew Gardens and Chiswick with its colony of houseboats. The river was busy with pleasure boats and rowers, including some training teams dressed in white and yellow with red pennants flying over their boats. An electric-blue kingfisher darted ahead of them. The breeze was mild, the water flow smooth. Swift watched Nora's steady arms and the sheen of sweat on her neck. He was in the best of company — his old friend and confidant, the Thames, and this smart, funny woman who made him smile.

CHAPTER 5

Adela Janssens ran her own carpentry business from her tiny terraced house in Harrow. The narrow front garden was filled with beautifully carved pumpkins of all shapes, sizes and colours. A few were done in the traditional jack-o'-lantern style but most were of intricate leaf or abstract designs. Swift stopped to admire them before he rang the bell.

Adela's workshop was at the bottom of the garden. Inside, he could see that she was packing up for the day. She brushed dust from a plane and offered him a beer from a small fridge. He sat on a tall stool, sipping his drink, breathing the sweet aroma of sawdust. The floor was covered in wood shavings. A sturdy workbench ran along one wall, with an orderly assembly of hammers, knives, framing squares, straight and circular saws, drills and chisels. The work in progress was a beautiful coffee table made of elm, with four long drawers in the base. Adela was sturdily built but trim, with short blonde hair and wide tawny eyes. She was wearing a red sock on one foot and a black one on the other. She saw him looking and smiled.

'Just a foible of mine, like carving pumpkins. I always wear odd socks. Don't ask me why. I started doing it when I was a child. Sadie Stanley used to tell me it made me look like a bag lady. You can always rely on Sadie to tell you what she's thinking. Has she had a chance to disapprove of you yet?' Adela had a booming voice that resonated in the small space.

'Not to any degree. I have a feeling she will in her own time. She's keeping me at arm's length until she's ready to talk to me. I understand she put a lot of money into Low Lake.'

Adela grabbed a bottle of moisturiser, drew another stool forward and sat on it, tucking her legs behind the struts. She sat very straight, working the cream into her hands and between her fingers. 'I don't know all the details, but I reckon Sadie owns more than half of it. She was married to a man who made a good living out of banking. He used to beat her up but after he obligingly popped off in his early sixties, she was a rich widow. Gill and Jakob wanted to move out of London. He'd had several unsuccessful business ventures and Gill wanted to do her home crafts, so she and Sadie came up with the plan to buy Low Lake. Sadie sold her place in Yorkshire and moved in. She's a miserable woman but she did have a hard life with her husband. Gill likes to live beyond her means, I can tell you that. She scratches together an income from her work, however much she bigs it up. She relies on her aunt for the goodies, so that makes Sadie a big cheese.'

'How long did you live at Low Lake for?'

'About a year, on and off. I visited over the years but I stayed for a while after I came back from teaching in Kenya. I was married to a guy from Nairobi but it didn't work out. I didn't want to go back to Brussels, where my family live. I needed a complete change so I decided to try my hand at carpentry. I'd always been good at working with wood. I was doing a course in Banbury, so living at Low Lake was handy for me — and cheap, of course.'

'And you were living there when Kim died?'

She nodded. 'I left a couple of months later. It was very sad. A terrible time. I hope she didn't suffer much.'

'If she'd had a seizure and was unconscious when she fell in the lake, she probably didn't.'

'It's ironic that Kim drowned, given what happened to her in childhood, don't you think? My first thought was that her mother had come back to finish off the job.'

'Her mother disappeared after leaving prison, didn't she?'

'As far as I know. A very disturbed woman, from what I gathered.'

'Did you know Pete Hussain?'

'The guy who was arrested but then let go? Never met him. Kim used to have conspicuous love bites on her neck at times, so I gathered she was seeing someone. Some girls might have tried to cover them up, but not Kim. I remember at breakfast one morning Sadie made some comment about flaunting disgusting behaviour. I could see from the glint in Kim's eyes that she'd been waiting for a reaction from her. She looked pleased.'

'Was Gill there? Did she comment?'

'She was there but she probably changed the subject. Gill always seemed uncomfortable around Kim, a bit guarded, watchful. I used to think that after she'd taken Kim in, Gill realised she was out of her depth but it was too late to pull out. She'd thought she could deal with Kim through her half-baked ideas about surrounding her with affection and a big family, but it didn't work. Kim was too tricky. So Gill kind of skirted around her. Kim could be scary, you know. She'd snap at you if she was crossed or when she wanted something, and it was best not to get in her way. She was deeply troubled. Hardly surprising. She didn't often show it but there were layers to her. The top one seemed calm, but underneath there was real agitation. That's what I thought, anyway.'

'Tell me about how Kim fitted into the family. Or didn't.'

Adela took a long drink from her bottle and sighed with pleasure. 'Woodworking builds up a thirst. Look, I'll be honest with you. I never felt comfortable at Low Lake and I was relieved when I was able to move away. It was good of Gill to put me up but I don't like her much. I haven't got kids so I'm no expert, but I thought Gill was a strange mixture of controlling and libertarian. The family was closed off, constraining.' She stopped and considered him for a moment, rather as he imagined she might contemplate a piece of wood before sawing it. 'For example, Gill homeschooled the children with loads of random choice and "pick what you want to do today" going on, and she'd say she wanted them to be creative and original. But at the same time she always wanted to know where they were, what they were doing, who they were seeing — except for Kim, of course. I think it made them secretive, the mixed messages. I imagine it's why Will escaped into the army at just sixteen, as soon as he could. He wanted some freedom, together with order and routine. And Steve managed to get away at last, I've heard. I could see that living there was grinding him down too.'

'He lives in Islington. You haven't met up since he moved to London?'

She shook her head. 'No, no reason to. We were never close. Once the kids were older, Gill's grip was inevitably loosened but she still tried to stay involved. Kim escaped all that. I kind of admired her, although I thought she was a chancer and I couldn't warm to her. Don't tell any of the family that I said this to you but I thought she had more gumption than Valery or my nephews. Will is plucky but not exactly brainy, Valery's a dreary mummy's girl and spiteful with it. Ben's engaging but chaotic and Steve is a nice enough but taciturn bloke, only interested in engines as far as I can see. I sound nasty saying all that but, well, it's the truth.'

He smiled. 'I always appreciate the truth.'

'I bet you don't always get it, though.'

No, he thought, *and I usually assume that people are telling me their own version of the truth, if not actually lying.* 'It depends on whether or not the person I'm talking to has something to conceal.'

She nodded. 'Hmm, I can see how that works. I thought Kim had done well to overcome a hard start in life and on top of that she had her epilepsy to deal with. She was a strong personality and she was a stoic. She never moaned or complained, unlike Valery, who's always griping. But I thought Gill didn't do Kim any favours by letting her roam around, making up her own rules, sleeping out in the woods. I reckon Gill was relieved when Kim was out of sight. No one knew what she was up to half the time. She could be devious, a bit under the radar. *Elusive.* Yes, that sums her up. It was probably a survival mechanism. Gill would make a token effort now and again and ask her what she was up to, but I think Kim lied a lot and Gill turned a blind eye. I used to tell Kim that I didn't think it was good for her. She and I rubbed along, although I didn't think much of it when she borrowed my stuff without asking — scarves, jackets and jumpers, things like that. She had no scruples about taking things and she never washed them, just dumped them on my bed or on the floor. When I had it out with her she'd shrug, as if I was making a fuss about nothing. I think she took money sometimes as well. When I complained to Gill, she'd babble on about how Kim was different because of her early childhood and needed special understanding. Bullshit. That's when I started to think Gill was scared of her.'

'How did Kim seem to you before she died?'

'I was busy with my course in Banbury. I didn't see much of her. She asked me for a lift to the station a couple of mornings before it happened, though. Said she was going to see an exhibition at the Museum of London. Cadged a tenner off me in the car. When she put it in her purse, I saw that she already had a bundle of notes in there. It annoyed me but I couldn't be bothered to argue the toss with her. That was the last time I saw her.' She bent and ran a hand over the tabletop, smoothing it.

'Tell me a bit more about Valery. She seems to have disliked Kim.'

'She did. Intensely. Kim was a slim, good-looking girl, striking in fact, and Val is a pudgy plain Jane. Hard to swallow that, and to have to make room for a lively cousin. And in my opinion, Val's a hypochondriac, which her mother encourages. Poor old Val, she's probably going to turn out as another Sadie unless she manages to kick-start herself. She's had no luck with romance, probably because she's so self-obsessed. I thought at one time that she fancied Phil Dunbar. He's married to Elaine, the archaeologist that Kim worked with. Val had no interest in archaeology or the museum, but she went to a talk there with me one evening. I thought she'd slathered on a lot of makeup for an educational outing, but then the penny dropped when I saw her making cow eyes at Phil. He looks like a faded matinee idol. A bit gangly and lined for my liking, but he obviously pressed Val's buttons. Sadly for her I'm not sure he noticed. Have you met Val yet?'

'Yes, with her mother. I've yet to talk to her on her own.'

'Well, good luck. If she doesn't like you, you won't get much change out of her.'

Swift took another drink. The beer was malty, with a gentle kick. 'Your cousin Jakob doesn't seem to have played much of a part in raising the children.'

Adela snorted. 'Jakob was always a weakling. A passive man. His first wife was a strong character. She died when he was in his twenties, leaving him with two young sons. He quickly remarried someone who'd be his mum and tell him what to do. Gill likes to have people dependent on her. She works on them subtly, pulling them in. Jakob wasn't the most stimulating of company and I'm not sure the family noticed his absence much when he died. Who's that member of the royal family they nicknamed "Fog?" Oh, I know — Mark Phillips, Princess Anne's ex. It was an apt name for Jakob too.'

'He wasn't too passive to have an affair,' Swift said.

'True, but I would imagine he was propositioned or wandered into it. He'd always choose the path of least resistance. He'd been exiled from the house when he died. I haven't been there for ages now but Ben sends me chatty emails now and again. Tells me about Gill and Sadie's arguments, usually over money. You can rely on Ben to be indiscreet. I don't think Gill's style of parenting did him much good either. He needed much more day-to-day structure instead of floating around in make-believe land and gluing bits of cardboard together. That's not much preparation for adult life. A school would have made him more resilient and realistic.' She smiled. 'Now I'm starting to sound like Sadie. She's a poisonous old battleaxe but sometimes there's an element of truth hidden amongst her rants. Another beer?'

'No thanks, I'm fine. Did you know about Kim's friend, Nadia?'

'The girl who died? I wasn't living there when it happened but it sounded shocking. It must have affected Kim deeply. I never heard her speak about it. But then you only ever knew what Kim wanted you to know.' She held up a finger. 'She did just say one thing to me once about Nadia's dad. What was his name?'

'Larry Barton.'

'That's it. He was coming out of the fish and chip shop in Great Howe one day when we were driving through. I didn't know him but Kim shrank down in her seat and said she didn't want Larry to see her. That was the only time I saw Kim look scared. Then she muttered something about Nadia knowing more than her dad realised about him playing the grieving widower. I've no idea what she meant. I did ask but she changed the subject.'

'Do you have any idea why anyone would want to harm Kim?'

'I don't, no. Given that it wasn't Pete Hussain, I was amazed when you said Jack thinks her death might not have been accidental. There seemed to be no question about it at the time. I hardly know Jack but I understand he was very fond of her. Sorry, I just can't help you there.'

They talked for a while about her work. She told him that she made all kinds of high-end domestic furniture and her next commission was three bookcases.

'I've had some lucky breaks and built a steady reputation,' she said as she showed him out. 'I do love it here in my little house.' Swift found it refreshing to meet someone who seemed content in her work and life.

He made his way back to Hammersmith, getting off the train at Putney and walking home along the Thames Path. The streetlights had come on and the wide river glittered. It had rained and the pavements had a glassy sheen. A sharp northerly breeze had blown in, chopping at the water. Kim Woodville had told Jack that she wanted to discuss something thorny. She didn't seem to have been a woman much given to confidences, so it must have been important to her. He thought that the word 'thorny' also applied to her. She'd stolen and cadged money and other people's possessions, but was that because of what they represented rather than because she needed them? He wondered what had happened to her laptop and why someone would have wanted to take it. Her medication lay in the desk in his office. He would come back to that. He already had an idea about it.

* * *

Swift parked in Great Howe and checked Larry Barton's address.

Barton had sounded gruff and unfriendly when he rang. He spent five minutes saying he didn't see why he should agree to meet, and then suddenly capitulated. Swift sensed that he grasped at any opportunity to talk about his dead daughter. He lived near the centre of Great Howe and Swift decided to look at the village before the meeting and piece together more of Kim's context. He had driven around the narrow streets, noting the signpost to the train station with its hourly service to London, and getting an idea of the place before parking in a small area behind the tiny white plastered museum.

The village sat cosily under the golden autumn sun, moderately busy. All the buildings had colourful hanging baskets. It was the kind of place that a film company might use when making a period drama or an Agatha Christie mystery. It had small houses built of golden stone and some half-timbered and thatched cottages. There was a square in the middle, with a clock tower, almshouses and a medieval church called Saint Osgyth situated on three of the sides. On the fourth was a heavily beamed tithe barn, no longer used for crops, which had been turned into a café. A group of Chinese tourists herded by a young man in a lime-green jacket were taking photos of each other outside the church.

There were individual shops of the kind that had disappeared from most places — a hardware store, a butcher, baker, greengrocer, and one called Belinda that sold women's clothing, including corsets and amazingly structured brassieres 'for the fuller figure.' Swift immediately thought of his stepmother. He spotted a floral tea dress in the window of the type that Sadie Stanley wore and wondered if she shopped there. It was as if the village had been frozen in the 1950s. Or perhaps it was preserved for the likes of Chinese tourists as a representation of a bygone age. *Very Miss Marple*, Swift thought. *Looks like they polish the roads.*

Kim had lost both her parents and had been propelled from the urban grit of Tottenham to this. It must have been like landing on another planet.

He stopped at the café for a coffee and a chicken sandwich and sat at one of the metal tables outside, watching people shopping and chatting. He thought about Branna, who had just started at a nursery. He hoped she was coping and that her hearing loss wasn't impeding her too much, or causing difficulties with the other children. One of the staff at the nursery knew sign language, which should ease things for her, but even so, she would face challenges. He recalled Jack North's reference to the 'sliding glance' and had to fight back an urge to ring the nursery and check that Branna was okay. He'd had no idea that his daughter would capture his heart and hold it to ransom in this way.

A group of eight racing cyclists in yellow and black Lycra arrived, looking like a swarm of bees, and providing a welcome distraction. They glowed with sweat and exhilaration, exuding a sense of energy and action. They clustered their bikes nearby, and then started ordering plates of food. When he had finished eating, Swift wandered back to the Bickmore Museum where Kim had worked. It was closed and he jotted down the opening times. A notice informed him that it was named after Victoria Bickmore, a local historian who had established it in the nineteenth century.

He walked on to Larry Barton's house, a stone cottage at one end of a group of three. It had a small, carefully tended front garden and a white door inside a wooden porch. Barton was formally dressed in grey flannels, white shirt and a gold-buttoned navy blazer with a tightly knotted striped tie. He was a big man, heavily built, and as Swift followed him into the house, he coughed wheezily. They sat in a small living room at the back. A conservatory had been added which should have enhanced the light but instead turned the room into a dim cave. The room contained an empty, dusty fireplace, dark furniture and few ornaments. A vase of tired-looking dried flowers sat on the mantelpiece next to two framed photos. One was of two women. The other showed three men sitting in a pub, Barton in the middle, holding up some kind of trophy. A large clock ticked in an alcove next to the fireplace. It was half an hour fast. The room was chilly and Swift was glad he had worn his leather jacket with a fleece lining.

'I'm sorry about what happened to your daughter,' Swift said.

'I'm sure you are. I don't really understand why you're here.' Barton's voice was rasping, with a slight burr.

'Jack North, one of Kim's family, is still unsure about the verdict regarding her death. He's asked me to take another look.'

Barton looked at him impassively. His clothes were crisp and fresh but his face was crumpled and his eyes heavy, as if he'd just woken from a deep sleep. 'What's that got to do with me?'

'I'm talking to people who knew Kim.'

Barton uttered a strange noise, somewhere between a sob and a laugh. 'I wish I'd never known her. I wish Nadia had never known her. I know it's a terrible thing to say but I'm glad she's dead. She deserved it after what she did.'

'I understand Nadia's death was a terrible accident. An allergic reaction.'

Barton ran his hands over his face. 'An accident, you say? Yes. An accident that would never have happened if she hadn't been in Kim Woodville's company. Nadia was impressionable, easily swayed. I could tell that she thought Kim was a bit . . . exotic. Living out at the grand house with grounds to play in, never been to school, as well as a tragic past and an incurable illness. Nadia would never have thought of a tattoo on her own. I'd forbidden her to go to London with the Woodville girl. Nadia didn't go against me until she got friendly with that wayward bitch.

Kim persuaded her to make the trip. I was at work that day, so it was all done behind my back.'

'How long had Nadia known Kim?'

'Not that long. About six months or so. They met through the museum. Nadia was doing a school project on the local area and went there to get material.'

'And you'd met Kim?'

'I'd seen her around the village now and again. She was drunk one night outside the chip shop, having a row with Pete Hussain. They were throwing food and beer at each other. Nice company she was keeping there, but I suppose like attracts like.' He shook his head in distaste. 'He did it to her, I'm sure of that. He might have got off through police sloppiness but he's the one you're looking for. You can tell Jack North that from me if you want. Not that I care one way or the other.'

Swift knew that blaming someone else could be a useful smokescreen. 'What makes you think that?'

'Hussain's a lowlife. That kind always causes trouble. I expect they had a bust-up and he pushed Kim in the water. He lives somewhere in London and used to come here to see his grandad, Robbie. Robbie was trouble in his day, too. Poaching and the like, getting into fights. Always just avoiding the law by the skin of his teeth. Hussain liked swaggering around the village, playing the big man from the city, winding people up. Handy with his fists too. Had a nasty temper on him. You could see he was amusing himself by picking arguments. His grandad died last year and Hussain hasn't shown his face round here since, thank goodness.'

Barton stared into the empty fireplace for a few moments. 'Kim was here once when I came home, drinking my whisky, getting Nadia to try some. I could smell marijuana. Kim was wearing clothes with deliberate rips in, as if looking like a tramp is clever. I threw her out.' He reached for the nearest photo and handed it to Swift.

'That's Nadia, with her mother. I lost my wife eighteen months before Nadia died.'

They had both been blonde, with wide faces and soft, open expressions. Mrs Barton was a stout, comfortable-looking woman. Nadia's long hair was in a neat ponytail and she wore a check shirt and denim skirt. She had the eager smile of a girl who likes to please. No makeup or jewellery, her mother's arm around her shoulder. You would take her for a well-brought-up, well-mannered girl.

'You had a terrible double blow,' Swift said, handing back the picture.

'Yes. Well. You can't say what's coming your way in life. All I know is that my daughter would be with me today if she hadn't been . . . been *corrupted*.' He spat the word and put the photo down heavily, clenching a fist.

'That's a strong word to use. Teenagers do strange things without seeing the consequences.'

Barton stared at Swift, unblinking. 'Look here. Nadia went off the rails after she met Kim. Until then we had a regular life. Work for me, school for Nadia. She was always here after school to do her homework and help me get the tea. She helped out at the cricket in the summer, making sandwiches and such. It was hard after her mum died but we were getting through day by day. That's what you do. After she met Kim, she never stopped talking about her. "Kim says this, Kim does that, Kim knows lots about Roman manuscripts, Kim knows the names of all the constellations, Kim maintains that rules are there to be broken." Her epilepsy fascinated Nadia and from the things she said, Kim gave her graphic descriptions of her seizures. All very dramatic. Nadia had her navel pierced, let her hair grow longer. It started to look kind of wild, her hair. Her schoolwork suffered and I'm sure she was truanting some of the time. She started wearing jewellery and makeup, cheapish stuff but lots of it. She stole money from me. I always kept some money, about fifty pounds, in a tin in the kitchen. Just for bits and pieces and in case

Nadia noticed we were running out of something. I realised that twenty-pound notes were going and I couldn't see what they'd been spent on. Nadia denied it when I challenged her, flared up at me. I knew who was behind it. She started staying out late so that I was worried out of my mind. Stayed out overnight once. I called the police. When she came back, she smelled of smoke and drink and said she'd camped out with Kim in the grounds at Low Lake and they'd lit a fire. What kind of family are they, allowing such goings-on? People round here have always said they were a rum bunch. That Sadie Stanley is a horrible woman. She's fallen out with all the village shops, accusing them of short-changing her or getting orders wrong. I told Nadia she wasn't allowed out for a fortnight after she stayed away for the night. All she said was, "Chill out, Dad," and laughed. She never used to speak to me like that. It felt as if my Nadia had been replaced with a strange girl I hardly knew.' He held a hand to his chest, as if the torrent of words had emptied him.

Swift waited a few moments to let him recover. 'How old was your daughter at that time?'

'Just seventeen.'

Swift thought that in his own way, Barton was as controlling as Gill Ramsay. Nadia's behaviour had hardly been that extreme for her age. There was a tightness to the man that indicated a need for order. Life had been unkind to him but a seventeen-year-old was always going to rebel in some way. A grieving Nadia had probably found an older, charismatic female friend to hero worship and copy. It would be odd to roam about with wayward Kim and come home to this claustrophobic atmosphere. Would Barton have been capable of taking revenge? He thought it possible.

'Did the police talk to you about Kim's death?'

'A detective called Josh Houghton came here. I told him I was here at home on my own that night. It would have been my pearl wedding anniversary. I was in this chair, thinking about my wife. That satisfied Josh, so I presume it will satisfy you too. Not that you've any right to ask. You've no right to be in my house at all.'

Swift ignored this. 'I understand that you went to Low Lake after Nadia died. You were upset, and rather aggressive.'

'I was beside myself. I had my say. I had a right to that. I told Gill Ramsay she should be ashamed of her child-rearing.' He looked at the clock on the mantelpiece, then at his watch, and rubbed the face with a finger.

Swift sat forward to catch his attention. 'Kim told someone that you were playing at being a grieving widower. She said your daughter knew it.'

Barton's head snapped up. His eyes were dark with animosity. 'Little bitch. What's that supposed to mean?'

'I thought you might tell me.'

'She'd have said anything to make herself feel better about what she'd done. I don't have to answer for any poison she came out with.' He stood abruptly. 'You have to leave now. I'm off to the doctor.'

Swift rose. Josh Houghton and Barton were friends, and it had been Josh Houghton who had interviewed Barton about his whereabouts on the night Kim died. That contravened police procedures. 'If Pete Hussain wasn't responsible for Kim's death, do you believe it was accidental?'

Barton gripped the back of his chair, his shoulders square and stiff. 'Like you said about my Nadia, a terrible accident.' For the first time, he smiled. There was no warmth in it. Then he led the way to the front door and banged it shut after Swift.

* * *

The village was quiet in the early afternoon, the streets deserted. Swift went to collect his car, and saw a man with a cardboard box balanced against his chest unlocking the

95

museum door. He introduced himself, saying he was hoping to speak to Elaine Dunbar.

'I'm her husband, Phil. Elaine's not around today. Can I help you?' He was tall and rangy, dressed in jeans and a tan cotton jacket. A pair of tortoiseshell-framed glasses were perched on top of his head.

'It's about Kim Woodville.'

'Kim?' The man looked surprised. 'Are you from her family?'

'No, I'm not family. I've been asked to take another look at her death. I'm a private investigator.'

'Well, you can come in for a minute if you want to. I'm not opening up, just dropping off some supplies for the office.'

Inside the door there was a narrow stone-flagged corridor leading to a scarred oak counter with a cash till and plans of the museum layout. Behind it lay a small office. Swift could see a sink, a single metal cupboard and a kettle. A notice by the office advised that the toilet was outside, at the rear. A spiral metal staircase led to an upper floor with a sign reading PRIVATE. STAFF ONLY. The place smelled of warmth and dust, with a hint of mildew from the stone floor. Phil Dunbar put the box on the counter and rubbed his hands. He had a pale, lined face, faded blue eyes and an easy smile.

'I understand Kim used to work here,' Swift said.

'That's right. It was after she came to a talk here. Elaine gives them every month. They got chatting and it went from there. Kim loved archaeology.'

'How old would she have been when she started working here?'

'I'm not sure. You'd have to check with Elaine. She's the one who owns and runs the museum. I just drop in now and again. Victoria Bickmore, who started the museum, was Elaine's great-grandmother.'

'You knew Kim, though?'

'A little, but Elaine was her friend. I know she thought Kim had real potential. Do you want to have a look around while I unpack this stuff?'

A surprising amount had been squeezed into just two rooms. Swift wandered through, looking at information about the local harvesting of flower seeds and the history of the wool trade in the village — there was a working loom and examples of covers made for church kneelers. There was a display of helmets and pikes from the civil war, cases of Neolithic flints, Bronze Age axe heads and daggers, tiles, mosaics and medieval pottery and trade tokens made from lead. It was well presented with brief, clear descriptions and historical context.

A section at the end of the second room was devoted to the excavations at Frynfold, with a history of the site, which a farmer had discovered in 2005. There were descriptions of how small and bulk finds were washed and processed and how pottery was analysed. Some Roman coins, reconstructed wine vessels, tesserae, fragments of shoes and bone hairpins with faces were on display. A large laminated card lay in the centre of a table with the caption:

An introduction to our work written for us by our dear friend and colleague, Kim Woodville, who was one of our committed Frynfold volunteers. Sadly, Kim died in July 2015. Rest in Peace.

My first ever dig was terribly daunting. I didn't know what to expect and I was very nervous. I had butterflies in my stomach. My first job was clearing weeds and nettles from part of the site at Frynfold. It was incredibly hot and I was bad-tempered by lunchtime as well as having nettle stings! When I was let loose on digging in the soil, I was all fingers and thumbs but after a couple of weeks, I felt like a pro.

The weather plays a major part in any dig and we all ran for cover in some of the downpours in summer 2013. You have to bring high factor sun cream and strong waterproofs. Of course, the heat did mean ice cream breaks!

There's real satisfaction in getting into the rhythm of mattock to shovel to wheelbarrow, even if your back aches. I loved the debates between supervisors about what different features and finds might or might not mean. It made me realise that archaeology isn't at all clear-cut and there can be a number of explanations for the same thing.

I fell in love with everything to do with archaeology. You never know what the next day will turn up. It's always fascinating and exciting as well as exhausting.

He moved away from the sad legacy and made his way back to the entrance, where worksheets for children were provided on a table with an open book for visitors to leave comments. Swift leaned over and read the most recent: *A little treasure of a place! B Traynor, Wisconsin.*

'Whereabouts is Frynfold?' Swift asked Dunbar.

'About three miles out of Great Howe, on the Banbury road. It has some interesting features and an area of floor mosaic is reasonably intact. Elaine is the lead archaeologist working the site. Kim used to volunteer there.'

'You're not in the archaeology business then?'

'No. I used to teach but now I work in the local garden centre. It's much easier talking to plants than mutinous kids.' He glanced at his watch. 'I have to be on my way. I can give you Elaine's number if you want to call her.'

Swift unlocked his car and watched Dunbar walk away with a light, springing tread. He had expressed no interest in why there might be any question about Kim's death. Perhaps she was already a distant memory.

CHAPTER 6

Swift woke at six thirty, had coffee and a banana and then did some stretches. He checked the river conditions and saw that flows were low and steady. He rubbed cream into the scar tissue on his thigh to keep it supple, then donned an old tracksuit and hooded top and walked to his club, Tamesas, just below Hammersmith Bridge. He rowed for an hour on a still, calm Thames, looking out for incoming migrant birds. He spotted some whooper swans and a flock of pink-footed geese and took a couple of photos to show Branna. He wondered if there was a sign for pink-footed goose and assumed that you'd have to combine several to indicate the species. His daughter was certainly widening his vocabulary.

Back home, he showered, ate buttery scrambled eggs and then headed up to Cedric's flat where he spent an hour cleaning, changing the bed and checking that there was no out-of-date food in the fridge. There were regular thumps and sounds of hammering from the builders next door. To drown them out, he switched on the Benny Goodman CD that was in Cedric's player, humming along to 'Moonglow' while he worked. The flat seemed strange and lifeless but expectant, too, as if waiting for Cedric's return.

He changed into clean jeans and shirt, donned his leather jacket and set off for Low Lake at eleven thirty. The sun was low but bright. As he drove, he had a feeling of virtuousness and wellbeing after his exercise and cleaning, despite a lack of enthusiasm at the prospect of Valery Ramsay's company. He wondered if she would be as rude on her own as she'd been in front of her mother.

She let him in without a greeting and sat curled on a sofa in the living room. It was a mild autumn day but she wore a shawl around her shoulders and clutched a hot water bottle encased in a felt Paddington bear cover to her abdomen. She sipped at a tall glass of some raspberry-coloured drink. It was as if a stage had been set: the frail woman bravely facing the brusque detective.

'I'm not sure I'm up to talking,' she told him ungraciously. 'I'm not well today.'

'I appreciate you giving me your time,' he said mildly.

She shot him a suspicious look. She was paddling her fingers against the hot water bottle, and it reminded him of a cat kneading its bedding before lying down. She had changed the coloured layers of her hair to blue and yellow. He thought that she probably stayed at home a lot, playing with her unprepossessing appearance. She took some more of her drink. He hadn't been offered anything. He settled himself into a comfortable armchair and said nothing for a few minutes. He guessed she wouldn't be able to maintain a silence and he was right.

'So, what do you want? Or have you just come here to meditate or something?'

He crossed his legs and retied a shoelace, taking his time with the knot before turning a smile on her. 'Your nose must have been put out of joint pretty badly when Kim came to live here.'

She looked startled and shifted on the sofa. 'Don't know what you mean.'

'You were the only girl in the family, the youngest with three brothers. That's quite special. Then another girl, the same age, turned up. A girl who must have attracted, maybe demanded, a lot of attention.'

'Hmm. Interesting angle. I always got enough attention. Mum explained it all to me, how we had to offer Kim a home. That's how we were brought up. We're an inclusive family, there's room for everyone.'

Faking it, he thought. 'But there's having things explained rationally and then there are feelings. I think I might have felt a bit fed up in your position.'

She folded her mouth inwards. 'You're not me though, are you?' She gave a little groan and ran her hand in a circular motion over Paddington's duffel coat.

'You didn't like Kim. You didn't get on with her,' he stated.

'That's right. There's no law that I had to *like* her. We didn't like each other, actually. It was mutual. She was underhand. A calculating bitch. I always reckoned she was secretly laughing at us.'

'Why would she be doing that?'

'She saw us — well Mum and Dad definitely — as the well-meaning do-gooders who took her in and let her get away with stuff because she'd been "abused and deprived."' She made quotation marks in the air.

'That's a bit contradictory.'

'Meaning?'

'A couple of minutes ago, you were saying you were such an inclusive family.'

'Life's contradictory.'

He watched her run her fingers through her hair, and examine the ends. 'Going back to what you said, Kim had been abused and her early years were spent in dreadful circumstances. You once told her you wished she had been drowned as a child.'

'I suppose you got that from blabbermouth Ben. Yes, I told her that. I didn't mean it. It was just something I said when I was angry.'

He thought she had meant it. 'And you once pushed her in the lake, despite knowing how terrified she was of water.'

'Ben tell you that too?'

'Jack North told me.'

'Kim's pet midget. He would. She charmed him. He thought the sun shone from her arse. He didn't see some of the things we saw, living with her all the time.' Her voice was filled with spite.

'And *did* you push her?'

She shrugged and yawned. 'We were messing about by the lake, pushing each other. She tripped. It was an accident.' She looked at him as if to say, *and you can't prove otherwise.*

He changed tack. 'Did you know Pete Hussain?'

'I saw him around the village and a couple of times down by the lake, at night. I knew they were seeing each other. Kim never told anyone much. She was secretive. I heard her on her phone to him one day, telling him to stay away from her. She had a big bruise on her wrist.' This was said with a certain satisfaction.

'You think he caused the bruise?'

'How would I know? I suppose. Maybe she was into kinky sex games or she liked being knocked about. She was pretty warped. Maybe she did it to herself when she was out and about, doing whatever she did. Or when she was pretending to be a famous archaeologist. As if! All she was doing was digging around in mud with a trowel but anyone would think she'd discovered Tutankhamun's grave all on her own.'

It was fascinating to see her let rip with malice. Her eyes shone. Kim might have been no saint, but Valery had her demons.

'I hear that Pete Hussain had a bad reputation around here.'

'Yeah, a dangerous bloke. He wasn't my type.'

'Oh? What is your type?'

'Not him. Coarse and mouthy and full of himself.'

From the way she said it and looked away, Swift thought she wouldn't have minded catching Pete Hussain's eye. He said nothing until she glanced back at him.

'I wish you'd stop looking at me like that.'

'Like what?'

'Like you're trying to see into my brain. Like you know stuff about me. Fancy yourself as a mind reader, do you?'

'Am I making you uncomfortable?'

She shifted on the sofa, making it creak. 'Yeah, as if.'

'I can't help the way I look at people. Going back to Pete Hussain, what did you think after the police let him go?'

'I don't know. I suppose if he and Kim were into rough stuff, something might have happened.' Her tone said she couldn't care less.

'How was Kim after you pushed her in the lake that time?'

Valery hunched her shoulders fiercely. 'I don't know why you're going over this stuff. It was years ago. Kids' squabbles.'

'I'm wondering if anyone had a reason to immerse Kim in water so that she drowned.'

'That's ridiculous. She was roaming around like she usually was. She had a fit, she drowned. Read what the coroner said.' She leaned forwards, rubbing her back and giving another low groan.

'Do you think Kim had a fit because she'd missed her medication?'

She turned her head and looked sideways at him from behind a curtain of hair. 'Maybe.'

'I suppose,' he said thoughtfully, 'that severe epilepsy is in a different league to period pains. More dramatic and worrying for the family. Tonic-clonic seizures would tend to steal the limelight from a bit of hormone trouble. I wonder if you felt eclipsed by Kim.'

Valery sat bolt upright, chewing her lip. 'That's a rotten thing to say. I have a serious health condition. I don't have to talk to you, you know. I only agreed because Mum said you'd go away if we cooperated with you. But don't push me around.'

'I appreciate your cooperation, Valery. I'm sure you're well-intentioned.' He held his hands out in a frank gesture. He didn't want her to close down just yet. 'Maybe what I said was a bit harsh but it was rotten that you called Kim piss pants after she'd had a seizure.'

She pulled at Paddington's ears. 'Children say things. It was just the heat of the moment. Kim had a sharp tongue when she needed it. I could tell you stuff she said . . .' She broke off and buried her nose in her drink.

'Go on, Valery, why don't you tell me? I'd like to hear it.'

She stroked the ends of her hair, silent.

'Okay, then. What about Phil Dunbar?'

Her shoulders twitched. 'What about him?'

'Do you find him attractive?'

'Can't say. Haven't thought about it. He's married anyway.'

'I met him. He's good-looking for his age. Well preserved. Nice smile.'

'If you say so. Fancy him, do you? Want me to be a go-between? Yuk, that would be manky, getting two oldies together.' She mimed vomiting, a finger in her mouth.

'He's not my type. But I think he might be yours.'

She pulled a face and yawned. 'You're boring me now. Have you finished?'

'Not quite.' Swift leaned forward, and pulled the medication pack from his pocket. 'If you won't talk to me about Dunbar, why don't you tell me why you took Kim's medication and hid it on Ape Island?'

She froze. 'What are you talking about?'

'I found it over there, where you'd hidden it. Did you forget what you'd done with it? I'm surprised you left it there, but I suppose a lot was happening after Kim died and you got distracted.'

'I don't know what you're on about. I don't know anything about Kim's medication and you needn't try to bully me into saying I do.' Valery was one of those people whose face drained of colour when they were caught in a lie, instead of blushing.

'Look me in the eye and tell me it wasn't you,' he said quietly, and leaned towards her.

'I don't feel well. I don't have to listen to this crap. You've got no right to come here pressurising me. I'm going to bed.' There were tears in her eyes. The tears of a spoilt child used to getting her own way. She leapt up, knocking over her glass and throwing the hot-water bottle onto the sofa. She ran awkwardly, knock-kneed, to the door and as she opened it, she looked back at him with a defiant scowl. 'If you really want to ask clever questions you should ask why Kim was in touch with her scummy mum just before she died.'

He heard her thunder upstairs. He waited a moment, and then went into the hallway. The radio was playing again on the roof, competing with music coming from a TV at the back of the house. Swift walked down the wide hall and into a huge kitchen. It was painted white throughout and looked brand new with black marble worktops, complicated-looking ovens and hobs, masses of shining gadgets, brass pans hanging from ceiling hooks and a central wooden island. Sliding doors opened on one side into a long sunroom. Ben was sitting on the table, eating a carton of pungent noodles and watching a Batman film on a TV fixed to the wall nearby.

'Hi,' he said, with his eyes still glued to the screen. 'How's the sleuthing?'

'So-so. I think I've upset your sister.'

'Everything upsets Val. And one of her rabbits died yesterday.' He giggled. 'Probably died of boredom or committed suicide, having to listen to her moaning all the time.'

The music soared. Batman confronted Scarecrow. Ben's fork was suspended in mid-air. He stared at the screen, his mouth open.

'Ben, do you know anything about Kim's mother?' No answer. Swift moved a hand in front of Ben's face. 'Ben! I need to speak to you. Can you turn that down?'

Ben nodded, watched another thirty seconds, and then lowered the volume. Swift moved between him and the TV and repeated the question.

'Only that she was a lowlife druggy and she tried to drown Kim and got jailed.' He picked up a tall chocolate milkshake topped with vanilla ice cream and drank.

'Valery says Kim was in contact with her mother before she died.'

Ben shrugged. 'Don't know anything about that. Val might be making it up. She can be a fantasist.' He had a bubble of light brown froth on his top lip.

'Says the grown man watching Batman. Is your mother in?'

'Nah. She's at the chiropodist. Just me and Val this afternoon. They let me go from the shoe shop yesterday. That's why I'm here. I got some prices muddled and a customer complained.' His gaze kept straying to the film. He didn't seem too bothered. He blinked and made an effort to concentrate. 'I haven't got anything for you. Haven't been able to think of anything that might help. I have tried. Got anything else I can help you with?'

It was just after two in the afternoon and the young man had nothing better to do than eat junk and watch Hollywood superheroes.

'Turn the bloody TV off,' Swift said impatiently, and sat down at the table.

Ben pressed the remote, swung down beside him, and began rocking on a chair.

'Are any of Kim's things still here?'

'Nah. Mum cleared her room after she died, gave away her clothes and books, and threw stuff out. Valery redecorated the room and uses it to fiddle about with her scraps of material and glue pots. She couldn't wait to get her hands on it. She calls it her studio. She blagged money from Mum and bought herself a new computer with design programs, a sound system and swanky furniture.'

'It seems odd that Kim's laptop vanished when she died.'

'Yeah. She used it a lot. Kept her archaeology notes on it and stuff. Records of what she did at the museum. She said it would all come in useful if she ever applied to college. She used to carry it round with her in a backpack but it had gone. Maybe it got nicked.' He snapped his fingers. 'Maybe she *was* murdered and the killer took it because it had evidence on it. This stuff's fascinating! I wish I could help more. Hey, I could, couldn't I? I'm on the spot. I might be able to turn something up.' He held his clasped hands out, beseeching.

'Okay, turn down the performance. Kim seems to have been concerned about something before she died. She mentioned it to Jack. She said she'd met two new people.' Swift found Jack's email and showed it to Ben. 'I've no idea what was on her mind or whether it was significant. You could help by asking people who knew her, people who saw her around then if she'd talked about anything worrying her or about anyone she'd met.'

Ben came alive, and rapped the table. 'Okay. I'm on it. Should I make notes?'

'If you want. If you think you might not remember. So, keep in touch. Are you looking for another job?'

'Mum said she was going to talk to the woman at the garage. They need someone for shelf stacking.'

'You could look for a job yourself.'

Ben dug a spoon into the melting ice cream in his glass. 'Hmm, this is the best bit, this chocolate gloop. I suppose I could. I'm just not much good at it. I never get the words out right. They trip me up.'

As Swift left the kitchen, Ben turned the TV volume back up. He heard the jarring screech of a car crash, a blare of music and Ben whooping with excitement. Swift slammed the front door, feeling bad about the way Ben was squandering his days, and generally ill-tempered about the Ramsays.

* * *

They had set the dominoes up on the adjustable bed table that Cedric ate his meals from. Swift watched while Cedric and Milo played and discussed a jazz festival on the South Bank.

'Will you be up to coming?' Milo asked, placing a four on the board.

'Try and stop me. It's three weeks away. I'll be fine. If all goes to plan, I'll be home by the end of the week.'

'You'll be glad to hear that next door's construction work is past the worst of the knocking about,' Swift told him. 'I've started preparations for your homecoming. I've bought you a new duvet cover, red with white peonies. I took a photo of it, look.'

Cedric examined the photo on Swift's phone. 'Lovely, and suitably garish. Don't be going to any trouble, dear boy. You know, I've been talking things over with Milo and we think that it might be a good idea if I move in with him.'

Milo nodded. 'I'm on the ground floor and I've got two bedrooms. We could prop each other up as we grow increasingly ancient.'

'But what would I do without you to annoy me?' Swift kept his tone light, although Cedric's suggestion had winded him.

Cedric smiled at him. 'You see, my dear Ty, I've been lying here in bed with nothing to do except plot and organise other people's lives for them. It occurred to me that if I vacated upstairs, Ruth and Branna might like to move in. Then you'd have your daughter nearby. Arrangements would be so much simpler. It makes a lot of sense, you know, and I'm not getting any younger. Those stairs might defeat me soon. And Milo's only half a mile away. I could still annoy you regularly.'

'Well, we'll see how you go,' Swift said.

'Of course. But we can discuss it further. You could have the flat redecorated, make it suitable for a younger person. My heart might be faulty, but my brain is working well again and I think it's worth considering. Milo, I believe I've won that round.'

'Time for a coffee,' Milo said. He had brought a flask of home-brewed Italian coffee and poured a cup for Cedric. 'I got decaffeinated. A sin, I know, but I thought we'd better not overstimulate you, given your condition.'

Cedric snorted. 'Condition! I'm fighting fit again. This pacemaker lark is wonderful. I think they've rejuvenated me.'

He looked so much better. His eyes were brighter and the fatigue had left his face.

'Joyce came to see me yesterday,' he told Swift. 'She was here for hours, talking at me. The trouble with being in hospital is you have to be appreciative. That sounds ungracious, but you know what I mean.'

Swift did know. He recalled a time when he had spent a couple of days in hospital, after having been attacked. His stepmother had sat at his bedside, wearing him down with kindness. 'Never mind, you'll be home soon and back in charge of your life.'

'Blissful thought,' Cedric said. 'One more game, Milo? I want to thrash you before you go home.'

Swift watched them play for a while, then wandered into the corridor and checked his phone. He'd had an email from Ben with the subject heading 'Investigation.'

On the case and starting my enquiries.
Ben Ramsay, API (Assistant Private Investigator)

He shook his head, smiling, and returned to say goodnight to his friend. 'I'll be in tomorrow afternoon. Anything in particular you want?'

'There is just one thing. I find that I'm craving a decent bacon sandwich. On soft white bread, with lovely crispy rind. Is that possible?'

'Of course. See you tomorrow then. Sleep well.'

* * *

Swift's phone woke him from a deep sleep at four thirty in the morning. He sat up and scrabbled for it in the dark.

A quiet male voice that he didn't recognise. 'I'm very sorry, Mr Swift, I'm afraid I'm ringing you from the hospital with sad news.'

Sad news. As a young police constable, he'd knocked on doors and said those words to any number of people. They meant only one thing.

'Yes?'

'It's concerning Mr Sheridan. He passed away just now. He had a fatal heart attack. There was nothing we could do.'

His mouth had dried up. 'I see. Was it sudden?'

'Yes. He didn't suffer. As you know, he had been making progress but unfortunately this does happen sometimes after a first cardiac episode.'

'I'll come to the hospital. I'd like to see him.'

'Of course. I have tried calling his next of kin, Oliver Sheridan, but I couldn't reach him. I left a message asking him to phone us urgently.'

'Fine. I'm on my way.'

He sat in the dark for a few moments, trying to take in the news. Cedric was a survivor. He had always been there. Only a few hours ago, he had won two games of dominoes. He wondered if he should ring Milo. It was the middle of the night and Milo was older than Cedric, but he would want to know. He dressed quickly and rang Milo from the car on his way to the hospital.

'But he was so lively last night. How could that happen? Darling Cedric. I'm coming to the hospital now.'

'Milo, it's okay. I'll see him. Why don't you wait until the morning?'

'I'm coming. I won't be long. He mustn't be alone.'

They sat for an hour with Cedric, in a little side room. He looked serene and absent. Milo took a comb from his pocket and gently smoothed his hair.

'We were lovers once, you know,' he told Swift.

'I thought you might have been. I used to think that Lily and Cedric were but then she told me that Cedric was bisexual and she stuck to straight men.'

Milo chuckled and coughed. 'It was back in the mists of time, when we were still illegal. I think that if we'd been born in a more enlightened age we would have been together. But when we were young, we were too fearful for our jobs, our families. You know, when we were at school, we used to play a game called "being dead" in the dormitory at night. You had to lie with your eyes closed for as long as possible, holding your breath. Cedric always beat me. I wish he'd open his eyes now and grin, the way he used to.'

Dawn was breaking outside, grey and overcast. A few raindrops spattered the window, streaking through the grime. The day held no promise.

'He didn't get his crispy bacon sandwich,' Swift said quietly.

'He had the promise of it. He went to sleep happy.'

A nurse knocked and came in. She gave Cedric's things to Swift. The books he had been trying to read despite a struggle to concentrate, his watch, glasses, playing cards, and toiletries in a brown leather case. A meagre set of possessions to have had by him as he ended such a long and full life.

'He seemed so well last night,' Milo said to the nurse. 'We were talking about him coming home. Making plans.'

'It's not uncommon for that to happen before someone dies. We call it "the last rally." I'm glad you enjoyed his final evening with him.'

'I remember the day he bought that toiletry case in Bond Street.' Milo opened it and sniffed. 'He always used Dior soap. That's Cedric, that smell.'

'His watch stopped when his heart gave way and he fell on the floor,' Swift said. 'It says ten fifteen.'

'You should give it to Oliver,' Milo said grimly. 'A souvenir of the moment his filial devotion reached new heights.'

* * *

Swift had applied for and received a copy of the coroner's inquest report on Kim. He brought it into the garden to read early the next evening. He lifted his gaze and looked at the building progress next door. There was now a tall window and a Juliet balcony. The trumpeter would have a good view over the rooftops while he rehearsed. Cedric would have opened his own window to listen to him. He might even have requested some jazz standards. The October breezes had scattered rose petals and crinkled leaves over the borders. Swift sat on the swing seat and watched the sky. The sun was sidling away and the evening was chilly, with light fragmented cloud. The air was redolent with smoke and regrets. He zipped up

112

his jacket, pulled up the thick collar and opened the report. The concluding paragraph, headed 'Finding of Fact,' confirmed what Jack North and Gill Ramsay had told him:

It is more likely than not that despite her apparent fear of water, Kim Woodville stepped near or into the shallows at Low Lake to cool off on a warm night. Ms Woodville frequently spent such nights sleeping in the grounds at her home, or in the summerhouse by the lake. Ms Woodville had not taken her medication for her epilepsy for several days. This may have caused confusion, making her temporarily forget her fears. It appears that she then experienced a tonic-clonic seizure, which rendered her unconscious. Ms Woodville then drowned in the water.

It was clearly stated, leaving no room for doubt. The coroner might have come to a different conclusion if she had known where Kim's medication had ended up.

Everyone was a blend of light and shade and Kim certainly had two sides to her. One face of the coin was a quick-witted, feisty, humorous, dedicated and kindly young woman, and the other, a damaged, self-contained, wayward, risk-loving lawbreaker. The Ramsays had taken her in but she had kept herself apart. There had been comments about her secretiveness. She seemed to have been fond of Jack and Ben, yet Swift felt that none of them had really known her. Jack was the only one who truly mourned her. Gill had spoken of cherishing her, but Swift could see little evidence of that. He thought that Adela had probably summed her up best. *Elusive.*

He had spoken to Ruth about Kim's sleeping problems. She had explained that, given Kim's childhood trauma at her mother's hands, her insomnia was probably caused by a need to stay vigilant. The roaming around in the grounds of Low Lake and keeping on the move could also be interpreted as a way of avoiding harm, a form of self-protection. Yet outsiders saw it as risky behaviour.

He didn't know if Kim's death had been accidental or not. At this point his instinct suggested that it wasn't. Both Valery and Larry Barton disliked her intensely, and she had known something about Barton's private life that had enraged the man. Either of them could have snapped and pushed her into the water. His phone rang.

Gill Ramsay breathed fire into his ear. 'Poor Valery is terribly distressed. I knew something was wrong but couldn't get her to tell me. She's just broken down in tears. She says you harassed and bullied her when you spoke to her. How dare you come to our home and behave like that!'

Swift rolled his eyes. 'No, that's not the case. I asked her some direct questions. They did upset her but that wasn't my intention.'

'Well, I don't want you here again. The poor girl's weeping her heart out, and she was already feeling very low because of her health problems. I almost cancelled your visit but she said she'd rather get it over with. I knew Jack was going to cause trouble with this. I don't like our family harmony being disturbed in this way. We've always been a close-knit group, all pulling together.'

Swift thought of the husband exiled in the stable flat, the sons who couldn't wait to escape, the animosity between Valery, Sadie and Kim, the drawings in the treehouse and the way Gill had allowed Kim to live by her own rules. The woman lived in a bubble of self-delusion.

'I would like to speak to the other family members.'

'You can find some other way to do it, if they're willing to talk to you. I just can't have this upset.'

'Has Valery told you that Kim was in touch with her mother before she died?'

There was a long silence. 'That can't be the case. Valery can't have told you that.'

'But she did. It was her parting shot to me. Unless she's making it up, but I have no idea why she would say such a thing if it's not true.'

'Well . . . she was very upset.'

'Mrs Ramsay. Please. This is important, and if Valery was telling the truth, she should have told the police at the time of Kim's death. I need to know what Valery knows about this. If she doesn't want to speak to me, she can email me. Can you tell her that? Otherwise, I will have to talk to the police about it.' He had no intention of doing so, but mentioning the law was usually a helpful nudge.

'I see. Threats now. Oh, I thought we were over all of this! I'll speak to Valery. We'll let you know.'

She banged the phone down. Sometimes it was productive to set the cat amongst the pigeons. As if reading his thoughts, Nigel, next door's plump cat, hopped over the wall and stalked his way across the garden to the neighbours on the other side. His usual evening stroll. When spring arrived, it would be his time for slaughtering nesting birds.

Before he headed to bed, Swift went up to Cedric's deep oak wardrobe and picked out one of his suits to take to the undertaker. He would want to look his best. His most cherished clothes were protected in polythene dust covers. Swift chose a houndstooth tweed suit in pale grey and green that Cedric had ordered bespoke from Savile Row in 1963. He matched it with a dark grey shirt and hung a scarlet tie around the neck. Kris had taught him a thing or two about this kind of thing. He could hear her voice now, with her clipped accent. *So you want harmony but you know, sometimes you add a splash of completely different colour just for edge, for interest.*

Cedric would appreciate a dash of interest and edge.

CHAPTER 7

The ashes were pale grey and looked like coarse sand. Cedric's will had stated that he wanted no fuss or bother when he died. He wished his ashes to be buried under one of the rose bushes in the back garden, so that he could feed the plants. Lily had planted the roses years ago and Cedric had said that he could think of no better resting place.

Swift had dug the hole that morning, choosing Cedric's favourite, the large pale pink tea rose. The earth was warm and damp and smelled of decaying leaves. A couple of weeks ago, he had watched Cedric raking the flowerbeds, preparing them for winter. Now he stood with his cousin Mary, her partner Simone, his stepmother Joyce, and Milo. A blackbird was singing above them and a light breeze rustled the leaves of the sycamore tree. All was quiet. The labourers next door had agreed to have a break while the ceremony took place. Swift bent and carefully tipped the ashes into the earth.

'Do you want to say something, Milo?' Swift asked.

Bent forward on his walking sticks, Milo was like a wrinkled tortoise. 'Bye, old friend. Sleep well. See you soon, I expect.'

Joyce was crying, dabbing at her eyes with a tissue. She was a small, stout woman and her sobs made her body ripple. Swift patted her hand, a little surprised by the strength of her grief. His own eyes brimmed and he swallowed hard.

Mary put an arm around his shoulders and kissed his cheek. Her brunette hair felt soft and warm. Swift was glad she was there, reassuring and calm, as always.

'Goodbye, Cedric,' he said. 'I'll miss hearing Ella Fitzgerald late at night.' Then he took the trowel and filled the hole in. Nigel approached, interested in the newly dug soil. Mary chased him away and he gave her a baleful glare as he heaved himself back over the wall.

They walked along the Thames Path to the Silver Mermaid for lunch. Swift and Cedric had shared many drinks and meals there over the years. When they arrived at the pub, he was glad to see that Nora was already there, leaning on a table, reading emails from an iPad. She was nibbling from a bowl of spicy mixed nuts. Her rucksack lay beside her, her gym gear and trainers visible. He knew that there would be a bag of fruit in there as well.

'Glad you could make it,' he said, and kissed her cheek.

'By the seat of my pants and I won't be able to linger, but I wanted to raise a glass to Cedric.' As usual, she had kicked her shoes off. Nora had the knack of making herself comfortable and at home wherever she was.

They looked at the menu and Mary congratulated Nora on her recent move to a serious crime squad.

'I'm getting stuck in,' she said. 'Loving it so far. Plenty to chew on.'

'Speaking of which, I'd avoid the beef in here,' Swift advised. 'Everything else is usually good.'

'Is all the meat free range?' Simone asked in her Geordie accent.

'I'm not sure. I know the chicken is but best to check.'

'No sign of Oliver?' Milo asked when they had ordered their food.

Swift shook his head. 'No. I emailed him about the burial, but I wasn't expecting him to turn up.'

Oliver had shown his face briefly at the chapel in the crematorium, lurking at the back and leaving just before the service ended. There had been at least sixty people at the funeral, crowding the small space. Ex colleagues in various stages of infirmity, Ruth and Branna, and many friends including Yana, a Syrian girl Cedric had befriended when he found her living on the streets. Yana had played her flute for him.

'Guilty conscience, I expect,' Mary said. 'Shouting Cedric into a heart attack. Pity that isn't a criminal offence.'

As their food was served, Swift heard Simone explaining the composition of human ashes to Nora. They were mainly calcium phosphates mixed with some minerals, she said. She was a forensic pathologist and had a habit of pronouncing on subjects authoritatively and in great detail. She shook her long hair out, running slender fingers through it. Then she turned to the rest of the group and began a disquisition on more ecologically friendly forms of cremation that some countries were using now.

'It's an alkaline hydrolysis process called "resomation." Lye is heated with the body at high pressure, breaking it down to its chemical compounds. I hope it will be used in the UK in the future, as it's much more environmentally responsible. We need to find less harmful ways of tidying ourselves away.'

There was an embarrassed silence. Mary glanced at Swift and touched Simone's arm. 'Maybe a bit too much information there, darling, given the occasion. Mmm, this crab salad looks good!'

Nora rolled her eyes at Swift and passed the bread around. 'You must try some — it has fennel seeds in and a delicious crust.'

Joyce was making her way through a gin and tonic. 'What goes around comes around,' she said. 'Oliver will regret his actions one day.'

Swift took a deep draught of lager. 'I hope he feels guilty, although knowing Oliver I doubt he'll be troubled for too long. I'm sure I'll hear from him eventually. He knows I'm Cedric's executor.'

He had read Cedric's will and for the moment, he was keeping quiet about the startling contents. When he'd shown it to Nora, making her promise not to talk about it, she'd raised her eyebrows and whistled. He would have to reveal the details in the next week or so and he knew there was going to be trouble. A while back, when Cedric was in hospital after a minor accident, Swift had discovered Oliver sniffing around his father's flat, looking for his will. Swift had thrown him out. Now he never wanted to see the man again. He was scum. He played at being a sculptor and appeared to fund his average talent by scrounging handouts. As far as Swift was concerned, it would be quite sufficient to communicate via email about Cedric's will. Oliver had tormented his father for years, visiting him only to pick quarrels, shout at him for not being a good enough parent and badger him for money. Swift suspected that he had physically hurt his father a number of times, but Cedric always defended his son and allowed him the benefit of the doubt. The previous year, Oliver had stolen a credit card from his father and bought himself an expensive holiday. There had been an awful inevitability about that last scene. Swift had always wished that Cedric would stand up to his son and ban him from visiting, but he had been too guilt-ridden, too generous and forgiving. Swift wasn't an aggressive man but he was so angry with Oliver that he thought he might hit him if he ever saw his face again.

'I'm going to miss Cedric's damson jam,' he said.

Mary squeezed his arm. 'And his crazy shirts.'

Milo sat staring at the table. Then he raised his glass. 'I loved him from the moment I met him at the start of the school term on the fifth of September 1933. I'm very cross with him for going before me. Very cross indeed.'

'He'd like that,' Nora said. 'He always loved getting one over on you.'

Swift watched them laughing. Nora's grey-green eyes were dancing. She was wearing one of her natty string bow ties, dark green with a raspberry stripe. Her short hair was in a pixie cut and tousled.

Joyce was sitting next to him, and her gardenia perfume overwhelmed him. She pulled her chair closer, took his arm and squeezed it. 'I didn't mean to cry earlier on. It came over me by surprise. Suddenly, I was reminded of your father. They say, don't they, that deaths often bring back old losses.'

She was wearing a dark grey suit in a stiff material that rustled when she moved. Her eyes were still watery and some mascara had pooled on her lower lids. Joyce was so unlike his mother that Swift had sometimes wondered if his father's rapid remarriage had been an effort to distract himself from his grief. As usual when he was in Joyce's company, he was affected by guilt and annoyance in equal measures. He looked down at her chubby face and slightly streaked foundation and felt a stab of compassion.

'Yes, I'm sorry, Joyce. I know how much you miss Dad.'

The moment was soon spoiled when she leaned even closer, her breath warm on his cheek.

'Ruth couldn't come today?'

'No. She was teaching this morning and she thought the funeral was the more important occasion. Branna's at the nursery.'

'Just as well, anyway, as Nora's here,' Joyce said, sotto voce. 'I'm so pleased about you and Nora. She's a lovely woman. Just right for you. About time you got away from Ruth and carved out a better future. Are you moving in together?'

'Early days, Joyce. No need to rush.'

She patted his cheek, not noticing him flinch. 'Oh, Ty, if she's the right one you need to snap her up before someone else does. You can't afford to wait around at your age.'

He grabbed his glass and drank, and turned away to speak to Milo.

Mary had to head back to work as soon as they had eaten. She was an assistant commissioner in the Met and chairing a focus group on radicalisation. To Swift's relief, Simone said she had to go too. They left with Nora, Simone leading the way, telling Nora where she could buy organic vegetables and have them delivered. Nora was nodding with a fixed smile. Swift knew she never went into the kitchen if she could help it.

'They're great women but I'm sort of relieved now they've gone,' Milo said. 'Surrounded by cops I'm always worried I'm going to confess to something, anything.'

'I don't cause you that worry?'

'Not these days. I was a bit wary of you when you were in the Met, but a private investigator can't arrest me.'

'I still can't believe you gave up your steady career,' Joyce said. 'This private investigating is such an unpredictable, hand-to-mouth business. I always thought you'd be the Met commissioner one day. You'd look so handsome and imposing in that full dress ceremonial uniform with silver trimmings, rows of medals, a plumed helmet and a sword!'

Swift thought it would make him look like a tinpot colonel leading a junta. 'Oh, I think that might be Mary's prize,' he said. 'I've never had much time for dressing up. Shall I grab you a cab?'

He handed Joyce into the taxi with a sigh of relief.

'A formidable woman, that Joyce,' Milo observed. 'The kind of woman who runs charities and clubs. She reminds me of my Akela when I was in the cubs. Very bossy and organising.'

'She has her moments. I just wish she'd stick to her golf and amateur dramatics and keep out of my personal life.'

Milo nodded. 'Hmm. That's the trouble with energetic busybodies. They're always looking for a cause.'

Swift and Milo walked slowly back beside the Thames, Milo swinging his sticks rhythmically. The tide was out, and the river grey under light clouds. Seagulls swooped under Hammersmith Bridge, looking for pickings.

'Cedric was a mischievous schoolboy,' Milo said. 'I was a conformist until I met him. I'm so glad he led me into naughty ways.' He stopped and looked up at Swift, blinking in the thin sunlight. 'You know, Ty, you were more of a son to him than Oliver. That's what he thought, what he felt. He never said it but I know. He cut Oliver far too much slack because he felt guilty about not being around for a lot of his childhood.'

'That was hardly Cedric's fault. Oliver's mother took him off to France when she left and from what I understand, she was always moving from place to place.'

'I know, I know, but in later years, Cedric worried that he hadn't made enough effort to keep in contact. The eternal guilt of the parent. I'm glad I never reproduced. Seems to me like giving yourself a permanent headache. Oliver's mother indulged him, you know, gave him whatever he asked for. She brought him up thinking that if you wanted something, it just landed in your lap. When she died in a car crash when he was eighteen, she left massive debts. I'm terribly glad Cedric had you. It comforted him, knowing you were there, standing by him.'

Swift could only nod, overwhelmed by loss. *I might have been there but I couldn't stop Oliver nagging him to death*, he thought.

Milo collected a couple of pots of jam and marmalade from Cedric's flat and went on his way, inching up the road. Swift made coffee and sat in Cedric's living room. He played Ella Fitzgerald, Count Basie, and the Mouldy Figs, a London-based group beloved of Cedric and Milo who had performed at Mary and Simone's wedding. One of Cedric's new shirts, patterned with lime and yellow stripes, hung by the bookcase. He had shown it to Swift, saying he planned to wear it to a friend's birthday. The crossword he had completed on the day he fell ill still lay on the arm of the sofa, with the Mont Blanc pen that was a retirement present beside it.

Dusk was falling, and the flat grew chilly. Swift switched on the electric fire and let the music flow through him. He had found a note from Cedric, tucked into the John Le Carré novel he'd had by his hospital bed. He took it from the book and read it again.

Dear boy, just a note before I go to sleep. I do think I should let Ruth and Branna have the flat. It makes sense and you'd get to see so much more of your lovely girl. I regret not having more input in my son's life. I think he might have benefited from a father figure. Branna needs you. Let's get on with the plan as soon as I'm out of this place. As my heart has made clear to me, there's no point in putting things off.
C

He left the note on his lap and sank into a reverie. He thought back to the first time he met Cedric. He was four years old and had been visiting Lily at the house. The three of them had eaten scrambled eggs on toast followed by a pink milk jelly, which looked peculiar but tasted wonderful. Cedric had made the toast at the fire, ferrying it to the table on the toasting fork. Swift had asked to be allowed to do it but Cedric had told him he would have to wait until he was seven, because then he would have reached the age of reason.

He thought of Cedric's will, folded in the drawer, and fetched it and read it through again. He'd had no prior knowledge of its contents, except that he was the executor. From a previous conversation with Cedric, he thought he had made his will some years back, but the one he found in Cedric's flat was dated just six months ago. It was written in Cedric's neat, flowing hand on a DIY form bought from a chain of stationers. Cedric hated solicitors, whom he regarded as money-grabbers.

The will was simple, and it was dynamite. Cedric had left twenty thousand pounds to Oliver, a hundred and fifty thousand each to Swift and Milo, ten thousand to Yana Ayo and ten thousand to Oxfam. The witnesses were two friends from the dominoes team in the Silver Mermaid. Swift had been shaken by the contents. He hadn't realised that Cedric felt so strongly about his son's behaviour. He must have been masking his anger and disappointment, waiting to express it through his last wishes. Swift decided that he would tell Milo and Yana about it in a couple of days and email Oliver a copy. Then he would wait for the explosion. *I do understand, Cedric, but it's a bit of a poisoned chalice*, he thought.

He sat listening to the music for a while longer. Finally, he roused himself, put the will away and tidied Cedric's kitchen. He took the soup from the freezer. He had been saving it for when Cedric came home. Instead, he would have it this evening to celebrate his memory, and he would add a generous dollop of cream. He looked around. He would have to decide what to do with the flat. He thought about what Cedric had urged but he needed to mull it over.

As he folded a tea towel, he thought again of that pink milk jelly. Lily had shaken it from a mould. It had fluted edges and air bubbles, and dissolved on the tongue. He had never tasted anything like it since. He reached to close the kitchen window and glanced out. Nigel was sniffing around the tea rose. He ran down to the garden and Nigel scarpered. The cat had been pawing the earth. Swift fetched a large empty plant pot and placed it upside down over Cedric. It would do until Nigel turned his attention to some other recently dug patch. He didn't think his friend would mind.

* * *

Swift had tracked down Pete Hussain. He worked in a pub, the Miller and Porter, at Blackfriars, and said he could spare half an hour just before he started his shift. When Swift wasn't rowing on the river, he took every opportunity to travel on it, so he caught a clipper from Putney to Blackfriars. It was a turbulent, uneasy day. The sky raced with mustard and grey clouds, there was a skittish wind and the river looked surly. The water slapped the boat, sending a fine spray upwards. The thrum of the engine vibrated through his shoes. Swift relished this kind of weather: it made him feel edgy and alive. The boat travelled past Chelsea Harbour and Westminster and he sat back, watching the people on the bridges waving, and smiling when someone returned a greeting. He wondered why people on dry land were always moved to salute boats. Perhaps it was envy. They wished they were on the restless waters, travelling. The hope of moving on.

Just before the boat docked, an email arrived from Ben Ramsay.

Investigation continuing. Several lines of enquiry.
Ben Ramsay, API.

He replied: *Okay, keep me posted.* He thought it unlikely that Ben would uncover anything useful, but at least something was getting him moving and exercising his brain.

The Miller and Porter had large, handsome windows framed by ivy. The glass was etched with silver lettering: *Wines, Spirits & Ales.* A plaque informing him that there had been a pub on this site since 1420 topped the swing doors with their ornate brass fittings. Another, smaller notice decorated with a tricolour said that the pub had been a meeting place for the French resistance during World War II. On either side of the doors stood two figures carved from wood. A plump, smiling miller in a long apron on the right and a porter with a bent back, hefting a box, on the left. The interior was dark but vibrant with amber and crimson lighting and a beautiful curved mahogany bar. Swift asked for Pete Hussain and studied the list of craft beers. He decided on a sticky-toffee-pudding ale and went outside to wait for Hussain, onto a decked, heated patio that overlooked the river.

'Hey, man, great view. I don't really notice it any more. Too used to it.'

Hussain sat down opposite him. He was extraordinarily handsome, with a Roman nose, a ready smile and long-lashed calculating eyes. He was dressed all in black, with black ringlets down below his shoulders, secured by a headband around his forehead. Dark, rough stubble covered his face. His fingers were laden with silver rings and he had a pale crescent-shaped scar above his top lip. His nails were oval and long, hardly practical for a barman. Swift wondered how hard he'd had to work on the Johnny Depp/Jack Sparrow look. All he lacked was a cutlass.

'So,' Hussain said. 'What do you want with me?'

Swift accepted his ale from a young woman who brought it out on a tray. She glanced at Hussain, who winked at her. She smiled as if they shared a secret.

'Jack North is unsure about Kim Woodville's death.'

'Little cousin Jack. Little Tom Thumb. Her mini friend. She was sweet on him, said he was free of bullshit. Mind you, it's not hard to be sweet on someone who follows you around like a puppy dog. Didn't some aristocrats used to keep dwarfs as pets?'

'I think royalty used to. I seem to recall that a dwarf often stood next to the king or queen on state occasions to emphasise the monarch's stature and position.'

'The good old days, when the lower orders knew their place. Some people still think like that.'

'Some people in Great Howe?' Swift assumed a look of complicity.

'Too right, man. Bunch of miserable, turnip-crunching throwbacks. Always ready to think the worst of you.'

'You found it like that?'

This made Hussain wary. He ran a finger down the buttons on his waistcoat. 'Sometimes.'

'Tell me about Kim.'

Hussain leant on the table and rested his chin in one hand. 'So sad about her. She was quite a girl, you know. Difficult, gutsy.' His voice was light but hard-edged, with a teasing note running beneath the words.

'Difficult in what way?'

'We knocked around together for a while, but I never really got near her. She was like water running through your fingers. Sometimes she didn't turn up when we'd agreed to meet. Phone turned off, no explanation. Or we'd meet and she'd be offhand, only stay around for an hour. She interested me to start with. She had a spark and she wasn't always obsessing about her looks the way a lot of women do. She had a *take me as you find me* attitude. I liked that. I'm the same way. She was a bit of a challenge. But then I got fed up with her unpredictable moods.'

'I heard that you knocked her around.'

Hussain turned one of his rings. 'Not true.'

Swift let that hang in the air. 'How did you get together?'

'She was in the pub in Great Howe one Saturday. Our eyes met across a crowded bar and all that. Most of the time we spent together we were pissed or drugged or both. We knocked booze back like there was no tomorrow. What else is there to do in a place like Great Howe? We argued a lot, the way two drunks do. I don't drink now, despite working in a pub.'

'You've given up?'

'Yeah. A girlfriend told me it turned me into a bore and made my breath stink.'

'Why do you think Kim drank?'

He shrugged. 'You know, man, why does any teenager drink? She was bored. Bright and bored, damaged and confused. Whenever I visited Great Howe I was bored out of my skull. Snoresville. The arse end of nowhere. I mean, Kim had all the archaeology stuff, sure, she lived and breathed it, but that can only fill so many hours of the day.'

Swift could identify with drinking because of damage and confusion. He was reminded of his younger self, propping up the bar at Warwick. Hussain was fluent and cocky, and obviously liked the sound of his own voice.

'So why did you visit the village?'

'I was fond of my grandad and he was on his own. He was a right old rascal. Used to tell me about when he went poaching and deer rustling at night. He got me started on drinking and smoking when I was twelve. I kept telling Kim she should come and live in London, get away from her weird family and that parasitic Elaine Dunbar, and spread her wings. She wanted to take some A levels and there'd have been plenty of opportunity to study in London. She could have stayed with me in Bow. She spent the odd night with me and she said she liked being in the city. We used to roam around. She loved Little Venice, said she'd like to live there one day when she was a famous archaeologist. She said she'd think about a move but she'd never make the decision.'

'Why do you think that was? From what I've learned about her, she seems to have been a forceful character.'

'Dunno. Maybe London held bad memories of when she was a kid. She was up for stuff but she doubted herself too.'

Swift rolled the ale on his tongue. It was creamy, dense, and a tad heavy on an empty stomach. 'What was parasitic about Elaine Dunbar? I've got the impression Kim liked her.'

Hussain ran his fingers through his hair. It was shiny and stiff with gel. He snagged a curl and twisted it. He looked clean enough but now and again Swift caught an unpleasant whiff of sweat.

'They were close in the sense that Elaine had her claws in her. Have you met la Dunbar?'

'Not yet. I've only spoken to her husband.'

'I reckon Elaine made use of Kim as cheap labour. I mean, she bigged up the archaeology and the museum for her as if they were going to lead to some glittering career. But in the end, Kim was just a poorly paid gofer. My grandad had known Elaine since she was young. Said she was always ambitious, a social climber. Her parents lived in a council house and worked in a car factory in Oxford and she shook them off as soon as she could. She and her husband are a couple of posers. I suppose that's why they suit each other. His parents run a takeaway in Banbury but the two of them act as if they're toffs. They used to live in an ordinary semi-detached on an estate just outside Great Howe. Then they had a huge, architect-designed place built in the village a few years back and started having regular parties. "At homes," Elaine calls them. She plays Lady Bountiful. Shows films of her digs and her finds to the local dignitaries, hosts charity galas, fundraises for various good causes. All that kind of Middle England crap. She had Kim handing out the nibbles, of course.'

'Sounds as if Kim got on with Elaine, though.'

'Yeah, I guess. She didn't like it when I told her what I thought of the cow.'

'Were you jealous?'

Hussain let out a high laugh. 'Of Elaine? No way, man. See, Kim was hard-headed in some ways but vulnerable in others. I didn't like the way she was being exploited.'

Swift didn't fully buy what Hussain was saying. He seemed very keen on presenting himself as Kim's defender. There was something feral about the man and Larry Barton had said he caused trouble whenever he visited the village. Yet Swift detected a hollowness behind the carefully cultivated appearance and the bravado. Bullies usually had fragile egos.

'What did you and Kim argue about?'

'Man, we were pissed out of our heads on cheap cider. How do you remember what you argued about when you wake up and can't remember getting home?'

'Whatever it was, it seems to have been enough for Kim to tell you to leave her alone.'

Hussain's mouth hardened. 'Like I said, she was changeable weather. Some women are like that, aren't they? One minute they want you, next minute they don't.'

'Is that why you bruised her?'

He laughed. 'We were just playing. Man, you should have seen the marks she left on me sometimes! We both got rough now and again. Spiced things up. It went a bit wrong now and then, like it does. Games getting out of hand, you know?'

'No, can't say I do. Did you leave her alone when she asked you to?'

'I backed right off, man. She was starting to bore me anyway. She was always waxing lyrical about Frynfold, and I can only get so excited about Roman bones and mosaics. When she was well pissed, she kept going on about that Nadia, the girl who died. Saying she'd never forgive herself and how she thought she'd meet some awful karma because of it. She droned on for ages one night about the randomness of life. How maybe it would have been better if her mother had managed to drown her when she was little, because then Nadia would be alive. She was real wary of Larry Barton, Nadia's dad. She told me that sometimes

130

he came into the museum and just stood there, staring at her. A couple of times he followed her to the bus stop and waited around, watching her. She said he never spoke, just stared. It was all a bit depressing. Man, I can't be doing with women who are hard work, you know? I don't need it.'

'When did you stop seeing her?'

'We hadn't seen that much of each other the spring and summer before she died. Just now and again. She kept making excuses. I last saw her a couple of weeks before she died.'

'Did she seem worried about anything?'

'Don't think so. If anything, she seemed a bit excited about something. You know, on edge and restless. We had a blazing row and that was that.'

'Did Kim say anything to you about being in touch with her mother?'

He narrowed his eyes. 'She never mentioned her mother. Only that stuff about the attempted drowning. What's all this about, man?'

'I've been waiting for you to mention the fact that the police questioned and arrested you over Kim's death. Why haven't you? It was a big event for you.'

Hussain adjusted his headband. 'You think so? I wasn't worried. I knew it was nothing to do with me. I could see that the feds couldn't tell their arses from their elbows. I'd lost my watch one time I'd been with Kim at the summerhouse. Or shag house, as we called it. We searched and couldn't find it. I was upset about that — it had sentimental value. The feds dragged in that Bailey guy who was losing his mind. My solicitor pointed out that Bailey had history with me, might hold a grudge. I'd punched him one night. I couldn't remember why but I could recall his ugly mug. Then they lost my watch for me. I had no worries, man. I was home alone, which was a problem but not that big a one. I could see the feds were losing the plot. I knew I'd walk.' He undid and retied his headband. 'What's little Tom Thumb fretting about? I mean, it was an accident, the way Kim died. I was with her once when she had a seizure. She was well out of it for a couple of minutes. She went up to the wire with her epilepsy, man. Messed about with her medication.'

Swift gave him a level look. 'The bruises on Kim's upper arms. Did you do that?'

He opened his hands and a ring flashed in the watery sunlight. 'I honestly can't remember. Cider, weed and arguments, man. Quite a combination. We exchanged some nasty remarks last time I saw her. I might have made those bruises or I might not. If I did, she probably left marks on me.'

Swift didn't respond. He finished his ale and watched the river. Hussain said he had to get to work and drifted away. A peal of bells sounded from a nearby church and one sonorous clang struck the hour. Hussain was a prickly character, he thought, effeminate-looking yet handy with his fists. He had the kind of vanity that a woman could easily wound. He'd lied about backing off when Kim asked him to. According to Josh Houghton's information, Hussain had seen her again after she'd texted him, telling him to stay away. Swift wasn't convinced that he had accepted Kim's brush-off as readily as he had made out, but that didn't mean he was a killer.

CHAPTER 8

Nora scraped the last of the chicken balti from the foil container and sighed with pleasure. She was still in her work suit, but had taken off her mustard and black string bow tie so that it didn't dip in the curry sauce.

'Some boogie-woogie and a spicy dinner. That was terrific food. It's one of the reasons I bought this flat. I spotted the takeaway on the corner and knew I'd always have a hot meal nearby.'

'What were the other reasons?'

'Modern, easy to look after and secure on the top floor. Women on their own should always live high up to avoid the bad men.'

Swift nodded, although it hadn't saved Kris Jelen from the bad man. She had lived in a top-floor flat and had let her killer in. He finished his last chunk of naan bread and took a drink of cold beer.

'I used to work with a sergeant who always said "I'm as full as a pea pod" when he'd eaten in the canteen. And I am now. Don't think I can move.' He lay back in the sofa, patting his stomach.

They'd been to a Jools Holland concert at the Albert Hall. Then Nora wanted to be back at home as she had an early start the next day. 'Tricky interviews to prepare for,' she'd said with a grimace that he understood.

Her flat was compact and tidy, probably because she spent little time in it. The walls were painted what she called all-purpose magnolia. The only personal touches were some stunning large framed posters of Irish landscapes by Paul Henry and some family photos. She rose, shoving her chair back noisily on the laminate flooring, and tidied up the empty containers, clumping to the kitchen with them. For such a slim woman, she had a heavy tread. He felt sorry for whoever lived beneath her.

'Another beer?' she called.

'No, I'm fine.'

His phone rang. Unknown number, but he answered.

'You bastard, Swift,' Oliver Sheridan spat. 'This will of my dad's is a fucking laugh.'

'That's not how it struck me.'

'Don't take me for an idiot. I know you had Dad tied up in knots. You always drove a wedge between us, made sure you badmouthed me. I'm not standing for it. Do you hear me? I'm going to see a solicitor and show you up for what you are.'

'You must do whatever you want.'

'I will, I will! You needn't take that high tone with me, mate, I don't have to stand for it any more. I only ever put up with you because of Dad!'

He was shouting. Swift's ear vibrated. Nora had come back with another beer for herself and sank down next to him.

Who is it? she mouthed.

He mouthed back, *Oliver Sheridan.* Sheridan was continuing to rant.

'You spent years schmoozing my dad, you bastard, making him rely on you. I know all of it, I can tell you. Every single thing. You reckoned you could do whatever you liked with Dad, getting him to leave money to some skanky refugee bitch . . .' Swift held the phone to Nora's ear. She listened for a few moments, grimacing, and then took the phone from Swift.

She spoke in a low, even tone. 'Mr Sheridan. This is DI Morrow from the Metropolitan police. This phone call sounds highly abusive to me. I hope I'm not going to have to get my handcuffs out. I'd advise you to ring off and calm yourself.'

She listened, widened her eyes and handed the phone back, laughing.

'Oliver, I've sent you the will and I'm applying for probate. That's my duty as executor. As I said in my email, let me know if you want anything from your dad's flat in the meantime.'

'Fucking game player with your cop pals. You think you're untouchable, with your cousin in the Met. Well, you've got another think coming. You won't like it when I drag your name through the courts and it's mud. It won't do your detective business much good when you're shown up as an inheritance chaser instead of Mr Crime Solver. No, I don't want any manky stuff from the flat. That's because I'm going to make sure I get the lot. All of it! I'll prove Dad was senile and you made him do what you wanted. I expect fucking Milo was in on it too, that old poofter—'

'I'm not listening to any more of this. You need to sort yourself out. I'd like to think your anger is coming from grief for your dad. If only that was the case, but I think I know better. Night, Oliver.' Swift ended the call.

'He called me a nasty name,' Nora said. 'Maybe I should knock on his door and feel his collar.'

'Please don't. I don't want to wind him up any more.'

She sipped her beer. 'Are you really worried by him?'

'If he does go to court and throws mud, some of it might stick, whatever the outcome. You know how it goes.

I wouldn't put it past him to contact a tabloid either. It might not be good for business.'

'I can't believe that any court would take him seriously.'

'Maybe not. I could do without it, that's all. Cedric has managed to tie me to Oliver in a way he didn't foresee.'

'Sure you don't need another beer? Glass of wine?'

'No, I'm good. Let's forget Oliver.' He put an arm around her and kissed the top of her head. 'Have you ever had a lover who was physically aggressive?'

She gave him a look. 'Strange question from left field.'

'I met this guy, Pete Hussain, earlier. He used to hurt Kim Woodville, the woman who drowned. Bruised her. I wondered why she put up with it. From what I've gathered about her, she wasn't needy or a shrinking violet, or an obvious victim.'

'Not the kind of woman who says walk all over me?'

'Far from it. She was troubled, though, and she'd had trauma in her life.'

'There you are then. That made her vulnerable.'

'Hmm. Anyway, you haven't answered me.'

'The answer's no. I went out with a boy when I was sixteen who used to pull my hair when he kissed me. It hurt. I walked. Some people like it though, don't they? I've known women who put up with stuff that worried me, usually because they didn't want to lose the man involved. Then there's the internet.'

'How do you mean?'

'It's normalising weird stuff, pushing boundaries. It can be fierce complicated. Maybe Kim was a bit of a masochist.' She laughed. 'Lovely conversation we're having.'

'Sorry. Bringing the job here with me. Bad behaviour.'

She nudged him in the ribs. 'And what about you? Have you ever let a woman beat you up?'

'I've not met one who wanted to.'

136

'Ruth kind of beat you up though, didn't she? Emotionally. Mentally.'

'I suppose that's true. I felt bruised and battered for a long time. She didn't set out to cause me pain, though. It wasn't deliberate.'

'You reckon? She must have known how much you'd be hurting.'

'I don't think she was thinking it through that much when she left me.'

'You know, Ty, you always make excuses for her. I wonder why that is? I expect a shrink would have a field day.'

He flinched. That was the thing about Nora, she was always quick and incisive. 'Maybe you're right. But emotions aren't always straightforward.'

'I know. I didn't mean to sound accusing. But sometimes a bit of blame is okay and probably therapeutic.' She turned to face him. 'And you and me? We're okay, are we?' She looked anxious, the tiredness of a long day suddenly showing in her eyes.

'Of course. Why do you ask?'

'Oh, it's just . . . I was reading this magazine while I was waiting to talk to a possible witness. There was an article headed "Does Your Relationship Need an MOT?" It said relationships need maintenance, just like a car, to keep them running healthily. It was common sense stuff really, how it's good to take a look at your partner, not take things for granted. Check out what the other person is thinking and feeling.'

'Pop psychology?'

'Don't mock. See, I think I did take things for granted with Alistair. I was busy, he was busy, and I didn't notice that things were sliding. Took my eye off the ball. It leaches your confidence. Mine, anyway.'

'I get it.'

'Do you?'

He put a hand out, cupped her head and pulled her close. 'There's nothing wrong with checking things out. I've made that mistake myself. I know Alistair knocked you back. I've no intention of doing the same. I'm happy to be with you, if that's what you're asking.'

'I was. And ditto.'

'It's mutual then.'

'Yes.'

'Well, that's sorted.'

* * *

Elaine Dunbar lived in a vast detached house called Dancer's End on the outskirts of Great Howe. A modern property of timber, stone and acres of glass, it was surrounded by a minimalist garden, mainly paving, interspersed with small areas of silvery shrubs and tall grasses. Inside, everything was white — walls, furnishings, the curtains. The sunlight, the glass and the whiteness gave the house an exposed, arctic appearance. It was obviously designed to impress, but Swift thought it offered little comfort.

He sat on a deep white sofa, worried that his jeans might smudge the pristine cover, and watched Elaine Dunbar pour coffee from an elegant silver pot into thin china cups. Her wide shoulders made her look square, and she was dressed in a black shirt and grey jeans. Her hair was cropped and silvery, framing a rounded, smooth face with a short, wide nose. No makeup or jewellery. She looked slightly mannish and formidable, a woman used to taking charge.

'I still miss Kim,' she was saying. 'She was an interesting and promising young woman.' She had a resonant voice and a slow drawl. He thought of her parents in the car factory and wondered how young she had been when she acquired her posh accent.

'You were close, then.'

'Up to a point. Kim was . . . well, she was always a little shut off. We met when she came in to the museum. She wasn't easy to get to know but we gradually became friends. She had a natural curiosity that I found appealing. She was keen to learn all she could about archaeology. But tell me, why is her friend raising questions about her death?' She sipped her coffee, holding the cup by its base. She had short, square nails and her large fingers looked chapped. He guessed that she liked to be hands on at Frynfold.

'He's never been convinced that it was accidental.'

'Because Kim hated water?'

'That's right.'

'Well . . . I attended the inquest. The coroner seemed sure.'

'I'm just asking around. How long had you known her?'

'Let me think.' She gazed over his shoulder. Swift suspected she knew the answer but was pretending to have to mull it over. 'About three years, yes. She started working part time in the museum around six months after we met.'

'And she helped you with digs?'

'Each season, under supervision of course. I've spent some years working on a Roman site at Frynfold. It's a villa that was occupied from around AD 130 to 300. I'm the project director. We've had some remarkable finds there and the excavation has featured in international journals. The BBC have expressed interest in including us in a programme. I also deliver lectures about Frynfold and Roman archaeology in general.' She spoke with evident pride, gesturing at the large, framed black and white photos on the walls. They showed beakers, pots, pieces of jewellery, animal bones, coins and mosaic. 'As you can see, it's my passion. My baby. I've been nurturing it along.'

'You must find your work very rewarding.'

'I do, yes.' She looked at him, her gaze intense. 'I'm committed to my profession. I find it absorbing. That includes the museum. I love engaging people in archaeology and helping them to understand how we work.'

'I thought the museum was impressive when I called in there. And Kim obviously shared your commitment — I saw the piece she'd written.'

She nodded, and touched the base of her neck. 'You see, I think Kim was looking for direction and purpose in her life. Her upbringing and education had been . . . how should I put it? Unconventional. Not that I'm criticising or saying that there's anything wrong with breaking convention but I thought Kim needed more structure. She was a very intelligent girl, yet her general knowledge was lacking. She'd achieved some GCSEs but she needed to study for A levels if she was going to try for a degree in archaeology. She enjoyed the discipline of our work — the methodology, the systematic and careful recording, the attention to detail. She brought great care and focus to what she did. I do believe she could have become a professional archaeologist, given time and attention to her studies.'

Swift thought of the other Kim, the wild girl who roamed at night, who took risks with her health, stole and got drunk and aggressive with her boyfriend. 'That's an interesting picture. I've heard that Kim had another side to her character.'

Elaine raised an eyebrow. 'How do you mean?'

'She had a volatile relationship with her boyfriend. She drank too much, smoked dope. She encouraged another girl, Nadia Barton, to defy her father and it ended badly.'

Elaine got up and straightened a perfectly level frame on the wall, folded back her shirt cuffs and sat on a different, higher chair. 'I can really only speak about Kim's work at the museum and at the site. I had no problems with her. I know that some people in Great Howe thought she was erratic but that's not how she was when she assisted me. Maybe the structure of our work gave her

140

focus. Maybe she responded to my high expectations. No, I didn't see any negative sides to Kim.'

Swift thought she was avoiding the issue. 'But this is a small village and you're very much part of it, from what I've been told. You must have heard about Kim's behaviour. You must know the Bartons.'

She frowned. Her narrow lips folded down. 'I'm sorry, what do you mean? What have you been told about me and by whom?'

'That you have been successful, that you moved to this house and you have parties. You fundraise for various causes, you're on charity committees. So, you know, you are part of this community. I tend to pick up information as I go along.'

She had coloured slightly, a faint rose shading her cheeks. 'I see. You always get pettiness and silly little jealousies in small communities. I suppose some people have inevitably begrudged my success. I am very involved in village life and I enjoy making a contribution. It brings me great satisfaction and I think I make a difference. As for Kim, I knew about what happened with Nadia Barton. A tragic accident. Kim disappeared for a couple of months afterwards. She phoned me and said she didn't want to work or face people. That was understandable. I told her to take her time. When she returned, she didn't talk about Nadia. I don't know about her boyfriend or drinking. I never smelled alcohol on her or thought she had been drinking. I'd have thought alcohol wasn't advisable, given her epilepsy. I suppose a lot of young people smoke some dope. I did when I was at college. Most youngsters break a few rules but that would have been a matter for the Ramsays. I was careful not to trespass on any areas I thought her family should deal with. I enjoyed cultivating Kim's interest in my field of study and I enjoyed her company. I have to go to Frynfold soon. Is that all?'

Surely, he thought, if you worked closely with someone, mentored them, you got to know them better than Elaine said she knew Kim. He didn't believe her cool denial of any knowledge about Kim's occasional volatility.

'Do you know the Ramsays?'

'Only in passing. We haven't mixed socially.' Her tone communicated *not my type* in that understated, very British way.

'Did Kim ever speak to you about her mother?'

'She told me that her mother had tried to drown her and that she had been in prison. She said once that she was glad her mother had no contact with her because she didn't want her in her life. But Kim rarely talked about personal matters, just now and again, usually when we were on our own in the museum, planning and sorting exhibits. Some people find it easier to talk when they are involved in an activity, don't they?'

'That's true. Did Kim ever come here, to your home? Your husband said he knew her slightly.'

She seemed not to like the question, although he wasn't sure which part made her uncomfortable. 'She came here about half a dozen times, when we had social gatherings in connection with Frynfold or the museum. I use these occasions for promotion, fundraising and generally publicising our profile and what we do. Kim liked to help me out and it gave her an opportunity to talk to some of my colleagues about their excavations and researches. Phil, my husband, gave her some advice about A level and further education courses.'

'When did you last see Kim?'

'Five days before she died. She worked at the museum in the afternoon from two to five. I just saw her in passing, as I was on my way to Cambridge to attend a symposium. Now, I really must go.' She stood up.

'Could I come and look at the site at Frynfold? I'm interested, and also I'd like to see where Kim worked. I could follow you in my car. I won't take up too much of your time.'

She nodded politely but seemed irritated by his request. He waited by the front door while she made a phone call and fetched a jacket, a smart one in brown and black tweed. The photographs ranked on the walls were all of Elaine with different groups of people in various settings — awards, conferences, charity events and meetings, and at the museum. Several showed her giving talks from a podium, against a backdrop of diagrams of digs.

'This is an impressive house,' he said, while she locked up. 'Did you design it yourselves?'

'Yes, we worked with an architect in Oxford. It was two years in the making. We love it. It's wonderful to have so much light. Some of the art we've found at Frynfold indicates that a dancer probably lived there at one time. Hence the name of our house.' She pressed her hand against the door in a gesture of affection, and then pointed her keys at the garage door. It opened to reveal a gleaming red Lamborghini coupé.

The journey to Frynfold took about ten minutes, along narrow, leaf-strewn roads. Swift followed the Lamborghini, admiring its sleek curves. Elaine drove just over the speed limit. He saw her reach up towards her sun visor and thought she was using a phone.

The excavated low walls of the villa lay about half a mile off the road. A high metal fence surrounded the site, topped with razor wire. There were CCTV cameras, an alarm system and a padlocked gate.

'You're well protected,' Swift said as he joined Elaine.

'We've had to have all this installed. We've had nighthawks around. You've heard of them?'

'You mean thieves?'

'Yes. People with metal detectors and no permits, who search archaeological sites under cover of darkness. Our worst nightmare. It's a terrible crime, it robs us of our heritage, and it's on the increase now that some of these digital detectors are so sophisticated.'

A sign by the gate informed Swift that an inscribed tablet found during the excavation said that this had once been 'a house of the tragic poet.'

'Do you think it meant that the poet had a tragic life, or that he or she wrote tragic poetry?' he asked.

Elaine smiled, and for the first time he caught a glimmer of warmth. 'I'm fairly sure that the poet wrote tragic verses. I like to think that the poet and the dancer were members of the same family. It would have made a harmonious household. Perhaps the dancer died young and that inspired the poet's writings. Most of the time I have to deal in facts and evidence, but I like to permit myself the odd flight of fancy. I think that archaeologists need imagination as well as practical skills. The people who owned this place must have been wealthy as well as artistic. Everything found here indicates that the villa was made of the highest quality materials. Bits of the stone they used came from more than a dozen different quarries in Britain.'

They walked through the site. Elaine explained that the main villa was built around three courtyards with a bathhouse at one end.

'The Romans were just like us, always adding to their homes and changing them around,' she said. 'We've found where new walls and passages were constructed during the lifetime of the villa, to add more room. I like to think that an owner of this villa consulted an architect, perhaps brought one from London to draw up the plans. I can feel a connection to them through the centuries.' Her voice was filled with passion and energy. She would be an engaging, inspiring lecturer and guide to the ancient world. He understood what had drawn Kim to her. Compared to Gill, she was vital, cerebral and animated.

She showed Swift where the kitchen had been situated. Many oyster and whelk shells had been found there — another sign of wealth. She pointed out the place where a well had been discovered, with copper plates and jewellery lying at the bottom. They may have been hidden during turbulent times or possibly left as an offering to water spirits. Finally, they came to a fenced-off section enclosing a preserved mosaic floor which had been part of the bathing area. The aquamarine and burnt orange of the tesserae was still clear in places. Swift saw pictures of seahorses, dolphins and river gods, and in the centre was a portrayal of a semi-clothed man and woman lying on a couch. It reminded Swift of Kim and Jack in the summerhouse.

'Kim did a lot of work on the mosaic flooring, especially cleaning,' Elaine said.

'Was she paid for her work?'

'Not here on the site. She was a volunteer. Archaeology depends on them. I paid her for her shifts at the museum, of course. Now, I must get on. I have work to do here.'

'One last thing. Just before she died, did Kim tell you about something she had on her mind?'

'No, I don't recall anything like that. She seemed her usual self. Why do you ask?'

'A couple of people have mentioned that something was troubling her.'

She shrugged. 'Really? I wouldn't have thought so. She showed no sign of it and her work was the same as usual.'

'Okay. Thanks for showing me around. Very interesting.'

Back in his car, Swift googled Elaine Dunbar and found an article about her in *Archaeology Now*, with a photo showing her outside the Bickmore Museum.

Meet Dr Elaine Dunbar. She took a first in Archaeology and Ancient History at Oxford. She specialises in archaeology of the Roman Empire, particularly in European provinces. She is project director at Frynfold, a Roman villa in Oxfordshire. Dr Dunbar is the author of Colonisation and Romanisation in Southeast

Britain *and* Understanding Romano-British Culture *as well as a number of research papers. She is a regular contributor on the lecture circuit.*

He looked at archaeologists' salaries. Digging up old stuff didn't pay that handsomely. He reckoned that Elaine Dunbar might earn around forty thousand a year, given the size of the Frynfold site, plus whatever she earned for research and lecturing. Her husband had been a teacher and now worked in a garden centre. The museum was run as a charity and entry was free, yet the Dunbars had had an impressive house built on modest incomes. The Lamborghini alone would have cost an eye-watering amount. Perhaps one of them had inherited money, although according to Pete Hussain, they were both from ordinary backgrounds. Elaine, of course, might have other sources of income from writing on her subject. He filed those thoughts away when his phone pinged, and he saw an email from Gill Ramsay.

I am sending this on Valery's behalf, as she is unwell and resting. She says that a couple of months before Kim died she saw her getting off the train in Great Howe. Kim looked as if she'd been crying. She said she'd been to London. When Valery asked her why, Kim swore at her, told her to mind her own business and said that she wished that her f*** mother had been locked up for good. Valery says that Kim had been drinking and she took this as meaning that Kim might have been in contact with her mother. But Kim didn't actually say that and Valery didn't think it was significant. Perhaps Kim was feeling emotional about something and it raised old traumas for her. That's all we have to say on the matter. Please don't contact Valery again.

Swift wondered if Valery ever fought her own battles. *Resting.* It made her sound like an elderly invalid. Maybe at some point he would tell Gill about Kim's medication, but for now he would save that piece of ammunition. He'd let Valery sweat it out. He sent a reply:

Can you give me full name and date of birth for Kim's mother and any addresses or other information you have about her?

It was silent and still out here amidst the fields. A tall scarecrow stood on the horizon, the arms of its coat flapping. Inky clouds moved fast, driven hard by an easterly wind. He closed his eyes for a few moments. He had been having vivid dreams about his mother, Kris Jelen and Cedric. He knew that a recent bereavement could trigger memories of other losses, bring back old griefs. His head felt full of voices that had gone. He listened to them for a while before starting the car and heading back into Great Howe.

* * *

Sadie Stanley had said she would meet him in the Tithe Barn at three o'clock sharp and he'd better be on time, because she wouldn't wait around. He was pleased to have arrived just before her, and could tell from her expression that it annoyed her. She was wearing a navy mac and a scarf patterned with prancing ponies. She left her coat buttoned and belted despite the warmth in the café.

'I can't stay long. I'm catching the bus at three forty-five.'

'You don't drive?'

'Don't see the point. The bus drops me by the gate. You can buy me a pot of tea.'

'Right. Do you want a cake?'

'No. Just tea. Breakfast.'

He ordered, with a coffee for himself, and noticed that she was cleaning the already spotless tabletop with a wet wipe from a purse in her bag.

147

'In my day they'd put a nice tablecloth on. Now it's this horrible plastic. No standards.'

'I'm surprised you agreed to talk to me,' he said.

'Are you? You're easily surprised then.' She gave her little satisfied smile. Her hair was in its usual severe style, with two brass grips pinning it tight. 'I'll be eighty-one in December,' she added.

He wondered if she was waiting for him to tell her she didn't look her age. It wouldn't be the truth. 'You and Kim didn't get on,' he said.

'That's an understatement.' She made a fuss with the teapot, which was like a small cafetière, with leaves and a plunger. 'Look at this newfangled nonsense. What's wrong with a straightforward pot and a tea strainer? Just lets them charge more.' Her hands were large and sinewy, with blue veins raised rigidly on the backs. They could maintain a firm grip on somebody, he thought. She pressed the plunger down and then sat back. 'Kim was trouble with a capital T.'

'She'd had a hard start in life. Didn't you sympathise with that?'

'Lots of folk have a hard start. Doesn't mean they have to carry on the way she did.' She gave a little sniff.

He almost smiled. This conversation was going to be oddly enjoyable. 'How did she carry on?'

'Backchat. Sarky. She was a know-it-all, was Kim. I didn't trust her as far as I could throw her. I could never understand why Gill took her in. Well, except for the extra cash. That interested Gill all right.'

'Meaning?'

She gave a smug smile. 'Gill's always been keen on money and never had enough, by her reckoning. Jakob had messed around with a few businesses that went down the pan and lost them money and he never earned much after that. That's why I stepped in and helped buy the house. Gill got an allowance from the welfare for taking Kim in. She got it every month until Kim was eighteen. So that was

148

a handy extra boost to her income. I'm not sure she thought she'd got a good deal when she balanced the books and realised how much trouble madam Kim had turned out to be.'

She sipped her tea, fingered the biscuit on the saucer and rejected it. 'Take in a stray, and you never know what you'll get. That brother of Gill's, Malcolm, was a wastrel and his wife was a slut who couldn't have looked after a puppy, let alone a daughter. Any child they produced was always going to spell trouble. When she first came to the house, she had no manners. Ate with her fingers like a savage, cramming food into her mouth, and she still wasn't properly toilet trained. She used the "F" word too. Must have heard that from the mother and her disgusting friends. Gill might have polished the veneer with Kim but she was still wild underneath, right until the day she died.'

'You believe in nature, not nurture, then.'

She shot him a poisonous look. 'You'd have got on with Kim. You have the same smart-alec style. Too clever for your own good. Of course, Gill was spoiled as a child. She was her daddy's pet and it made her think she could do no wrong. The way she runs that family is shocking. Far too much pampering and claptrap about self-fulfilment, whatever that is when it's at home.' She snorted and blew on her tea. 'Ben should have been sent to some kind of special school and Valery needs a good slap, fresh air and exercise. They were all allowed to learn what they liked and eat whatever they wanted. In my day, children didn't refuse the food on their plates and there was none of this nonsense of being offered a choice. We were grateful for what we were given and my father took the strap to us if we were rude. If I'd had my way, those children would have had to eat whatever was on the table or go hungry.'

Swift suspected that if allowed, she would carry on in this vein for some time. He agreed with her about Valery, except for the slap.

'What do you remember about Nadia Barton's death?'

She looked pleased. 'Well now, there's an example of what I mean by Kim spelling trouble. I was right, whether your sort like it or not. She had no reason except sheer wilfulness and mischief-making for getting that Nadia to go against her father's wishes. I heard them talking about it in the post office. I don't know her father except to nod to but he seems a decent sort of man. He's a verger in the church, you know. He was in a terrible state when he came to the house.'

'When was that?'

'A couple of weeks after Nadia's funeral. He rang Gill before the funeral, saying he didn't want Kim or anyone from our family to attend. Gill was upset about that but I thought the man was in the right. He turned up one evening, and started hammering on the door. I answered. He was yelling that he wanted to see Kim, tell her what she'd done. He said she had blood on her hands. I remember him shouting that she should have to pay for causing Nadia's death, that it wasn't right that she should get away with it. I could see tears in his eyes. He pushed his way in, shoved me against the wall and I bashed my arm but I didn't cause a fuss. Gill sat him down and gave him a brandy. Kim was out and about as usual, up to God knows what. It would have done her good to have to face him, face the music. In my day, you weren't let off the hook so easily. Gill just let him rant for a while, heard him out until he ran out of steam. Thank goodness she didn't try any of the old guff about "accidents will happen" on him. Even she realised that would have been a red rag to a bull. Mr Barton never came back and Kim lay low for a while. Didn't dare show her face around here.' She leaned in to the table. 'If I was Larry Barton, I'd never forgive Kim for what she did. Some things are unpardonable. I'd have wanted justice.'

'What kind of justice would you be thinking of?'

'Oh well, that's not for me to say, is it? Some might think an eye for an eye . . .' She sat back and nodded, rearranging her slippery scarf.

He imagined how she would have enjoyed the drama of Larry Barton's visit to the house, relishing Kim's mortification. 'Did Kim seem upset in any way before she died?'

'How would I know? We barely spoke and she was always off doing whatever it was she wasted her time at. Hobnobbing with that posh archaeologist and mucking about in a field, I suppose. She should have been told to go and get a regular job but then again, I don't suppose a lot of employers would have put up with her bad manners and her attitude.' She leaned forward and tapped the table with a wrinkled finger. 'Or perhaps she was mucking about with the archaeologist's *husband*. There's an old ruin, if ever I saw one.' She smirked. 'Don't gawp with your mouth open,' she said in her flat Yorkshire accent. 'You'll catch flies.' She laughed her humourless laugh, as if pleased with the witticism.

He knew she had been saving this piece of information for him and waiting for her moment. 'Are you saying that Kim was involved with Phil Dunbar?'

She tapped her nose. 'I'm not saying anything. All I will say is that I saw them together one Saturday night just up the road from the house. I'd been for a stroll. His car was parked on the verge. They were sitting in it, chatting, heads very close. They seemed very *intense*. He was slapping the dashboard with his hand and she was shaking her head like this.' She demonstrated. 'They didn't notice me — too absorbed in whatever they were up to.'

'When was that?'

'Hmm . . . the spring before she died. March or April, I reckon. He was supposed to be helping her with her education, or maybe he was giving her *other* kinds of lessons. In my day, no self-respecting girl would have been in a car with a married man at night. I didn't make any

151

comment to her. No point. I'd only have got a smart response or a mouthful of abuse. I thought of mentioning it to Gill but there again, she's too busy cosseting Valery and doing her painting workshops or whatever it is she pretends to make a living at. It's all playing around, and I've told her so. I said to her, I don't know why you can't get some sense into your head and do a proper job, something that brings in real money, instead of tinkering around with dye and bits of sewing. Anyone would think she was living in the nineteenth century with her cottage industry. She told me to mind my own business. That was a bit rich, given the money I've ploughed into that house. The roof would be leaking if I wasn't paying for the repairs. As for the setup she had with Jakob, I've never known anything like it. What a way that was to carry on a marriage, no wonder he dropped dead . . .'

He tuned her out while she talked on about her ungrateful niece. She was building up a head of steam, enjoying her memories of the arguments she'd had. She clearly relished bickering. He could see how it energised her. Her face had grown animated and there was a malicious spark in her eye. He sipped his coffee, thinking about Phil Dunbar's faded good looks and Elaine's unease when he had asked about Kim visiting their house. It added up to something, but he had no idea what.

'You know,' she said suddenly, 'you're a good-looking man. You've got all the basics. But look at you! That jacket's seen better days. Your shirt cuffs are fraying and a bird could nest on your head. If you smartened yourself up a bit and had a decent haircut you might pass muster. In my day, men made more of an effort.'

'I'll think about it.'

'I'm sure. I just saw a pig fly past the window.'

'The dressed-down look is fashionable these days, you know.'

'Don't take the mickey. There's nothing wrong with standards. Anyway, I can't stop here all afternoon yarning to you.' She checked her bag, looking for her bus pass. 'People might talk. I mustn't miss my bus. It's the last one today.'

'Where's the garden centre that Phil Dunbar works at?'

'It's called Green Fingers, about half a mile away. Green Fingers! Some of the plants I've bought from there have died. I don't think they water them enough. Sad-looking, scrawny things once I got them home. I took them back and they argued the toss with me, saying I hadn't treated them properly but I got the manager to reimburse me in the end. I know when I'm in the right. I wasn't going to back down.'

He watched her stride away, a strong and vigorous woman despite her age. Most of the Ramsays seemed to have disliked Kim. If what Sadie said was true, Gill had been motivated to offer her a home by more than kindness. Kim had been shrewd and might well have understood that. No wonder her Facebook posts had been bleak. Gill Ramsay was good at talking the talk but she had presented him with a sanitised version of Kim and he suspected that her focus had always been on Valery. From her own description, she had been hands off with her niece. It seemed to him that in many ways, Kim had been adrift and without proper guidance. Had Kim and Valery fallen out over Phil Dunbar? Badly enough to lead to violence?

He checked his watch. He needed to be back by seven. He had contacted a decorator who was coming to give him a quote for the basement and Cedric's flat. He planned to get the top floor refurbished and discuss it with Ruth. He had just about enough time to get to the garden centre.

CHAPTER 9

Green Fingers was proud to tell its visitors that it was a family-run business. Swift walked through a foyer of tubs filled with shrubs and flowers and a couple of burbling water features and stopped at a display of highly scented indoor plants. A woman in a green and white tabard was spraying mist on them and checking leaves. Swift's eyes started itching.

'Hi. I'm looking for Phil Dunbar. I think he works here. I just wanted a quick word if he's around. He's a friend of mine.'

She smiled at him. 'I think he's out back, sorting through the climbers.'

Swift had an attack of sneezes. 'Thanks.'

'Allergic, are you? Lots of people start sneezing around here. It's the lilies.'

He nodded, blowing his nose. 'I rarely visit garden centres. Too many things to set me off.'

She laughed. 'Just as well I don't have allergies — I'd be out of a job.'

Swift walked on, holding a tissue over his nose and blinking. He was glad to exit through the back doors and into the raw, damp air. The rear of the shop was separated into different areas with timber signposts — perennials, annuals, rock gardens, shrubs, winter bulbs, seasonal specials, roses and climbers. Swift saw with dismay that there was already a display of tacky Christmas decorations, including a life-size plastic Santa sitting on a sleigh, illuminated by flashing lights. He headed for the climbers and spotted Phil Dunbar lifting plants from a trolley and positioning them on a shelf.

'I wondered if you've got a minute,' Swift said.

Dunbar looked surprised. 'I thought you were seeing Elaine today.'

'I saw her, yes. I needed to see you, too.'

'I can't imagine why.' He gave his faded, quizzical smile and pushed back his floppy ash-blond hair. He was wearing jeans and a leather jerkin. Twists of orange twine trailed from the pockets.

'I wondered if you knew more about Kim Woodville than you told me.'

Dunbar fiddled with a plant label. 'I don't understand what you're asking me.'

He moved away as he adjusted the plant and Swift followed him, closing the space. 'You indicated that you didn't know Kim that well, but she visited your home.'

Dunbar glanced at him. 'Yes, she did. But as Elaine's protégé. I just gave her the odd pointer about educational courses. I'm sure Elaine told you that.' He smiled again, wrinkling his nose.

'So you only saw Kim at the museum or sometimes at your home?'

'That's right.' Dunbar turned towards him. 'Why are you quizzing me like this? I'm not sure I like it and I am at work, you know. I have a job to do.'

'I know and I won't keep you. It's just that someone told me that they saw you in your car with Kim one night near Low Lake. It wasn't long before she died.'

The fine lines at his eyes deepened. There was a little frown of irritation now. 'Who told you that?'

'I have my sources. Is it true?'

'Hmm, let me think.' He turned away and lifted another climber, the mass of leaves hiding his expression. 'Oh yes, that's right, she was looking into A-level courses and phoned me with some questions. I was driving back that way from seeing friends so I agreed to have a word with her. She said that would be good because then I could give her a lift into the village.'

'So you were talking about education?'

'That's right.'

'The person who saw you said it all looked a bit intense. You and Kim seemed agitated, maybe upset.'

Dunbar dumped the climber on the shelf. 'Country gossip! Heaven save me from it. I suppose your informant decided we were having a liaison?'

'Possibly. Were you?'

Dunbar laughed and Swift could hear relief. It was the wrong question. 'Mr Swift, I am a happily married man.'

'That's never stopped men having affairs.'

He rubbed soil from his hands. 'Perhaps not, but not this man, I can assure you. My memory of that meeting isn't terribly clear. I think I was telling Kim that she should aim for a mix of science and art A-level subjects. She wasn't keen on sciences and didn't want to study them but I pointed out to her that unless she knew a particular specialism she wanted to pursue in archaeology, it was better to have a mix of exams behind her. She didn't like being told what she should and shouldn't do, you know, she was quite stubborn like that. But I wasn't going to mislead her about her prospects. So maybe your snooper saw her getting annoyed because I wasn't telling her what she wanted to hear. That's the trouble with reading things into situations. You know, there's a narcissus flower called Peeping Tom. Perhaps you should buy one for your informant. People are such busybodies!' He shook his head ruefully, but with a satisfied grin.

It didn't ring true and it didn't explain why Dunbar would have been agitated.

'Have you ever been involved with Valery Ramsay?'

Dunbar laughed. This time it sounded genuine. 'I see you've cast me as the local lothario. You give me credit for more energy than I possess. I suppose I should be flattered, but actually I find it insulting to both my wife and me. I barely know Valery, certainly not well enough to get up close and personal with her. Someone's misleading you.'

A hefty man in brown overalls approached and nodded. He told Dunbar that he was needed at customer services to give some advice about wall climbers.

'Must go,' Dunbar said. 'Hope I've been able to help.' He was shaking his head as he walked away.

Swift headed back to his car, dissatisfied. It was hard to imagine that Kim would have gone for a lightweight like Dunbar, with his affected schoolboy charm. Unless she was tempted because he was such a contrast to rough diamond Hussain. He could imagine Valery having a crush on Dunbar. Fatherless girls often gravitated towards older men. It was possible that Sadie Stanley's description of the night she had seen Kim with Dunbar had been embellished. Maybe she had been mischief-making, but he thought her comments had the ring of truth. He would just have to let Dunbar's story lie for now, and see if anything more about him bubbled to the surface.

There were so many strands and possibilities in this case — Barton, Valery, Hussain and possibly Dunbar and Sadie all had reasons to harm Kim. If there had been a crime, it seemed unplanned and spur of the moment. Anger and jealousy that had festered over time could have resulted in a sudden eruption of rage by the lake. A few moments, and Kim would have been unconscious and drowning.

* * *

The Saturday outing with Nora and Branna had gone well until the evening. They had visited Kew Gardens in hazy sunshine, taking in the treetop walkway where, to Branna's delight, Nora had pretended to be a monkey. Swift was pleased to see that the two were growing more accustomed to each other with each meeting. They looked at the child-sized badger sett and the woodland house, and stopped for tea and cakes before heading back to Hammersmith.

When Swift had said it was time to go home, Branna had become fractious for a few minutes. She'd yelled huskily until the car journey back lulled her. Now that she had found her voice and was responding more to language, she could be loud and noisy. In the last week, she had learned to say *dada*, which she delivered with a laugh and at ear-splitting volume. The audiologist had smiled at the last appointment when Ruth mentioned this. She had told them that this was a natural tendency in a child with hearing loss, because she couldn't hear herself clearly. Also, Branna was a confident girl who had encouragement and support, and therefore she wasn't shy about communicating. They should be pleased, she had added, that Branna was determined and socially at ease. It was good groundwork because nursery might knock her confidence to start with, although Swift had seen no sign of this. He had explained all this to Nora but he had been aware of her wincing at times and closing her eyes, reading her emails while he calmed his daughter and distracted her with her picture book.

Nora rarely cooked but she had one failsafe recipe, coronation chicken, which she said she would throw together when they got back to his flat while he sorted Branna out.

He bathed his daughter, and they spoke and signed, intermingling the two forms of communication.

'You know, you're a highly intelligent girl, if a little forceful at times,' he told her. 'I wouldn't have you any other way. I wouldn't want a shy, retiring type. That wouldn't do at all. You've exceeded your developmental milestones. And this is lovely bubbly water.' He made small circle shapes in the air for *bubbles*.

Branna laughed and splashed water at him, then lifted a bubble on her finger, chanting, 'Dadadadabubbabubbababubba.'

'You've definitely got my eyes and your mum's mouth,' he said. 'And I'm sure I catch a glimpse of my dad when you give me your stern look.'

She furrowed her brows at him, making him laugh. He sat on the floor, watching her play, pretending to wash her hair. His mind strayed to the drawing on the wall of the treehouse on Ape Island. He pictured a woman on her knees, holding a struggling child down in the bath. He shivered, thinking of the terror that had been wired into Kim's brain at a tender age, wondering if she had recalled that previous immersion as she collapsed into the lake.

They ate when Branna had gone to sleep, exhausted by her day out. The chicken was creamy and spicy and they shared a bottle of white wine.

'Thanks for this, it's lovely to be cooked for,' he said.

'My pleasure. Although basically, I opened cartons. When can we go rowing again?'

'As soon as you can make the time. Speaking of which, I've ordered something for your birthday. I know it's a while away yet but I happened to see it. It's to do with rowing.'

Nora rubbed her hands. 'Give me a clue!'

'It's connected to the discussion we had about rowing on other rivers, exploring.'

She narrowed her eyes. 'A map? A boat? A year's subscription to other rowing clubs?'

'No. Not even warm. You'll have to wait until your birthday.'

She pulled a pretend scowl. 'That's a torment now. But a nice one.' She drank some wine and leaned back. 'Lovely peace and quiet now the little one has gone to dreamland.'

'You should have been here yesterday. There was tremendous banging from next door. It would have stunned Branna into silence.'

She poured them both more wine. 'You're great with Branna, you know. I admire your patience.'

'Well, she's my girl. It's painful sometimes, with her deafness. I can see she gets frustrated and I feel for her. And of course, I worry about how it will affect her life. I know from talking to Jack North how hard it can be if you're different.'

'Have you ever regretted having her?'

Swift was taken aback, a little offended. 'No, never. How could I regret Branna?'

'Some parents might, when they find out their child has a disability. I have a friend in Dublin who has a son with learning difficulties. She can't handle it at all, finds it frustrating. The kid spends most of the time with his grandmother.'

'I can't imagine being distanced like that from Branna, but I suppose that for some people, a disability is a problem they can't work with.'

'A couple of generations ago, kids with disabilities often got stuck in care homes. Out of sight, out of mind. I had an aunt with cerebral palsy in a home in Wicklow. I never even knew she existed until I was in my twenties. At least we've moved on from that.'

The subject seemed to cast a cloud over the table. They ate in silence for a while.

'This rice is lovely and dry,' Swift said finally.

Nora laughed. 'Cheat's rice — microwaved. As you've gathered, I'm not a woman to stand over steaming pans. I can never understand people who go through long rigmaroles of washing rice or slaving over homemade puff pastry or triple cooking chips. I take it Simone is like that.'

'She is. She's into sourcing her meat and vegetables. Everything has to be organic. When she cooks, it's like a military operation. She makes her own profiteroles. They are wonderful.'

'That one's as mad as a hatter, always mouthing off about every subject under the sun,' Nora said. 'I don't know how Mary sticks it. If I lived with her, I'd be homicidal.' She finished eating and leaned back, sipping her wine, smiling at him. 'What's with the paint colour charts?'

He was glad she'd changed the subject. He was wary of Simone and didn't hit it off with her. She had once visited him unannounced when she and Mary wanted to have a child. She'd sat in this room and proposed that he be the father. He could sleep with her, and Mary need never know. When he rejected the idea, she had thrown her wine over him. It had taken some months for a thaw to set in. Swift certainly didn't want to spoil an enjoyable day by discussing her. He was feeling relaxed, and warmed by the mellow wine. Nora's hair was tousled after their walk, her cheeks rosy from the fresh air and steam from the cooking. He reached out and took her firm, dry hand.

'I'm planning some decorating and I've had an idea. I want to redecorate my basement office and Cedric's flat. I thought of a paint called London Stone downstairs and pale grey and white upstairs, with a new carpet in the living room. A guy called Vlad Codreanu is doing it, starting next week. The landlord at the Silver Mermaid recommended him, said he's neat and efficient. Good value, too.'

'Oh, right. Sounds very tasteful. Neutral colours are always best if you're renting out the top. You're getting another tenant?'

'In a way, yes. I've asked Ruth if she'd like to move in with Branna, and she's thinking it over.'

As if a thermostat had been switched, the temperature in the room seemed to plummet to freezing. Nora pulled her hand away.

'You've asked Ruth to move in with you?'

'No. Not with me. Upstairs, in her own place. She'd pay some rent.'

'Is this for real?'

'Yes, of course.'

'Tell me you're joking.'

'No, I'm not. What's the matter?'

She shook her head and stared at him. 'The matter? Have a think, see if you can find a clue as to why I might think it's bloody peculiar that you're moving your ex in.'

Her eyes were blazing. He tried to catch her hand again but she pulled it away and folded her arms.

'I'm not moving her in. I've suggested it. She hasn't decided yet.'

'Oh, I think I can guess what her decision will be. Why wouldn't she opt to have you exactly where she likes you, at her beck and call?'

'Don't be nasty about it. It makes sense, that's all. Nora, it's not any kind of attempt to reignite things with Ruth, if that's what you're thinking. Those times have gone. Ruth's husband still lives in their house and given his illness, she doesn't feel that she can ask him to divorce her or sell. So her money is tied up in the property and she's paying an exorbitant rent on that shoebox in Hendon. If they live upstairs, it means I can help to look after Branna much more easily and have more time with her, day to day. It has to be better for her. It will be much easier to share drop-off and collection from the nursery. Ruth's hoping to secure more work and my hours are flexible.'

'That's all good for Ruth and Branna. And you, of course. Where exactly do I fit in?'

'Well of course you fit in. You're part of it all. I don't see that it makes any difference to us. We have our lives, Ruth has hers. I share Branna's parenting. It was Cedric's idea originally. He broached it in the hospital before he died. He was keen for me to pursue it. He said he could move to Milo's. I'm not sure I'd have thought of it otherwise.'

'God, this gets better and better! That's handy, blaming the whole thing on a dead man. Talk about emotional blackmail! I mean, whatever I say now, I'm going to sound cold-hearted, aren't I?'

He gazed at her. There was a frozen, blank look on her face that he'd never seen before. It chilled him. 'That's a horrible thing to say. Making me out to be manipulative. Cedric thought of it because he wanted to be helpful to me and he was worried he might not manage the stairs much longer.'

'So, let's see, you've known about this for weeks and been thinking about it but you didn't think to discuss it with me? You know, me, Nora, the woman who's supposed to be your partner. Or maybe you don't see me that way. Maybe I'm a temporary interest, another woman to fill in the gaps while you hang about waiting to see if Ruth might reconsider you.'

'Nora, stop. You know that's not true. You know I care about you. I *am* discussing it, or trying to.'

She held her hands to her head. 'Oh yes, as a done deal. Not to ask my opinion or check how I feel about it. You really don't see it, do you? How can a fierce intelligent man be so *dense*? I already share you with Branna. That's okay, she's your child. But I'm not bloody well playing gooseberry to you and Ruth. Come on, Ty. How am I going to feel, knowing that Ruth is literally perched over my head? I mean, talk about an anaphrodisiac!'

He shoved his glass away, spilling wine. He could feel the evening souring, slipping away. He didn't understand. He'd thought that Nora trusted him, knew that he was genuine about their relationship and would see his point of view. He rose and took Cedric's note from the bookshelf, and held it out to Nora.

'Look. If you need proof, Cedric wrote this note to me before he died.'

She scanned it and threw it on the table. 'So what? Is it supposed to make me feel better? I just love the way you two men thought you could move us women around like domino tiles. So Cedric felt guilty about his son and thought he'd had a good idea? Doesn't mean you have to run with it. He was old and ill, a bit confused, not thinking straight. If he'd recovered, he'd probably have realised his idea had a major flaw. Me!'

Swift felt suddenly weary and cross. 'There was nothing wrong with Cedric's reasoning. And by the way, I'm glad you're *okay* about Branna. That's so generous of you. You know it's complicated with Ruth and Branna. If anything, this is an attempt to make things simpler. And they'll have a bigger place to live and a garden.'

'Oh, it gets better and better!' Nora shoved her chair back with a screech, stood and picked up her bag, and snatched her jacket from the chair. 'So it will be a happy little ménage. We'll be here billing and cooing, and Ruth and Branna will be tiptoeing down the stairs and through to the garden so as not to disturb us. It's like the script of some bloody farce. I thought Simone was as mad as a hatter but I think it's you who needs certifying! You know, I believed you when you told me that you were completely over Ruth. I really thought you'd moved on. You were very convincing, but then cops usually make good liars, don't we? We listen to so much fabrication we know the form.' She was at the door now, and yanked it open. 'There's posh delicatessen apple tart if you want it. I hope it gives you fierce indigestion!'

The door slammed and she was gone. He stared at the remains of the meal. The chicken looked jaundiced in its congealing yellow sauce. He poured the rest of the wine into his glass. It tasted bitter and tainted now but he knocked it back. How dare she speak of Branna in that way, as if his daughter was an encumbrance! It had never once crossed his mind that Nora would take his plan about Cedric's flat in the wrong way. She was being ridiculous and petty. If she had so little faith in him, so little trust, it didn't bode well for a mutual future. He thought of her acknowledged low tolerance level for children, her quick temper and the expression on her face earlier, when Branna had yelled. Maybe he had been fooling himself. Maybe it could never work.

Well, Nora, he thought grimly, *if you don't want to have to share me, you'd better find someone with a blank history, someone all clean, uncomplicated, and shiny new. And good luck with that.*

* * *

He'd had no reply from Gill Ramsay about Kim's mother and she had failed to respond to two phone messages. He had done a quick search for a Paula Woodville in the London area but failed to turn up anyone in the right age bracket. He needed to trace the woman and check out if Valery's impression was correct. He rang Jack North, who was taken aback at the possibility that Kim had been in touch with her mother.

'I'm sure Kim would have said something to me. It would have been a huge thing for her.'

Swift wasn't so sure. He thought that North underestimated both Kim's ability to guard her privacy and how much the distance between them had affected their friendship. Easy intimacy could dwindle when people were miles apart. He knew that only too well from his experience with Ruth.

'Maybe if it's true, Kim needed to think it over before she talked to anyone,' said Swift. 'If Valery is right, we don't know which of them made contact.'

'Maybe that's what she was hinting at in that email to me. I do wish I'd phoned her, asked her what was bothering her. Some friend I turned out to be.'

'It's possible that she wanted to discuss her mother. What do you know about her?'

'Not much except that she was a monster. I don't know any details, just that her name was Paula. Do you want me to contact Gill?' North asked.

'No, it's okay. I'll follow up. Quite a few of the people I've spoken to weren't as keen on Kim as you were, Jack. It sounds as if she could be difficult company.'

North sounded subdued. 'I know some of the family and people around there didn't get on with her. I can only say how I found her. She'd had a rough start in life and she was never going to be an angel. But she was *my* angel and I hate the idea that some of them are speaking ill of her.'

'From what I've heard about her, I'm not sure she'd mind. She might even enjoy it.' Swift smiled to himself.

'That's probably true. You've got the right idea about her. She'd take it as a challenge.'

'One thing you didn't mention to me which could be significant was what happened to Nadia Barton.'

A pause. 'Who's Nadia Barton?'

'You don't know about her?'

'No. I've never heard of her.'

'She was a friend of Kim's who died.' Swift explained about the girl's death and her father's anguish. There was a long, tense silence.

'I didn't know anything about that,' North said at last. 'I was in Liverpool by then. Kim never mentioned it. Why didn't she tell me?' His voice was trembling.

'I don't know. Maybe she was embarrassed or she felt too traumatised by it. She said little about it to the immediate family or anyone else, as far as I can gather.'

'But . . . I mean we always talked about important things. Confided in each other. I just don't get it. That was a big, big thing in her life. She must have felt terrible, in shock. Why wouldn't she have reached out to me?'

That was the trouble with asking questions about people, Swift thought. Sometimes you heard unexpected things that rocked your view of them and your relationship. It confirmed that Kim and North hadn't been as close in later years as North thought.

'Sorry to upset you, Jack. I wondered if you knew but I couldn't keep it from you.'

'Yes . . . okay . . . I see. Well, I'll just have to puzzle over why she didn't tell me. What's your thinking about Kim's death now?'

'I don't know, Jack. Nothing is clear at the moment. She was certainly on the receiving end of animosity from a number of people.'

'Okay. I see. Sorry, it's a lot to take in.'

Swift could hear the pain in his voice. His loss of Kim was being compounded by the fact that she hadn't shared one major life event with him, and possibly more than one. He would brood and worry about what else she hadn't told him. Swift was beginning to wonder about that too.

'Take it easy, Jack. No one ever tells another person everything, no matter how close they are. We all guard compartments in ourselves. Life would be unbearable otherwise.'

'I know, but such major, really important stuff. I feel as if I'm on shifting sands. Kim was such a constant figure in my life. I relied so much on her, even when we were far apart. I told her everything, all my dreams and doubts. I thought it went both ways.'

He sounded tearful. Swift ended the call, relieved to escape from the distraught man. The problem with angels was that their haloes sometimes slipped or grew tarnished.

The trumpet player next door was practising scales. He was considerate, using a mute until his soundproofed loft was ready. He started playing a tune that Swift thought he recognised, then realised it was the spiritual song 'Nobody Knows the Trouble I've Seen.' He tapped his foot to it, thinking, *Seems to me that you were Trouble with a capital T, Kim Woodville.* The rehearsing stopped abruptly and he checked his diary. He'd made an appointment to see Steve Ramsay in Islington. He'd go by bus, he decided. Horizontal, drifting rain swept the streets outside.

* * *

Swift got off the bus at the Angel and walked along Upper Street, past gluten- and sugar-free bakeries, high-end boutiques, Chinese and French restaurants, salad bars, retro clothes shops, patisseries and a wine merchant with a display of champagnes in the window.

Halfway along the main road he cut down a turning and into the street where Steve Ramsay lived. After Upper Street, it looked ordinary, a mixture of two and three-storey slate-roofed houses. Some were ill kempt and in multiple occupancy, some were newly painted and others had skips standing outside. Signs of an area on its way up. The street inhabited a territory between the chi-chi, expensive terraces where champagne was sold, and the council estates. Ramsay's house was at the end of a terrace, attached to a double garage. Swift could hear an engine running. He knocked on the heavy steel door and pulled it back. A man in navy overalls was peering into the engine of a white Porsche parked over an inspection pit. The air was heavy with oil and exhaust fumes. Swift moved round the car and caught his attention.

'Steve Ramsay?'

'That's right. Hang on a minute.' Ramsay leaned in and turned off the car engine.

'I'm Tyrone Swift. I'm the private investigator working for Jack North.'

'Right. Mum rang me and said you'd been asking questions about Kim and stirring things up. Your name's mud at Low Lake. You've given Mum the jitters and I understand that Valery's had the worst sulks in years. I hear that Ben's been banging on about helping you. Apparently he's like a recording playing on a loop, saying he might start his own detective agency. As if! He has the attention span of a mayfly. Congratulations on shaking

168

them up.' He was dark, with a thin face and high cheekbones.

'You're not too bothered?'

'Me? No. I'm just a grease monkey. I prefer engines to people. They're easy to work out and they don't talk back.' Ramsay grinned.

'So is it okay if I ask you a few questions?'

'Fire away.' He propped himself against the bonnet of the car, took some chewing gum from his pocket and offered a stick to Swift.

'Thanks. Your mum didn't seem too happy that you'd moved to London.'

'Well, no. When I told her I'd met someone and I was moving here, you'd think I'd said I was going to another continent. Lots of sighs and long-suffering looks.'

'When did you leave home?'

'About eighteen months ago.'

'Do you go back much?'

'Rarely. I like my independence. Got Kirsty, my girlfriend, our own house, my own space. No one breathing down my neck.'

'You don't miss your family?'

'Nope. A phone call now and again and the odd visit is as much contact as I like. I certainly don't miss that poisonous old bat Sadie.' His eyes were dark, almost black, and seemed watchful.

'What did you make of Kim's death?'

Ramsay unwrapped his gum, folded it into his mouth and chewed for a moment. 'I reckoned it might have been suicide.'

'I've not heard that theory. Tell me your thinking.'

'It didn't occur to me at the time but later on, when I mulled it over, it seemed possible. Kim was dead moody just before she died. More than usual. You know about Nadia Barton's death?'

Swift nodded.

'I think she was a lot more down about what happened to Nadia than she ever let on. I wondered if she got really depressed and topped herself.'

'Your mother told me that Kim was her usual self before she died.'

Ramsay snorted. 'What would she know? She always turned a blind eye to whatever Kim was up to. And she was up to something.'

'Oh? Any idea what?'

'I don't know, but she'd borrowed one of my cars before she died, an Audi TT. I don't know when exactly, because I was away at the time at car auctions. But when I came back the day she was found, the speedometer had a few more miles on the clock.'

'How do you know Kim had used it?'

'No one else would have. She'd taken one before, used it to drive to Great Howe. She didn't have a driving licence. She couldn't get one because of her epilepsy, but that didn't stop her. She went joyriding with that creep, Hussain. I warned her off but she was like that — taking and using other people's stuff whenever she felt like it.'

'Did any of the family see her driving the Audi?'

'No, but they wouldn't necessarily. I'd just finished reconditioning it and it was in one of the garages near the front entrance. I expect Kim sneaked it out at night, like she did before. I told the police but they never mentioned it again so I suppose it wasn't important.'

'I've been getting different views of how Kim was before she died. Ben told me he thought she was excited about something. She sent Jack an email saying she'd met new people.'

'Don't know anything about that. As I said, I thought she seemed a bit down.'

'Did you know that Kim might have met her birth mother shortly before she died?'

Ramsay's chin had a light shading of stubble. He scratched it. 'Who told you that?'

'Valery suggested it.'

He shook his head. 'Sounds unlikely. Val says stuff to cause a bit of trouble and get some attention. I don't think Kim would have gone anywhere near her mother. But then she wouldn't have confided in me about it.'

'Did you know Pete Hussain?'

'Not personally. I'd seen him around. He was a tosser. He liked to be noticed and his reputation went before him. It didn't surprise me when Kim took up with him. She was attracted to the dark side.'

A gust of wind and rain blew the door back. Ramsay propped it shut with a brick and switched the lights on, setting shadows dancing.

'I saw your sketch of your family on Ape Island. Pretty scathing.'

Ramsay shrugged and laughed. 'I did that when I was sixteen. Adolescent turmoil. I think it was accurate though. We're an odd bunch. You must have worked that out by now.'

'And Kim was the cuckoo in the nest?'

Ramsay took a rag and wiped one of the Porsche's headlights. 'I didn't have much time for Kim when she was growing up. I thought she should never have come to live with us. I reckon Dad agreed with me but he always let Mum overrule him. Kim could be a pain in the arse. We all got on pretty much okay before she arrived. Then she turned up, and there was tension from then on. She never fitted in, but Mum and Dad pretended that she did. There was always this jolly fiction that we were different and interesting. That's what the drawing was about. I didn't want my family to be different. I wanted it to blend in. Children always want to be like everyone else. Whenever we went to the village as kids, the oiks were always name-calling. "Freakies" was a common one, or the good old "hippies." Mum would tell us that people often resented anyone unusual. That's okay for her, she hardly ever sets foot in Great Howe, spends all her time pottering around her estate.' He sounded brittle, angry.

'I suppose the homeschooling set you apart as well.'

'Yes. If you can call it schooling. More like messing about most of the time. I'm amazed that we could even read.' He glanced at Swift. 'I'm glad I got away from Low Lake. The bloody place sucks the energy out of you. Mum's like one of those animals that eat their young. She'll be feeding off Ben and Valery now. I saved up and got out as soon as I could. Tell you another thing, if I have kids they'll have a boring, conventional life, rules they have to keep to and they'll go to school wearing a uniform, with polished shoes.'

Life was just a back and forth of reactions, Swift thought. Ramsay's response to his upbringing was to seek mundane routine. 'So, you do cars up for a living?'

'Yeah, and I do okay from it. Make enough to get a decent mortgage.'

'Well, thanks for talking to me. Oh, by the way, did you ever think that Kim was having a relationship with Phil Dunbar?'

For the first time, Ramsay tensed up. 'Dunbar? That skinny old guy? I shouldn't think so. What makes you ask that?'

'Nothing. It's okay. See you.'

He turned back at the doors. Ramsay was watching him carefully. Then he shrugged and bent back over the Porsche.

Swift left him tinkering with the car and walked back to Upper Street. Ramsay seemed to be the most well-adjusted member of his family. He'd considered the family dynamics and taken a mature decision to create his own space. There was no love lost where his mother was concerned, and there had been bitter rancour in Ramsay's voice when he spoke about her. He wondered why Ramsay thought that Kim might have been suicidal. He hadn't sounded that convinced by his own theory. If she had been, Swift was sure she would have chosen any method other than drowning. And Ramsay had flinched at Dunbar's name. There was something there, a kind of miasma surrounding the Dunbars. He wished he could understand it.

CHAPTER 10

The Ramsays were a strange bunch and he was tiring of their company, but he needed to visit their territory again. He drove to Low Lake with the windscreen wipers on fast, in pouring rain. The countryside looked bleak and hunkered down, readying itself for winter. When he parked in front of the house, he noted that the scaffolding had gone. Dripping tubs of dahlias, salvias and asters now stood on the gravel. Sadie Stanley was perched inside one of the front windows, tapping a finger against her lip and gazing out gloomily. She opened the window slightly and called out to him.

'If you're wanting Gill, she's working.' She gestured with a thumb towards the stables.

'Valery?'

'Her too. Playing with glue or whatever.' With that, she slammed the window shut and vanished.

He walked to the stable which had a hand-painted sign over the solid timber door: RAMSAY RURAL CRAFTS. The door opened straight into a high-ceilinged airy room lined with long tables. The white plaster walls were covered with colourful examples of crochet, découpage and framed prints. Around a dozen women were engaged in decorating various objects with coloured paper, paint and gold leaf. Gill Ramsay and Valery were helping students at the far end of the room. The woman nearest him was working on a mirror in a white frame, carefully moulding a paper corner. She noticed him and smiled.

'You're a bit late for class. There's only fifteen minutes left.'

'That's okay, I'm not a student. Is that découpage?'

'That's right. I'm making this for my granddaughter's bedroom.'

'Very nice.'

He saw that Gill had spotted him and was walking towards him, tight-lipped. Today's crocheted shawl was grey and silver, tied across the front with a clasp, a dove made of wood.

'Morning. You haven't answered my calls,' he said.

She waved her hands fussily, moving him back towards the door. 'How dare you interrupt our work! I told you not to come here again. You're not welcome.'

'I need details of Kim's mother. I'm sure you must have some.'

'Just leave things alone. Stop raking over the past. It's pointless.'

Several of the students had paused in their work and were glancing towards them. Valery stomped up the room and stood beside her mother. Her hair was tied back under a bandana and she was wearing a sparkling blue eyeshadow that glinted in the light and made her eyes look smaller, meaner.

'Why don't you piss off,' she hissed.

'I will, when I have the information I want.'

'Well, you're not getting it from us,' Gill Ramsay muttered. She turned to the room, calling cheerily, 'Sorry about this, ladies. Just carry on. I'll be with you in a minute.'

'Okay, if that's how you want it. In that case, I'll have to speak to the police about why Valery stole Kim's medication and hid it on Ape Island.'

'What are you talking about now?' Gill looked at her daughter, then back at Swift.

'Valery knows. I'll see you at the house when class finishes.'

He left her with her mouth gaping. Outside, he stood for a moment with his back to the door, peering through the slanting rain. He went and sat in his car, listening to a play about the Russian revolution, until he saw the class dispersing and the Ramsay women go to the house. Valery turned and scowled at him, Gill stared straight ahead. He waited five minutes, and then rang the doorbell.

Gill opened the door and thrust a piece of paper at him. 'No need to come in. This is the information I have about Paula. Valery tells me that you found Kim's medication on Ape Island, but she has no idea how it got there. Oh, and can you stop giving Ben silly ideas? He's been telling everyone he's your deputy and pestering us with questions about Kim's death. It's terribly upsetting. There's enough foolish behaviour with him as it is, I don't need you egging him on.'

She stepped back and pushed the door. Swift stuck his foot in the gap.

'I will go, but I just want a minute of Valery's time. Not even a minute. It's important. I won't upset her.'

She glared at him and turned away. He stood with his shoulder against the doorjamb. After a couple of minutes, Valery appeared, carrying a glass of milk and eating a biscuit.

Swift tried an encouraging smile and a lie. 'I don't think you harmed Kim. But I do think you hid her medication because you disliked her so much. Just nod if it was you. It won't go any further and then I can stop bothering you.'

Her eyes narrowed, she stuck up two fingers and slammed the door. He shrugged and darted back to the car through the insistent rain. He examined the note Gill had given him.

Paula Christine Woodville. Or may be using her maiden name, Flanders. I don't know her DOB but I think she was born in 1977 or 78.
Last address I know of: 21 Manley Road, Tottenham.
Now leave us alone!

* * *

Swift had been waiting for the inevitable from Oliver Sheridan, and it arrived that Saturday morning: a letter from a firm of solicitors, informing him that they were acting on behalf of Mr Oliver Sheridan.

We have lodged a caveat at the Probate Registry regarding Mr Cedric Sheridan's will. This means that you cannot proceed with probate. The caveat is based on two grounds, one that Mr Oliver Sheridan believes that undue influence was brought to bear on his father in the making of the will and two, under the terms of the 1975 Inheritance Act, that Mr Cedric Sheridan's will fails to make reasonable financial provision for his son.

Swift rang Milo on Saturday morning to let him know.

'Listen, Ty, I don't need the money and you don't need this trouble. It was lovely of Cedric to think of me but I have enough to get by on and I don't need that much. I can give my share to Oliver if it will shut him up. It will pain me to do so but I'll survive.'

'That's very kind of you but it doesn't work like that, Milo. The will is a legal document and as executor, I can't go against Cedric's wishes regarding the other beneficiaries. I have to carry them out to the letter, unless a judge says otherwise. Obviously, you can do what you like with the money once this has been settled and you can give it to Oliver then if you want to.'

'Oh Lord. A terrible situation for you. What do they mean by "undue influence?"'

'I suspect they mean me. Oliver will have given them a tale of woe about me pressurising Cedric, getting him to give me his car and so forth.'

'Except that you and I know that it was Oliver exerting pressure.'

'Yes, but I was the only witness to that, which could put me in a difficult position as both a beneficiary and executor. I considered giving my own portion to Oliver after probate was complete, hoping to get him off my back for good. My solicitor pointed out that this might be seen as admitting that I did influence Cedric. And to be honest, although I don't really need the money either, Oliver's attitude makes me so angry I don't feel like being generous to him.'

'There's nothing you can do?'

'I don't think so. I'll take further legal advice. I just have to wait to hear more. I may have to go to court eventually.'

His phone buzzed as he finished the call and he saw that he'd had an email from Ben Ramsay.

Someone has been covering up! Got important info for you. Not sure what it means. Thought I'd visit the big metropolis so will call at your place later this afternoon. You'll want to hear this!
Ben Ramsay, API

Swift replied:

Okay, I'm out during the day but I'll be home around six so any time after then. If you get here early, there's a decorator in the house and he can let you in. I'll tell him just in case.

He went upstairs to Vlad Codreanu, who was on a ladder in the kitchen, and explained that he had a visitor arriving later. Then he set out for a row, hoping that Ben wasn't getting excited about very little.

* * *

He met Mary for a coffee that afternoon. He thought it was going to be just his cousin with her son Louis, but as he arrived he saw that Simone was there too. Mary and Simone had used a donor to have their son the year before. Louis was busy with crayons and a sheet of paper, although most of the colour was spreading on the table. Both women treasured him but Simone went to extremes. She made sure that he ate only organic foods, had no saturated fat, sugar or fizzy drinks, and he went to sleep listening to educational stories on an app called Wise Owl. She dressed him in the kind of traditional 1950s outfits that royal children were now wearing. Expensive, monogrammed shorts, shirts, and T-bar shoes. He was always gleaming and clean. He was around the same age as Branna but sturdier and, Swift thought, more placid. Perhaps a little boring even. He flapped his hand at Swift in a regal wave and returned to his scribbles.

'I'm sure his coordination is better than it was yesterday,' Simone said with maternal pride. 'They change all the time at this age, don't they? Do you notice that about Branna?'

'Of course. Her sign language skills are really coming on.' He was missing his daughter. Ruth had gone to Shropshire with Branna for a couple of weeks, to see her mother. She said she would think about his offer of the flat upstairs while she was away.

'How are you doing?' Mary asked. 'I often think about Cedric. You must miss him so much, Ty.'

'Every day. The house is so quiet — well, apart from the work next door and before Vlad Codreanu, my decorator, started. He's improving his English by listening

179

to a language course. He has a deep voice so I hear regular bursts of "It's great to see you, you're looking well" and "Can you tell me where the railway station is?"' He stirred his coffee. 'I've encountered a bit of a problem regarding Cedric's will.' He explained the letter from the solicitor.

Simone waded straight in. 'I've heard of this kind of thing. Apparently, contesting wills is becoming quite common and DIY wills are the worst culprits. A colleague at work had a major fallout with her family because of her father's. It doesn't make any sense, not getting a solicitor to draw up a will, especially if you think it might be contentious. I mean, Cedric must have realised it would rub Oliver up the wrong way. I'd have thought he'd be more savvy. Unless he was setting out to cause trouble, I suppose. People do sometimes. They get cranky as they get older and they decide to wield retribution and power from beyond the grave.'

As usual, Simone was managing to rub Swift up the wrong way. 'I don't think that was Cedric's intention. He must have had enough of Oliver's behaviour, even if he didn't speak of it. He was always a generous man but I think Oliver pushed him too far, especially when he stole from him.'

'Well, maybe. But even so, it's left you in a pickle and I don't think Cedric should have done that.' Simone waved her teaspoon at him. He particularly disliked the way she brandished cutlery to emphasise a point. 'It could drag on for months, even years, you know. If it goes to court it will be very expensive and all kinds of dirty laundry will get washed in public.'

Swift took a sip of coffee and a deep breath. 'Well, Simone, it will be Oliver's dirty laundry and that's fine with me.'

She continued as if he hadn't spoken. 'You don't know, a court might think you *were* in a position to influence Cedric. I mean, we know you didn't but it's hard to disprove when you were so close and he was your tenant. And of course, he gave you his car last year. That might not look too good.'

'Anyway,' Mary said quickly, collecting a couple of crayons that were about to roll off the table, 'we'll see. I think mediation is sometimes offered in these circumstances, to try and resolve matters out of court. That might settle things. Simone, I think Louis needs changing and I believe it's your turn!'

Simone's eyes narrowed but she picked Louis up and swept him off to the Ladies. There was a silence while Mary and Swift both sipped coffee.

'And have you talked to Nora?' Mary asked. Swift had mentioned their row when he called her.

He shook his head. 'We haven't been in contact since our disagreement. I didn't like her attitude to Branna. Anyway, she's the one who walked out. I've been busy on a case.'

'You mean you've been avoiding the issue. Has Ruth decided about the flat?'

'Not yet. I think it makes a lot of sense, though.'

Mary sat back and gazed at him. He knew that look. It meant she didn't agree with him. Today she was wearing her dark-framed glasses and they made her seem sterner. She smoothed Louis' colouring paper.

'I can see Nora's point of view. You did rather drop the proposed plan on her without any discussion.'

'You're saying I've been insensitive.'

'Yes, I am and I'm surprised you can't see it. Except . .
.'

'Go on.'

Mary took a breath. 'You can be blinkered where Ruth's concerned.'

'So people tell me.'

'Maybe you should listen to them.'

'But this is really about Branna. The idea about the flat is mainly for her benefit, not Ruth's.'

181

'Hmm. It's hard for Nora to see it that way. I'm not sure you've thought it through properly. It might seem a bit crowded in your house, in your life. Not the best of starts to a newish relationship.'

'There has to be give and take. I explained it all to Nora. She turned nasty, more or less said I was using Cedric's idea to try and pressurise her. Branna's welfare is important. I'm not sure that Nora likes being around children. She's said she doesn't want any herself.'

'Well, that's not a fault, it's just how she is. At least she's honest. I can see it could take time to adjust to someone else's child, delightful though Branna is. It can't be easy, fitting in to your complicated personal life.'

'That's up to Nora. She knew about Branna from the start.'

'But it's not as simple as that, surely? Branna's one thing. Ruth's another. I think I'd feel vulnerable if I was Nora. You can't just steamroller this through because it's what you want.'

'Is that what you think I'm doing?'

'Yes, frankly. I think you've made Nora feel like a bit player. And come on, it isn't just up to Nora to resolve things. How would you feel if it was the other way around? What if Nora was moving that bloke who left her — what was his name — into a flat near her? What if he came back from New York and was living in her block?'

'Alistair. And it's not the same.'

'I know that. I'm talking about emotions. I remember you saying you felt knocked back the first time you saw her with Alistair. You were about to ask her out and then you saw her with him.'

'Nora's only responsible for herself. I've got other people to think about too.'

Mary sighed. 'I can see you're not in a receptive mood. Not talking to Nora is no answer, though. Someone has to be grown up and break the silence. I suppose it comes down to whether or not you really want her in your life. Only you know that.'

Swift was feeling irritable. He'd been looking forward to time with Mary and this wasn't the pleasant interlude he had been expecting. First Simone holding forth, now Mary quizzing him. 'Exactly. Let's leave it there. Another coffee?'

She sighed and said she'd have an orange juice, Simone would probably like another decaf latte and Louis could have a pure fruit smoothie, the only brand that Simone approved of. He could feel Mary's eyes on him as he went to the counter. He felt confused about Nora and angry with her. He wanted to speak to her but didn't know what to say. And after all, she was the one who'd had a temper tantrum and stormed out. He would let things lie a while longer, let the dust settle.

As he paid for the drinks and took his change from a tall young waitress with long dark hair, he wondered what Kim had been doing in Steve's car before she died, and where she had gone.

* * *

Swift put his car in the garage at six thirty, nodding to a neighbour who was walking his dog. He was home later than he'd intended. Simone had taken Louis to visit a friend and Mary had suggested a walk on Hampstead Heath. The breeze had blown away his touchiness, ending the afternoon on a more pleasant note.

The hallway smelled of fresh paint. There was no sign of Ben. Vlad Codreanu had left the spare house keys with a note on the hall table, saying he had finished the basement and almost completed upstairs. He had just a couple of hours' work to do and would be back in the morning. He had also accepted a delivery, a long, heavy cardboard box, and left it propped against the wall. Swift checked the label. Nora's birthday present. He'd seen a special offer and now that she had a car, he had ordered it early, relishing a bargain as much as the next man. He took it into his flat and left it on the floor in the living room.

When Ben hadn't arrived by seven, Swift rang him and got his voicemail. He left a message, saying he was in and would be at home for the evening. He made beans on toast, poured a glass of wine and put Bruce Springsteen on. He googled Paula C Flanders while he ate, eventually finding a likely-looking woman in Wood Green. He tried Ben's phone again at nine, but still got voicemail. He left another message.

'Hi, Ben, I assume you got sidetracked or delayed. Give me a call when you can. You don't have to come all the way here with your news. We can talk on the phone or Skype.'

Swift went down to check out the basement. It looked transformed and reassuringly businesslike. He sat there for a while, admiring the clean surfaces, allowing his thoughts to wander. *Where were you driving to, Kim, and who were you seeing? What were you moody about? Who were the new people in your life? What was your thorny issue? Where did your laptop go? Did you bring someone back to Low Lake and have an argument with them? Did they spot that you were starting to fit and take advantage?* Too many questions. He roused himself and went to have a shower, followed by another glass of wine and a late-night chat show on TV.

Vlad Codreanu arrived the following morning at nine in his paint-spattered jeans and T-shirt.

'Is okay if I finish today? Means I can start new job tomorrow.'

'No problem. I'm around this morning, so just give me a shout when you've finished. You didn't see that young man I told you about yesterday, Ben Ramsay? He was supposed to call in to see me.'

Vlad shook his head. 'No visitors. Just parcel. I sign for it.'

'What time did you finish?'

'About quarter past five.'

Swift gave him the key to the upstairs flat and spent the morning making a pan of soup to last him though the week. Then he cleaned, put laundry on to wash and sorted out the recycling bin. As he passed through the hallway, he could hear Vlad's sonorous tones from the top floor, copying his lesson in English tenses. 'I *am making* an appointment to see her next week. I *will make* an appointment to see her next week. I *have made* an appointment to see her next week. I *had made* an appointment to see her next week.'

At eleven thirty, Vlad called him up to show him the finished flat. He had removed the dustcovers and fixed a new blind to the kitchen window. The work was skilled. The rooms looked more spacious and full of light. Cedric would have approved, Swift thought with a twist of misery.

'You happy?' Vlad asked.

'Very, and with the basement. Thanks so much.'

'Lovely flat. Make nice home for someone.'

'I hope so.'

He settled the bill with Vlad, and then checked his phone. Nothing from Ben. He tried ringing him again, with no success. He would leave it for now, he thought. Ben was fanciful and haphazard. Perhaps he'd decided that his important news wasn't so important after all and had been distracted by a superhero film.

Downstairs, he made a coffee and sipped it as he stood and looked around his living room. Vlad's pristine work above and below him made his own slightly shabby decor look even more faded. He liked Lily's art nouveau furnishings, the William Morris wallpaper and the beautiful fireplace with original, slightly chipped Victorian tiles. The room was a comfort zone. Maybe he'd make some changes in here. Maybe.

The heavy parcel that had been delivered lay beside his sofa. There had still been no word from Nora. Nor had he contacted her. Stalemate. Maybe he should just send the present back. Yet that would be an admission of an ending, and he didn't want that. Or thought he didn't. He really wasn't sure. Ever since Ruth first left him, uncertainty had dogged him. It was like a mist that never cleared, but with Nora the mist had definitely been thinning. The robotic tones of Vlad's cyber teacher echoed sarcastically in his head: *I am* unsure, *I have been* unsure, *I will be* unsure. *Enough*, he told himself. He threw back his coffee, found a pair of scissors and carried the parcel to the garage where he hacked it open. He spent the next half hour labouring over its construction, pleased that it could be removed easily when not needed.

That evening he heated up the last of the meals that had been stored in Cedric's freezer, a lamb stew with rosemary and pearl barley. It was rich, sticky and delicious. While he stirred it, he emailed Nora.

I miss you. I would like to see you and talk to you. Next week any good for you?

He poured a glass of Bordeaux to go with the lamb and toasted Cedric's memory. He switched on a playlist and ate sitting on the sofa, his feet up on the coffee table, plate balanced on his lap. As Cedric would have said, the pleasures of being a single man. As he was mopping up the dark gravy with a hunk of bread, his phone rang and he heard Gill Ramsay. She sounded breathless.

'Have you seen anything of Ben?'

'No. I was expecting him here yesterday evening but he didn't show. Is there a problem?'

'He's gone missing. I'm about to call the police.'

Swift put his plate on the table and sat forward. 'When did you last see him?'

'Sadie saw him yesterday morning, around noon. He was on his bike. He said he was off to the station and going somewhere on important business. Sadie said he was excited. When I didn't see him last night, I assumed he was sleeping on Ape Island. Then I had a class this morning. I didn't get worried until early this afternoon when I realised no one had seen him since yesterday. He's not answering his phone.'

'You've checked the island?'

'Of course. Valery went over there. No sign of him and the boat is moored by the summerhouse. I've just rung the local hospitals but got nowhere.'

'Ben contacted me to say he was coming to see me yesterday evening. He didn't turn up and his phone has been on voicemail. I assumed he'd changed his mind.'

'If something's happened to Ben because of this Kim nonsense, you'll be to blame, Mr Swift. You put ridiculous ideas into his head and I will tell the police that.'

'Ben is a grown man. Maybe he's with friends. Does he know people in London? What about family?'

Her voice was getting higher and thinner. 'I've spoken to Adela and Steve. They haven't heard from him. Ben doesn't have many friends and certainly none in London. This isn't like him. Ben's a home bird. He never misses our roast at four o'clock every Sunday. He knew it would be pork today, his favourite, and he's always first to the table. I must go.'

'Please let me know—'

She had cut him off.

Swift finished his wine. He was worried. It was true that Ben was a grown man but he was immature and had the instincts of a juvenile. He thought of trying Ben's number again but decided not to. If Gill was phoning the police, it was best to leave contact to them. He scrolled to Ben's last email and read it again.

Someone has been covering up.

* * *

When Swift rang Low Lake the following morning, he got Sadie Stanley.

'Gill's not available. She's talking to the police.'

'Ben's not back?'

'No. Gone two nights. That's bad news. More trouble for this family. I've never known anything like it. Valery's been crying her eyes out, saying something terrible must have happened to him. The usual histrionics. Mind you, it's not like him to take off. Now, with Kim, that wouldn't have been at all strange but Ben . . . he's a different kettle of fish. Of course, you've been a bad influence on him. Turning his head with notions about Kim. I said to the sergeant, that know-it-all meddler from London—'

'Thanks,' he said. 'I'd appreciate it if you could let me know if Ben turns up. Who is your police contact?'

'That numpty, Josh Houghton. He couldn't find a goldfish in a bowl.'

Swift took the bus to Wood Green, Ben still on his mind. There had seemed no harm in allowing him to ask questions but if that meant he had fallen foul of someone . . . He rang DS Houghton but was told he was busy. He left a message and read an email from Nora.

I'm on a complicated case at present, working 24/7 and knackered. I'll ring you when I see the light of day. Yes, we need to talk.

He wondered if it was true that she was so busy, or if she was avoiding him and giving herself time. He'd made the effort, and all he could do now was wait. The bus trundled along the northern edge of Woodside Park, past a parade of charity shops, and then plunged into a sprawling concrete estate. Paula Flanders lived on the ground floor of a block of flats built around a central courtyard. The courtyard contained a couple of stunted trees and a generous scattering of litter but an effort had been made to cultivate a corner with vegetables and fruit bushes. Two women were digging raised beds and tipping compost into the soil.

A man in an immaculate white shirt and jeans answered the door. His gaze was mild behind large round glasses. Swift introduced himself and showed his ID.

'Does Paula Flanders live here?'

'That's correct.'

'I'd like to speak to her. It's about her daughter, Kim.' Swift read the NHS name badge the man was wearing around his neck. VIS PERERA, COMMUNITY PSYCHIATRIC NURSE.

The man looked puzzled. 'Oh, I see. I didn't know Paula was in touch with her daughter. She's never referred to her.'

'She might not have been in touch. That's what I've come to clarify. How long have you known Paula Flanders?'

'Just over a year. I come to check on her welfare.' He glanced over his shoulder and stepped out further. 'Paula has some memory lapses. She may not be able to help you as much as you hope.'

'She has mental health problems? I can see that you're a nurse.'

'Paula has her difficulties.'

'I haven't come to add to them. Her daughter Kim died two years ago. She drowned.'

Perera's eyes widened. 'But I thought that's what almost happened when . . . okay, carry on.'

'I'm trying to find out if there was anything suspicious about Kim's death. She might have been in contact with her mother just before she died. Presumably you know Paula's family history? And that she was in prison?'

Perera nodded. 'So Paula might not know that Kim is dead?'

'Good question. Possibly not. Kim was living with extended family and they've had no contact with Paula. I just don't know until I speak to her.'

'As I said, you might have difficulty. Paula's recall is often poor. It varies.'

A thin woman shuffled into the hallway behind Perera. She was barefoot, wearing a diamond-patterned lilac and white fleecy onesie and sucking on a cigarette.

'Who is it, Vis? Someone for me? Someone for me, Vis?'

'It's a gentleman, a Mr Swift who'd like to talk to you. Can he come in?'

'Course he can. I don't get many gents calling on me. Not these days. Come on in, love. Come and see me in my home sweet home.'

He followed Perera and Paula into a low-ceilinged sitting room. It was sparsely furnished with faded orange chairs and an oak sideboard holding a small TV. A neat stack of vividly coloured word puzzle magazines stood beside the television with two pens lined up beside them. The room smelled of the cheap children's sweets Swift used to buy at the corner shop with his pocket money — Love Hearts. He remembered the fizzy sherbet taste of them when they dissolved on the tongue.

'I have to get on,' Perera told Paula. 'I'll be back in a fortnight. I've put it on the calendar. I've filled your medication box.' He touched her arm and tried to hold her gaze but her eyes flickered away from him, darting about the room.

'That's lovely. You're good to me, Vis, you really are.' She swivelled towards Swift. 'He's the genuine article, is Vis. Have a seat, take the weight off. The chair comes at no extra charge!' She laughed, sat in an upright armchair and reached for another cigarette.

Perera picked up his bag and jacket and handed Swift a card, asking if he could call him later. Paula listened for the door to close, lit her cigarette and straightened the cigarette packet. Then she placed the lighter on top of the packet, repositioning it several times until she was satisfied. There were a dozen large bottles of a cheap shop brand of cola ranked by her chair. She held her cigarette between her lips and lifted a bottle, adding to a half-full pint glass by her side, watching the bubbles dance.

'My only vice these days — well, and the fags. Nobody's perfect. Can't stand the sight of that Perera bloke,' she said. 'Can't stand do-gooders. But when you're like me, you have to toe the line. I learned that inside. Take my medicine like a good girl. Obey the rules. My life's not my own.' The front of her onesie was dotted with cigarette burns, as was the beige rug under her chair. 'Who are you then? One of those . . . things . . . students they send from the surgery? Come to see a nutter on her home ground and make notes? I reckon more people have written notes about me than I've had hot dinners. I saw my file once. It was that thick.' She held her hands out a couple of inches apart.

'I'm not a student, and I'm not adding to your file.' He told her who he was and showed his ID. 'I've come to talk to you about your daughter, Kim.'

She looked around the room, rubbing the callused heel of her right foot hard against the toes of her left. Her eyes were vacant and moist. She was bony with thin, yellowish skin and the burnt-out look of an addict. Two of her front teeth were missing and another was broken. Yet her brunette hair was in a neat bob and looked as if it had been styled recently. She contemplated her cigarette, rolling it in her nicotine-stained fingers.

'Long time since anyone asked me about Kim. Years. One time, that was all they asked me about. That and my addictions. I spent hours with those . . . things . . . therapists and in groups. Chatter chatter chatter. Going over old ground. Where does it all get you, eh?'

'That was when you were in prison?'

She seemed to take it for granted that he knew about her past. She'd have forgotten what privacy was like. She took a gulp of her drink and wiped her mouth with the back of her hand. 'Back then. Lots of questions. Lots of talk. What prison was I in? The first one?'

'I don't know.'

'Oh. That makes two of us. What kind of thing do you want to know about Kim?'

'Some general information about her.'

'So, you're asking for my help?'

'That's right.'

Paula put a hand to her cheek and pushed her lips out in a little pout. 'It'll cost you.'

Swift hadn't seen that coming. 'I see. I thought you might want to talk to me, as you're Kim's mother.'

'Yeah, I'll talk to you. Not for free, though. Nothing comes free these days, does it? I have to make ends meet. I can't afford anything nice. I have to buy this naff brand of cola and it's nothing like the real stuff. Bargain-basement Betty, that's me. Like that song, second-hand . . . thing . . . Who do I mean?'

'"Second Hand Rose?"'

'That's it. Life's expensive and information's never cheap, eh? Give us thirty quid.'

He thought she'd pitch higher. 'Twenty.'

'Twenty-five.'

If she had memory loss, he wasn't sure that her information would be worth that much. He reached for his wallet and took out ten pounds. 'Take this for now. I'll give you the other fifteen when we've finished.'

'You're canny,' she said, and snatched the money from his hand. She folded the note into small squares and tucked it into a pocket in her onesie. 'Fire away, then.'

'I've been talking to the Ramsay family. I know about Kim's history.'

'Oh, *history*!' she said, tapping her right temple. 'I know what you're on about. See, thing is, I don't remember what I did to Kim. Not that day with the . . . you know, bath business. I mean, I know I sometimes locked her in and left her on her own but I was an addict, see. I had to get gear. What else could I do? Her dad dropped dead and I was on my own. Life was a struggle. I was out of control. I was off my face on gear the day the bath thing happened. I know what I tried to do. They told me. But I don't remember. I don't remember filling the bath or putting her in it. I was sorry that I did it. She was a game little thing, never still. I'm sure I didn't mean to harm her. That's what I told her when she came here. Up to her if she believed me. I suppose she didn't. She pissed off again.'

'You saw Kim? When was that?'

'Search me. A while back. Could you make me a cuppa? I'm fed up with the cola for now. Gives me wind. I've got a condition. What's it called? Kors . . . kors something anyway. Vis wrote it down.' She picked up a notepad from a low table beside her chair. 'Korsakoff's. That's it. Sounds like a Russian president. You heard of it?'

'I have. It affects your memory.'

'So they say. So they say. Doctor told me it was because of the booze.' She laughed. 'I reckoned she'd say all the gear I'd taken, but it was the booze! Well, who'd have thought it? If they don't get you one way, they get you another. Doc said it's early stage. God knows what'll happen when it's late stage. Suppose they'll carry me off in a . . . thing . . . straitjacket and lock me away. I'm off the booze now. They give me injections so I won't want it. I just rot my teeth and lungs instead.' She rubbed her heel on her toes again, *scritch scritch*. Her gaze drifted up to the ceiling. She sang in a falsetto, 'Memories are made of this . . .'

He stood. 'Do you take milk in tea?'

'I do, kind sir. Plenty of milk and three sugars. And a biccy. They're in the tin by the cooker.'

Swift expected the kitchen to be a tip but it was tiny and ordered, with saucepans and utensils neatly ranked on shelves. The white dishcloth was folded over the mixer tap and jars of tea, coffee and cocoa were labelled and standing in a straight line by the kettle. A foil tray of frozen macaroni cheese sat defrosting exactly in the centre of the gleaming sink. Swift looked in the cupboards. There were dozens of cheap tins of soup, baked beans and casseroles, all facing forward and aligned. He guessed that they would be placed according to use-by date. Swift recalled that prisoners who survived incarceration by conforming to the rules often developed OCD. He saw that the mugs on the hooks were from Starbucks, there was a pile of plastic sachets of ketchup, salad cream, mustard and vinegar from Marks and Spencer and Costa and the sugar in the jar was in tiny paper packets from Café Rouge. He imagined that Paula always took a large bag with her when she went shopping and acquired more than she paid for.

He made tea and a coffee for himself. The granules were damp and clumped. He was reminded of cat litter and grimaced but they smelled okay. He didn't want the coffee but he thought Paula would like it if he kept her company. She looked as if she could be hard work, so he'd do whatever it took to keep her onside. He found a biscuit assortment in a dented tin, fetched a tray from the worktop, took a deep breath and brought the drinks and biscuits through.

CHAPTER 11

Paula was examining the ends of her hair. 'Split ends. Can't stop them. Must be lack of something. Vitamins. I ought to eat better but I can't afford it. I was healthier when I was inside. I liked the grub in jail. Plenty of mash and gravy. Some of them complained about it but I didn't see anything wrong with three square meals a day and no . . . thing . . . washing up. Ooh, lovely. This is nice, isn't it? I don't often get waited on, not these days.'

'It is. Careful with the tea, it's hot.'

'What's your name again?'

'Tyrone.'

'Funny.'

'It's Irish.'

'Oh, right. Name of a place, isn't it?'

'There's a County Tyrone in Northern Ireland.'

'And Tyrone Power. He was handsome, but small. Not like you. I like a man with a bit of height.' She selected a chocolate biscuit, dunked it in her tea and moved the tin a couple of centimetres to the right.

The coffee was cheap and bitter. He took a sip and put it down. 'How did you come to see Kim?'

'Oh, well. I asked if she could lend me some money. I was hard up. Sent her a note.'

'I thought you weren't supposed to contact her?'

Her eyes flickered. 'When I sized it up, I reckoned what would they do to me if they found out? Put me back inside? I wouldn't mind, to be honest. Less of a struggle. Decided it was worth a punt.'

'Where did you send the note?'

'No. I didn't *send* it.' She fished a chunk of biscuit from her tea and licked her fingers.

'I thought you said you did.'

'Marie took it for me.'

'Who's Marie?'

'My little sister. She's another one who's pissed off. Why do they all piss off?' Her eyes were full of sudden tears. 'I paid for what I did,' she said morosely, holding her mug close to her lips. 'I did pay. I did my time, years of it. I'm entitled to some life. If that's what you can call this, sitting here on my tod and trying to make ends meet.'

He edged the biscuits towards her. 'So Marie took a note to Kim. To where she lives?'

'I didn't want that cow Gill knowing about it. Miss High and Mighty. That's why I didn't post it. Marie went to . . . thing . . . what's the name of the village?'

'Great Howe.'

'That's it. She asked around. Found some place where Kim was working.'

'So Kim came here?'

'I told you that. Pay attention, why don't you? I'm supposed to be the one with a bad memory. She made me a cuppa as well. Mind you, she probably spat in it, or worse. They did that inside sometimes when they didn't like people. I knew a woman who got mouse droppings in her dinner.'

'Did Kim lend you money?'

'Yeah. That surprised me. I can't remember how much, around a thousand. Well, she threw it at me, right in my face. We didn't exactly hit it off. She said I'd been a right bitch to her. I agreed. Nothing else I could say. I mean, she had me bang to rights, nowhere to hide. I had to eat humble pie. She stood there in front of me, towering over me, told me I was a waste of space. She's turned out tall, like Marie. I bawled my eyes out. But then she said I was too pathetic for her to hold a grudge. Told me I'd ended up with the life I deserved. That cow, Gill. She came years ago, told me I was a . . . thing . . . a trollop.'

'It was kind of her to give Kim a home.'

'Suppose. Posh place, isn't it? Big place in the country. Plenty of dosh there. All right for some.' She put her mug down on the table and moved it around, sitting back and checking its position.

Now and again there was a glint of craftiness in her eyes. Swift wondered what it must have been like for Kim, finally being contacted by her abusive, self-pitying mother. And not because she wanted to apologise or try to make amends, but because she wanted to tap her for money. He thought that Kim had shown good judgement, if she had truly decided her mother was too pathetic to worry over.

'What was your name again?'

'Tyrone Swift. How many times did Kim come here?'

'Don't know. Maybe three. She only brought money the first time. Marie was here a couple of times when she came. Wanted to get another look at her niece. They hit it off, those two, had a bit of a laugh together. Kim helped Marie do her hair with one of those home dyes. Stank the place out. We had bangers and mash. Or was it fish and chips? Anyway. Then they both buggered off. Left me in the lurch. That's rotten, whatever way you look at it. I never get a bit of company. Might as well be a . . . thing . . . a bloody nun, or live on a desert island.'

She was rubbing her yellowing heel again, digging it against her toes. He found it distracting and wondered that she didn't tear the skin.

'Did Kim seem worried about anything?'

'What did she have to worry about? Nice comfy home. Enough dosh. No, she had no worries.'

Only a lifelong illness and an enduring fear of water, Swift thought. He took a breath. He had no idea how this would go down, but she had to be told. Even if she found it hard to remember afterwards, she needed to know.

'I'm sorry to tell you this, but Kim died a couple of years ago. I think it was not long after she came here. She drowned in the lake where she lived. Her death might not have been accidental. Someone might have pushed her in the water. That's why I'm asking questions.'

Paula turned the handle of her mug and moved the biscuit tin a fraction. She looked puzzled. 'So that's why she didn't come back, then.'

'Yes. She had a seizure in the water.'

Paula looked around the room, rubbing her foot faster. 'Oh, well, that'll be why she drowned then. Marie's got epilepsy. It's in the family. Missed me. My gran used to call it "the shiver twitch." Her dad had it. But why hasn't Marie been in touch? She might have told me. I miss her. She's my little sister and we were always close. I looked out for her, looked after her a lot before I left home. She came to see me in jail, regular as clockwork once a month. Never failed.'

He might have told her that her daughter had broken an arm rather than died and possibly been murdered. Her moving foot was the only sign that she found the news upsetting. He wondered if Marie had been in contact and Paula had forgotten. 'Where does Marie live?'

'Not sure. She moves around, here and there. Dosses. Lots of jobs and blokes. Sometimes the blokes are the job, ha ha! She used to pop in regular, must have been every couple of weeks, and we'd have a chat. She'd do my nails for me, make some dinner, give me a bit of a sub when I needed it and she was flush. Maybe Kim turned her against me. Yes, I bet that's what happened. Marie stopped coming to see me. I reckon it was soon after Kim was here. Can't remember now with this bloody brain rot but yeah, it was around then. I bet Kim told her awful stories. I never thought of that before. I'm a fool to myself.' She stared at him, frowning. 'Funny, Kim drowning after all those years. You reckon someone might have pushed her in? I didn't do it. They can't come after me again.'

No, Swift didn't think Paula had gone back to finish the job. He doubted she'd have found her way and anyway, why cut off a potential source of money?

Paula took a tissue from her sleeve and wiped the tray, then finished her flat, caramel-coloured cola. 'It's dinner time. I always make my dinner now. I eat at twelve or I feel funny.' She held a hand up in front of him, rubbing her fingers together, and he gave her fifteen pounds. She tucked it into her pocket. 'Anyway, what's your name. Did you get your money's worth?' She put her head back and winked at him.

He thought she was heartless and appalling and that her illness was bringing out her rotten core. He'd seen and dealt with numerous sickening people and situations but Paula was something else: self-absorbed and calculating. He couldn't detect an iota of motherly feeling.

'My money's worth? I'm not sure. I'm not sure anyone ever would with you. It sounds as if you got yours from Kim.'

She smiled, as if he'd complimented her, and got up, twisting her fingers together. 'I've got to eat. I'm starting to feel wobbly.' She probably still heard a bell sounding, the clatter of feet and cutlery as she got in a queue and jostled to get to the serving hatch. She started towards the kitchen, and then paused. 'If you see that Marie, tell her to come round. She's my sister. She ought to be helping me. I had to look after her often enough when our mum was at work. I never hurt her. She knows I've had a hard life. She's got no reason to stay away. Do *you* think Kim put her off coming?'

'I've no idea. Is your sister's name Marie Flanders?'

'Don't know about her last name these days. She never married but she's had a few live-ins and she took some blokes' names when it suited her. When she wanted to cheat the welfare. She liked to pretend she was all proper and married. But she knew no bloke would put up with her long term — she's too gobby. We were a gobby lot in our family. I think Kim must have poured poison about me in her ear. I rang Marie's . . . thing . . . mobile but she never replied and then it went dead. There was no need for Kim to go and do that. I paid for what I did to her and I'm sure I never meant it. I was ill. Addiction's an illness, you know. I've had a rotten life and, I mean, Kim fell on her feet when all's said and done. She'd never have got to live in a posh house if she'd stayed with me. I did her a favour in a way, set her on the right road. It all turned out all right for her. I'm the one living hand to mouth.'

'You do understand that Kim is dead?' he asked. He didn't care now if she was upset.

'I heard you. Well, it was nothing to do with me. They can't say it was. I'm not taking the blame for something I didn't do.'

She opened the door to the kitchen, muttering to herself, and slammed it behind her. Swift let himself out and walked fast to the bus stop, Paula's whine echoing in his ears.

He phoned Vis Perera while he waited for the bus. 'Paula told me that she has Korsakoff's syndrome. I explained that Kim had drowned. She didn't seem to react much.'

'Thanks for letting me know. The Korsakoff's was diagnosed recently. Paula's emotions are somewhat flattened by her illness. She may or may not remember what you've told her. It's very difficult to call how her memory will be from one day to the next. I'll make an extra visit to her, in case it distressed her.'

Swift couldn't imagine Paula being genuinely troubled. He almost laughed at the concern in the man's voice but bit his lip. Someone had to care about Kim's awful mother.

'Has Paula ever mentioned her sister, Marie?'

'Quite often. Mainly to complain about her and say that she never visits nowadays. They seem to have been close. Paula gets tearful about her at times. I think she really misses her. I don't know when Marie was last there, but she hasn't shown up since I've been involved.'

'But she might have been there and Paula could have forgotten?'

'That's true, but there's never been any sign of another visitor. Paula is lonely, quite isolated.'

It was all she deserved, Swift thought. 'If Marie does turn up, could you ask her for a phone number and an address and give me a call? Marie made contact with Kim and I'd like to talk to her.'

'If I see Marie and she's willing to give me the information, I'll contact you. But I usually visit fortnightly so even if she does call, I might not see her.'

He sat on the bus, rain rendering the streets almost invisible. When Kim had said that she'd met new people, had she meant her mother? Or Marie? Or a new man to replace Pete? And where had Kim come by a thousand pounds to give to her mother? Condensation clouded the window. He was rubbing it clear with his sleeve when DS Houghton rang him.

'Any news of Ben Ramsay?' Swift asked.

'Nothing. His phone's switched off and the last signal was between Low Lake and Great Howe. He'd told Mrs Stanley that he was going to Great Howe station but there's no sign of his bike there and nothing on CCTV. The ticket office was open around the time he should have arrived and the station staff know him. None of them saw him. We've been searching the area. I understand he sent you an email.'

Swift explained that Ben had said he was on his way to London. 'But I heard nothing more from him.'

'Why was he coming to see you?'

'He said he had information about Kim Woodville. I'll forward you his email.'

Houghton clicked his tongue. 'Why was Ben getting involved with your investigation?'

'He wanted to help. He seemed to be at a loose end so I agreed that if he found anything out, he should let me know. He'd been asking questions.'

Houghton sighed, loudly. 'Right. Just what we needed. Inspector Clouseau bumbling around. All this fuss and bother about a clear-cut death. A local plod from round your way will be in touch with you sometime today. Make yourself available.'

The line went dead. He had planned to return to Great Howe but he thought he had better stay in London and talk to the police. As he reached home, he had an email from Ruth with a photo of Branna attached. His daughter was wearing a saucepan on her head.

Hi, see Branna reorganising her gran's kitchen. Having a good break. I've thought about the flat and if the offer's still there, I think it would be a good idea. Talk more next week. R.

He replied.

The flat has been redecorated and looks good. Glad you think moving in is a good idea. Give Branna a big hug and kiss for me.

At least he knew now what he would tell Nora when he saw her. He had no idea if it would mean the end of their relationship. Sometimes he could recall her eyes, the sheen of her hair and the colours of her bow ties but he struggled to picture her complete face. He wasn't sure what that meant but it gave him a knot in his chest.

He pushed her out of his mind, allowing concern about Ben to flood back in. He had been missing for too long now. He had a bad feeling about the young man.

* * *

DS Maddon and probationer PC Saddler sat side by side on Swift's sofa. They'd refused tea or coffee so he pulled up a dining chair and seated himself opposite them. DS Maddon was tight-lipped and snappy and looked as if she hadn't slept in a while. The sallow bags under her eyes resembled smudged thumbprints. Swift guessed she'd instructed her colleague to keep quiet and observe. Saddler had a coffin-shaped face and a lugubrious expression to go with it. He seemed ill at ease, and sat fiddling with his uniform cap.

'I'll tell you for starters, I don't hold with bloody private investigators. I think they should be banned,' was DS Maddon's opening gambit.

Swift tried not to roll his eyes. Always good to get the interviewee in a cooperative mood, he thought. 'You're entitled to your point of view.'

'I took a look at your self-satisfied website. Clever old you. All your successes. You're not modest, that's for sure. The Met not good enough for you?'

This kind of sparring was pointless but if she wanted to play the game, fine. 'We all need to know when it's time to move on. The job can exhaust you, can't it? Too little sleep makes you bad-tempered and jaded.'

Saddler's eyes darted between the two of them, like a man watching tennis.

DS Maddon threw Swift a hostile look and flipped open a notebook.

'This young man, Ben Ramsay. There's no sign of him and his bike hasn't been found. We've checked with his family and friends, including a Ms Janssens, a Steve Ramsay and a Jack North but none of them have seen him. Any ideas?'

'No. This is the email he sent me, where he said he was on his way to see me.' Swift held his phone out. DS Maddon waved her hand.

'Yeah, I've read it. Oxfordshire forwarded it. Talk me through how you know Ben and what you did after you got the email.'

Swift explained his contact with Jack North and the Ramsay family and his movements after he received Ben's email. 'I checked with Vlad Codreanu, the decorator who was working at the house on Saturday. He didn't see Ben. I'm very concerned about him. Is there any evidence that he arrived in London?'

DS Maddon ignored the question. Saddler sat very still, staring at him.

'Do you reckon it was sensible to involve a vulnerable, disabled man in your investigation? Didn't you think it might put him in harm's way? What were you up to? Getting your dirty work done on the cheap?' DS Maddon snapped the top of her pen up and down.

'Ben Ramsay isn't disabled. He struck me as a bored young man looking for something to occupy him. He wanted to ask some questions.'

'So you set him running around for you.'

'That's not how I'd put it.'

'No, I don't suppose it is. And you've heard nothing more from him.'

'No.'

'No idea what he meant in his email? Sounds very dramatic and full of himself. A bit like you.' She gave him a mean smile.

'No. I wish I did.'

'I bet. People who go missing are always a nightmare, and we have to spend hours looking for needles in haystacks. Maybe Ben fancied cutting loose from his mummy and taking off, and the email to you was a cover story.'

Swift shook his head. 'I don't think so. It sounded genuine and Ben liked his home comforts too much.'

'Any problems at home?'

'Not for Ben, as far as I know. He didn't mention any. I thought it was a problem that he didn't have a proper job but he didn't seem bothered.'

'Right. Mind if we take a look around? We've only got your word that Ben didn't turn up, and there was no one else here with you.'

'Are you suggesting I might have harmed him?'

She shrugged. 'Best to cover all bases. And as we're here . . .'

She had no right to look. Swift thought she wanted to rile him. He couldn't be bothered to argue the toss about a search warrant. Might as well get it over with. 'I'm happy to show you around the house. Follow me.'

He led them around his flat, down to his office in the basement, then up to the top floor. They proceeded in silence, except for when Saddler tripped on a stair, earning a glare from his sergeant. Maddon opened every door and peered round the rooms.

'You can look under the beds if you like,' Swift said.

'That won't be necessary. Nice house. Must be worth a bob or two. You're doing okay out of your private meddling.' She sounded bitter.

'That's right. Not that I asked for your opinion.'

In the hallway, Maddon asked for Vlad Codreanu's contact details. 'What do you know about this guy?' she asked.

'Only that he's a decorator, and a good one.'

'Where's he from?'

'He's Romanian. He showed me his passport. He has a right to work here.'

'Got transport, has he?'

'He has a van.'

'Right. Well, we'd better check that he didn't find our Ben on your doorstep, decide to do him in and stick him in his van. You can follow up tracking him down, Saddler. He's finished the work here, right?'

'Yes.'

'He did a nice job.' PC Saddler finally spoke, blushing.

'I think so,' Swift said.

'You want Vlad the Impaler round yours, do you, Saddler? Want him to give you a lick of paint? God help us. We'll probably be in touch again,' Maddon said, and yanked the door open. 'In the meantime, stay away from the Ramsays. From what I hear, you've caused enough trouble there already.'

* * *

Some people said that rowing was the sport of masochists and at times, Swift agreed with them. Rowers were obsessed, determined, and grew cranky and twitchy if they hadn't had the oars gripped in their hands for a couple of days. He was feeling restless and confined. Sleep had eluded him, his brain crowded with concern for Ben, tangled strands and knots of ideas about Kim, anxiety about Nora and sadness because Cedric had gone from his life. When he closed his eyes, he saw a child held under water, its huge eyes looking up in terror. His bed seemed to grow harder, his pillow hotter. The duvet kept snagging into coils, trapping him. He had given up on rest and risen just after dawn. Fifteen minutes of stretches and warm-ups, strong black coffee and a shower brought him to life.

Despite reading of cold and difficult weather conditions, he had picked his boat up by seven and driven to a stretch of the Thames north of London. It was one of the rows he had discussed doing with Nora. He decided that he would try out her birthday present and navigate the river in her absence.

'Sport of masochists,' he muttered to himself. A cross-head wind was whipping the river, causing a heavy swell. Visibility was poor and rain was falling steadily, drumming on his hood and stinging his face. A strong stream was flowing. He carried on, maintaining the rhythm and momentum of the oars. He focused on his breathing and the path of his boat and his heart pumped strong and steady. He counted the strokes of the oars to keep his mind off his aching shoulder and calf muscles.

He neared the two hills called the Wittenham Clumps, and the reward kicked in quietly. He felt the deep and complete harmony of mind and body that he found only in his boat on the river. At times such as this hours could pass without him noticing and he would return to the ordinary, troubled world, surprised and cleansed. He was alone on the full, racing waters, curtained by chill rain, his warm blood surging and his mind clear. The rest of humanity could vanish and he wouldn't know. He threw his head back and laughed, licked the rain from his lips and journeyed on.

After a while, the rain pounded even heavier and he had to turn the boat, deciding not to risk negotiating a lock in such conditions. He pulled in by the sodden riverbank, which was lined with beech and alders and dotted with tall, bedraggled spires of rosebay willow herb. A grey wagtail was braving the downpour, dancing up and down on a stone, its tail splayed like a fan. He ate a banana and drank water, following its energetic movements. He pulled the hood of his jacket back and lifted his face to the sky, enjoying the drenching. *This kind of focused activity would be good for Ben,* he thought, *make him concentrate his thinking.* If he ever turned up.

He adjusted the oars, while his thoughts turned to Kim. She had been surrounded by people at Low Lake and yet she had been oddly alone. The cuckoo in the nest. The charity case, partly funded by the state. She must have been aware of the resentment surrounding her. Not one person there apart from Jack had spoken of her with genuine affection. Not even Pete. She had battled with the guilt of Nadia's death and the devious attentions of her mother without support or comfort. He felt for her, even though she could clearly be underhand and exasperating. Her life had been a struggle and her courageous attempts to shape a future for herself had been ended abruptly.

* * *

Swift's daughter was back in his arms. Her hair was longer and curlier and she had a tiny new front tooth. Her cheeks were still inflamed with the effort this had taken.

'I always think it's unfair that babies go through so much pain to grow a set of teeth that will fall out,' he told her, opening his mouth and rubbing his forefinger sideways to sign *tooth*. 'Can you sign *tooth* with me? I know Mummy's taught you.'

But Branna was in a cranky and uncooperative mood, unsettled by the journey and her time away. She looked around, watching her mother.

'I think she's tired,' Ruth said. 'She didn't sleep in the car and she's been out of her routine at my mum's. I'll take her home soon, but I thought I'd just call in. I knew you'd want to see her. Can I take a peep upstairs? I'm excited about moving in now.'

'Of course. Here's the key.'

As her mother moved away, Branna wailed, kicked her legs and held her arms out.

'You want to come with me?' Ruth asked. 'Well, why not? It will be your home too. I expect you want to give your approval.'

'I'll make coffee while you look. Some lunch for Branna?'

'Yes, she'll be ready to eat soon. Whatever you have. Cheese is a favourite right now, the stronger the better. She's been refusing meat recently.'

'Maybe she's going to be a vegetarian, like you.'

'Ah, I'm not a strict veggie any more. I only gave up meat because Emlyn's a vegetarian. I've lapsed since I left him. I eat chicken and fish now.'

Swift put the kettle on and took a slab of cheddar from the fridge. He sliced brown bread and buttered it lightly, cutting it into manageable squares. He was washing an apple when he heard a door slam upstairs. Ruth was calling him, her voice high and choked with distress.

'Ty! Ty! Come here!'

He dashed to the stairs. Ruth was standing at the top, swaying slightly, clutching Branna tight and looking down at him. Her face was drained of colour. He ran up to her.

'What is it? Ruth, what is it?'

She stepped clumsily past him onto the landing, tears starting down her cheeks. Branna was weaving her hair into knots.

'In there. Cedric's bedroom. The wardrobe. My God. Look in there.' She turned her head away and pressed her face into Branna's shoulder.

He went to the door of Cedric's room and slowly pushed it open. Opposite him were the deep, handsome fitted oak wardrobes where he had found Cedric's funeral suit. They had been built into the house in 1895 and covered the wall adjoining the house next door. He had cleared Cedric's clothes and shoes from them just before Vlad Codreanu started the decorating. The wardrobes usually smelled of their own woody aroma and the scent of Cedric's Dior soap. But now they smelt of something else. Something sour, like food that had gone rotten.

The end set of double doors was open. Inside, lying on his back on the floor was a man wearing jeans and a blue fleece jacket. His right arm was straight by his side. His left had fallen out when the door was opened, the hand dangling onto the floor. His legs were slightly apart, his feet invisible in the closed section of the wardrobe.

Swift stepped closer, his heart thudding. The man's face was encased in a large transparent plastic bag. It was secured tightly around his neck with brown masking tape. His skin was pale and congested, his open eyes popping and bloodshot. There was no sign that he had struggled.

No marks or scratches on his hands or on the inside of the doors, no visible blood. Swift stared, unable to believe his eyes. He was dimly aware of the sound of Branna's chattering from the landing. For a moment he felt dizzy, and focused on his breathing. He crouched and felt for a pulse. He knew there was no point but it was an automatic response. The skin was cold and slack, with no beat of life.

Ben Ramsay was silent and was going to remain that way.

Swift backed away, his mouth dry. He returned to Ruth who was still on the landing, slumped against the wall. Branna was straining over her shoulder, slapping a hand against the doorframe.

Ruth stared at him, tears in her eyes. 'Who is that?' she whispered.

'Come away, come downstairs,' he said, and closed the door of the flat, blotting out the awful scene behind them. He took Branna, glad of her solid, reassuring weight and held Ruth's elbow, guiding her gently forwards. She clung to the banister on the way down.

In the living room he handed Branna back to Ruth, who walked her up and down.

'Who is that?' Ruth asked again. 'Do you know him?'

'I know him. In a minute, Ruth. I have to ring the police.'

She stared at him angrily, shook her head and walked with Branna to the window. He went to the kitchen and phoned the police. When he had finished talking, he stood for a moment, watching the steam that was still rising from the kettle. He was trying to think about the past few days and his movements, but he was filled with confusion. The top of his scalp tingled, as if it was lifting up. Branna started crying, the wail that meant she was hungry. It made him wince. He roused himself and took her plate of food through.

'Did she see?' he asked Ruth.

'No. She was looking the other way. Thank goodness. Just give me some bread and cheese in a bowl for her. I want to go. I want to get Branna away from here. She can eat in the car.' She looked around anxiously for her bag, and searched for her keys, hands trembling.

'Ruth, you can't go. You have to stay. You found him. The police have to talk to you. Please, sit down. The sooner you talk to them, the sooner you can get home.'

She bit her lip. There were tears rolling down her cheeks. 'I can't believe this. I can't believe it. It's like a . . . contamination. My God, to think I walked in there with Branna . . .'

'I'm so sorry. You're in shock. Sit down, come on. I'll see to Branna.' He unfolded the portable high chair he had bought, attached it to the table and secured it. He sat his daughter in it and watched her busying herself with chunks of cheese. Then he crouched in front of Ruth, who had slumped on the sofa.

'His name is Ben Ramsay. He's been involved in the investigation I'm working on. He went missing a couple of days ago. The police are on their way.'

'But how . . . ?'

He shook his head. 'I don't know. I just don't know.'

She winced. 'He suffocated?'

'I think so. He may have other injuries.'

She looked away, as if seeing it again. 'I just opened the wardrobe door. I don't even know why. It's just the kind of thing you do. I was wondering how much storage there would be . . . Oh God, why did I have to open the door? His arm fell . . . it made a little noise. I thought he was alive, and then I saw his eyes.'

'I know. I'll make you a coffee. I'm so sorry.'

Branna laughed as she tore a piece of cheese and stuffed it into her mouth, thumping her plate with pleasure. Upstairs a dead man, down here a lively, happy child. The discordancy jarred him. He made coffee, poured milk for Branna. He seemed to be watching himself

211

moving, functioning, feigning calm. He had a mouthful of coffee and felt instantly nauseous but made himself swallow more. He thought of how he had showed DS Maddon around upstairs and asked if she wanted to look under the bed, while Ben lay just feet away from them. He took the drinks through. Ruth was sitting, her hands over her eyes, while Branna mangled bread. He touched Ruth's arm and she jolted.

'Branna's fine, she's fine,' he said.

'He's been up there and you've been down here.'

'Yes.'

'How long? How long has he been there?'

'A couple of days, I think.'

'Oh God. His poor family. How old is he?'

'In his twenties.'

'But why . . . ? My God, did you not *sense* anything with a dead man lying in your house?'

'Ruth, I'm an investigator, not a psychic. Drink your coffee. The police will be here soon. I don't know what happened. I don't have answers.' He gave Branna her milk. He kept his voice light and steady. 'You were a hungry girl. I see you like strong cheddar. Some apple now?'

She nodded. Her random gurgling and chatting filled the room. He sliced the apple and the sharp, fresh aroma scented the air. He was glad of her innocent noise, muffling his dull, nagging thoughts.

Ruth shot from the sofa, hand to her mouth. 'I'm going to be sick.'

CHAPTER 12

DI Baptiste was a well-built woman with braided hair drawn back in a ponytail, huge knees and legs like tree trunks. She had powerful shoulders and a low-key, mature manner that Swift appreciated when he saw her quickly summing up the situation and Ruth's emotional state. She asked Ruth a few questions, then said she could go home as soon as she liked.

'We'll get a statement from you tomorrow. How old is the little one?'

Branna had fallen asleep on the sofa, tucked in with cushions.

'Nearly a year and a half,' Ruth told her.

'And you're the father?' She turned to Swift with an assessing gaze.

'Yes. But Ruth and Branna live in Hendon.'

'So I gather. Well, Ruth, are you okay to drive yourself home? I can get someone to take you.'

'No, that's not necessary. I'm okay.'

'You sure? You look washed out, you know. You might get shaky after a nasty shock like this.'

'No, I'd rather drive myself. I just want to get away from all of this, including the police.'

DI Baptiste nodded. 'Okay. Good woman. But I'm going to send someone to follow you home, just to be on the safe side. They won't bother you. They'll just make sure you're in your place okay. Best to get an early night. Try not to think about it, focus on baby. Have you got anyone else who can be with you, someone we can call?'

'No. That's okay, I don't need anyone.'

'I'll call you later,' Swift told her. 'Take it steady.'

Ruth stood, moving gingerly, like an old woman. 'I'll never forget the sight of that man. So awful. Such a vicious way to die.'

When she and Branna had left the house, DI Baptiste turned to Swift.

'We need to talk. I understand you're ex Met. You'll have seen a dead body before.'

'More than once.'

There were footsteps and the noise of equipment being moved overhead while the crime scene was processed. A photographer murmured to a colleague on the stairs. Swift thought of Ben's fascination with police procedures. He had never expected to be their subject.

Ruth had spoken of contamination. He knew that his house would never be the same again. Anger flared in him at the thought of someone invading his home and leaving a young man to die, the life literally sucked from his body. And his young child could easily have seen the corpse. He forced himself to stay calm. He needed to focus on Baptiste.

DI Baptiste rested her hands on her thighs. 'I've been told that DS Maddon was here recently, looking around.'

'Yes. She visited because Ben Ramsay was missing. She asked if she could look round the house.'

'A bit remiss of her not to find a body upstairs. I'm assuming that Mr Ramsay was dead and in your wardrobe by then. Though forensics might say different.'

'I think he must have been. Unless he was murdered somewhere else and then brought here.'

'The science will tell us.'

'To be fair to DS Maddon, and I don't know why I'm bothering because she was rude and insulting, she wasn't looking into a murder at that point.'

'No. Even so, there will be questions. Right, let's sit down and get a timeline here. Tell me when you met Ben Ramsay.'

Swift told her about his involvement with the family and Ben's eagerness to help him. He brought up his work diary on his phone and gave her the dates of his visits to Low Lake, and explained his contact with Paula Flanders. 'Ben was supposed to visit me on Saturday evening. He didn't show. He said he'd found something out and he was keen to give me information.' He showed her Ben's email.

'You've no idea what he's referring to, when he talks about a cover-up?'

'No.'

'When was the last time you spoke to him?'

'On the fifteenth, when I visited Low Lake. That's the day I agreed that he could help me and ask people questions about Kim Woodville.'

'Where were you on Saturday, and what have you been doing since then?'

He talked her through it slowly. Her unblinking gaze never left his face, even when he told her that he had spent Saturday afternoon with his cousin, who was an assistant commissioner in the Met. He recalled that a neighbour walking his dog had seen him arriving home at six thirtyish. Baptiste's steady stare was a good tactic, one he had used himself. He didn't much like being on the receiving end.

'When you got home on Saturday, was your flat secure?'

'Yes.'

'This Paula Flanders is Kim Woodville's mother?'

'That's right.'

'Ramsay, Flanders, Woodville, I can't be doing with people having different family names. Gets on my nerves. So when you were out rowing, did anyone see you?'

'I doubt it. I suppose you'll find my car on motorway CCTV but once I was on the river, I didn't see or speak to anyone.'

'Has anyone else had access to your house?'

'Yes, a decorator, Vlad Codreanu. He was here on Saturday and again on Sunday. I gave him keys on Saturday because I was going out. He locked up and left them in the hall before I came home. I was at home all the time he was here on Sunday. DS Maddon took his details. He's hardly likely to have murdered Ben on a whim and left him in the very place where he was working.' DI Baptiste was watching him impassively, no doubt wondering if she was looking at her prime suspect. Swift returned her look. 'I think someone must have come here with Ben or followed him,' he said. 'Probably someone from Great Howe, because that's where he was asking questions. There must be a reason for killing him in my home. I'm reading this as a warning to me as well as a way of silencing Ben.'

'Maybe. We have to wait for our colleagues upstairs and the autopsy. Who would want to give you this kind of warning?'

'I don't know. But my investigation has worried someone enough to kill. That surely suggests that Kim Woodville's death wasn't accidental. If someone did kill her, it could be the same person. Or Ben had stumbled across information about someone, something I'm not aware of, and they didn't want me to find out.'

'Theories are just that until there's evidence. I prefer facts.' She reached into her pocket, took out an evidence bag and held it in front of him. 'A couple of these were found in Ben's pocket. Have you seen one before?'

He looked at a card, the kind you could get printed at a kiosk, light blue script on a navy background.

Ben Ramsay
Assistant Private Investigator
Hire me if you've got a question!

Oh, Ben, he thought sadly, *you silly idiot, what were you up to?* He shook his head. 'No, I've not seen a card like that. Ben took off with the idea of being an investigator. It excited him, fired his imagination. His head was full of movie heroes. He didn't have a job. Maybe this was his way of making himself feel useful. He told me he tried to join the police once.'

'Sounds more like a giddy boy than a man in his twenties.' Baptiste pocketed the bag. 'Who else knew that you had a decorator in here?'

He thought about it. 'Ruth knew. So did Nora Morrow, a friend who's a DI in the Met. I'd mentioned it to Mary. That's it. Oh, and I told Ben in my email to him. I said that Vlad could let him in if he got here early.'

'Okay. I'll get my sergeant to sort out an appointment at the station with you ASAP. We'll need fingerprints and a full statement. And a DNA sample if that's okay. We might as well take one while you're enjoying our hospitality.'

He nodded. His anger had turned into tiredness. It trickled through him like icy water.

'We'll be sealing off the upstairs once the body has been removed. We'll need any sets of keys you have to the top of the house. Maybe you'll want to stay somewhere else for now?'

'No. I'll stay here.' He shook his head. 'I used to have CCTV outside but the camera broke and I didn't think I needed to replace it. Also, my friend who used to live upstairs hated it.' He'd had the camera installed when the man employed by Ruth's ex was harassing him — the man who had killed Kris Jelen. Cedric had said it was like living in a police state. *Do I have to be spied on, dear boy? Will a street committee denounce me if I come home drunk?*

'Might be an idea to replace it, in your line of business. You must make enemies. It's more personal than being in the force.'

'I'll consider it.'

'And did you kill Ben?' she asked conversationally.

He looked her in the eye. 'I didn't kill Ben. I liked him. I wish I knew what he wanted to tell me. I wish I hadn't agreed that he could ask questions about Kim, but he was eager to be involved. Clearly, he was playing out of his league. I regret that now.'

Baptiste snapped her notebook shut. 'If you didn't kill him, you don't need to have regrets.'

Her phone rang and she walked to the kitchen to take the call. Swift sat, watching her beefy back straining at her jacket. He pictured Ben cycling to Great Howe station on Saturday, and began piecing together a scenario. Someone in a car pulls up near Ben along one of those narrow roads. Someone Ben knows. He/she knows or suspects what Ben has discovered and asks him where he's off to. What Ben says rings alarm bells. He/she offers to drive Ben to the station — no, he/she says, 'I'm going to London so save yourself the fare, put the bike in the boot and hop in.' Maybe Ben is knocked unconscious at that point and stuffed in the boot with his bike. Or does the perpetrator wait until they get to London? If so, Ben was killed in the house. But how did they access the flat? And who drives around with a plastic bag and masking tape ready to suffocate someone?

Dusk was falling by the time he saw the police out. He waited until the hallway was clear, and then searched for Vlad Codreanu's number. He didn't care if DI Baptiste found out and barracked him for it. He didn't believe that Codreanu had anything to do with Ben's death. His killer was close to home, as were most killers.

'Hi, Vlad. It's Tyrone Swift. Have the police been in touch with you?'

Codreanu sounded as if he was in a drain, his voice echoing. 'Yes, police call me. Ask me about the weekend. They ask about my van. What is this trouble?'

'I'm sorry you've been dragged into it. A young man was missing and he's been found dead. Vlad, did you leave the flat any time on Saturday afternoon? Was the house unlocked?'

'You had a thief there?'

'No, that's not it. I just need to know.'

A mumbling and the noise of a train. 'I go to my van for more paint and a smaller roller. I have quick coffee. Then I see guy laying floor next door. He ask me if I want to see loft so I go in there to look.'

'Do you remember what time that was?'

'Just after four.'

'How long were you out of the house?'

'Ten, fifteen minutes maybe. Maybe a bit longer. Guy was explaining how they line the walls and floor. Very interesting.'

'Did you leave my doors open while you were out?'

'I think, maybe. On the latch, you know. Yes, so is easier to get in carrying things. Is this a problem?'

'It's okay. Thanks for that. Just tell the police what you've told me.'

He recalled Codreanu's van when he left the house on Saturday morning. It had been parked a little way up the road. There would have been enough time for someone to access the house without being seen, especially if Vlad was on the second floor next door, in the loft that faced out the back. He pictured Ben alive, walking in through the front door with his friendly driver, saying thanks for the lift, eager to impart his information. Then the assault. He wondered how long it had taken for him to asphyxiate.

He closed the curtains against the night and rang Ruth.

'We're okay,' she said. 'Branna's fast asleep. I'm wobbly and I have a terrible headache but I've taken a painkiller. What did the police say to you?'

'All the usual things. And Branna's okay? You're sure?'

'Yes. She could tell I was upset but she went off to sleep. It helped that she was tired from the journey. She's at the nursery in the morning, back in her routine.'

'Good. I just wanted to say sorry again.'

'I know. Look, Ty, you can't help what happened. But I've been thinking. There's just no way I could move into that flat now. I wouldn't feel at ease. I think I'd have nightmares. I wouldn't want Branna to be in that place either, a place of such violence. What happened with Cedric was bad enough but a murder . . .'

'Okay, Ruth. I understand. It was a good idea while it lasted.'

'Yes, and it was good of you to offer. I've been mulling it over, distracting myself from the memory of that body. I'm going to ask Emlyn if we can release some money on the house so that I can buy nearer London. We're on reasonable terms these days so I'm hoping he'll agree. I'll give it a shot.'

'Well, good luck. I'll call you tomorrow.'

'Have the police gone now?'

'Yes, and they've taken Ben's body. The flat has been secured as a crime scene. Tape across the door and all that.'

'I'm sorry for you, that it's happened in your lovely home. I hope you sleep. Your job, Ty . . . you seem to meet so much violence. You've been stabbed and beaten up. You could have burned to death last year. What's that going to be like for Branna as she grows up? What if she was staying with you and something awful happened there again?'

'It's not likely, Ruth.'

'Isn't it? There's already been that criminal Emlyn set on you and now this. It worries me.'

He couldn't think of anything he could say to reassure her. He said goodnight and looked out of the window. The night was chilly and clear. He poured a glass of wine, took the bottle with him and sat out in the garden for a while, on the damp swing seat. It was cold but he needed to breathe untainted air. He was angry, empty and too tired to eat. Had Kim and Ben been killed by the same hand? There was a similarity in the methods. Lungs filled with water, lungs deprived of air. Perhaps all this tracked back in some way to the same source: Kim's mother. He couldn't see how. If he could speak to Marie, he might glean more about Kim's behaviour and state of mind two years ago. He googled Marie Flanders but could find no trace.

He poured another glass of wine, hoping that Ruth would be able to sleep. He wondered how Nora would react when he told her there was now no chance of Ruth and Branna living upstairs. He felt so distant from Nora now. She might as well be on the other side of the planet.

He sat, drinking and staring at the pale sickle moon. It trailed wisps of dark cloud like a ragged cloak, reminding him of Gill Ramsay's shawls.

* * *

Swift woke early in the morning, in a grim mood. He thought immediately of Ben, the body lying above his own head, the face stilled behind the clinging plastic. He had been phoning Ben and leaving him messages while he was just a flight of stairs away. The young man had been so harmless, so aimless and full of foolish ideas. The placing of the body just there was a threat, a taunt and an insult. It would have been so easy for Branna to have seen it, and he knew that Ruth would be haunted by the sight for a long time. Whoever had done it would pay.

He made himself eat toast, although he didn't want it and it tasted like cardboard. He rang Gill Ramsay, to give his condolences. He had drunk too much the previous night and could still taste the sourness of the wine in his mouth. Valery answered the phone and said that her mother didn't want to speak to anyone and especially not him.

'Has anyone told Jack?' he asked.

'That troublemaking midget? We've got enough on our plates without having to talk to the dwarf.'

'You've a nasty tongue. Tell your mother I'm very sorry about Ben.'

'Yeah, it stinks. Do you get many murders in your house?'

She slammed the phone down. Pretty much the response he'd expected, but then a call from Vis Perera took his mind off Ben for the time being.

'I'm with Paula,' he said. 'She doesn't have credit on her phone at the moment and she's not well enough to go out. She'd like to speak to you. I was looking through a drawer with her, trying to find a prescription, and we found a memory stick. She thinks Kim left it here.'

'Paula remembered me?'

'Yes. As I've said, this is early stage Korsakoff's. Memory loss is intermittent and unpredictable. Hold on, here she is.'

'Is that Mr Swift?'

'Yes. I understand you've found something.'

'That's right. I must have put that . . . thing in the drawer. I think I found it under a cushion after Kim was here. I didn't know what it was. Vis said you might be interested in it. Can you come round today?'

He agreed to visit that afternoon and asked to speak to Perera again.

'Any news of Marie?'

'Nothing. Paula says she still hasn't contacted her and there's no sign that anyone has been here.' His voice dropped to a whisper. 'I think Paula has forgotten that Kim is dead. There wouldn't be any point in telling her again and renewing the shock.'

'I can't say that she seemed all that shocked when I told her, but I won't mention it unless she does.'

* * *

Swift arranged to see Jack North later in the morning, saying only that he had some important news. They met in a café near North's surgery in Twickenham. Rain was drumming against the windows, which were masked with condensation. North looked as if he hadn't slept. His eyes were strained and raw, and his hair was lank and shone with raindrops. They ordered coffees and sat at a table near two women whose umbrellas were dripping puddles on the floor.

'Jack, I'm sorry to have to tell you this. I have some bad news. Ben Ramsay is dead.' He explained how Ben had wanted to help him and how his body was found.

'Oh my God. Poor Ben. I'm so sorry. Finding him in your own home . . .' North's eyes were brimming. He held on to the edge of the table as if it were a lifebelt, pressing so hard his fingers turned white. 'I can't believe this.'

'The police are investigating. I think Ben's death has to be related to Kim's and that's why he was left in my house. I don't know how that works. Not yet.'

'Ben wouldn't hurt a fly. He was always upbeat, up for a laugh. Just a zany, inoffensive bloke.'

'I know. He lived in his own world, full of fictions. I liked him.'

The café was warm and busy with people sheltering from the rain. Alison Krauss was singing in the background, exhorting people to go to the river to pray. North was staring into his coffee, turning the teaspoon over and over in his hand.

'Jack, I met Paula Flanders, Kim's mother. She's a dreadful, spiteful woman. She confirmed that she contacted Kim, and that Kim visited her a couple of times before she died.'

He knew that this would upset North even more. He had decided not to mention the memory stick in case it was irrelevant. The little man burst into tears and lowered his head into his hands, his shoulders trembling. One of the women at the next table glanced across and glared at Swift. She said something to her friend and they both looked over. He ignored them and leaned closer to North.

'I'm sorry. This is hard for you. But I will find out what happened to Kim. And Ben, too. If the police don't find the perpetrator, I'll search until I do.' He was being paid for Kim. With Ben, it was personal.

North fumbled for a paper napkin and dragged it across his face. 'Why did Kim just shut me out? I'd have been there for her if only she'd told me. She must have been dealing with so much pain in her life. That girl Nadia dying and then her mum . . . That would have been massive for her. I'd never have thought she'd agree to meet her mum. She hated her. I just don't understand.'

'People change, Jack. Kim still had a relationship with her mother, even if it was long distance and bitter. She may not have seen her for years, but her shadow was always there. The lure of seeing a biological parent can be very strong, no matter the damage and hurt. Life gets in the way, trips you up. Maybe Kim wanted to resolve some things and then tell you. Maybe she was too confused to talk about it, or she thought you had enough to think about with your studies and she didn't want to burden you. The truth is, you'll never know now.'

North blew his nose and swallowed. He drew his spoon across the film that had formed on his coffee. 'Kim and I hated it when there was skin on custard or milky drinks. We used to say it was like snot. We liked the same foods, the same flavours.' He smiled, tears streaking his cheeks again. 'Different memories come back at random. I remember one day I was in Great Howe with Kim, and a couple of boys were calling me names. The usual stuff. I just wanted to get away from them but Kim shouted at them to apologise. I was frightened because they were teenagers, older than we were. I tried to pull Kim away but when they laughed at her, she went for them. She punched one in the face, gave him a bloody nose, and kicked the other in the crotch. They were so astonished they didn't retaliate. Then she grabbed my hand and we ran and hid in the library. We crouched down behind a bookshelf and started laughing. Kim had blood on her hand and she wiped it on the carpet. The librarian found us and threw us out.'

'How old was Kim then?'

'Around ten.'

'Brave of her.'

'That was Kim.'

Swift smiled. 'It's a good memory. One to treasure.'

'Yeah. She always took my part. I'd give anything to talk to her again, ask her what was happening in her life before she died.'

The women at the next table were leaving, heads close together and murmuring to each other. The one who had glared at Swift stopped by North and stooped down.

'Are you alright? Is this man bothering you?' She used the kind of tone you might employ with a child.

North looked up at her blankly. 'Pardon?'

'Are you okay? Are you okay with this man? You look upset.'

North drew himself up. 'I'm fine. This is a business acquaintance. I've had bad news.'

'Oh, I see. I'm sorry.'

Swift shrugged at her and she blushed and hurried away.

'Patronising kindness,' North said wearily. 'I wish I had a fiver for every time I've experienced that in my life. I know people mean well, but . . .' He drank some coffee and looked at Swift with eyes full of pain. 'Just find out what happened to Kim, please. Then maybe I can understand what went on, why she kept things from me, and then I can lay her to rest.'

* * *

Swift drove to Paula's home this time, unable to face the rambling bus journey. His head ached and now and again a dull pain throbbed in his lower back. He had an old injury there and it usually kicked in when he was tired or stressed. He wondered about Paula's forgetfulness and how selective it was. It seemed to him that it suited her to have problems remembering people and situations she didn't want to dwell on. He felt a flicker of anticipation. Perhaps the memory stick would contain information about Kim's concerns at the time of her death.

Paula was dressed in another onesie, this one yellow with a red trim, and her hair was pulled back under a red scarf. She opened the door holding a glass of cola and pattered back to her chair, barefooted.

'What's the weather like?' she asked. 'I haven't been out for a week. My nerves are too bad. I come over all weak and jittery.'

'Chilly but dry today.' He took the chair opposite her. The white memory stick lay on a little table beside her.

'I hate the winter. It didn't matter when I was banged up, I hardly noticed the seasons. But now . . . It gets dark so early. Everything feels shut down, like everyone's gone away. I get lonely on my own. I could be dead in here and no one would know. Or care. Funny, isn't it? Sometimes when I was inside I used to long for a bit of peace and quiet, but now I'm dying for some company. Some nights I'd love to be back on the wing, all nice and warm and cosy, chatting to the girls, having a game of . . . thing . . . bingo, or watching some slop on the telly. Even having a laugh with the screws. Some of them were a real gas when things were quiet and you got them in the right mood. I've read about some ex-cons who commit a crime just to get back inside. Now I know why.'

He couldn't muster any sympathy, and just nodded. 'The memory stick,' he said. 'I would like to take it away and have a look at what's on it. I'd return it to you. Although I don't think you've got a computer so it's not much use to you.'

'I tried having a go on a computer inside but I couldn't get the hang of it. They said I could build my skills. Whatever. Memory stick. Funny name for a bit of plastic. Pity I can't plug one in here and rewire my brain.' She jabbed at her temple and laughed. 'That would be good, wouldn't it? Vis would get a shock when he came round with his . . . thing . . . syringe. What is it, anyway, this memory thing?'

'It's a storage system. Once you plug it into a computer and open it, you can read whatever documents are stored on it. Are you sure it was Kim's?'

She pursed her lips. Nodded. 'I reckon. Yeah, I reckon. She used to carry one of those small computers around with her.'

'A laptop?'

'That's it. She had a special case for carrying it. So it's just a load of writing on it?'

'Probably.'

'Are they expensive, these memory sticks?'

He could see where this was going. 'Not particularly. It depends how much storage space it has.'

She picked it up and balanced it in her hand, as if she could gauge its worth by weight. 'You want to have a look though.'

'Yes, I'd like to have a look.'

'I'll sell it to you. Fifty quid.'

'But I might find it isn't Kim's after all, or that it's empty or full of useless stuff.'

'Ah well, that's a gamble.' She smiled and sipped her cola.

He recalled his first visit, taking care about informing her of Kim's death, concerned that she might react badly. Disgust and impatience flared in him. 'You know, if Kim didn't die accidentally, there might be something on here that would help me find whoever drowned her. You'd still want me to pay you?'

She rearranged herself in her chair, pressed the soles of her feet together and fingered the zip of her onesie. 'Life's a struggle. I've got to get by. I've got no one to rely on. Nothing can bring Kim back, can it?'

'No, nothing can bring her back. Although I'm not sure you give a toss about that. I'll give you twenty pounds and if I find anything useful on the stick I'll send you another twenty.'

She put her head on one side. 'How do I know you'll keep your word?'

'You don't. It's a gamble. Here.' He took the money from his wallet and held it out in one hand, extending the other for the memory stick.

She grinned, passed it to him and whisked the note away. 'I reckon you're a gent. I'll trust you. When I can get out, I'll be able to buy a couple of decent lamb chops and some cakes. Chocolate eclairs are my favourite. Tell you what, can you make me a cuppa? That was lovely, the one you made last time. Almost as good as Marie's. The rotten cow still hasn't been near me, you know. I'll give her a piece of my mind if she ever turns up.'

'Sorry, I can't today, I've got to get on.'

'Love me and leave me, that it? Get what you want and scarper. I've lost count of the times that's happened.'

'Something like that.' He turned at the door. He was going to ask her if she ever missed Kim but she was bent down, fiddling with the cola bottles by her chair, making micro adjustments to them so that the labels faced outwards. He knew the answer anyway.

The rasping of her callused feet followed him through the door. Callous and callused, he thought.

Swift was eager to look at the memory stick but he had to attend the interview at the police station first. He was there for two hours. He sat in a small, featureless room with DI Baptiste and a sergeant. His fingerprints and a DNA sample were taken, then he was given a statement to sign.

'Handy having an alibi from the assistant commissioner,' Baptiste said. 'Given that, and the time Ms Adair says you left her, plus your neighbour verifying that he saw you arrive home at six thirty, I'm not including you further in my enquiry.'

'Can you tell me what happened to Ben and the approximate time of death?' he asked.

'I can,' Baptiste said. 'He was hit over the head, a blow which left him unconscious. Then the plastic bag was secured. We don't know what he was hit with yet. Something blunt. The wound on his head didn't bleed much but the carpet in the bedroom had minute traces of his blood. So it looks as if he was bashed over the head in that room, and then placed in the wardrobe to suffocate. Given the lack of any attempt to remove the bag or get out of the wardrobe, it looks like he didn't regain consciousness. Small mercy. He died between four and six pm on Saturday.'

'What have you got from forensics?'

Baptiste tapped her nose. 'My business.'

'Have you interviewed Vlad Codreanu yet?'

'We're talking to him, yes. We're finished here now. Stay away from the Ramsay family and don't trespass on my territory. I know you phoned Codreanu. I'll let you off with that, but don't try my patience.'

CHAPTER 13

Swift drove home, thinking of the brief period when Codreanu had left the house unsecured, around four o'clock. He couldn't understand why Ben had arrived so early, but five or ten minutes would have been enough time for an efficient killer to manoeuvre him into the wardrobe.

Inside, he stood in the hallway, looking up. The police had stretched a tape barrier across the bottom of the stairs as well as over the door at the top. It seemed only yesterday that Cedric was coming down those stairs, smart in a paisley shirt and linen jacket, off to buy his paper and sit with it over a late breakfast. *Morning, dear boy. Fancy pancakes and maple syrup? My treat.*

He took a deep breath, headed for his kitchen and made coffee and a ham sandwich. He still wasn't hungry but running on empty wouldn't help him focus. Down in his office, he sat at the desk and ate. Opening his laptop, he took the memory stick from his pocket and smoothed it with his thumb for a moment. He decided to make the phone call he had been thinking about first and was surprised when Nora picked up almost immediately, sounding muffled.

'Hi? Are you okay to talk?'

'Just having a snack so got a couple of minutes,' she said, mouth full.

'How are you?'

'Okay. Flat out on this enquiry but I think there's light at the end of the tunnel. You?'

'I need to let you know a few things.' He brought her up to date. 'It was Ruth that found Ben's body, so she no longer wants to live upstairs.'

'That's understandable.'

'She's going to talk to her husband about releasing some money so she can buy a place. I think it will take her a long time to get over the shock.'

'I'm sure it will. That was a tough call.' She coughed. 'Sorry, chunk of tuna went down the wrong way. Is Branna okay?'

He was pleased that Nora had asked after her. 'She's fine. I just wanted you to know the situation.'

'Thanks for that. Hang on.'

There was the sound of phones ringing and another voice. He thought he could hear the whine of a printer. He pictured a buzzing open-plan office with cluttered desks, the kind he used to work in. There were odd moments when he missed the camaraderie and the opportunity to bounce ideas around.

Nora came back. 'Listen, I have to go and talk to a solicitor and his scummy client. Look after yourself. I'll be in touch.'

She was gone. No hint of *I miss you* or *that news changes things*. For all he knew, she was already seeing someone else, some detective she'd been thrown together with recently for long hours. He knew the intimacy that could bring, the way a colleague could start to feel like family. Late nights together, takeaways and beer, a growing warmth and co- dependency, the momentum of bringing in the right suspect and sensing that a case was about to break . . . He told himself to stop it. He'd done what he could. After all, she could hardly whisper sweet nothings in the middle of her office. He'd have to wait for her to contact him and say whatever she had to say.

He inserted the memory stick into his laptop. It held five documents: three named KimDigger 2013, 2014 and 2015, the fourth Bickmore and the fifth AFI. He clicked into each of the KimDigger documents and glanced through them. They consisted of detailed descriptions of the seasonal digs at Frynfold, the notes that Ben said Kim had kept. Swift saw records of weather conditions, soil types and found objects. The Bickmore document was a history of the museum, the exhibitions Kim had helped curate and notes on some of the finds. He clicked on the AFI document. It was a couple of pages long, an undated commentary rather than a diary. He read, sipping his coffee, stopping now and again to reread a paragraph.

Audentes Fortuna Iuvat (Virgil). Fortune Favours the Bold.

Good old Virgil. Top man. I don't know all that much about him except that he was a famous Roman poet. Gill's education system, if you could call it that, didn't include the classics. All those years spent pissing about, doing collages, pointless 'projects,' writing stories and filling books with copied maps. If Gill knew how much I loathed her and her pathetic folksy wisdom, she'd cry into one of her ugly homespun shawls. I reckon she should be prosecuted for child abuse. Boring children out of their skulls must be a crime. I never could warm to Gill because she's such a phony. I knew early on, without being able to put it into words, that she'd taken me in to make herself feel good. 'Look at me, aren't I kind, giving a home to this poor little abandoned child of druggie parents!' Then there was the boost to her income, her dowry from the state for being so charitable. She looks just like my dad in drag and a bad wig. I don't remember him but I've seen photos. I wanted my dad but instead I got a rotten facsimile.

I've always encountered the same reaction when someone has found out about my childhood. It goes like this: 'Oh, that sounds terrible, how sad. But you were lucky that your aunt was there for you and gave you a lovely home.' This delivered with the unspoken message that she'd also been brave to take on a strange girl with epilepsy. I'm supposed to look grateful. Pete was the only one who got it right. He said I jumped out of the frying pan into the pressure cooker. A bit of an exaggeration. No one at Low Lake has tried to kill me. I think Valery would like to. I bet she dreams about getting rid of me. Killing me would be too direct for Valery, though. She's a sly bitch, a fucking manipulator.

I'd tell anyone who cared to ask that it would be better to grow up with a damaged parent who wanted you than spend your childhood as a charity case, never quite fitting in with the family. Having to be appreciative. Gill never said it out loud but I could see it in the way she'd glance at me with her wounded look. She'd expected me to be more indebted. That poisonous old cow Sadie's always been keen on telling me I should be more grateful. Part of the problem is that I've never been the appreciative kind.

But no one has cared to ask.

I came across Virgil when I was reading up about Roman poetry, one of the residents of Frynfold having been a tragic poet. Phil advised that colleges always like to see evidence of background reading. I like that phrase — fortune favours the bold. I've decided to make it my motto in life. Stop fucking dithering about, KW, or you might end up wearing woolly shawls. Take action!

It's not simple or easy. But then, it shouldn't be. Big decisions. Big leap into the dark. Make your mind up time.

Around 400 people drown every year in the UK. That's about 1 person every 20 hours. 1 in 10 people knows someone who has drowned, 1 in 5 someone who has nearly drowned. So I count as a statistic for the 1 in 5. You can drown in just 5cm of water. When you're drowning, you panic and you hold your breath. You probably don't make any sounds because you're trying to control your breathing. Then you can't hold out and you try to breathe and swallow water. Your lungs fill, like water rising in a glass. The body

233

shuts down. If you have any awareness, you might feel peaceful due to lack of oxygen in the brain. If you're lucky.

I don't remember being in that bath or how I felt. I can only remember that huge shadow over me. I know I had a cough for a long time afterwards. I used to wake up in the night coughing and feeling scared. Maybe I was trying to get rid of the last drop of water from my lungs.

Sometimes I dream about my dad. Usually I dream that my mum drowned him. I see her holding him down in one of those old-fashioned deep enamel baths, pressing on him. She's cackling, like a crazy cartoon character or the wicked witch in The Wizard of Oz. Dad's legs and arms are jerking out of the water but his face is sinking down and down. Then sometimes he has my face. I wake up hot and sweating, gasping for air. I never have the dream when I sleep outside. Then I always wake up cool, untangled. No panic under the stars.

Paula. OMG, what a disappointment. The evil bitch didn't even try to stand up for herself. I think I could have admired a woman who tried to front it out or even just admitted she's wicked. But Paula was all about what a rotten life she's had and she's ever so sorry for what she did but she was out of her head and struggling after my dad went and died on her. (She made it sound as if he'd croaked on purpose.) And look at her now, living hand to mouth and all on her ownio. All those years I hated her and feared her, never wanted to see her again, longed to see her again and was desperate for her to love me. Waste of emotion and time. I'd imagine that she'd write to me one day, explaining it all: 'Sorry I fucked up your life. I have missed you. What can I do to make amends?' Then I get a note and I open it with a dry mouth and my heart pounding like I'm running a marathon and she's saying she's skint and can I lend her some money. I liked that: 'lend.' I had to laugh. She's just a sad sap, one of life's whingers. I don't know how she summoned the energy to try and drown me.

I was glad to give her the money and I made sure some of it was Gill's. She leaves so much cash lying about. She doesn't always notice how much I've taken. One useless mother paying off another. Nice closed circle there. It felt like a way of finishing off any business I had

234

with both of them. And a dismissive gesture to Paula to say fuck off for good and goodbye. Part of me was hoping that she'd splurge the cash on drugs and booze and kill herself. Not that it matters.

Now Marie, she's much more like me. Very like me. She's got a bit of spirit and brains — underused but they're there — and gumption. I like her take on life and we clicked straight away. We even have epilepsy in common. I told her we were a couple of mutated genes. Weird. Too weird for comfort.

Ancient people called epilepsy 'the Sacred Disease' because they believed the gods sent it as punishment for some sin or slight. I quite like that. Makes it sound special, mysterious and significant. Unfortunately, in 400 BC, Hippocrates rubbished that idea and said that epilepsy was due to heredity and occurred when the body's humours were disturbed. Boring!

People used to think that if you had epilepsy, you were full of evil spirits or demons or just retarded. It was thought to be connected to lunar phases. There are times when I've felt like howling at the moon. Some societies thought it was contagious and shunned the sufferer or locked them up. One delightful theory was that masturbation caused seizures and men who had epilepsy were castrated. The Romans had a custom of spitting if they saw someone having a seizure. They thought this kept demons at bay and prevented infection. I wonder if Virgil did that. In some places, the sufferer might have had a hole cut in their skull to release the demons.

Such a lovely gift that my delightful mummy Paula passed on to me. So kind of her to blight my life in so many ways. That woman's pure fucking poison. My only inheritance from her, and inevitably a tainted burden. The old tonic-clonic dance. My one repulsive, reliable partner through life. I picture it dressed in black and purple, waiting to swing me into the next rollercoaster ride.

Isn't it odd that someone can be around for years and suddenly it's as if you never really saw them before? Then one day you look and they look and wow! Big explosion. Love has hit me over the head. Amazing and terrifying and wonderful.

It's been a bit like a dig. Finding pieces, fitting them together. It's taken time but I'm almost there. It's sheer fluke that I stumbled over it when I was looking at records for Frynfold. I've kept a copy of that day's site record, August 20th 2011, and done some comparisons. I'm going to be bold, Mr Virgil, but being bold has its dangers. Elaine's dirty little secret. She shouldn't have encouraged me to be so rigorous. She isn't anyone's fool. She's got a lot to lose. Reputation, job, social standing. I reckon she'd kill to protect her baby. She won't see me coming but once she knows, I'd better watch my back and I've been thinking about how I should do that. I've done my research so I'm ready. Move over Virgil, bring on Augustus Caesar.

I think I hate Elaine now more than Gill and Paula. There's a lot of people to hate. Form a queue! I know I'm extreme emotionally. Either I really like people or I have no time for them. Sometimes I like myself, more often I loathe myself. Maybe it's because I had extreme experiences when I was a child. Or maybe I was just born that way. It's why I stuck with Pete for so long. He answered my craving for excess and my need for self-disgust. He was what I felt worthy of. Until I looked and saw. Now I just need to shake him off for good.

I hate Elaine because she shattered my dream. There's a poem about treading on someone's dreams and that's what she's done. I really rated her. Looked up to her. Held her in great esteem. Wanted to be like her. Digging is what I want to do with my life. I won't let her ruin it but she's been my biggest disappointment. Bigger than Paula even because I respected and trusted her. But she'll pay for what she's done. Literally.

I'm thinking it through. I reckon it will work. I've sweated over it, nearly lost my bottle once or twice. It's bold, Mr Virgil.

I'm sorry about Jack. I feel bad about him but he'll be okay. I thought of telling him, nearly phoned him once, but it wouldn't work. It would weigh him down. Best to keep it tight. He's the only one of them I've ever had any time for. We had lovely years, lovely times. My little man. Sex with him was sweet and cosy. We were attracted because we were a pair of misfits. It was different after he went to Liverpool, though. I felt jealous because he was getting on in life, pursuing his studies and spreading his little wings while I was stuck here, going nowhere fast. I felt as if he'd abandoned me, which was crazy because I was glad for him as well. Crazy, mixed-up emotions.

I gradually cut myself off from him. I couldn't handle the feelings. Not fair on him really. There's no sense in it. I've been a two-faced bitch to Jack. It's not rational, how I react. That's just how I am, who I am. I look for slights and I expect people to turn their backs, let me down. So I get in there first and reject them. Until now, anyway.

Jack's got a kind nature. It should do him good in life. Either that or life will eat him up and spit him out.

It's not what you find, it's what you find out. Elaine knows what I've found out now. It's going to get very interesting!

Swift got up, walked to the window and back again and then stood, tapping his desk. Such a perplexing young woman; intelligent, damaged and insightful. Full of hate, too. A woman who knew about Virgil yet kept company with the likes of Pete Hussain. A woman whose emotions had veered between admiration and hatred with little room in between. Images and thoughts of drowning shadowed her days. She'd set her heart on a career in archaeology, yet seemed unable to take action to secure the education she needed. What he had read indicated that Kim had become a danger to herself and Elaine Dunbar. She had discovered that Elaine had a secret, something to do with her work at Frynfold, and she was probably contemplating blackmail. For the first time, he was grasping at something concrete.

He glanced through the final page of the document again. Kim had been smart and perceptive but she had also been a thief with a need for money. It meant power, love and security. You could say she'd been obsessed by money. She'd stolen from Gill Ramsay and encouraged Nadia Barton to start stealing from her father. She'd borrowed from Adela when she hadn't needed it and probably stolen from her. She'd had enough to give away a substantial sum to her mother, yet she hadn't been earning much at the museum. Money kept cropping up in this investigation. The Dunbars had acquired enough to build their dream home.

Frynfold held the answers to why Kim had come to hate Elaine, was excited about challenging her and possibly why she had died.

There was a thread of hope running through the tangle of emotions in the document. It seemed that Kim had met someone who had ousted Pete from her life. She'd managed to conceal the new relationship, but then flying under the radar had been her forte. It was intensely frustrating that she gave no clue as to who it had been but Pete might well have known, or suspected, and resented it.

Swift copied the memory stick onto his laptop and emailed the documents to himself. Remembering Jack North's look of misery, he decided to copy the section where Kim spoke honestly and fondly of him and attached it to an email.

Hi Jack,

I've come across a memory stick that belonged to Kim. One of the documents refers to you and I thought you'd like to see that part. The way she speaks about you shows how much you meant to her. Kim was planning something and I think it might have put her in danger. More of that when I can look into it further. In the meantime, this might be of some comfort to you.

TS.

He locked the memory stick and laptop in his desk drawer, and checked news websites for a mention of Ben. The police hadn't made his death public yet. He turned over an idea and made a decision.

He needed to see Pete Hussain again, but first it was time to visit Dancer's End.

* * *

There was no reply at Dancer's End the next morning. The wind blustered, rattling the wooden window shutters and spitting the odd raindrop. Swift didn't want to give Elaine notice of his visit so he headed to the museum and saw that it was open. An older man with a curved back and thick, greying hair was in the office, sorting leaflets.

'Hi. I'm looking for Elaine Dunbar. Is she around?'

The man stepped out of the office. His chunky knitted cardigan was the same steel colour as his hair and he had braces attached to high-waisted fawn trousers. 'I'm expecting Dr Dunbar soon. Do you have an appointment?'

'No. I was just passing and wanted to have a word.'

'Well, the doctor's a busy woman.' The man folded his arms like a good gatekeeper.

'I'm sure. Is it okay if I wait? I've been here before, Elaine knows me.'

'Well, I suppose that's all right. Are you an archaeologist?' He looked Swift up and down with a dubious expression.

'No, but I'm very interested in the work at Frynfold. My name's Tyrone Swift. Do you work here, Mr . . . ?'

'Clarke, Len Clarke. I'm a volunteer. Been here for fifteen-odd years. You have to keep yourself occupied when you retire and my wife doesn't like me getting under her feet around the house.' A slight frown crossed his face.

Swift leaned against the wall, ankles crossed, nodding understandingly, man to man. 'I've heard many a bloke say that. It's best to keep the wife sweet. It's good that you maintain interests. Keeps you young and agile, doesn't it? Keeps the brain sharp.'

Mr Clarke was thawing out. He put his hands in his cardigan pockets and nodded. 'Don't know about agile with my back, but you have to have something to get up for.'

'Too true. You've got the right attitude. And this museum is all in a good cause. I wonder, did you know Kim Woodville? She used to work here. I'm a family friend.'

'Oh, I knew Kim. She called me Clarkie. Cheeky young madam, that one, but I couldn't help liking her. She did good work in here, very efficient. She'd make me a nice strong cup of tea when she brewed up.'

'It was so sad how she died.'

'It was a waste. A terrible waste. I miss her, you know. She always cheered me up.'

It was good to hear someone say they missed Kim. 'I know she loved working here and her fieldwork at Frynfold.'

Clarke fingered one of the buttons on his cardigan. 'You're right. She lived and breathed her digging. I haven't heard her mentioned for a while now. It's good to hear her name. You say you know the family. I always wondered if Kim's aunt managed to get to know her before she died.'

For a moment, Swift was puzzled, thinking of Gill, then the penny dropped. 'You mean her aunt Marie?'

'That's right. She came here one day looking for Kim. Tall woman, a bit loud and brash but polite enough.'

'Kim wasn't here?'

'No, she was having a break in the café over the road. I sent her aunt over there.'

'You know, I've been wanting to contact Marie but I couldn't remember her surname and the family at Low Lake can't recall it. You don't happen to remember if Marie told you her last name?'

'I never forget a name or a face. Pride myself on it. I used to sell insurance and you have to remember your customers if you want them to come back to you.'

The phone rang in the office and Clarke turned away to answer it. Swift listened to him giving information about the museum and the opening times. He waited impatiently while Clarke chatted about the weather and other places of interest in the area.

'Tourists,' he said, when the call ended. 'Swedish this time but you get them from all over. They seem to love Oxfordshire. I suppose it's not too far from London, you can do it in a day.'

'Yes, a quick trip up the motorway to take in the sights. You were saying about Kim's aunt, Marie?'

'That's right. When she came in she introduced herself, said her name was Marie Piper and she was looking for her niece. She said she'd never met her and was excited about finding her. I asked Kim about it next time I saw her but she didn't reply, changed the subject. She could be like that, a bit offhand. Best not to rub her up the wrong way, I always found.'

'People can be tricky, can't they?' Swift decided that while he was on this unexpected winning streak, he'd probe a bit more. He gestured around. 'It's good to see that Elaine's been so successful in her career. I've visited her at Dancer's End. It's a lovely home.'

'Dr Dunbar's very proud of it. She's certainly done well for herself but she works hard, puts in the hours and she carries a lot of responsibility. She works late at night here sometimes, especially when it's the digging season.'

'I suppose she has to catalogue any finds.'

'Of course, and make sure anything valuable is locked away. She never delegates the final recording. She goes through all that herself. That's why she burns the midnight oil.'

'How does it work then, recording the finds?'

'The supervisor on the site on any given day makes a record of everything that's found, with the sector it was found in and photographs. Then Dr Dunbar goes through and makes a final summary.'

'Have there been any very valuable finds?'

'I think the biggest was a number of silver and gold coins a while back. I remember there was a lot of excitement and Dr Dunbar was thrilled to bits. She went to London to talk to people at the British Museum.'

Swift felt a little thrill of his own. 'One last thing. Do you know Ben Ramsay? I wondered if he'd spoken to you recently.'

'Daft Ben? Last time I saw him, he was dithering about in the Co-op, trying to decide which sandwich to buy. That was months ago.'

A couple came in, unzipping their coats, and asked for tickets. Swift moved away and stood by the doorway. He rang Pete Hussain but his phone went to voicemail. Swift left a message, asking Hussain to ring him, then googled *Frynfold* and found a link to a national tabloid, dated 28 August 2011.

OXFORDSHIRE DIG STRIKES GOLD

Archaeologists digging at the site of a Roman villa at Frynfold near Banbury have unearthed a cache of valuable coins, many of them gold and dating from the reigns of several emperors. They are still to be valued but one is a very rare silver coin, from the time of the Emperor Proculus, and is thought to be worth hundreds of thousands of pounds.

The director of the project, Dr Elaine Dunbar, said that she and her colleagues are delighted with the find, which has come after months of painstaking work. At a press conference, she stated, 'Every find at Frynfold is important but these coins will really put us on the map and they are a very significant contribution to our understanding of the Romans in Britain.'

The coins will be displayed eventually in the British Museum.

Swift spent another couple of minutes on Google, finding the information he needed, until Elaine Dunbar swept up in her Lamborghini. She glanced at him without acknowledgement, opened the boot of the car and took out a hefty briefcase. She was wearing a long olive waxed raincoat with a wide cape and hood. It was undone and as she strode towards him, it streamed behind her in the stiff breeze.

'Hallo, Dr Dunbar. I wondered if I might have a word with you.'

She gave him a thin smile. 'Mr Swift. I'm afraid I haven't time. I'm preparing for a conference and my schedule is packed all week. You need to make an appointment.'

'I'm afraid this really can't wait. It's about Kim Woodville and some records I've found, referring to you.'

She had been about to walk past him but she stopped, swinging her briefcase in front of her. 'Records? What kind of records?'

'It's a document that Kim wrote. Part of it refers to August 2011 at Frynfold.'

'I don't know what you mean. Kim wasn't working with us then.' She pushed a hand through her short springy hair.

'I know. But I do need to discuss the detail Kim refers to. It's worrying, Dr Dunbar.'

Len Clarke was standing at the desk, fanning out brochures and watching them. Elaine glanced at him and seemed to debate with herself.

'Len, I'm just taking Mr Swift up to my office. We won't be long. Can you ring Felix Medalio for me and ask him if he can delay his call for thirty minutes?' She asked graciously but it was a command.

'Of course, Dr Dunbar. I'll do that straight away.'

Swift followed her up the spiral staircase to a low-beamed room that ran the length of the building. Sun spilled in through three skylights. Filing cabinets and tall ranks of shallow, labelled wooden drawers filled two walls, with a wide walnut desk against another, holding a computer with a printer on a table beside it. A safe was inset into the wall just above it. The fourth wall was lined with crammed bookshelves from floor to ceiling. It was a room for serious work and study. There were two upright armchairs by the bookshelves and Elaine gestured to them as she slipped her coat off and draped it on the back of her desk chair.

'Well?' she said. She was wearing a navy linen trouser suit and white shirt, paired with bright red and navy leather trainers.

'I suppose this is where you record the finds made at Frynfold. Do valuable items go in the safe?'

'Correct.'

'I've seen a number of documents that Kim wrote. In one, she expresses a lot of anger towards you. She says that you have a dirty secret and that you've trodden on her dreams.'

Elaine's fingers were linked together in her lap, pointing upwards. She raised an eyebrow. 'That sounds unpleasant and highly dramatic. Not like the Kim I knew. I've no idea what you're talking about. How did you come by these documents?'

'I can't tell you that. But I believe they're genuine.'

'May I see this particular document?'

'No, I can't show it to you. Kim alludes to having discovered something about Frynfold.'

She lifted her shoulders. 'Alludes. I see. Or rather, I don't. You need to make yourself clearer. I have no clue about any of this. As I say to my students, "Elucidate and explain."'

Swift thought she might well maintain the stern educator attitude for some time. He settled back in his chair, crossed his legs and sighed. 'You're a very wealthy woman, considering that you grew up in a council house.'

She stared at him, and then laughed. 'Have you come here to be offensive?'

'No. I've come here because I've read something that indicates that Kim may have put herself in danger. She was preparing to challenge you about something she had discovered concerning Frynfold. She said you were going to pay for it. I think she may have been pushed into that lake. I'm wondering now if you pushed her.'

Elaine shook her head. 'This sounds crazy. It also sounds as if you're on a fishing expedition. I resent your tone. If you won't show me this document you *claim* to have found, I can't help you.'

St Osgyth's bells erupted, clanging the hour. The room reverberated and Swift waited until the deep peals stopped.

'When I came to your lovely home, you were clearly very proud of your work and your achievements.'

'Yes. And?'

'Well, I just find it a bit odd that when you were talking about Frynfold there and when we were at the site, you never mentioned the important find of coins in 2011. I heard a lot about poets and dancers as well as mosaics and other artefacts but not about the rare and valuable coins. I'd have thought you'd highlight that to a visitor. Maybe you do, usually. Maybe I was the wrong kind of visitor, asking the wrong kinds of questions.'

She waved a hand dismissively. 'My work is extensive. There have been a number of finds. I don't assume that everyone's interested or wants to hear about them all.'

'You're saying you're modest?'

Anger flared for a moment in her expression. 'I'm busy. People who want to hear the full details of our work buy a ticket and come to my lectures. So if that's all . . .'

'Have you spoken to Ben Ramsay recently?'

'Is he one of the family at Low Lake? I don't think I've met Ben. Kim might have mentioned him once or twice. Why do you ask if I've spoken to him?'

Swift wanted to tell her that Ben was dead so as to gauge her reaction, but knew he needed to keep on the right side of DI Baptiste. If Elaine already knew, she was a good actor. 'I just wondered. So. What Kim wrote about you having a secret and being a terrible disappointment to her means nothing to you?'

'No, it doesn't. As I've told you before, we had a good relationship and we worked well together. I can't throw any light on this document Kim is *supposed* to have written.'

He nodded, deciding not to reveal any more details for now. 'How did you come by the money for a house like Dancer's End and a Lamborghini? Archaeology and selling plants don't seem to account for it.'

Elaine slapped her hands down on the arms of her chair and stood. 'I'm not putting up with this. What I earn and how I live is none of your business. You have absolutely no right to be here asking me questions at all. Kim died tragically. I know nothing about a document or any danger. As far as I know, the only discoveries Kim made were during the digs. She found little of any importance and it was all recorded.' She levelled her chin at him but he could see the tension in her.

'Was your husband having an affair with Kim?'

She strode across the room, switched on her computer and turned to him. 'Of course not. You're ridiculous and rude. I've given you more time than you merit. Get out.'

He stood. 'Okay, I'll go. When I went to Frynfold with you, you explained that you needed good security around the site because of intruders, nighthawks. I wondered if daylight thieves were the real problem.'

She shrugged. 'Yet again, I don't understand you.'

'No? Then I'll leave you with two words. Augustus Caesar.'

It was a random thrust but by the look on her face, it went home. She wasn't quick enough to conceal a flicker of anxiety. Then she rallied, gripping the high back of her chair. She was used to being in charge and holding an audience.

'Documents, dreams, danger and Roman emperors.' She counted them off on her fingers. 'Sounds like the plot of a Dan Brown novel. You're talking in riddles. Let me give you some alternative Roman names to play with, Mr Swift. Previously you mentioned Mr Barton and his unfortunate daughter. There's an angry, dangerous man if you want to associate someone with Kim's death. Maybe you should think about bothering him instead of wasting my time. Perhaps he really does have a secret. Here's a bit of homework for you. Try looking up Catullus and Juventius.'

CHAPTER 14

Swift ordered a bowl of rice and chilli in the Tithe Barn. He was fairly sure that Catullus had been a Roman poet. He sat by the window and googled the name while he waited for his order.

The Roman poet Catullus lived in the time of Julius Caesar. He wrote a number of love poems which are remarkable for their explicit and erotic imagery. Many of his love poems are written to a woman called Lesbia but Catullus may have been bisexual. A number of poems talk about his feelings for a boy called Juventius, describing how the poet would like to give him 'a thousand kisses.' In other poems, Catullus writes about gay love and enduring relationships between people of the same sex.

Presumably Elaine Dunbar was hinting that Larry Barton was gay. If his daughter had realised this and told Kim, it could explain the remark about him 'playing the grieving widower.' If the man was gay, it was his own business, unless it provided him with a reason to attack Kim.

The TV positioned above the counter was suddenly loud, distracting Swift. The three staff members stopped what they were doing to look at the screen. A newsreader with glowing orange skin appeared with a regional bulletin.

Police have announced the death of a local man, Ben Ramsay. Mr Ramsay, twenty-six, was found dead in suspicious circumstances in West London after being reported missing from his home near Great Howe last Sunday. Police are appealing for anyone with information about Mr Ramsay to contact them. They are particularly interested in Mr Ramsay's movements last week and would like to talk to anyone who had contact with him.

A photo of Ben flashed up on the screen. A head shot, Ben smiling, hair tousled, his eyes merry.

'Oh gosh!' The waiter who had brought his order swivelled sideways and stared at the TV. 'I can't believe it. Poor old Ben!'

'You knew him?'

'Yeah. We used to play football sometimes in a local team. He wasn't much good but he was keen. He could never remember the rules and once he scored an own goal.' The young man was still holding the tray of food, suspended mid-air. 'I hadn't talked to him for a while but I saw him last week. I suppose I should tell the police.'

'You should, yes. You should ring them now.' Swift held up a hand. 'Shall I take the food?'

'What? Oh, yes, sorry. It's a bit of a shock.' He put the tray down and stood rubbing his cheek.

'I knew Ben too, although not very well. Where did you see him?'

'I think it was last Thursday. Yes it was, 'cause I was buying stuff for my mum's birthday at the garden centre. Ben was chatting to a guy who works in there. I can't remember his name.'

'Tall, slim, middle-aged man, faded blond hair?'

'Yeah, that's right. Do you know him?'

'Sort of. Make that call to the police now.'

'Right. Yeah. God, poor Ben. I wonder if they mean he was murdered.'

The young man wandered away, taking his phone from his pocket.

Swift scooped up a fork of chilli and sour cream and blinked at the heat from the spices. He juggled strands of thoughts and the information he had come by that morning. He could see across to the museum from his window seat and he watched Elaine Dunbar hurry through the door and speed away in her car. He wondered if she was heading to Green Fingers. He'd have liked to follow her and almost abandoned his lunch, but decided that he needed to concentrate on Kim and make another local call. It was time he talked to Larry Barton about his threatening behaviour towards Kim after Nadia's death, and the reason why his daughter had thought he was pretending to grieve for his wife. It might be an explosive meeting.

He scraped the last of the rice from his bowl and looked up Marie Piper in London. There were a couple of Anne Maries but only one M Piper, with an address in Lambeth. He made a note, flicked to Facebook and found several Marie Pipers in the UK. One photo looked likely and when he selected the page, he saw the head-and-shoulders image of a woman who bore a close resemblance to Kim. The same shape face, dark brows and strong looks. The hair was a similar length but a light hazel colour. Facebook's privacy settings meant he couldn't access any other information. He debated sending a message but decided he would try the address first. He finished his lunch and paid his bill. The staff behind the counter were still clustered around the till, discussing the news about Ben.

* * *

As he approached the lane leading to Larry Barton's house, Swift saw a man pulling the door behind him and double-locking it. He was medium height and well-built with short brown hair brushed straight back from his face, a ridged nose and Van Dyke beard. He nodded at Swift as he walked quickly past, his eyes flickering up and down. Swift smiled and carried on. When he reached the house he glanced back, but the man had vanished.

He rang Barton's bell and knocked on the door but got no reply. He tried Barton's phone but it went to voicemail and he decided not to leave a message. He walked back to his car. Something about the man he had just passed was niggling at him. He was sure he had seen that distinctive beard before but couldn't think where. He sat for a moment in his car, and then it came to him. He was one of the men in the photo on Barton's mantelpiece. Three men in a pub holding a trophy. The bearded man was sitting on Larry Barton's right. He recalled that DS Houghton had said that he and Barton played in the pub quiz team. He tapped the steering wheel, thinking. Houghton had accepted Barton's alibi for the night of Kim's death, when he was supposedly alone at home. If Barton was actively gay, he might have a partner and if the man he had just passed was Houghton, he had a key to the house. That suggested a certain intimacy. There had been suggestions of various possible liaisons during this case — Valery and Phil Dunbar, Kim and Dunbar. What if they had been pointing him in the wrong direction? It was worth a try. He rang Houghton's mobile number.

'Yes?' It sounded as if he was driving.

'Hi, a couple of things have come up about Kim Woodville and Ben Ramsay. I wondered if I might have a few words with you. I'm in the area at the moment.'

'DI Baptiste is heading Ben's enquiry.'

'Yes, I know. I just wanted your local knowledge. Maybe I could buy you a drink? I won't take up much of your time.'

'Ahmm . . . let me think. I'm heading to the station now and I've got to make some calls. I could make a quick drink after work. Do you know Banbury?'

'No, but tell me where to meet and I'll find it.'

'There's a bar called the Purple Grape just off Castle Quay. I'll see you in there at five thirty.'

Swift got to the Purple Grape early. It was in a row of shops alongside the banks of the Oxford Canal. He chose a seat at the bar, facing the door, wanting to surprise Houghton. There were a range of local ales on offer but he decided it was a wine kind of evening. He ordered a glass of Sauvignon, enjoying the first cold hit of gooseberry on his tongue. It was a soulless bar, the dark red walls lined with badly hung black and white photos of Hollywood stars. The paintwork was patchy, one of the strip lights was flickering and there was a faint smell of frying fat. The place seemed in keeping with the town, which had a dusty, jaded appearance. The canal was its saving grace, busy with boats and walkers with stout boots and rucksacks. The Purple Grape's only other customer was a middle-aged woman with bags of shopping who was arguing with someone on her phone.

At five thirty precisely, the bearded man came through the door, wearing a black wool overcoat. He saw Swift and stopped in his tracks, then walked over, frowning.

'Hi, I'm Tyrone Swift. We met earlier in Great Howe.'

'What is this? What's going on?'

'I thought you might tell me. Sit down. Let me buy you a drink.'

Houghton stood, looking hesitant, and then pulled out a stool. He was in his thirties, Swift gauged, possibly about the same age as himself.

'What will you have?'

He cleared his throat. 'A half-pint of Old Hooky will be fine.'

Swift ordered. 'Thanks for coming, I appreciate it was short notice.'

Houghton seemed nervous, shifting on his stool. 'What's this "local knowledge" you're after? Something to do with Ben Ramsay?'

Swift drank some wine. 'I'll be honest with you. When I saw you earlier, I recognised you from the photo on Larry Barton's mantelpiece and I wondered if you were DS Houghton. I wanted to check that out. I think you're in a relationship with Larry Barton and that's probably been the case for some time. I was calling on Mr Barton to put the same idea to him but he wasn't in. Or he was pretending not to be in. You'll know, as you'd just been at the house. Listen, I don't care if you're gay or not. I do care that you accepted his explanation that he was at home on his own the night Kim Woodville died.'

Houghton took a gulp of his beer and swallowed loudly. He was collecting himself, buying time, weighing up how to play things. And as Nora had pointed out, police made good liars. He fingered his beard and cleared his throat.

'Why would you think I'm gay?'

Swift couldn't blame the man for being defensive. Even these days, being gay and in the police could be difficult, especially in a rural area. Mary was okay in the liberal metropolis but you didn't have to go far from London to hit a wall of prejudice.

'Barton gave me and the wider community the impression that he was still mourning his wife, but Nadia Barton told Kim Woodville that her father was pretending to be a grieving widower. Someone else suggested to me that he might be gay. I don't know how my source knew that. Then I saw you with keys to the house. Why would you have those? Unless you're going to tell me you're related to Barton, in which case your involvement over the Kim Woodville enquiry would be equally questionable.'

Houghton traced a finger down the side of his glass. Swift could see a slight tremor. He caught a drip of moisture and brought it to his tongue. 'Larry Barton didn't touch Kim Woodville. He's all bluster. He wouldn't harm anyone.'

'Oh, come on. You're a cop. You know that's what a lot of family members say when they're faced with the reality that one of them has caused harm.'

'I'm not related to Larry. That's all I'm saying on the subject. You've got a bloody cheek asking me these questions.'

Swift's jaw tightened. He leaned in, his voice angry. 'Have I? I've been finding information that makes me think someone pushed Kim in that lake and I want to know who did. If you're a half-decent cop, you should want to know that too. And I think that Ben Ramsay's death is associated with hers. I'm bloody angry about his death. I'm furious that someone left his body in my house and my baby daughter was there when he was found. So I have every right to ask questions, and I can get a lot worse than cheeky if you try me.' He folded his arms, and stared hard at Houghton. 'Larry Barton held a real, bitter grudge against Kim. He followed her around sometimes. He turned up where she worked, looking hostile. He believed she was responsible for the death of his only daughter. Any proper investigation would have to include him as a suspect.' Swift saw that Houghton was looking alarmed and he decided to press his advantage. 'Look, I don't often tell people this but my cousin is Mary Adair, assistant commissioner in the Met. She's gay and out there. I was best man at her wedding. I'm no homophobe and I'm not going to out you for the sake of it. Just level with me and if I think you're being honest I'll trade you some information I came by earlier in Great Howe. DI Baptiste may already have heard it but if not, it might earn you some kudos.'

Houghton looked down. Swift could almost hear his thoughts whirring. 'Let me get another drink first. You want one?'

'Okay, thanks.'

Houghton ordered, and then took off his coat, revealing a well-cut grey suit and cream shirt. He loosened his tie. 'You're barking up the wrong tree. I know Larry didn't kill Kim.' He looked around, and pulled his stool closer to the table. 'I know because we were together the night she died. I was in the house from eight o'clock until four the next morning.'

'Right. Of course, you could be covering for him. I need more than that.'

Houghton shrugged, took a deep draught of beer and stared down into the glass. 'I could be lying, but I'm not. I've been with Larry for six years almost, through the deaths of his wife and then Nadia. He's a good man. Yes, he was angry with Kim and behaved in ways he shouldn't have, but he was gutted. I know he's never been able to forgive Kim and he still struggles to deal with his grief over Nadia's death but he's not a violent man. I know, I've met enough of them. Larry has tremendous patience. He puts up with me refusing to leave my marriage and my children. He's brave, too, or would be if I'd let him. He'd like to come out and for us to be a proper couple. Believe me, that would cause quite a stir in Great Howe. But I can't lose my family. My kids are young. I love them. I can't bear the thought of being parted from them. Larry understands because his wife never knew he was gay, or at least if she did, she never let on.'

'Yet it seems that his daughter knew, or took an educated guess.'

'I don't know how Nadia worked it out. Maybe she saw or heard something, even though we thought we were discreet. She was a bright girl. When you love someone it's difficult to keep it completely under wraps.' He looked at Swift, his expression anxious. 'It's hard to describe what it's like, living a double life, feeling pulled in two directions and guilty all the time. People think coming out as gay is easier now but you should hear the stuff that goes down at my station. And my wife . . . I can't imagine how I would tell her and the kids. So I live a lie, and Larry puts up with it because he loves me. He's willing to go on living in secret, even though he's on his own now. He'd be free to come out and maybe find a man who wouldn't deny him every single day. We spent that whole night together. We don't manage to do that often but it was another night when I told my wife that I was on late operations or doing surveillance. I have a box of lies I dip into.'

He closed his eyes and ran his hand across them. Swift was silent, affected by the torment in his voice. He thought Houghton was genuine.

'Thanks for telling me the truth. I appreciate it's hard.'

'Do you? I doubt it. Easy to say.' Houghton gave him a cold look, the shutters on his face back down.

Swift changed the subject. 'I was in the Tithe Barn earlier. A news bulletin came on about Ben Ramsay. A waiter in there told me he'd seen Ben in the garden centre last week. He was talking to Phil Dunbar. It might mean something or nothing. I told the waiter to call the police.'

Houghton collected himself, adjusted his tie. 'Dunbar's married to the archaeologist, right?'

'Elaine Dunbar, yes. Kim worked with her.' Swift kept the information about Kim's document to himself for now. He needed to do some research.

'I'll check what's happening.' Houghton looked shrewd now, his expression rigid. 'Stay away from Larry, Swift. Stay away from us. You need to search in some other direction for Kim Woodville's killer, if there is one.'

He grabbed his coat and walked out. His second drink stood on the bar, half finished. Swift reckoned he could cross Larry Barton off his list of suspects. One way or another, it had been a productive day and he needed to sift through what he had learned. He drained his glass and decided to walk along the canal path for a while.

A light drizzle was falling as he headed out of the town, past derelict warehouses, of which some were being converted into flats. The towpath was damp and muddy, fringed with dripping foliage and fallen leaves. A glorious Virginia creeper blazed amber and gold across the front of a lock-keeper's cottage. He stopped at the lock to watch a narrowboat negotiate the rushing waters, wishing that he was out in his own boat in the mild evening air. He leaned on the fence, watching foam lap the timbers below, and mulled over ancient sites and artefacts. He rang Bella Reynolds and left a message, asking if she could help him with a few questions, then strode on.

* * *

Pete Hussain still hadn't returned his call. Swift rang the Miller and Porter and asked if he could speak to him.

'He's not here anymore. He quit,' a man told him. 'Left us in the lurch and all.'

'When was that?'

'Couple of weeks ago.'

'Do you have any contact details for him? I'm a friend of his. I've lost his address and can't raise him on his phone.'

'No idea. Sharon, the manager, might be able to help you. She'll be in later.'

Swift left his details and set off for the Silver Mermaid, where he had agreed to meet Bella for dinner. After heavy rain, the evening was quiet with a grey and mauve sky. The lights of some evening rowers glinted on the river. This was a stretch of the Thames he had rowed a few times with Nora. Cedric had vanished suddenly from his life and now she had too. Work could mask the gap up to a point but he felt their loss at dusk, when the day slowed and the sky assumed the colours of mourning. He missed Nora. Her birthday was approaching and her present awaited, but there was still no word.

Bella was dressed in a vivid emerald-green shirt with matching earrings. She lit up their corner of the room. They ate sea bream, and shared a bottle of Viognier.

'Jack was hoping to drop by but he had to attend a seminar in Birmingham. I said I'll give him the feedback.'

'How is he?'

'Confused, a bit down because of the things he didn't know about Kim — and about Ben, of course. That must have been awful for you.'

'Pretty grim.'

'He appreciated the email you sent him with the stuff Kim had written. He's been studying it over and over again. Obsessing, almost.'

'I thought it might help him. He replied, saying he didn't understand some of it but it helped to know that she was thinking of him.'

'Have the police made any headway regarding Ben Ramsay?'

'I don't know. I need to be careful not to cross a line with them and I already have, in a way. I've got information I should give them. It's in some documents I came across, written by Kim.'

'That's where you got the excerpt you sent Jack?'

'That's right. I will show them to the police but I need to think something through first, see how it plays. That's why I wanted to pick your brain.'

Bella's eyes lit up. She looked pleased. 'Is there something new about Kim?'

He told her more about the memory stick and the remarks Kim had made regarding Frynfold and Elaine Dunbar. 'Kim was clearly very upset and had some kind of plan about tackling Elaine. Elaine has acquired impressive wealth. I've been wondering how she came by it. I went to see her. She threw me out but I could see that she was rattled, especially when I mentioned Augustus Caesar.'

'I looked him up after you mentioned him on the phone. I was a bit hazy about where he came in the list of Roman emperors.'

'I was more than hazy — I had no idea. As you've probably read, he was Julius Caesar's great-nephew and

Julius adopted him as his son and heir. Kim mentioned that there was a find of highly valuable coins at Frynfold in 2012 and I looked that up too. I think that Elaine Dunbar did something illegal — sold some coins possibly — and that Kim worked it out when she was looking at the records. She must have seen a discrepancy and followed it up. Kim liked money, she had a nose for it, and she had quite a bit just before she died. Enough to give some away to her mother. I'm working on the idea that she blackmailed Elaine Dunbar. That's why I was asking you about the market in illegally traded ancient artefacts. How would I sell a rare coin if I found one?'

Bella ran a hand through her hair and helped herself to more creamed spinach. 'I'm seeing the whole picture now. I knew a bit anyway because some of the big auction houses have unwittingly been caught up in illegally traded antiquities, especially the ones that actively seek business. Actually, I'm being too generous. Some of them must have known at times that stuff they were selling was of dubious provenance. I could bore you in detail about that as it's a favourite bugbear of mine but I won't. The whole market became particularly complex and fraught after stuff appeared from the conflicts in Iraq and Syria — Assyrian gold, cuneiform tablets, for example. Some of that's tied into terrorism. It's how they fill their coffers. But putting the auction houses aside, there's always been private illegal trade of high-quality objects. It's called "the invisible market" and as you can imagine, the internet has assisted that trade enormously, making it even more invisible. An important hoard of Celtic coins was illegally excavated in Norfolk and dispersed on the market not that long ago. It's hard to guess how much valuable stuff has been traded in this way and been lost to collections but I'd say it's massive. I did some research and talked to a colleague in Dresden who specialises in coins. She told me that a rare gold coin imprinted with Augustus Caesar, called an aureus, was sold for £600,000 to someone in Austria about seven years ago. That one was all above board, of course. But if Dr Dunbar did filch a coin or coins and sold them through a website or connection, she could have made a fortune.'

'Enough to build an impressive house, buy a Lamborghini, pay off a blackmailer and still have money in the bank?'

'Certainly. But hang on, why would a highly respected professor do that? If she was found out she'd stand to lose everything. Her reputation would be in tatters and she'd be prosecuted and jailed.'

'I know, and Elaine Dunbar is very status conscious and proud of her standing in the local community and the archaeological world. But we can't forget simple greed and opportunity. Those are the motivations for most thefts. She was in charge of the finds at Frynfold. She catalogued them and controls the safe where valuable items are kept. Presumably she could "disappear" a coin, especially if there were a number of them, without anyone knowing. No one would have any reason to think that the highly respected professor would do such a thing. I think she ran the risk because the profits were so huge. She's ambitious and she has a high opinion of herself. She enjoys social status and I imagine she felt she deserved big rewards after so much hard work. People can always find justifications for doing things. An inner voice urges them on and they believe their own lies. Of course, this is all supposition. I have no evidence and I doubt she'd ever admit it. The police would have to track it down by seizing her computer and records.'

Bella was gazing at him. 'It would be a strong motive for her to kill Kim. She might have paid Kim off but what if Kim wanted more money or Elaine just decided it was too risky?'

'That's a possibility.' Niggling at him was the issue of what Kim had done with the money. No one had discovered a stash in a bank account after she died. Of course, she could have had an account that no one knew about and the money was sitting there, gathering interest.

'Are you having pudding?' Bella asked, reaching for the menu.

'Share one?'

'Agreed. Have I got spinach stuck to my teeth?'

'No, but there's a shred on your chin.'

'Oh God, that's the kind of thing I dread when I go on a date.'

'Have you been on any recently?'

She rolled her eyes. 'Don't ask. Last week I met up with an intense guy who spent the evening telling me about his passion for potholing. I reckon if I'd left a cardboard cut-out of myself when he went to the loo, and scarpered, he wouldn't have noticed. He seemed to think it had gone really well. He was disappointed when I didn't want to see him again.'

'Sorry. Keep trying. You'll meet someone.'

'You reckon? I'm not so sure.'

They ordered pudding and tucked in at either side of a bowl of cherry pie. Bella licked cream from her spoon and touched his arm lightly.

'I'm glad Jack got in touch with you. Wherever this goes, it's best for him that he finds out the truth, even if his dead heroine has feet of clay.'

He patted her hand, and then jumped. A familiar voice snapped just behind him.

'How lovely and cosy. Nice to see you relaxed and enjoying yourself. Expensive wine, too.'

Swift looked around. Nora was standing there, rucksack slung over her shoulder, looking exhausted and furious. He was aware of Bella's hand on his arm and the cherry pie between them, both their spoons dipping in. He stood.

'Hi, Nora, it's good to see you. Has your case resolved?'

'Yeah. Sweet result. Looks like you've got one too.'
She tapped her foot and cast a cold glance at Bella.

'This is Bella, an old friend from university days. Bella,
this is Nora.' He went to kiss Nora's cheek but she backed
away.

She ignored Bella, glaring at him. 'An old friend. I see.
How original. I called by because I've just wrapped on the
case and I thought I might catch you in here. And I have,
I'd say. I was looking forward to seeing you but it's clear
how much you've missed me. Didn't take you long to find
consolation elsewhere. I shouldn't be surprised. It's what
blokes do. Very nice, very intimate. Enjoy.'

She turned away and he caught her arm. He could see
the tiredness around her eyes. 'Nora, don't go. Don't jump
to conclusions.'

'Why not? I've seen the evidence, Detective.'

He shook his head. 'No, you've seen nothing. You're
wired and knackered at the end of a long investigation. I
know what that's like, remember? Don't embarrass
yourself.'

She shook his hand away. Her voice dripped ice.
'Don't try the false empathy. I'm not that stupid. And I'm
not embarrassed. You should be. I'll let you get back to
your supper for two.'

Bella cleared her throat and spoke in a small voice.
'This is two friends having dinner. Honestly, that's all it is.'

'I wasn't asking you, gingernut,' Nora hissed. 'I saw
the way you were looking at him.' She hefted her rucksack.
'Don't bother calling me, Ty.'

She was gone. The air hummed with her anger. Swift
sat down heavily.

'Crumbs,' Bella said, wide-eyed. 'That's quite a
temper.'

'Nora takes no prisoners. I'd say she's still in full
interview mode. It's hard to come down from that.'

'I'm sorry. She certainly did make me feel like a criminal. I wouldn't like to face her if I had anything to hide.'

'That's why she's highly rated in her job.'

'Should you go after her?'

'I don't think so.' He was incensed with Nora, turning up and jumping to conclusions after she'd stayed away for so long. She should have gone home, got some sleep, worked the tension of her job out of her system. He was tired of her crossness, of being judged and found wanting.

'I suppose it did look suspicious when she walked in and saw us. We do look cosy, but what's wrong with friends looking that way?'

'Nothing. It only looks suspicious if you've got a suspicious mind. Nora and I have had some differences. I haven't seen her for a while.'

Bella pushed the unfinished pie away. 'I feel bad now. I always have a need to explain myself to people when they're angry with me. I fret about it otherwise.'

'Bella, it's okay. Not your problem. Nora's angry with me, not you. That's for me to deal with, but not tonight.'

'Well . . . if you're sure.'

'I am. Fancy another drink?'

'Why not? But not a Brain Haemorrhage!'

They laughed at the memory, and the tension eased. Suddenly, he wanted to get drunk. He and Bella had managed that with great ease and resolve years ago. He was sure they could do it again.

* * *

Swift woke the next morning to the deep whine of a drill next door. At first, he thought it was in his head, which felt as if someone had nailed it to the pillow. He unglued his eyes and squinted at the clock. Just gone seven. His body felt hollow and his tongue filled his dry mouth. He lay flat on his back, blinking at the ceiling and trying to focus his gaze. Vague memories drifted in. He and Bella, dancing in the living room to Lenny Kravitz and Red Hot Chili Peppers. A bottle of whisky liqueur featured, poured over ice cubes. He groaned and rubbed his gritty eyes, crawled to the edge of the bed and sat up slowly. He fell back at the first attempt, and then tried again, managing to achieve a sitting position. He pulled on the jeans lying at the end of the bed and stood, swaying for a few moments before heading to the kitchen for water. In the living room, he stopped in his weaving tracks. Bella lay asleep on the sofa under a throw, still wearing her emerald shirt but with her jeans draped over a chair. She was snoring and puffing.

He left her to it and drank three large glasses of water, his stomach turning over. He peered into the bathroom mirror and saw a pale, haggard face, bleary eyes and wild hair. He brushed his teeth and his tongue and made liberal use of mouthwash. Then he stood under a scalding shower, turning it to cold for the last few minutes, making himself suffer. He was beginning to feel semi-human, although his head was still rotating. He took a couple of painkillers while he brewed coffee, his forehead resting against the cool granite of the work surface. Nora. The memory of the pub came back to him. Just as well she wasn't ringing the doorbell today. Now he recalled numerous bottles of wine, and leaving the pub with Bella, then music, dancing and whisky. Every bit of him ached.

He took water and coffee through to Bella and gently nudged her awake. She groaned and burrowed her head into the cushion. The drill was still whining through the walls. He sat and watched her go through the same procedure as he had as she struggled to get her head up. It seemed to take forever.

'Whass time?'

'Half sevenish. I guess you feel as lousy as me.' He picked up the empty bottle of whisky liqueur and showed it to her.

'Oh God.' She pushed herself up. Her hair was sticking out as if she'd been plugged into the mains. 'My lips . . . glued together.'

'Here, drink this water. Then coffee.'

'Oh. Everything hurts. I'm all limp.' She drank the water, closing her eyes. 'Is that a dentist or a serial killer next door?'

'They're finishing a loft conversion.'

She sipped from her mug, eyes still closed, wincing. He pushed the pack of painkillers into her hand and drank his own coffee in silence.

'What are we like?' she said at last.

'Don't. Don't ask.'

'I didn't get hungover like this back at uni. I feel as if I've been poisoned.'

'It's the ageing process.'

'Too cruel. Amazing to think I used to do all that and still have energetic sex.'

He remembered her, limbs tangled in sheets, the blaze of her hair in lamplight. She glanced at him and smiled as if she was sharing the recollection. Another long silence. She moved her head carefully in a small circle and sighed.

'I can't remember the last time I got this drunk.'

'Nor me.'

'Can't remember the last time I danced.'

'Me neither. I seem to recall we did the Macarena.'

They looked at each other and groaned.

'There should be a law against using a drill so early in the morning,' she said. 'I'd better have a shower and get home, I've got an evaluation at eleven. Got to resemble a functioning human.' She crammed a couple of painkillers in her mouth, wrapped the throw around her waist and struggled up.

'I'll call you a cab. Twenty minutes?'

She nodded, then yelped and held her head before setting off to totter to the bathroom. She stopped at a photo on the wall — him, holding Branna.

'Is this your daughter?'

'That's her. That's my Branna.'

'She's gorgeous. Got your eyes.' She looked wistful. 'Makes me feel how much I want my own. My own little one. You're a lucky man to have her.'

Maybe you should try telling that to Nora, he thought. He cleared away the empty bottles and sticky glasses and opened the kitchen window. Raw, cold air snaked in and he took a lungful. Rain was slanting across the garden, dripping from the sycamore branches. The bird feeders were empty. Cedric had usually filled them. Another vacuum he had left.

On her way out, Bella kissed his cheek and hiccupped. He bent and hugged her.

'We both still smell of whisky,' he said. 'We'll be laying a vapour trail of it all over London. Thanks for your help.'

Bella giggled, and then yawned. 'Good luck with nailing Dr Dunbar. And that Nora . . . she should know when she's got a good 'un. Tell her to get real. If she vanishes over the horizon, ring me. Ring me anyway.'

He unlocked and opened the front door, and immediately there was a buzz of activity. Cameras clicked and several voices shouted, competing for his attention. There were five of them, waiting eagerly on the pavement.

'Mr Swift? Any comment about Ben Ramsay?'

'How do you feel about a body being discovered in your home?'

'Is it a case you're working on? You're a private detective, yeah?'

'This Mrs Swift? How are you feeling, Mrs Swift?'

A photographer came up the steps, angling her camera to try to get a shot of the police tape. Swift held his arms out, blocking her away. He could see Bella's cab arriving. She was just behind him, looking stunned.

'Just go, go, go,' he said, and nudged her forwards. She darted past the journalists, head down, while cameras tracked her.

'Mr Swift! What can you tell us—?'

'No comment,' he said, and stepped back and slammed the door.

They rang the bell, knocked on the door and called through the letterbox for a couple of minutes. He was glad that he hadn't yet drawn back the front curtains. His phone rang several times and he ignored it. Trying to block them out, he finished tidying up and retreated to the kitchen at the back, closing the door.

A vicious hangover needed feeding so he made porridge. As he stirred honey into it, he wondered who had alerted the press. Perhaps one of the neighbours who had seen police activity or gleaned information during the door-to-door enquiries that Baptiste would have ordered along the street. Maybe a cop had fed the story to reporters. Would Houghton have done it to retaliate for yesterday? He didn't think so. The man was no fool and would want to keep the status quo after their meeting. He could only hope that the journalists would get bored loitering outside in the rain or have bigger fish to fry.

He ate standing in the kitchen while he emailed DI Baptiste, attaching Kim's documents and summarising his suspicions and his visit to Elaine. He included the information Bella had given him and added:

Ben Ramsay spoke to Phil Dunbar last week. If Phil let slip something to do with Elaine, that might account for Ben referring to a cover-up. I don't know if either of them had anything to do with Kim Woodville's death but they must be suspects regarding Ben's if they thought he had come anywhere near knowing about Elaine's activities.

By the way, I was doorstepped by reporters this morning. They knew that Ben had been found here. I think you need to check if you have a leaking colleague.

Swift's lower back was groaning again and he wondered if the Macarena had caused it. His phone signalled an email. It was from Nora.

I do think I deserve an explanation. Let's meet. I've got free evenings the rest of the week.

He read it, shaking his head. He didn't have any explaining to do. Nora had ignored him for weeks and now she wanted to click her fingers. He thought of Bella. There were women who weren't temperamental and who liked children. Nora could wait. She could certainly wait until his head stopped throbbing. Then he pictured one of those photos appearing in the press. He and Bella on the doorstep, looking awkward and guilty, as people always did when taken unawares. If Nora saw one of those, he was toast anyway.

Swift collected his thoughts. He wanted to visit Marie Piper but first he would go for a row to work the alcohol out of his system and give his muscles something else to think about. That was if he could get out of his house. He went through to the front window and glanced from the side. The pavement was empty, strewn with cigarette ends and snack wrappers left by his unwanted visitors.

CHAPTER 15

Marie Piper's address turned out to be a grim block of flats near Waterloo station. Swift negotiated the heaving concourse and walked in the direction of the London Eye before cutting off into a maze of side streets full of small workshops, garages and light industrial units. Cold rain was falling and the streets looked drab. He found Chalford House and checked the numbers on the cracked, graffiti-scrawled map of the building. Number forty-three was on the third floor. He ignored the lift, convinced that in a building like this it would break down and leave him suspended between floors. He climbed the stained concrete stairs to the third floor, wishing that he didn't feel so ancient. A row, another shower and more water and painkillers had improved his self-inflicted aches but there was still a lingering exhaustion.

Forty-three was along a narrow, puddled walkway. The door had been painted blood orange at one time but the paint had peeled, exposing spots of rusting grey metal. The doorbell chimed the Skye boat song, an unusually cheery sound for such a depressing place. A woman with pink hair, raddled skin and five gold studs in her nose answered the door. At least she looked rougher than he did. A heavy waft of meat and onions snaked past her. His stomach coiled.

'Hi. I'm looking for Marie Piper.'

'Oh yeah? So am I. 'Spect other buggers are too.'

'I thought she lived here.'

'Yeah, she did. She pissed off. Left without paying the rent she owed me.'

'When was that?'

''Bout three years ago. Why are you after her? She owe you an' all?'

'No. It's a family matter. How long did she live here for?'

'A year or so, on and off. She used to vanish every now and again, and then turn up like a bad penny. I didn't care as long as I got the rent off her. But I came back one day and she'd cleared her mangy stuff out.'

'And you've no idea where I might find her?'

She shrugged. 'Search me.'

'Did she work somewhere?'

The woman gave a deep belly laugh. 'Work? I reckon that would be a dirty word for our Marie. I ain't got a clue what she did. I never asked.'

'How about the neighbours? Would any of them know?' He knew it was too long ago. Paula had said her sister moved around a lot.

'Dunno. Doubt it. Bunch of druggies, from what I can tell. I don't know none of them. Keep meself to meself.' She drew back, her hand on the door. 'Good luck with it, mate. She's a slippery one. If you find her, let me know. I'll have that couple of hundred quid the cow owes me.'

She slammed the door and he made his way back down to the ground floor where a fox was rummaging in a torn rubbish bag. Marie must have been hanging out somewhere else when she got in touch with Kim. It would be difficult, although not impossible, to track her if she'd been in a squat or just staying with someone. She might even have changed her name again by now. Paula had told him that she swapped it on a whim. Frustrated, Swift stopped for a coffee on the mezzanine level at Waterloo station. He bought a large sticky bun to go with it, reckoning that a sugar rush might help the day and his gritty eyes along. As he filled his mouth with soft icing, his phone rang.

'This is Sharon Dunne, returning your call. I'm the manager at the Miller and Porter.'

He swallowed hastily, the bun sticky on his teeth. 'I'm a friend of Pete Hussain's. I'm trying to get in touch with him.'

'He doesn't work here anymore. He rang one morning and told me he was quitting. Just like that. I told him I needed a week's notice and I'd dock his pay but he didn't care. Left me scratching around for an agency worker for the lunchtime rush.' She sounded peeved.

'When was that?'

'Last week of September.'

Shortly after he had seen Hussain at the pub. His interest quickened.

'Do you have an address for him?'

'I thought I did. We sent his P45 to a place in Bow but it came back saying he didn't live there anymore. Melissa might know. She's one of our bar staff. They had a bit of a thing going.'

He pictured the waitress who had smiled at Hussain on the day they met. 'Is Melissa around? This is a bit embarrassing. I don't like to ask but the thing is, Pete owes me quite a bit of money and I'm short of cash. He's not returning my calls. I'm fed up with him. Nice way to treat a friend.'

That did the trick. 'There's a surprise. He was always more trouble than he was worth. Hang on and I'll ask Melissa.'

He waited for a few minutes, listening to voices and the clinking of bottles, the electronic beeps of a fruit machine.

'Hi. You're looking for Pete?' A light, sweet voice and a trace of a Spanish accent.

'That's right. Do you know where I can find him? He's not answering my calls and he owes me.'

'Tell me about it. He's not answering mine either. I haven't heard from him since he left here without telling me he was going. He's such a prick.'

'You were seeing each other?'

'That's right. I thought we had something going.'

'Do you know where he lives?'

'I'm not sure. I went to his place in Bow and they said he'd left. Charming. I was cleaning my room a couple of weeks ago and I found a bit of paper behind my laundry basket. It was Pete's writing, with an address on. He must have dropped it last time he was at mine, telling me how *special* I was.'

'Can you remember the address?'

She gave it to him, saying she'd thought of going there herself. 'But in the end, I told myself he's not worth it. I wouldn't lower myself. If a guy's serious about you he doesn't just vanish without saying anything. He returns your calls, right?'

Swift noted the address, agreeing that that was indeed the case. He rang off, his lips moving, recalling a conversation and something he had been told. He finished the bun, licking his fingers and chewing thoughtfully, and then ordered a second coffee. The rush hour was beginning and he looked down on the crowds streaming through the station entrances in the persistent drizzle. They formed an intricate, flowing pattern, weaving and shifting endlessly. Now and again, someone stopped momentarily to take an evening paper from a vendor, causing the huddle behind them to stumble and sway. The tannoy crackled and boomed into life, informing of delays through Vauxhall because of a previously broken-down train and signal failure.

He looked through his emails and the notes he had made, tying up information, and then went back to the video and the photo Jack North had given him. He glanced through Kim's commentary. Two people, Hussain and Marie, had gone off the radar suddenly and without warning. He stared again at the address that Melissa had given him. The location was unlikely to be a coincidence. He thought of a possibility and held his breath. Could it be? It was unlikely and daring but it could fit the facts. He sat, staring straight ahead, turning the idea around and examining it from various angles. The noise of the station faded.

He rang Paula Flanders, hoping that she would answer. He didn't want to have to visit her and he was relieved when she picked up. He asked her one question, nodded at her reply and cut her off when she tried to prolong the conversation. There was a fit, a possible fit. An arrow seemed to be pointing in a direction he thought worth following.

He spent a couple of minutes composing an email to Simone with several attachments, asking her if she could do him a big favour, and the reason for the request. They might not be the best of friends but she liked being asked for professional help and usually took it as a compliment. She'd helped him out once before but this was a big ask. He hoped she'd be unable to resist.

He sat watching the crowds ebb and flow. His aches and pains were forgotten, replaced with a slow and exciting tingle at the prospect of a bizarre chain of events.

* * *

The following morning's post brought a letter from his solicitor. She wrote to say that unfortunately, Mr Oliver Sheridan did not wish to attempt to settle his objections to his father's will through mediation. No surprise there,

Swift thought. Oliver was the type who'd want his day in court so that he could strut and posture, even if it cost him dearly. Enclosed in the envelope was a claim form from Oliver's solicitor, marking the start of court proceedings. The claim form was a list of allegations against Swift, stating that he had prevented Oliver from seeing his father and had pressurised Cedric into giving him a car. It alleged also that as his landlord and living on the premises, Swift had been controlling towards Cedric. He had influenced him into changing a previous will, which had been made through a solicitor and named Oliver as the main beneficiary. Swift's solicitor had jotted on an attached compliment slip:

I don't think he stands a chance in court and he's throwing money away. He appears to have no credible witnesses or evidence to back his allegations. He has a copy of the previous will but that doesn't necessarily mean he has a case. Depends on how good he is on the day at pulling the judge's heartstrings.

Swift threw the letter in a drawer. There was nothing he could do about it except deny the allegations in court and hope for a sensible judge.

He was anxious to hear from Simone. She'd said she thought she might be able to help and would try to get back to him before the end of the day if she could. He didn't want to act until he had her opinion. He had agreed to pick Branna up from nursery later in the afternoon and he decided to clean his boat until then. He went to the front window and checked the street again. There were no reporters outside the house. He guessed they'd come to the conclusion that he wasn't worth staking out.

In the garden, he filled the bird feeders with peanuts and sunflower seeds and stood by Cedric's resting place for a few minutes. Then he put on old jeans and a sweatshirt and went to his rowing club, where he placed his boat on trestles and removed the seats and slides. He washed it with soapy water and disinfected the oar handles. *Clean equipment is happy equipment* was the mantra he'd been taught when he first started rowing. He dried the boat thoroughly, and applied a coat of wax to the hull before replacing the seats.

Simone's email arrived while he was sitting with Branna in Ruth's living room, reading a story and sharing slices of pineapple with her. He scanned through the email, his pulse quickening. He wanted to punch the air. So unlikely and risky and yet so slick. He emailed Simone his thanks, saying he owed her a bottle of wine and to name her choice. Branna pulled his chin with sticky fingers, annoyed at the interruption. He continued with the story about a very naughty bear, his brain meanwhile engaged with the convoluted tangle of events at Low Lake. Branna closed her hands and held her arms across her chest, making the sign for *bear*. She had started signing without prompting, a major step forward. He kissed the top of her head and she yawned and crept closer in to him. They were both dozing when Ruth came in.

She smiled at them. 'It's okay for some, isn't it? Lazing about while others work.'

'I'm off to work this evening,' he said. 'Are you feeling okay now, Ruth?'

She shrugged her coat off. 'More or less. Now and again I get a bit shaky. I still wake up in the early hours, thinking about the body. That plastic bag . . . Is there any news?'

'No, but I think there might be soon.'

He kissed Branna, washed pineapple juice from his hands and face and drove to West London through heavy traffic. He had that scent in his nostrils, the scent of a case cracking wide open.

* * *

The house was in a cloistered, moneyed area. It sat behind a line of majestic weeping willows, looking onto the tranquil waterway. It was four storeys high, Regency style, painted white and stucco-fronted, with pedimented windows. Impressive stone corbels supported the projecting eaves. It was divided into flats and 1A was the garden flat. He heard a dog bark as he pressed the bell, bracing himself. If he'd got this wrong, he was back at square one.

A woman opened the door. Tall, dark hair, black jeans, a tie-dyed long-sleeved T-shirt.

'Hi, I'm looking for Marie Piper.'

'Who are you?' She moved into the doorway, blocking the hall behind her.

'My name's Tyrone Swift. It's about Marie's sister, Paula.'

'What about her?'

'I wondered if I could have a word. You are Marie, aren't you? I've seen your Facebook photo.'

She nodded, drawing her dark brows together. It gave her a fierce look. 'That's my name.' Her long hair rippled in the stiff breeze blowing off the canal.

'I've seen Paula recently. I have some news for you.' He needed to get through the door. 'It's important.'

'How did you find my address?'

'I'm a private investigator. There are always ways of finding people. Can I come in for a moment?'

He held out his card, ready to push the door. She hesitated, fingering the belt of her jeans, then stood back and gestured inwards. She pulled a door closed as she led him into the back of the flat to a small square sitting room overlooking steps down into the garden. The room had an elegant high ceiling but was messy with clothes and books strewn everywhere. A massive Alsatian dog with a glossy black and fawn coat sat on a padded cushion by the French windows, its glistening eyes fixed on Swift. The room smelled of dog, a sourish, heavy odour. Dark was gathering and one lamp was lit but the curtains were open. The pale blooms of late white roses glimmered through the glass doors. He glimpsed something in the garden that pleased him very much indeed.

'You'd better sit down,' she said ungraciously, perching on a chaise longue by the dog and fondling its ear. Her voice was toneless and tight, as if she begrudged every word. Despite the impression that she had been sitting and reading when he rang the bell, she wore strong, heavy-soled lace-up boots.

He moved a couple of books, glancing at the titles, and sat on a sofa. He looked at her intently and she held his gaze with flinty eyes. In the flesh, her mouth was fuller, with pale, slightly dry lips.

'This is a lovely home. Are you renting it?'

She shook her head. 'Why should you be interested?'

'Oh, it's just that a woman at an address you used to live at near Waterloo said you owed her money. It was a poor kind of area. And from what your sister has told me about you moving around, I wouldn't have expected to find you at this upmarket postcode. How have you managed to make it here?'

'Are you against social mobility?'

'Not at all. But it interests me. It reminds me of someone else I've met recently in Oxfordshire.'

Marie's brows drew together. 'I work with an agency these days. I'm a professional house-sitter, looking after the place while the owner's away.'

'Are you dog-sitting as well?'

'No. Rocco is mine. Aren't you, my lovely?' She bent and kissed the top of the dog's head and he licked her face with a long meat-coloured tongue. 'So, what's this about Paula?'

He wondered if she'd prepared the story about house-sitting or if she'd thought of it on the spot. Either way, it was good and covered lots of bases. He had to hand it to her, she was intelligent and astute. If she hadn't been a criminal, he would have admired her. 'Paula's concerned because she hasn't heard from you for a long time and you haven't returned her calls. She misses you.'

'The feeling isn't mutual.'

'Oh? I gathered you'd been close at one time. She told me that you visited her in prison and then regularly after she was released. She said she mothered you when you were little. That's a strong bond, I'd have thought.'

'That's Paula's version of things. You don't want to believe everything she tells you. Her stories change but they always cast her in a favourable light.'

'So what's your version? Did you fall out? Paula didn't mention any arguments. She said you just disappeared. Around two years ago.'

She examined the dog's ear for a moment, and then turned back to him. 'Why is this any of your business?'

'I make all kinds of things my business. It sounds as if you've gone off your sister.'

'Maybe I have. Sisters fall out sometimes.'

'I suppose. Do you house-sit on your own here?'

'That's right. Look, if you've come to tell me Paula misses me you've delivered the message. I've got nothing to say about her so you can head off and enjoy your evening. Is it still raining?'

'Trying to. I don't mind the rain. There are just a couple more things. I understand that you met your niece, Kim Woodville, at Great Howe?'

'That's right. I acted as a go-between for Paula. I suppose she told you. Did she tell you she had her begging bowl out, asking Kim for money?'

'She did say that, and that Kim had given her a substantial amount. It was actually Valery Ramsay, Kim's cousin, who first suggested that Kim might have been in touch with her mother.'

'Oh?'

'Well, Valery's a funny one. A bit of a stirrer when it comes to it.'

She looked at him poker-faced, but she was blinking. 'I wouldn't know.'

'Did you know Kim died?'

She put a hand to her mouth and gasped. 'No. When?'

'Just over two years ago. She drowned at Low Lake. That was sad, especially given her history. I told your sister about it but I'm not sure she'll remember. She has memory problems these days.'

'I'm not sure Paula will care much.' She paused, swallowed. 'That is awful. I liked Kim when I met her but then I moved on and she didn't get in touch. I thought it was because she didn't want to keep up a connection with Paula and her family. I could understand that.'

Swift nodded. 'Well, I'm sorry to be the bearer of bad news. Jack North, one of the Ramsay cousins, doesn't believe Kim's death was an accident. He was a good, close friend of hers. He asked me to look into it.'

She nodded in silence, running her fingers along the dog's neck.

'There's more as well, I'm afraid. Did you know Ben Ramsay, Kim's cousin?'

'No, I didn't. I didn't meet the Ramsays.' She took a deep breath. He sensed exasperation and tension. She didn't want him there but she knew she had to look interested.

'He's dead too. Suffocated and his body left in my home. The police are investigating it. I think his death might be connected to Kim's.'

She stroked Rocco's head with gentle, circular movements. The dog shuffled and looked up at her adoringly. 'That's very sad too. Awful for his family.'

'So much sadness at Low Lake. More for Ben than Kim, of course. Not many people there liked her. I've been told some pretty negative things about her.'

Marie's eyes narrowed. 'Really? Well, none of the women in our family are easy to get on with.'

'Your sister said something like that.' He leaned forward confidentially. 'As I said, I'm looking into what happened to Kim. I agree with Jack North. I don't think her drowning was accidental either.'

'Really?'

'Hmm.' He picked up a book and flipped the pages. 'I've heard a lot about you. I wouldn't have had you down as a reader. More of a good-time person, a bit of a social butterfly, someone who moves between men, jobs and addresses.'

'Those books belong to the owner.'

'Oh?' He looked at the cover, and then smiled at her. 'Shall we stop playing games now?'

'Sorry?'

He waved the book. '*Aerial Archaeology.*'

'That's right. The owner's an archaeologist.'

'Amazing. What a coincidence.'

She sat up straighter. The dog growled. 'What is?'

Swift stared at her. She held his gaze for a while before she looked away.

'Come on, you know that I know.'

'Haven't the faintest idea what you're on about.'

'Yes, you have. You see, I got to thinking about how the subject of money cropped up so frequently in this investigation. Women, money and power. Gill never had enough money or thought she didn't, Sadie could throw her weight around because of it, Kim stole it, Elaine Dunbar has grown rich and built a statement house, and Paula Flanders was always looking for ways of making it.'

She shrugged. 'There's nothing wrong with liking and wanting money.'

'Depends on how you come by it.'

'You've lost me.'

'No I haven't. That tent out in the garden at this time of year is a bit of a giveaway, as well as the books. I see you still like sleeping outside, Kim. You know, we could spar for ages but I don't think we want to do that. Elaine's money has bought you a classy flat here in Little Venice. Pete said this was your favourite area of London and that you'd live here if you could ever afford it.'

'I honestly haven't a clue why you're saying this stuff.' She put her hands flat on her thighs. Her nails were short and chewed.

He crossed his legs. 'You should have worked on your accent a bit better. Marie would sound more London Estuary. You've got Oxfordshire refinement after your years away from Tottenham. Pete's living here now, isn't he? I bet alarm bells rang when he came back and told you I'd been asking questions. You told him to leave his job sharpish. I can't imagine why you took up with him again. Your bad medicine. He was two-timing you, seeing a woman at work. Maybe you got lonely, living here alone, not knowing many people in the big city.'

She cleared her throat. 'I don't know what you're talking about.'

'You were a bit careless. You can't afford to be careless if you want to get away with a crime. Paula found a memory stick you'd dropped at her place during one of your visits. True to form, she charged me for it. You'll appreciate that. I read your documents. They were helpful, especially the one about Virgil. It pointed me in the right direction regarding Frynfold.' He gestured at the table. 'I suppose that might even be the same laptop you had back at Low Lake, the one that vanished when you "died," although you've probably traded up now.'

'Sounds fascinating. Whatever you're on about.' She patted the seat beside her, and said, 'Up, Rocco.' The dog jumped up heavily, and draped a gigantic paw across her lap.

'Ben Ramsay is dead because of you. He was asking questions about you. I'm wondering if you saw him off because he was getting too close.'

She put her arm around the dog. 'Now you're away with the fairies.'

'We could keep up the verbal ping pong all day. But it's over, Kim. I can see in your eyes that you know it. I have forensic information from a comparison of your Facebook photo and Marie's, a video Jack had of you and a photo of the woman who died in the lake. Ben took it when he found the body. You know Ben, always carried away in the moment. There are sophisticated body recognition techniques now. They confirm that despite the outward similarities, the body in the lake was Marie's.' What Simone had actually said was: *I'd need more data and time on this. Within the time and content restrictions of the material you've given me, I'm reasonably certain that the body is Marie Piper's.* 'Marie drowned at Low Lake, Kim. Not you.'

Her gaze flickered. 'Complete bollocks. I don't have to talk to you about anything.'

'No. But I think you want to. I know, so very soon the police will know too. Jack will know. How could you do that to him? He's been in mourning for you. His loss has been immense.'

She scowled and compressed her lips, looked down at the dog. Swift saw the brusque, withdrawn Kim that people had described. The frightening Kim. But the mention of Jack had made her hesitate.

He shrugged. 'Okay. I'm going to tell you a story. Bear with me. Indulge me. There are bits only you can fill in and if you want to do that during formal questioning by the police, that's up to you. Let's see. You saw something in the Frynfold records that made you suspect that Elaine Dunbar had made a mint by selling finds, probably coins, from the site. You'd heard people comment on how she'd come up in the world and you realised where the wealth had originated. That disgusted and angered you at first but when you mulled it over you saw it from a different viewpoint, one that would benefit you. You decided you wanted a share of the goods so you blackmailed her. During the weeks when that transaction was getting underway, you met your aunt Marie when she came looking for you in Great Howe. She gave you a letter from your mother, asking you for money. You took to Marie at once, and got to know her better over a couple of months. You looked very alike in build and facial features — so alike you found it weird. You see, your notes were very useful. The police have them now, by the way. You both suffered with the same type of epilepsy. I checked with your mother and she told me that Marie was only three when you were born so there was hardly any age gap.'

Kim's face was stony. 'Great story.'

'It gets better. I don't know when you thought about killing Marie and taking her identity — I guess by the time you got her to dye her hair the same colour as yours. The hair colour was the one obvious difference. By then you were worried about Elaine and what the future looked like. I wouldn't like to cross Elaine. She's powerful and you'd riled her, made an enemy for life. You had the edge on her but maybe you thought you'd have an accident if you stayed around, or that she'd do something to block your career. Compared to you, she's a big cheese in the world of archaeology. It would be better to vanish as a wealthy woman and start over than follow your ambitions. A clean slate. I can see the appeal of that. You had the finances and you could shake off your troubles, including the awful fallout from Nadia Barton's death. Also, you'd met someone. Only you can tell me who that was but it was another incentive and a reason to dump Pete. You could step into Marie's shoes and pursue your studies in London. Elaine would never know you were still around. All problems solved. How am I doing?'

She shrugged. 'You're boring me rigid.'

'Sorry to hear that. I'm almost finished. You lured Marie to Low Lake. I think you used one of Steve's cars to give her a lift to the house. You knew Ben's routines and habits. You knew he'd be on Ape Island that night and that he'd find the body when he rowed back. It was a gamble but people usually see what they expect to see and floating face down, Marie looked enough like you for Ben to assume it was you. It was a risky but clever plan, Kim, and you almost got away with it. If Jack hadn't loved you so much, he wouldn't have hired me and you'd have been home free. You underestimated the power and depth of Jack's love. That's sad for you because I suspect it's the deepest, most genuine love you'll have in your life. It'll be something to think about in prison.'

Kim looked up then, her eyes glittering. Her shoulders relaxed and she breathed deeply, all pretence abandoned. He recognised the signs. She wanted to tell him her story. It might be a relief.

'What do you know about my experience of love? You might be surprised if I told you.' Her voice softened. 'How is little Jack?'

'Not good. Still missing you. He's been finding out things you didn't tell him. You know, about Nadia. When he hears about all of this, he'll be in pieces. He's blamed himself since your apparent death — he felt he didn't offer you enough help. I'm not sure that anyone else missed you much at Low Lake, except Ben. You've been so cruel to him and Jack.'

'Don't talk to me about cruelty,' she snapped at him, and Rocco shifted and growled.

'Oh, I know. You've got the T-shirt. Your mother abused you. You can't dine out on that forever, and it doesn't excuse what you've done. And Ben's dead too because of it. Did you kill Ben?'

'You're the detective. You decide. Maybe Ben intruded on someone else. He could be such a fucking pain in the arse. He lived in la-la land and wasted his life. The hard, real world never affected him.'

'It certainly did when someone suffocated him. They tied a plastic bag around his head and left him to die. They stuffed him in a wardrobe in my house as if he was a bit of garbage. Even a pain in the arse doesn't deserve to die like that.'

She remained impassive. 'Bad shit happens. It happens every day to loads of people. I haven't got any sympathy going spare.'

'No. You keep that all for yourself, don't you? Kim's the only one allowed to be the hard-done-by victim.'

'Yeah, whatever. You don't know anything about me. You have a bit of a mangled story for me, I must say. Some parts are right. Wouldn't you love to know which? Being a detective must be a bit like being an archaeologist. Both professions dig into mysteries. You find random pieces and have to make a jigsaw. You make some discoveries but you can read them in different ways and you might come to wrong conclusions.'

Swift looked at her. 'As you wrote, "Dig deep and deeper still. It's not what you find, it's what you find out."'

'That's right. How flattering to be quoted by you. So you're going to the feds with all this, are you?'

'What do you think?' he said.

'I think you're a self-satisfied prick.'

'Better than being a blackmailer and a murderer.'

Suddenly she yelled, 'Attack!' The Alsatian was on Swift before he could react. It grabbed his left arm in its powerful jaws and bit him through his jacket. Kim then shouted, 'Stop. Guard!' and the dog dropped his arm. It stood in front of Swift, snarling, teeth bared, ears back and tail held high. Swift sat very still. His arm throbbed. There were puncture marks in his jacket, and blood seeped through.

'Don't attempt to move or I'll give him another command. He'll do whatever I say and it will hurt much more,' Kim said.

Swift remembered advice he had been given by a colleague when he joined the Met. *A lot of the low lives we come across have equally nasty dogs. If you get cornered, don't make eye contact or make any sudden movements.* Then she had laughed. *On the other hand, if there's a big stick nearby ram it through the dog's jaws or clobber it and run like hell.* He didn't

285

think the second piece of advice was much use in this situation. He felt dizzy, and breathed deeply. He cradled his damaged arm, avoiding the dog's eyes and trying not to show his fear.

'You must be living in such constant anxiety,' he said. 'Is that why you've trained your dog like this?'

She tossed her hair. 'I've always lived in fear. Of my mother, of my epilepsy, of water, that Gill might get tired of me and hand me back to the state. Then fear of Elaine, although that was pain for gain. I know all about fear. It keeps you in its hold, and whenever you forget about it, it gives you a shake. Can you imagine what that's like? Since I "died" and became Marie, I've felt almost secure for the first time in my life. I've remade myself and I'm in control. Rocco helps me. Woman's best friend and all that.' Rocco made a low noise in his throat when she said his name. 'Good dog, Rocco. Good dog. Sit, stay and guard.' The dog sat, front legs straight, head held high, alert. 'That's it, good boy. How did you find me?'

'Pete dropped a piece of paper at his girlfriend's place. It had this address on it. She's called Melissa, by the way. Stupid mistake but then, I don't think Pete's that bright. Handsome, but not sharp like you. He likes the sound of his own voice too much.'

The hand on her thigh made a fist. 'Fuckwit.'

'He's turned out to be a weak link in your chain. I got to thinking about Pete's timing in leaving his job and his mention of Little Venice. He can't help himself, can he? Likes to tease, to go up to the edge and look over. Thinks he's smarter than everyone else. Then I considered the fact that Marie vanished from Paula's life around the same time that you did. Paula told me that you'd dyed Marie's hair. As you said, fortune favours the brave. You needed to act. Pretending that Marie's body was yours was certainly a bold manoeuvre. I added the rest up and contacted a friend who's in forensics.'

'Such a busy man.'

Swift caught his breath as a stab of pain shot through his arm. 'Doesn't it bother you, living so near water? Being able to see it from the window?'

'I like to keep the enemy in my sights. Near but not near enough to kill me.' Kim stood abruptly. 'You stay where you are. Don't attempt to move. It wouldn't work out well and we haven't finished our chat.'

CHAPTER 16

Kim went to a bookshelf beside the fireplace. She took a long, thin joint from a tin and lit it, inhaled deeply, and then sat down. She had lithe, fluid movements and strong shoulders. She regarded him coolly as the acrid smell of the marijuana snaked through the air.

'Some of what you've said is bollocks. Elaine gave me money rather than be exposed as a thief, but it was Phil who threatened me.'

'How much did she give you?'

'MYOB. Elaine wouldn't get her hands dirty by delivering a threat. She gave Phil his instructions. I didn't think he'd have it in him but he's under Elaine's thumb so I suppose I shouldn't have been surprised. He had a go at me in his car one night after I'd banked the money. Told me if I didn't make myself scarce and clear out of the area, they'd do me damage and I wouldn't see it coming. I knew he meant it and they knew I wasn't going to go public about Elaine and dob myself in at the same time. He gave me a couple of months to sort something out and go away. He said we were to keep everything looking normal, with me carrying on with the museum while I made my arrangements. I didn't know how I was going to manage it. It wasn't easy, working it out. Then I met Marie and was amazed at how similar we were in looks and build. I thought I liked her to start with but then she got round to asking me for loans and I saw how like her sister she was. Flaky and a whinger, on the make and take. They both thought I'd be loaded because I lived in a country house with the Ramsays. I was loaded by then but through my own efforts.'

'If you call blackmail an effort.'

'Believe me, I do. I just woke up one night and saw how I could do it, how I could kill Marie and pass her off as me. She was living hand to mouth, doing drugs, always on the move. People like her go missing all the time and no one notices. They're like leaves you see blowing around the street, piling up in doorways. I'd seen where she was dossing. She was on her own in a skanky squat in Peckham. She didn't have a job or a boyfriend and I reckoned no one would even notice she wasn't around. I knew Paula might start bleating but who was going to pay any attention to her? I was a lot fitter and stronger than Marie and I thought that if I got her by surprise, I could overpower her and push her in the lake, hold her down while she drowned. If I bruised her, that would fit with my history with Pete. I knew that there were enough people in the area who disliked me for the feds not to look any further for my murderer.' She smiled and clicked her fingers in a way that reminded Swift of Ben. 'And yes, it solved a lot of problems in one go. I could cut off all contact with my fucking mother. I *wanted* to be dead to her and it also meant I could take away the one person who had any time for her. Serve her right. I could escape the shitty setup at Low Lake and never have to see them again. I'd loathed it there for years. And I could cut loose from that bloody awful mess about Nadia with her dad giving me the evils every time he saw me.'

'Adela said you could be scary. I should have taken more notice.'

'I can see you've been getting everyone to share their memories of me. What's she up to now?'

'She's set up a carpentry business. She's made her own money and done it honestly.'

'Good for her. She was okay, actually. No bullshit with her.' Kim relit the joint, sucking until she got a satisfactory glow. 'I did a good job of cultivating Marie. Visited her a couple of times in Peckham. Helped myself to her birth certificate, passport and driver's licence. I timed her death for when Gill had her operation and would be out of circulation. I didn't want her nosing around. Valery had done her usual nasty trick of stealing my meds so on the last visit I made to Marie, I nicked her medication. I could use it and it meant she'd be unmedicated, which suited me fine. We were even on the same drugs. Neat.' She took a deep pull on the joint, and murmured with pleasure. 'You needn't look at me like that. Judgemental.'

'At one point, when I was finding out about you, I thought I'd have liked to meet you. I admired how you coped with what life dealt you, including the Ramsays. Now all I feel is disgust. Maybe a trace of pity. You're no better than your mother is. Although you're not a moaner, I'll give you that.'

'I'd be more polite if I was in your position. Rocco might not like to hear me being insulted.' The dog's ears flicked and she laughed. 'Anyway, I might as well finish telling you since you're so riveted. Marie was excited that I was bringing her to Low Lake, somewhere dead posh. I built it up for her, talking about the grounds and how big the house was. Gardeners and boating on the lake. She thought all her Christmases had come at once. She saw herself coming up in the world, latching on to endless freebies. I said that she could meet the family later but first I wanted to show her the summerhouse. I'd given her an outfit of mine — Wrangler jeans and one of my archaeology vests — to make sure the resemblance was as close as possible. She knew the clothes were good quality so I had no trouble getting her to wear them and I played on the "we could almost be sisters" idea. She loved that. I borrowed one of Steve's cars and picked her up from the station. I'd wanted her unmedicated so that she'd be easier to handle, but I didn't know she'd have a seizure, or that she got mouthy before she had one. When we got to the lake she started arguing with me, saying I'd had it easy and I should be kinder to Paula, spend more time with her. That was a laugh.'

'So you *were* having a row with someone.'

'Yeah. That Bailey guy did hear an argument. I cracked my sides laughing when I read that he'd said it was Pete. Then Marie started fitting, which was too good to be true. Made it *so* easy. I grabbed her from behind and pushed her in the lake, the way that bitch Valery did to me once, back in the day. She staggered forwards and fell face down in the water. I didn't even have to hold her down. It was as if she was cooperating with me.'

'There was a major flaw to your plan, surely? It entailed you going into the water.'

'I know. But I had to be brave to get what I wanted. And then I was truly brave. I gritted my teeth and waded in to where she was. I shoved my wallet with my library card in her back pocket, a belt and braces for ID. I did freeze then, standing there with my legs in water, realising that I was in the lake. God, I was fucking scared. I was afraid for a minute that I wouldn't be able to walk back out. But I did. I put one foot in front of the other and I did it. That was an achievement.' She nodded, evidently still thrilled at the memory of her courage.

'If you say so.'

'Oh, I do. Old Virgil said you have to be brave and I was. I waited long enough to make quite sure she was dead. Then I walked to Great Howe and slept in a little copse behind the station for a couple of hours. I caught the early train to London. I'd bought a ticket from the machine and there's no staff there at that hour of the morning. I knew where the CCTV camera was so I avoided it.' She smiled at him. 'Impressed? Not that I give a fuck either way.'

Swift shifted his wounded arm, wincing, keeping an eye on the dog. Rocco's tail swished across the floor and he panted, his breath hot and pungent. The smell and the sight of his huge yellowing teeth made Swift's stomach turn. 'You clearly think you should get a medal. It was a bold plan. But somebody had to identify you. It was Steve. What if he'd realised the body wasn't you?'

She smiled to herself, smoothed her hair back. 'A risk worth taking. Like you said, people see what they expect to see, especially when they're shocked and looking at a corpse. I kept an eye on the news. If the worst happened, well, I had a healthy bank balance, I would have gone abroad. But,' she shrugged, 'everything worked in my favour. About time life handed me a lucky break.'

'So where did you stay in London? In Peckham?'

'Yeah. I stayed in Marie's dive for a night, then got myself some new clothes and booked into a hotel. Then I went flat hunting.'

'Did you have any regrets when you read that Pete had been arrested?'

'God, that was hysterical. I thought he'd got what he deserved. It was good that he sweated a bit.'

'Yet you contacted him?'

She put her head to one side and picked a shred of tobacco from her lip. 'No. That wasn't the plan. Funnily enough, Pete saw me in the street near Paddington when I was out walking Rocco. He told me Jack was causing waves. It was just before you showed up to talk to him. You wouldn't think that you'd just bump into someone in a big city but there we go, paths are sometimes meant to cross. I was fucking furious but what could I do? We talked, something sparked again and I expect my wealth fanned the flames for him. I wasn't going to turn him away now he knew I was still alive. Couldn't afford to. He moved in here the following week. I told him I wasn't going to keep him so he stayed at his job but then you contacted him. I don't give a toss about all the Melissas. Pete's the sort who'll always play away. I can deal with Pete.'

'I can see it would make sense to keep him close by, given what he knows. What's he doing now?'

'Courier work.'

'What happened to the new person in your life? The one you described as being suddenly there? You seemed thrilled by it. You'd fallen in love.'

Kim's voice flattened. 'It didn't work out. When I thought it over, I decided I'd have too much baggage to carry. A tough decision, but best to travel alone. You win some, you lose some.'

'So who was this person who was presumably left grieving for you? Yet another person you deceived and abandoned.'

'No one you'll have come across. None of your business. Not everything is, you know.'

'Doesn't matter. The police will find out. And you're studying?'

'That's right. I took A levels and did some archaeological fieldwork as Marie. I'm living the dream.' She waved her arm. 'I'm well off, own a place I love and I'm going to be an archaeologist. Result!'

'Sorry to mess it up for you.'

'Have you, though? From where I'm sitting, you're the one who looks messy. That bite's nasty. I'd hand you some tissues if I gave a fuck. I've worked hard for what I've got here. I've sweated, put up with years of shite from the Ramsays and then my lovely mother. I'm not letting it slip through my fingers now.'

'I don't think you have much choice, Kim. It's all unravelling.'

'Shut the fuck up, will you? Shut up and let me think.'

She finished the joint, taking one last deep draw, and stubbed it out in a glass ashtray. She got up and stared out at the garden, running her hand along the back of the chaise longue. Swift could sense the dog's eyes, still fixed on him. It was hard not to look at the animal's face, so close to his. Its rank, damp breath was like a creeping mist. His hand was wet with the blood from the wound on his arm and he pressed on it.

'I suppose I could get Rocco to rip your throat out,' Kim said. 'But there would be a terrible mess.'

'It would be hard to conceal and forensics would have a field day.'

Kim seemed about to say something else when she put a hand to her head, shaking it from side to side. She made a strange noise, almost like a high bark. In an instant, she seemed to freeze. She turned pale. Her right leg, then her left jerked and her arms spasmed. Her head rolled and jolted as if she were a marionette being pulled this way and that by strings. The twitching seemed to go on for minutes, and then she became rigid. She stared at Swift and tried to speak but groaned, then fell to the floor and lay still. Rocco turned and looked at her. He barked but didn't budge. Swift was paralysed. He didn't know what to do. If he moved, the dog might attack again. He called Kim's name but she seemed to be unconscious.

Rocco barked again, and raised his haunches. He had swivelled back towards Swift, and was staring up, past him. Swift sensed a movement at his back and turned to look. The blow fell from behind and he slid down the sofa, into unconsciousness.

* * *

Swift came to with a jolt. The cold was intense. His mouth and nostrils were full of water, and he was being dragged down. His limbs wouldn't work and his head was like a rock. It took a split second to realise that he was drowning. He panicked, took in a mouthful of water and thrashed with his legs. He looked upwards, and thought he could see the reflection of streetlights. His lungs were burning. Then he remembered the rule. *Fight your instincts, not the water.* He leaned back, pushed his stomach up and extended his arms and legs. Pain shot through his left arm but he moved his hands and feet and broke through the surface, spluttering and coughing. His chest heaved while he continued to float, gulping air. He turned his head and saw the towpath. It seemed to be rippling, dancing. Was this the Thames? He must have fallen from his boat. Where was it? He kicked his legs but they felt solid in the water. He'd used all his strength. He thought he was moving towards the side but he wasn't sure, and he was so sleepy. His limbs were heavy, like stone. He could feel his body dipping into the water again. He closed his eyes and felt himself drifting, the cold deep in his bones. Now he could breathe it was nice, a floating, peaceful feeling. He just wanted to sleep now, borne on the current. If he could just have a little sleep, he'd be okay . . .

'Hallo! Can you hear me?' A woman's voice. 'Hallo! Seb, get a lifebelt. Get something. Call emergency. Hallo, can you hear me?'

Swift was annoyed. She was making such a racket. He looked towards the voice. The moonlight hurt his eyes. He tried to make a sound but his tongue was in the way. He splashed his right hand in the water. It was *so* annoying. He just wanted to rest.

'The guy's alive!'

There was a loud splash, and then an arm was below his chin, pulling him backwards. A woman was shouting, 'Move your legs! Help me, move your legs!' He tried but he was too tired and numb. He wished this woman would stop fussing. There was panting in his ear, then another splash. A hand lifted his head and rested it on something,

something soft. A pillow. How lovely. He leaned back, eyes so heavy he couldn't open them. He was warm now, just happy to have a nap.

* * *

Swift's chest was burning, as if it was running with hot lava. Sweat was trickling down his back, he had a terrible headache and he thought he might be sick but he also felt elated. He smiled, opened his eyes and blinked in daylight.

'I'm glad you can smile, while I've been sitting here biting my nails,' Mary said, but not unkindly. 'Thank goodness you've woken up.'

He looked at her. She was out of focus. He licked his lips but could find no moisture.

'Here, have some water. And before you ask, you're in hospital. You were fished out of the canal at Little Venice. You ruined a couple's engagement. They'd come all the way from Auckland to do the deed. He'd just proposed to her in the moonlight when she saw you and jumped in to save you.'

He raised his head and drank through a striped candy-pink straw. 'That's a very pretty pink,' he croaked, stirring it around the glass.

'Pretty pink!' Mary snorted. 'Listen to you. You were trying to sing a lullaby a little while ago. Branna should have been here. That's the drug talking.'

'What drug?'

'Someone gave you GHB. I'd have assumed you'd been mixing with suspect company and it was a date rape except that you also have a nasty dog bite on your arm and someone bashed you over the head. I presume you were following enquiries.'

Swift lay back, looked at his left arm and saw that it was bandaged. He touched his head and felt another dressing. His thoughts were hazy but he recalled a large dog and then intense cold. He wanted to tell Mary something important but he couldn't think what it was and he felt deliciously sleepy. He struggled to keep his eyes open.

One clear memory suddenly came to him. 'Kim isn't dead,' he muttered as he drifted away.

When he woke again, the light was brighter. He stared around and closed and opened his eyes a few times, making sense of where he was.

Mary appeared again, unbuttoning her coat. 'Hallo, Mr Battered and Bruised. You've had a lovely drug-induced sleep but it would be good if you could wake up now and tell us what happened.' She leaned forward and kissed him lightly on the forehead. 'First things first. A doctor wants to talk to you.'

'What time is it?'

'Three pm. You were found at eleven thirty last night. See you soon.'

She waved her fingers and slipped away as a tall, cadaverous man who looked like an undertaker swished the curtain around his bed and announced himself. Swift was glad that he hadn't opened his eyes to this mournful-looking gaunt figure.

He examined Swift. 'The dog bite's the nastiest thing. We've stitched it up and we'll have to check it doesn't get infected, especially since the open wound was in canal water. We gave you a tetanus injection and pumped you with antibiotics. Can you tell me your name, date of birth and address?'

Swift told him, and began dredging up memories. His mind was sharper, even though he felt weak and his legs were still heavy. Then it all flooded in, all the details, crystal clear. He could even smell Rocco's breath. 'I need to talk to the police immediately,' he said.

'In a minute.'

'No, right now. It's urgent. Has the GHB worn off?'

'Pretty much. It won't be out of your system completely for another couple of days. You'll sleep a lot and you might well get nausea, hallucinations, sweats. Are you sure you're up to talking to the police? A DI Baptiste has been bothering me.'

'Yes! And right now! Where is Baptiste?'

The doctor looked startled. 'I'll get her. She's down the corridor.'

Mary appeared again as soon as the doctor had hurried away. She put a bottle of fruit juice on the cabinet by his bed and a carrier bag with clothes and shoes in the cupboard. 'I went to yours and got you some clean stuff and a washbag. Ahm . . . I rang Nora to tell her what had happened. I thought I should. She said to wish you better but she was sure Bella would be playing nursemaid and keeping you company. Who's Bella?'

He groaned. 'Doesn't matter. Where's Baptiste?'

'She's on her way so I'm off. I'll call you. Get better.'

She was gone before he could reply. He took a drink of water and DI Baptiste arrived and pulled up a chair. It creaked as she settled her bulk into it.

'Doc says I can have ten minutes max so we'll say twenty. Do you know who did you over?'

Swift gave her an outline of the previous night and Kim's address. The words came slowly. Baptiste immediately called for officers to go to the property, then tucked her phone away and folded her arms, nodding to him. He adjusted his wounded arm against the pillow, wincing.

'I think Pete Hussain hit me. He has a history of drug dealing so I guess there was a stash in the flat. One of them must have given me the GHB to keep me compliant. I don't know how long Kim would have been out of it after her seizure. One or both of them tipped me in the canal. Not a very efficient way of disposing of me.'

'I don't know. You were lucky. If the water hadn't woken you, you might have drowned. You might still have drowned if that couple hadn't been around.'

'If Kim and Hussain know I survived, they'll have gone.'

'Maybe. I'm going to keep that quiet for now. What made you think Kim had set the whole thing up?'

'I got to thinking about the fact that Marie had vanished around the same time as Kim drowned. Kim had commented on how alike she and Marie were. I recalled things that had been said, and then I went back over Kim's documents. I saw Elaine Dunbar and I came away convinced that she'd been selling finds from Frynfold. I suspected that Kim had blackmailed Elaine. Hussain had said that Kim loved Little Venice and strangely enough, his ex-girlfriend thought he'd vanished to an address there. Jack North said that Kim's death might have benefited someone and I got to thinking that it benefited her most of all. It would mean she was financially secure and free of the past. Then Simone compared the photos for me.'

'Did you ask Kim about Ben?'

'She didn't admit to killing him.'

Baptiste rubbed her nose. 'We're interviewing the Dunbars. Elaine's as cool as ice, playing the role of an important person whose time is being wasted by the plods. But we're going through the Frynfold records and her internet history so I think we'll get somewhere with her. Phil Dunbar's DNA was on Ben's jeans and we found traces of Ben's DNA in his car, even though he'd had it cleaned. He's denying murdering Ben. He claims that after Ben visited him at the garden centre he helped him carry some plants he was delivering to his car. He gave Ben a lift into town at the same time. He said that he had his car cleaned because of soil and mud from the plants. It's plausible. We're checking it out. He had a panic attack while we were talking to him so we had to let him go home with medical treatment but we'll have him back in as soon as the doctor says he's fit again.'

'You still don't know what Ben uncovered? I've been trying to work that out. I thought it might be something Phil Dunbar let slip when he went to see him.'

'Dunbar reckons he told Ben he couldn't help him, but I didn't believe him. The man's already wobbling like a jelly so I think we'll make progress once we can get him back in. You're going to be here for a couple of days, I hear. I'll keep you posted. I need Paula Flanders's address just in case her daughter has bolted there.'

'I think that's very unlikely.'

When she'd gone, Swift sat up and put his feet gingerly on the floor. It didn't tilt. He walked slowly to the bathroom. The face in the mirror was blanched, eyes bloodshot, hair tangled and filthy. Not a pretty sight. He smelled of cabbage, or rotting vegetation, courtesy of the canal. He supposed that Kim had thought another drowning, the theme running through her life, would close the circle. He splashed his face with water and cleaned his teeth. The activity made him hot and exhausted. He made his way back to bed, dizzy now, walking close to the wall. He found his mobile phone in his cabinet and rang Ruth, leaving a message to tell her what had happened and that he was okay. Then he dialled Jack North. He wanted to get to him before the police or the Ramsays did. The man was going to be shattered. North's voicemail clicked in. Swift left a message asking him to call, and then slid onto his pillow and back into sleep.

* * *

When Swift woke, it was dark and his skin was burning. He knew he was going to be sick and just managed to get to the bathroom where he retched for several minutes, clinging to a washbasin. His stomach was empty. When he straightened up, the room began to spin. He closed his eyes and waited until he thought he could make it back to bed. Just as he was moving to the door, his abdomen churned and he had to get to the toilet. Five minutes later, he dragged himself back to the ward. He had never felt so empty, dry and hot. He rang for a nurse and explained.

'Let's take your temperature,' he said, shaking a thermometer. When he read it, he nodded. 'It's forty centigrade. You have a fever all right. I'll call a doctor.'

The same cadaverous man who had seen him previously appeared and decided to run various tests.

'It's not still the GHB causing this, surely?' Swift croaked.

'No. We need to wait for the results of the tests, but given that you swallowed water in the canal and your symptoms, I suspect cryptosporidium. It's a parasitic infection. Drink lots of water and we'll give you something to lower your temperature. I'm going to get you moved to a side ward and ask visitors to stay away for now, until we know what this is. Cryptosporidium is highly contagious.'

Swift's heart sank. He knew several rowers who had been unfortunate enough to catch the infection when they had capsized. There was no quick fix.

He spent a restless night, punctuated by vomiting, stomach cramps and diarrhoea. His arm and head throbbed. He was too hot to get comfortable and drifted in and out of a feverish doze. He longed to be at home, lying down on the cool bathroom floor by an open window. He had wild nightmares in which he and Kim were struggling in water. She was strangling him with her hair and trying to push him under. Rocco was riding on her back, barking at him as he tried to fight her off.

Dawn finally broke, and he drank a glass of water, his hand trembling. He was given more medication. He slept again and when he woke, he felt a little less hot. He lay ordering his thoughts, trying to remember the events that had brought him to hospital. He replayed the scene with Kim, going over her version of how she had faked her own death. He thought that she had seemed too glib at times, and something about the conversation niggled at him. But another urgent trip to the bathroom interrupted his reflections.

Towards late afternoon, a different doctor appeared and confirmed that he did indeed have cryptosporidium.

'We'll start you on an anti-parasitic drug now. It will alleviate your symptoms and it attacks the metabolic processes of the parasite.'

'How long will this last?'

She tapped a pen against her chin. 'Well, you're otherwise fit and healthy so you should recover in about a fortnight. There's no hard and fast rule about this so you need to take it easy, especially as you've also had a head wound and a nasty bite.'

'When can I go home?'

'We'd like you to stay for another twenty-four hours. Then you can go home with medication. You don't have to isolate yourself but wash your hands a lot and don't prepare food for other people unless you absolutely have to.'

'Can I see my daughter? She's one and a half.'

'You're not the main caregiver?'

'No. She lives with her mother.'

'Well, it's up to you, but I'd leave it a couple of weeks just to be on the safe side.'

When she had gone, he checked his phone and saw missed calls from Jack North, Mary and Ruth. North had left a message, saying that DI Baptiste had spoken to him and told him that Kim was alive. Sounding subdued, he wished Swift a speedy recovery and rang off abruptly. Swift texted Mary and Ruth to tell them his diagnosis, adding not to visit and that he'd be in touch once he was home. He rang North and caught him as he was leaving the surgery. He was walking along outside somewhere, and Swift heard the hum of traffic and squeal of brakes in the background.

'Are you okay?' North asked. He sounded strained, his voice tight.

'Sort of. I've got an infection from the canal water.'

'Cryptosporidium?'

'That's right.'

'I've treated quite a few dogs who've picked it up when they've been swimming in rivers.'

'Don't mention dogs to me. I'm sorry I couldn't tell you about Kim myself. It must have been a terrible shock.'

'Yeah. I didn't want to go to work but Bella persuaded me to. I'm glad she did. I'd only have been going over it in my head all the time if I'd stayed at home. I don't think it's really sunk in yet. I feel sort of dazed. The best friend I've ever had killed her aunt and tried to kill you. How did she become that person?'

'I could hazard some guesses but I'm not sure there's much point.'

'She didn't care that much about me. I got that all wrong. She was happy to just write me out of her life when it suited her.'

'I think she did care, Jack. Remember what she wrote about you. When I saw her, the only time she softened was when she asked about you. I'd say that she misses you but she'd chosen a path that there was no going back from.'

'Right. Whatever. *I* don't care anymore now.'

Swift knew that North's problem was that he did care, very much. The pain would never leave him, just fade a little with time. 'Have you heard anything else from the police?'

'There's no sign of Kim or Pete Hussain at the house in Little Venice. DI Baptiste asked me if I could think of anywhere Kim might hide out. I couldn't think of anywhere apart from the grounds around Low Lake, and she's not likely to have gone there. I'm at the Tube station now, the signal will go. I'll talk to you soon. Look after yourself. Bella sends her love.'

'You too. And thank Bella.'

He slept deeply, disturbed only once with stomach cramps, and woke at seven the following morning. His temperature had dropped, his head was clear and when he went to the bathroom, the image in the mirror was slightly less frightening. He washed but decided he didn't have the energy to shave. He touched the dressing on his arm and flinched, recalling Rocco's jaws and Kim's practised control of the dog.

He rested against the cold porcelain of the sink, going over their meeting from start to end, his tired brain chasing connections. He remembered Kim's face when she described how she had carried out her plan, and the moment when she'd laughed to herself. She'd told him he only had parts of the story correct. He had missed something, he knew, mistaken something he had found out. There were words that hadn't rung true. It was bothering him. He needed to go back to Kim's commentary.

He sat on the edge of his bed, drinking water and flexing his leg muscles, and opened his email folder with Kim's documents, clicking on AFI. He scrolled through until he came to the paragraph he wanted.

Isn't it odd that someone can be around for years and suddenly it's as if you never really saw them before? Then one day you look and they look and wow! Big explosion. Love has hit me over the head. Amazing and terrifying and wonderful.

He juggled thoughts and the echoes of Kim's flat voice. While Rocco stood guard over him, she had smiled and said that he might be surprised if he knew her experience of love. In his brain the cogs slowly wheeled and one clicked softly into place. He suspected that he did know who it was, that person she had looked at and who had returned her gaze. When he'd pressed her, she'd become vague and casually dismissive. Too casual. Would Kim really have abandoned someone she had found amazing? Wouldn't she have wanted this overwhelming, wonderful relationship to be part of her new life? A woman who'd found love for the first time would hardly throw it away so easily. At long last, she'd have felt wanted, cherished. She'd value it, knowing it wasn't easily come by.

He didn't buy that she'd got back together with Pete Hussain, a man who had abused her. He might have come across her in the street but that wouldn't mean she would make room for him again, not in her new life. She was so much brighter than him. She aspired to a college degree and a professional career. Would she have wanted that limited, aggressive, drug-dealing man at her side, reminding her of damage and cruelty? Swift found it hard to believe. And if Hussain wasn't with her, where was he? When it came down to it, Swift couldn't find that many candidates for Kim's amazing, big explosion. She'd said that he wouldn't have come across this person, but he didn't believe her. From what he'd learned of her life, she had socialised only around Great Howe and he was sure he'd met all the people she regularly interacted with. This lover's proximity would explain the absence of emails, texts or calls. They wouldn't have been needed.

Kim had been protecting the last of her secrets. He thought he might know where to look. If he was right, then he had to hand it to her, she was an even shrewder strategist than he'd imagined.

He took a breath and reached for his clothes, glad that Mary had brought a large sweatshirt that was easy to put on. He went to the nurses' station and after a brief argument with a tired doctor, he signed a form saying that he was discharging himself. An hour later, he was in a taxi with boxes of medication, giving the driver an address in Islington.

CHAPTER 17

At Steve Ramsay's home, the garage doors were locked. Swift rang the bell and a tall young man answered. He had a prominent nose, shoulder-length hair and John Lennon style glasses. He seemed alarmed and Swift realised he must look disreputable, with his unshaven face, strange smell, crusted hair, bandages, bloodshot eyes and general air of having been knocked about.

Swift attempted a smile. 'Hi, I'm looking for Steve Ramsay.'

'He's not here at the moment.'

'Are you expecting him?'

'Not particularly. Any reason why I should be?' The man looked puzzled.

'He does live here?'

'Steve? No. What gave you that idea?'

'I had this as his address.'

'Well, you've been misinformed.'

Swift reached for his ID and held it out. 'I'm Tyrone Swift, a private investigator looking into a death. Do you mind if I come in for a minute? I've just left hospital after being attacked and I wouldn't mind sitting down. It's urgent that I find Steve.'

The man pushed his glasses up, examined the ID, and then nodded. He led him into a living room decorated in grey and silver, with black leather furniture. The walls were covered with photos and posters of vintage cars, and car magazines were stacked on a long chrome coffee table.

'Have a seat. You look done in.'

'Thanks. I've been better. Could I have a glass of water?'

'Sure. I've just made coffee if you want one.'

'Just water, thanks.'

'Won't be a minute.' He paused at the door. 'I'm Nat, Nat Carlton. I own this house.'

Swift closed his eyes, weary again. He'd walked so easily into Steve and Kim's trap. He needed to concentrate. Carlton brought in a glass of water and a mug of coffee for himself. Swift drank half the water and took a tablet.

'Steve Ramsay gave this address to his family in Oxfordshire. They think he lives here. I came here to see him not long ago about an enquiry. He said that this was his house and he lived here with his girlfriend, Kirsty. He was working on a Porsche in the garage so I didn't enter the house.'

Carlton scratched his head. 'Steve's never lived here, and I've never heard of a Kirsty. He works on cars for me sometimes when I need him. I'm away a lot. Aside from my business, my mum's in Sussex and quite frail so I spend as much time as I can with her. There's a key in a key safe by the side of the garage so that Steve can come in and make a drink, use the loo. He's stayed the odd night when he wanted to complete work the following day. I haven't seen him since he finished the Porsche.'

'How do you know him?'

'I trade vintage cars. I buy them, do them up and then sell them on. We met a couple of years ago at a car auction in Northamptonshire and got friendly over an Alfa

Romeo. Then we kept meeting up at auctions and car shows. We both know a lot about cars and give each other the heads-up on stuff coming on the market. I'm a pretty good mechanic but Steve's got expertise I lack. He's really skilled with gearboxes, so now and again he helps me out. We've actually bought one or two cars together — a Mercedes and a Ferrari — and split the profits when we turned them around. I thought Steve still lived in Oxfordshire. That's why I said it was okay if he took the spare room when he needed it. He told me he has his own garage at home.' He put his coffee down, looking worried. 'What's this all about?'

'I'm not sure. Steve clearly didn't want his family to know where he was living. I think he's been staying in Little Venice.'

Carlton frowned. 'Little Venice? How could he afford to live around there? I mean, he told me he did okay out of his cars but he wasn't in the big league. Neither of us is.'

'I think he has a wealthy girlfriend.'

'Really? He's never mentioned anyone. We tend to talk cars mainly, but I thought he'd have said something. Why would he lie to me?'

'That's a good question. Here's my card. If he contacts you or turns up, could you ring me straight away without letting him know? He might be involved in a crime.' *Like hitting me over the head and throwing me in a canal.*

'What kind of crime? Car related?'

'No. Not that simple. Thanks for the water. I'll just call a cab. Make sure you wash that glass thoroughly, I have a parasitic infection.'

Carlton looked concerned. 'You look terribly pale, like you should be in bed.'

Swift nodded and rang for a cab, thinking he'd be happy to take some bed rest once this case was resolved. He felt as if he could sleep for a month.

Looking bemused, Carlton showed him to the door and watched while Swift got into the taxi and gave his home address. He sank back against the seat and closed his eyes for a few minutes. He felt hot again. He rang Steve Ramsay's number, to see if he'd pick up. If Ramsay answered, he'd end the call. The number was unobtainable. He phoned DI Baptiste.

'I think it was Steve Ramsay who hit me and threw me in the canal, not Pete Hussain.'

'Hang on, let me close a door.' There was a thud, and then she was back. 'What are you talking about? Aren't you in hospital?'

'I discharged myself. Any news of Kim?'

'No one at the house. No dog. There are signs that they packed hastily. We're still doing a thorough search. We found a collection of mobiles with no SIM cards. No one in the street has seen Kim, but then it's not exactly the kind of place where people mingle. She hasn't turned up at Low Lake. She's just started an archaeology degree at University College and hasn't attended any lectures in the last few days. We went to her mother's and to Hussain's old address in Bow but they haven't seen her. We were just about to check with Adela Janssens and Steve Ramsay. What do you mean about him?'

'You can forget going to his address. I've just been there. He's been lying, it isn't his house. I met the guy who owns it, a Nat Carlton. Ramsay just stays there now and again.' He explained his previous visit to Steve and his reasoning, referring to Kim's commentary. 'I think she meant that she and Steve had suddenly fallen for each other. They had lived in the same house all those years and one day, something clicked. They fell in love. That's why she dumped Hussain. Steve identified Marie Piper's body as Kim's. He was in on the plan, her rock-solid guarantee. He left Low Lake six months after Kim was supposed to have died. He invented a girlfriend, gave his family a false address and moved in with Kim. Now his phone isn't working. It adds up.'

'Well, I could see that she's had a bloke there from some of the stuff in the bathroom but we couldn't find anything to identify him. So what about Hussain?'

'I'd dredge the canal. It seems to be their preferred method of trying to dispose of unwanted guests. I think Kim told me the truth when she said that Hussain saw her near Paddington. But that was the only true part. She must have been beside herself when he tripped over her, but she's a quick thinker. She decided to give him the idea that she was still interested in him and lured him to Little Venice with the promise of a rich lifestyle. Then she and Ramsay got rid of him. They'd have seen no other way of dealing with him once he knew their secret. Hussain dealt in drugs. I expect the GHB they used on me was from his supply.'

DI Baptiste sighed. 'I don't know. I suppose it's possible.'

'Come on, yet another person who suddenly disappears and doesn't answer phone calls. Dredge the canal. Have you got any further with the Dunbars?'

'Phil Dunbar's story checks out so far. Elaine's still playing the queen of cool. I'm waiting for information from her computer. Lots of stuff has been deleted but I'm hoping the nerds can retrieve it. But she was in meetings in Oxford when Ben disappeared, so she's got a watertight alibi. I'm waiting to talk to a Claire Beeston, who's a cleaner at the museum. She's just got back from a holiday in Tenerife and rang this morning. She says she spoke to Ben just before he went off the radar. I have to go. Do yourself a favour and get your head down, Swift. Take your medication.'

* * *

When he reached home, Swift lay down on the living-room sofa and woke four hours later with a dry mouth. His arm was stiff and achy and he was shivery. He drank a glass of water and took his antibiotics, listening to his stomach gurgling. At least the vomiting and diarrhoea had stopped. He couldn't remember when he had last eaten. A nurse had advised him to eat sparingly and avoid anything spicy. He had half a banana. When nothing terrible happened, he ate the other half.

He saw that his answer phone light was blinking and listened to the message from Joyce.

'Ty, my dear, I heard that you've been in hospital. You should have told me. I'd have come to see you straight away. It does worry me so when you're injured. I do wish you wouldn't be so secretive but I know it's your way. I hope you're all right. I wondered if you and Nora would like to come round for dinner soon. Ring me when you get this.'

He wondered how Joyce had found out about the hospital. She had an unnerving way of tracking what was happening in his life. He didn't feel up to talking to her and answering lots of personal questions. He deleted the message. He checked the waterproof dressing on his arm and stood under a hot shower. He leaned against the tiles and turned his face up to the water, thinking of Kim, who always turned her back in the shower. He knew so many things about her but he had no idea where she might have run to. Perhaps she and Steve had already left the country, but he didn't think that was the case. He guessed they would be in shock. Kim must have been stunned when he turned up and identified her. First Pete Hussain, and then him, just as things were going so well. She had started a degree course, on the path to realising her long-held ambition. She would know now that that wasn't going to happen. With all her plans shattered, she'd need time to regroup. Perhaps in the end she was very like her mother, persuading herself that she was hard done by, justified in whatever she did to shore up her own selfish desires.

The police had given him details of the woman who had saved him from the canal. He ordered flowers and a thank you note to be delivered to her at her hotel. Then he had a Skype call with Ruth and Branna. He longed to hold his daughter but told Ruth that he didn't want to risk making her ill. He could see the expression on Ruth's face when he told her about the dog attack and being fished from the canal.

'I've said it before, Ty. I hate the job you do, the life it makes you live.'

He didn't respond. He was too tired to start defending himself. Detective work could be dangerous. So was firefighting and he knew medical staff in hospitals who'd been attacked by drunks and drug abusers. He chatted to Branna, then slept again.

When he woke, he could feel his strength returning. He took some chicken soup from the freezer and had a bowl with toast. His stomach had settled into the odd cramp and groan. As he ate, he went back over his notes on the investigation and returned to Kim's documents but could find nothing to help him. Where could Kim and Steve have gone? He was finishing his food when Nora rang.

'I called the hospital but they said you'd discharged yourself. How are you doing?' She sounded polite, distant.

'So-so. I needed to follow up a lead and I'm glad I did. It was fruitful.'

'Right. I admire your persistence, but don't run yourself into the ground.'

'Is that the advice you'd give yourself?'

'Probably not. How long does cryptosporidium last?'

'Maybe two weeks. The medication should get rid of it by then. I'm able to eat now, which is something at least.' He took a breath. 'You know, you did get the wrong impression about Bella. I wouldn't do that to you. She's a friend and she'd done some research for me on the case.'

'Okay. Maybe I was a bit hasty. But you know, Ty, I was dumped not that long ago by a man I trusted. It still hurts. It's hard to rely on someone again after that happens and I thought you'd be honest with me.'

'I have been. I am being. I'm only involved with Bella as a friend. That's all.'

'Okay. Let's draw a line then.'

He sighed with relief. 'It's your birthday at the end of the week. I don't think I'll be up to baking a cake but I would like to give you your present.'

'Okay, that sounds good. See how you are, though, and let me know.' Her voice softened, became hesitant. 'I'm sorry about what's happened. Sorry we fell out. I know this isn't a good time to talk. We should wait until you're better.'

'Okay. I'm sorry too. I'll call you.'

Too tired to clear up, he fell into bed in the early evening and didn't wake until his phone rang. He reached for it, and saw that dawn was creeping in, just after six am.

'Mr Swift? This is Nat, Nat Carlton.'

'Hi, yes.'

'I'm sorry to call so early but I couldn't sleep and it seemed a bit early to ring the police with something that might not be important. Look, I've no idea if this is relevant but I've been worrying about Steve. I really like the guy and obviously, I thought he was okay. He's always seemed decent, honest. But the police called yesterday. He seems to be mixed up in something awful.'

'Yes, I think he is. Have you got some information?'

'I'm not sure. I've been awake half the night, thinking about the auctions we met at. There was one near Colchester a few years ago. Steve had been to it quite a few times. I remember that he brought a tent and was camping near a small village called Thorpe Langham. It was bad weather and I asked him why he didn't book a bed and breakfast. He said he was trying to save money and he knew the guy who owned the land from a previous car deal. You get to know people when you travel around the auctions. The guy let him camp there for free whenever he wanted. Steve said it was a beautiful, peaceful spot and he liked the sound of rain on a tent.'

Swift gripped his phone. Kim also liked sleeping outside, under the open sky. She'd even erected a tent in her London garden.

'Have you any idea where this place is?'

'I've been up since four, going through my accounts. I bought a Jensen Interceptor from the guy who owns the land and I found my record of the transaction. His name's Doug Grant, and he owns a farm called Brantham End. I've no idea if that's any help.'

'It might be.' Swift grabbed a pen, made a note and thanked Carlton, who sounded half asleep. While he made coffee, he googled Brantham End. It was in Suffolk, about ten miles north of Colchester. Most of the route was on the motorway, and he reckoned that if he left immediately, he could get there in under two hours. He splashed his face with water, dressed and grabbed a croissant to eat in the car.

Just as he was leaving the kitchen, he recalled Rocco's hefty jaws and reached into the cupboard for a pack of ground pepper, tucking it into his pocket.

* * *

Once he was on the M25, he debated whether to ring DI Baptiste. He decided to wait until he'd established whether there was any sign of Steve and Kim at the farm. The motorway was already busy but the traffic was flowing. The day was dry, crisp and unseasonably warm with high, pale clouds. As he left the motorway and drove into Suffolk, the air cooled a little and the flat ploughed fields stretched away to the horizon. The wound on his arm pulled and hurt whenever he changed gear. He recalled the calm, controlled way that Kim had set the dog on him. He wanted to be the one who found her, the one who ensured that she would pay for disposing of people to get what she wanted, and for breaking Jack's trust.

Brantham End was situated along a road framed by dense hedges, oak and beech trees. The farmhouse was half timbered, with plasterwork painted a dull ochre. The sign inside the gate informed Swift that it was a rare breeds farm, specialising in Norfolk Horn sheep, White Park cows and Berkshire pigs. There was also a farm shop selling free-range meat, organic vegetables and honey and there was a small animals enclosure for children to visit. Simone would approve. He drove towards the house and pulled up near a woman wearing a quilted jacket and bright purple wellingtons etched with pink flowers. She was scattering food to a noisy group of young piglets in a pen.

'Farm shop's not open yet.' She spoke through a heavy cold as he got out of the car.

'I'm here on a personal matter. Is Mr Grant in?'

'Doug? No, he's away this week, buying stock. I'm his sister. Can I help you?' Her nose was pink and raw-looking and her words were interspersed with sniffs.

'I hope so. I'm looking for a friend, Steve Ramsay. We think he might be camping somewhere on the farm. We know he has in the past. There's been a family emergency and Steve left his phone at home so we can't reach him.'

'Oh dear. Is someone ill?'

'Yes, very ill, I'm afraid. Do you know Steve?'

'Not that well — he's Doug's friend. But yes, I know him. When he camps, he comes to us to buy milk and food. He says ours is the best steak he's eaten and this is the most peaceful place he's ever stayed. He's a considerate man and careful about the countryside so we're happy to let him use our land occasionally. You wouldn't know he's been here after he leaves. I haven't seen him recently, though. I don't think he can be here.'

The piglets were squealing and knocking each other out of the way, annoyed that their food had stopped coming. A couple were attempting to stand on the backs of their siblings, as if they were practising an acrobatics act.

'He might have only just arrived. Could you tell me where I'd find him if he's here? Would that be okay? It is a matter of urgency.'

'Of course, no problem.' She turned to the piglets and threw them a handful of pellets. 'Oh, do shut up, you lot!'

'They're like a bunch of noisy kids in a playground.'

'Tell me about it. They drive me crazy some days with their squabbling and noise. A couple of them are real mischief-makers. Sometimes I wish I could hand out detentions!' She took a hanky from her pocket and blew her nose. 'Sorry, I'm rambling on and you said it's urgent. If you go back to the entrance and turn left, you'll see a layby after about half a mile and a gate set back from the road. There's a patch of woodland in there. It's an ancient broadleaf wood so we're preserving it. We keep the area wild. That's where Steve pitches his tent. Sometimes we let pigs roam in there to forage but there aren't any there at the moment. If Steve's there, tell him to call by.'

'I will. Thanks. Sorry to have disturbed you.'

She waved, and scolded the piglets in the tone of a long-suffering mother. Swift turned the car and followed the road, slowing when he spotted the layby. He could see no sign of a car. If Ramsay and Kim were here, they must have parked somewhere else or come by public transport. He pulled in just past the layby and closed the car door quietly. There was no other traffic. The only sound was the rustling of red and gold leaves and the creak of tree branches. A couple of squirrels were bustling about at the base of a huge horse-chestnut tree. They darted away when they saw him.

He found the gate and climbed over, stepping into soft leaf mould. There was no path, just spaces between the hazel, ash and sycamores. The air was damp and smelled of moss and rotting vegetation. He opened the pepper in his pocket and kept one hand on it, stepping lightly, listening out for Rocco. He passed a fallen tree trunk, its decaying bark covered in huge alien-looking speckled cream and mud-brown fungi. A sudden rustling made him stop in his tracks. A small roe deer appeared, as startled as he was, and vanished as suddenly as it had arrived.

He went deeper into the trees, stopping often to listen. Nothing. He had misjudged. The birds hadn't flown to Suffolk. He felt feverish again: his temperature was back. He wiped his brow and leaned against a lichen-covered beech. Then he heard the sound, a muted sob. It seemed that someone was crying. He followed the faint sighs of distress, placing his feet carefully, and then saw the pale blue dome of a tent, glimmering in the half-light. He decided that Rocco couldn't be here or he'd have barked by now. He retraced his steps, stood behind a broad tree trunk and called DI Baptiste. When she answered he whispered that he was sure he'd found Steve and Kim, and gave her details of where to find the farm.

'Don't approach any nearer,' she said. 'Stay where you are and leave this to us. I'll get onto the local force now.'

Swift rang off. He hadn't come this far just to stand back and hand over to the police. He switched his phone to mute and went back through the trees until he could see the tent again. Now he heard rustling and murmuring. He crept forward, closer to the small clearing. The tent flap was open, and Swift could see sleeping bags, a Primus stove, and a large plastic container of water.

Steve Ramsay was kneeling on the ground with his back to him, swaying backwards and forwards. As Swift edged nearer, he saw Kim lying in front of him, arms by her sides, eyes closed. Her face was pale and still. Ramsay was taking flowers and berries from a small pile beside him and gently placing them around her head and on her body, and twining them through her dark hair. He set out tiny violet flowers, sprigs of golden yellow honeysuckle, branches of dark green ivy and clusters of scarlet rosehips and berries. Then he placed two pale golden leaves over her eyes. It looked like a pagan ritual. Swift was reminded of Ben's photo of 'Kim's' body, framed with flowers and hearts. Ramsay sighed and rocked, whispering softly.

Swift circled him quietly and stepped out facing him. Ramsay looked up. His face was crumpled and tear-stained. He stared at Swift, then closed his eyes for a moment and gave a defeated shrug.

'Oh, it's you.'

'It's me. Fresh from the canal and worse for wear. What's happened here?'

Ramsay didn't reply. He took Kim's hands, placed them over her chest and tucked a spray of honeysuckle beneath them. He shuffled on his knees and stroked the ends of her hair, murmuring to her.

'Steve, what's happened?'

'You. You ruined everything. You and the midget. Why couldn't you leave well alone?'

'What happened to Kim?'

'Nothing. Everything. Kim died.'

'How?' But Swift thought he knew.

Ramsay ran a finger across her lips, bent and kissed her forehead. 'Seizures. She's had four in the last few days. Then, a couple of hours ago, she had one after another. We were having a stupid argument about where to go next. Nothing I could do. I just held her.' He started sobbing. 'She ran out of her bloody medication. Why did she let that happen? Why?'

Swift stepped nearer. 'I don't know.'

'No. No one knows. Sometimes I think . . . I think she had a death wish. Well, doesn't matter now.'

'You should be more careful with words. You suggested that Kim might have been suicidal when I visited you in Islington. You thought you were blowing smoke in my eyes but maybe there was a kernel of truth in there.' He looked around. 'Where's Rocco?'

'In kennels.' Ramsay took Kim's hands gently and rubbed them. 'Stupid, but I don't want her to get cold. You know?'

'Yes, I know. She looks peaceful.' *Unlike her victims.*

'Doesn't she? My Kim. My lovely Kim.'

318

'Steve, where's Pete Hussain?'

'Dead and gone. Where he belongs.'

'Like I should have been?'

'You shouldn't have come poking your nose in. I thought I'd got rid of you at the garage.'

'You're a good liar. You had me fooled for a while. You even threw in that detail about Kim borrowing your car. I reckon she tutored you well.'

'I couldn't believe it when I came home and saw you. I had to do something. Kim was out of it that night. Fucking epilepsy. Blighted her life. I had to decide. Protect her.'

'When did you and Kim fall in love?'

At this, a shadow of a smile crossed Ramsay's face. He cupped her chin carefully in his hand. 'She came into the garage at Low Lake one morning, the February before she faked her death. Trying to persuade me to lend her a motor. She pushed the cuff of her shirt up and I saw that she had a nasty dark bruise on her wrist. I asked her about it and she said that bastard Hussain had done it. I don't know what happened, but something about that bruise just suddenly hit me. I looked at her, into her eyes, and everything changed. Like in chemistry, you know, when two elements combine. I touched the bruise and then I kissed it. Kissed her. I'd never been in love before. Sometimes I thought I wasn't capable of feeling it. But then . . . It was magical. As if I'd been carrying ice in my heart and it melted away. Suddenly, everything fell into place and made sense. Life made sense for the first time. It was the same for her. Maybe I'd always loved Kim and just didn't know it. That's what she said. We just wanted to be together then.' He gave a low sigh. 'All those years I ignored her, thought she was a nuisance, wished her gone. Why was I so blind? All that wasted time. I wish I could turn back the clock. I could have looked after her, kept her safe, made her happy.'

'I doubt that. I think Kim was too troubled. How did you keep your relationship a secret?'

He wiped at his eyes. 'It was hard, but we didn't want people nosing around us, making comments, or Gill finding out and latching onto us, or any of Sadie's cutting remarks. There was so much to deal with. Kim had just found out about Elaine, what she'd been up to. Hussain kept hanging around. She needed to get rid of him, the bastard, turning up like a bad smell. He got what was coming to him. We used to meet at the museum. Kim had a key. That's where she told me about Elaine, the coins, and Phil's threats. About her mum and Marie. How she could take Marie's identity and then we could shake them all off. We thought it all through, and reckoned it could work. I was scared for her, being by the water with Marie. I worried that she might panic. I wanted to be there, to help her, but she insisted I should make sure to be away from home. She didn't want any chance of me becoming a suspect. My job was to be the one who identified her body. That would be the clincher. We both hated Low Lake, and it was a way to escape the place, once and for all. Our chance to set ourselves up, make a future.'

Swift shook his head. 'A future built on the backs of other people, their deaths. Did you or Kim kill Ben?'

Ramsay bent down and kissed her hands. 'No. I don't know who killed Ben. If I knew who did, I'd have gone after them myself. That's disgusting, what was done to him. He was a fucking idiot and looking for trouble, but he never harmed anyone. He always meant well.' He shook his head, and began to sob. 'Stop asking questions. I can't . . . It's all pointless. She's gone. Everything's pointless now.'

'Poor you. Time to stop feeling sorry for yourself, Steve. This big love story of yours has caused a trail of damage. It's pointless, true — for Marie, Ben and Pete and it could have been for me. How many more people would the two of you have been willing to get rid of for this sunny future of yours?'

'Nothing you say can touch me now. I just want to die. I just want to lie down beside her and die. At least she died out under the sky. I don't want anyone touching her, disturbing her. I'm going to get a shovel and bury her here, in the woods. Then she'll be completely peaceful. No one will disturb her.' He pulled more leaves and mulch in around her head, a soft, decaying pillow. 'It was going so well, so sweet. We were so happy together in our flat. Now it's all gone. I'm sorry, Kim. So sorry. I should have looked after you better. I left it all too late and now you've left me.' He started whispering to her again, bent low over her body.

Swift thought he could detect footsteps, soft and careful, approaching through the trees. He stepped back, watching Ramsay, who was rearranging foliage and berries. Then he stiffened, and his head went up. A branch cracked. He looked at Swift, understanding dawning in his eyes. His ravaged face became a sudden mask of anger.

'You bastard. You sneaky bastard. You've been spinning me. Kim said you were a fucking blight. I should have made sure I finished you off last time.'

He sprang up and paced, casting around. He snatched a hefty, thick length of wood from the ground and rushed forward. Swift backed away and dodged, knowing he didn't stand much chance of defending himself with his injured arm. He aimed for the cover of a sturdy tree, but tripped on a thick root and fell. He rolled and put up his good arm to defend himself as Ramsay, breathing harshly, hoisted the wood in both arms and swung the splintered end towards him. It glanced off his upper arm with a heavy thud, sending a sharp pain through his torso. Ramsay stumbled, off balance. Swift rolled again, groaning in pain. Ramsay recovered and took another swing. This time Swift managed to twist out of the way and the wood smacked against the ground. Ramsay swore and hoisted it up to hit him again. Swift reached clumsily in his pocket for the pepper. Ramsay came at him. Swift dragged himself onto one knee and threw it in his face. Ramsay screamed and fell back, clutching at his eyes. Swift got to his feet and staggered back against a tree for support while Ramsay clawed his face and cried out for help.

The clearing was suddenly full of uniforms and shouts of 'Police! Police!' A radio crackled. Ramsay was face down on the ground, his arms behind his back, in handcuffs.

'Water! Pour water on his eyes, I threw pepper at him,' Swift shouted to a constable.

Even while they sat him up and the water was washing his eyes, Ramsay was yelling, 'Don't touch Kim! Don't touch her! Leave her alone! Leave her!'

Swift sat on a tree stump and watched him being taken away, howling and sobbing. A couple of constables secured the tent. Swift eased his jacket off, wincing, and opened his shirt to check his bitten arm. The dressing was still in place and there was no sign of blood. A massive red bruise was blooming on the other arm where Ramsay had struck him.

'You okay? You need anything?' a constable asked.

'An ice pack would be handy.'

'Sorry, don't carry those. But we've called paramedics for Ramsay, because of the pepper. You should let one of them check you.'

'Okay. I'm not rushing off.'

Both his arms were throbbing — a matching pair, and he was burning up again but he didn't care. He'd done what he'd come to do. A shaft of noon sun was slanting through the trees. It touched Kim's face. Some of the flowers had fallen from her body but her hands still held a spray of honeysuckle.

CHAPTER 18

A couple of evenings later, Jack North and Bella sat with Swift in his living room. It had turned cold with a brisk east wind and bursts of fine sleet. He'd lit a fire, the first of the season, and it crackled and hummed in the grate.

He was stretched out on the sofa. His temperature was back to normal but he still felt tired. The red bruise on his arm was slowly turning purple. Luckily, the stitches in the bite wound had survived his encounter with Ramsay.

North had been crying again. Swift reflected that he'd never seen Kim shed a tear.

'I don't think I'll go to Kim's second funeral,' North said. 'I couldn't bear it.'

Bella touched his hand. 'Don't, Jack. Don't put yourself through that. She doesn't deserve your pity or regrets after what she did to you and Marie. And to Ty.' She looked at Swift. 'Has Steve told the police anything more?'

'Apparently, unlike Elaine Dunbar, Steve couldn't stop talking once they started questioning him. I think he's basically a decent man who fell head over heels for Kim and got caught up in her maelstrom. Like her, he was desperate to get away from the claustrophobic setup at Low Lake and she showed him a way.'

'Steve was always such a straightforward, boring bloke,' North said. 'I rarely heard him make any conversation and then it was usually about exhaust systems or oil changes.'

Swift tilted his head. 'Those drawings in the treehouse showed another side to Steve, an edge, a bitter slow-burning resentment. He might have seemed like a dull mechanic but he had imagination too. That can be dangerous.'

'Imagination and falling in love for the first time. That's a big deal.' Bella clapped her hands together.

Swift nodded. 'Steve said that falling in love was like a chemical reaction.'

Beside Bella, North sank back in the sofa. She glanced anxiously at him, then at Swift.

'What about Ben? Any news on him?'

'Not yet.'

'Did Kim kill Pete Hussain?'

'She was party to it. She left the actual disposal to Steve. I thought Pete would be in the canal but the police recovered his body from the River Lea. Kim pumped Pete full of a cocktail of drugs from his own stash and Steve drove him to Enfield Lock. His death was planned, so unlike with me, they'd had the time and presence of mind to weigh him down and he drowned.'

'I can't believe they thought they'd get away with it,' Bella said.

'They could have. Kim never thought that anyone would look into her supposed death several years on. She must have felt secure. She acknowledged as much to me. Then, when Pete Hussain told her I was asking questions she thought I was the big threat. But in fact, Hussain filled that role. If he hadn't seen her by chance and noted the address she gave him, she and Steve could still be living in Little Venice with Kim pursuing her career as Marie.'

North was staring at the floor. 'Maybe if you kill once, it's easier to do it the next time.'

'I think there is some truth in that. Luckily, we're wired to be compassionate but when that goes wrong . . .' Swift shrugged.

'If we were being kind, we might say it could all be traced back to her childhood,' Bella said. 'She didn't get much compassion from her mother, did she? She had an early brush with death.'

'I don't buy into that,' North said sadly.

'No, I don't either,' Swift added. 'There are reasons for behaviour but not excuses.' Sadie Stanley must be having a field day, he thought. Low Lake would be ringing with talk about bad blood and unheeded predictions of disaster. 'I didn't take to Gill Ramsay but this will be a lot to recover from. Kim dead, one son dead, another facing prison. Not quite the compact family unit she persuaded herself she had established.'

'I had an email from her,' North said. 'It was so awful I deleted it. She was blaming me for everything. She said she never wanted to see me again.'

'She's grieving, Jack. She's angry,' Bella said. 'But, you know, it might be best not to go back to Low Lake anyway. Best to stay away from the memories. Put it behind you.'

North didn't look convinced. Swift suspected that he might be drawn back there eventually, dogged by regrets. North's phone buzzed. He was on call and said he had to go and see to a hamster with a damaged eye. Swift saw him to the door. Rain was falling, dark and misty.

'I still find it hard to believe that the Kim I knew could have done all that,' North said, looking up at Swift as if beseeching him to say that it had all been a terrible mistake.

'Probably best to try and remember Kim's warmth and her fondness for you,' Swift suggested. He watched the little man go to his car with his swinging walk, knowing that the crimes would always overshadow the girl who had been thoughtful and generous. He went back inside and slumped down on the sofa.

'You look worse for wear,' Bella said.

'I'm okay. I've been better, though. It would be nice not to wake up aching. On the plus side, my parasite seems to have died off.'

She dipped into her bag and pulled out a bottle of rum. 'Fancy a hot spiced rum? I make a mean one. It will kill or cure you.'

'Go on, then. I'll make-believe it's medicine. It's an evening for it.'

As they sipped their drinks, Bella gestured at the fireplace.

'Lovely, having a real fire. Reminds me of childhood and my gran's house.'

'Hmm. It's cosy.'

The faint notes of a trumpet came from next door.

'I'm not sure the soundproofing works,' Swift said. 'Although I can't tell the tune.'

Bella put a hand behind an ear. 'I think it might be "Waterloo Sunset."'

'You've got better hearing than me.'

'Ty, I know this is a terrible thing to say, but I'm glad that Kim died. If she hadn't, I think Jack might have been visiting her in prison for years to come. She'd still have had a hold on him. At least he can let her go now. Mourn her properly.'

Swift nodded. The only death he truly cared about was Ben's, because he had known and liked him and he felt that he had contributed to it. He sipped the delicious rum and watched the blue and orange flames of the fire. He was dimly aware of the doorbell.

'I'll get it if you like. You're half asleep.'

Bella went to the front door, and he heard voices. He opened his eyes and turned to see Nora standing in the doorway, rain dripping from her hood with Bella behind her, biting her lip. Nora took a step into the room. He saw her take in the glasses, the fire, and the lamplight.

'This is nice. The glow of the fire, a warming drink, good company. You must be feeling better. There was me, thinking you might be on your own and a bit feeble and in need of cheering up. Ah well, I see I was wrong — again.'

'I was going to ring you later,' he said, standing up. 'I wanted to make an arrangement for your birthday. A lot has happened.' The words sounded unconvincing.

'Yes, that's true. And most of it behind my back. Well, I don't want to intrude.'

'Of course you're not intruding. I'm glad you're here. We were just going over what happened in the Kim Woodville case. Stay and have a drink. Bella's made hot rum if you'd like one.'

'Has she? She's fierce at home here by the looks of it. Playing the hostess and all, busying herself in the kitchen. Quite the domestic goddess. Too much competition for me. I don't think I'll accept the invitation.' She zipped up her coat and stuck her hands in her pockets. 'I wanted to say hallo, make my peace, see how you were. But I shouldn't just drop by. It doesn't seem to go well. I suppose the two of you are conducting more in-depth research. I'll leave you to it.'

'Nora, please . . .'

She put a hand up. 'I'm never an unwanted guest. Save your breath.'

She turned and stamped away. Bella stood rooted to the spot, biting her lip. The door slammed.

Swift sank onto the sofa. 'What is it with Nora? It's as if she's setting out to distrust me.'

'I'm so sorry,' Bella said. 'Nora can certainly do sarcasm.'

'She has a gift for it. It can be entertaining if you're not on the receiving end.'

'I'm sorry, Ty. That's the last thing you needed.'

'You don't need to be sorry. Not your fault. Sit down and finish your drink.'

'No, it's okay. I think it's better if I head off now.'

'In case Nora's conducting a surveillance operation to check whether or not you leave tonight?'

She blushed. 'I've things to do for work. You should get some sleep.'

'That's true.'

Bella let herself out. The distant tune played on next door, like a ghost trumpet. He stared at the fire for a while, and then rang Nora.

'Yes?' she said curtly.

'There's nothing between Bella and me. If you'd arrived earlier her flatmate, Jack North, would have been with us too. North employed me. We were discussing the resolution of the case. Bella just happened to stay on for a while.'

'You make it sound so credible, but it's really a bit hard to believe. I've seen you together twice now. It didn't take you long to move on, did it? You know, when you told me that Ruth wouldn't be living upstairs I was so relieved. I really thought we had a chance. Fat chance!'

'Nora, you're being ridiculous. Bella's a friend from the past and I only met her again because of this case.'

'Don't tell me I'm being ridiculous. I know what I saw.'

'No, that's the point. You've got it wrong. You've seen something and jumped to the wrong conclusion. You're just being difficult—'

'Oh, please! Listen to the man who wanted to move his ex in and then sits all huggermugger with yet another woman. And I'm the difficult one! I don't know how you find time to fit in any work at all with the juggling of your romantic interests. You must be one of those multitaskers.'

'Nora, please listen to me.'

'No, *you* listen. A colleague showed me a photo on some trashy newspaper website yesterday. You and your friend Bella on your front doorstep in the early morning, looking fierce bleary-eyed and shifty. She's all doe-eyed and shagged-out looking. Must have been quite a night. So, you know, you're bang to rights. That awkward stuff called visual evidence. I called round earlier to see what you'd have to say about it. What lies you'd tell me.'

'I can explain that. We got drunk and it was late . . .'

She snorted. 'Yeah, I can imagine. Spare me the details! You and your explanations, you've always got one, haven't you? You're a smooth talker, I'll give you that. You always sound so bloody plausible but you don't fool me. The trouble with you is you don't know who or what you want.'

'Well, you clearly don't seem to want me. Apart from a brief phone call and a quick visit to disapprove of me, you haven't been near me since someone tried to finish me off.'

'Oh, don't try playing the "poor me" sympathy card just because I've caught you out. That's really low.'

'You've got to be joking. I wouldn't bother looking for sympathy from you.'

'No need. You get plenty from the slinky Bella by the looks of it. Hot rum and hot everything else. She's welcome to you.'

Swift ended the call, threw the phone down and kicked the coffee table. Then he made himself another hot rum. It didn't taste as good as Bella's. As he turned back to the sofa, he saw that she had left her briefcase on one of the dining chairs. He had just picked up his phone to call her, when the doorbell rang.

It was Bella, holding her coat collar close to her neck. There was a bright full moon overhead. The rain slanted silver behind her.

'My briefcase. I left it. I'm so bloody stupid. I need some papers in it for tomorrow.' She was panting slightly.

'I know, I just spotted it.'

329

'I was on the Tube when I realised. I was worried you'd have gone to bed already. I ran back from the station.' She laughed, then shivered and stamped her feet.

Her hair was burnished in the moonlight, and drops of rain glistened on the ends. She was smiling at him. He remembered that smile on a pillow, her face turned to him, the thin mattress shaking with her laughter. The second rum was making the world seem so much better.

He held the door wider. 'It's late and filthy. Why don't you come in? Why don't you stay?'

* * *

In the garage, Swift boxed up the boat roof rack that he had bought for Nora's birthday. It went back fairly neatly into its original packaging. His arms protested at the effort and he swallowed a painkiller. He thought of how he had planned to show her the boat rack in situ and take her out for the day on the River Wey in Surrey. He sighed, shook his head. Now Nora could sell it on eBay if she wanted. He put a card in with it for her.

Happy Birthday. This is your present, for exploring other waterways. I hope you like it and have good times with it. It fits on any car, so you'll be fine with it.

You don't trust me. I wish you could. I'm sorry.

Ty

He'd done what she suspected him of now. He was as guilty as she'd made him out to be. It seemed that their relationship had failed its MOT. He sealed the box, wishing he could leave his regrets inside. It wasn't that simple. He stood at the garage door, waiting for the parcel courier to arrive, watching the world go by. His phone rang.

DI Baptiste's treacle tones. 'How are you doing?'

'Much better, thanks.'

'You disobeyed orders but you brought in the two runaways so respect for that.'

'I wasn't aware that you gave me orders.'

She laughed. 'I like your nerve, Swift. It rubs me up the right way. Just thought I'd let you know, Elaine Dunbar has talked, finally. Through gritted teeth and rather haughtily. She's obviously used to having the highest status in the room. But she faltered when we told her about the treasure trove of deleted emails we found on her hard drive. She started her illegal trading long before Kim stumbled over it. There might be stuff going way back, from other sites she's managed. I'd say she started building her personal fortune early in her career. We know she sold a Roman clasp and a brooch, something called a fibula, about ten years ago. They went to Vancouver for 900k. Then there were two coins that Kim tracked. One went to Argentina, the other to Moscow. She made over a million on the deals. We're still doing the sums. She says she gave Kim 700k.'

'Enough to buy a small flat in London and have a money cushion in the bank.'

'Nice. It will take a while to track how Elaine handled the money. She's holding out on that. We think we're on to an account in the husband's name in the British Virgin Islands. And moving on to him, we've found Ben's killer.'

'Dunbar killed Ben?'

'He confessed late yesterday. Cried his eyes out. I had to get another box of tissues.'

'What tipped him into telling you?'

'Forensics found minute traces of Ben's blood on his shoes. And Claire, the cleaner at the museum, was very useful when she got back from her holiday with her lovely tan.'

'What was his motive? Had Ben found out something about Elaine's illegal trade?'

'No, nothing to do with that directly, although Dunbar worried that it might lead there. He had his own secret. She's called Adela Janssens.'

Swift sat on the car bonnet. 'Adela? That never crossed my radar.'

'Hadn't crossed anyone's. They were as careful as Kim and Steve at staying low-key. Dunbar really hates you, you know. He spat when he said your name. For a mild kind of bloke, he certainly got worked up about you.'

'Did I stir things best left unstirred?'

'Exactly.'

'And presumably Ben was part of the stirring?'

'He went to the Bickmore Museum asking questions and met Claire of the lovely tan. She does another part-time job in a hotel near Oxford. She told Ben that she'd seen Phil Dunbar and Adela in there one afternoon about three months ago. He had his arm around her and they were checking in. Claire's lived in Great Howe all her life and she knew Adela from when she stayed at Low Lake. She didn't give it much thought at the time. She just wanted to get on with her work and mind her own business. But Ben's questions triggered her memory. Of course, Ben could never keep anything to himself for long. He went to see Dunbar and asked him about it. Dunbar told him that he and Adela being lovers had nothing to do with Kim's death, but Ben said you needed to know. He told Dunbar he was going to visit you on the Saturday afternoon. Being Ben, he created some drama around it. He rang Adela as well, got her all worked up and she hurried over to talk to Dunbar.'

Swift could imagine Ben talking about witnesses and evidence, alarming them both. 'If only Ben had just emailed me with what he'd found out. At face value, it was hardly that important. His death might have been avoided.'

'Yes, probably. He was too keen on whipping up the suspense. All those films he'd watched. Dunbar was furious at Ben. He was steadily siphoning money from an account he had with Elaine to fund a future with Adela. He'd been seeing her since before Kim died. He was planning to leave Elaine and move in with Adela when he had enough in the bank. Adela knew nothing about Elaine's thefts and Dunbar wanted to keep it that way.'

Ah, Swift thought, *clever Adela. Carving her pumpkins, carving her plan. She deliberately misled me about that talk at the museum when she said Valery was eyeing Dunbar. She made sure I was looking in the wrong direction.*

'And then Ben came muscling in and meddling and potentially upsetting all his plans.'

'Correct. The relationship with Adela was going to be blown out of the water and years of planning with it. And Dunbar was frantic that once you heard and asked more questions, the link to Elaine's trading might start unravelling and the whole lot would explode in their faces. That man Dunbar hates his wife almost as much as you. I'm amazed that she never noticed, except that she seems to be a complete narcissist. He was at her beck and call for years. He said that she treated him like a worm, but the worm finally turned. He wanted his money's worth for all the years of misery with her before he told her he was leaving.'

'So he decided that he had to shut Ben up.'

'From his point of view there was no other option. He took a decorative garden stone, a plastic bag and tape from his workplace and put them in a rucksack. He knew that Ben would cycle to the station when he was heading to see you so he waited for him on the road. He offered him a lift, saying that he wanted to travel with him to London to meet you and explain about him and Adela. Ben said yes, not knowing that he'd stirred a very deep pot and how much was at stake for Dunbar. Dunbar's plan, such as it was, was to kill Ben somewhere on the way and dispose of the body and the bike. So Ben's bike went in the boot of Dunbar's car.'

'So how did they end up here?'

'By then, you'd texted Ben. He told Dunbar you were out until the evening but there was a decorator in your house who could let him in. Dunbar began to play with the idea of Ben's body being found in your house. He liked it. Liked what he saw as justified payback for your prying and meddling in his life. It would put you in your place, cause a lot of mayhem. You'd be a suspect. You'd be put through the mill.'

'It was all highly risky. He could easily have been seen.'

'Yeah, well, he's not a born killer and he didn't have much time to plan. He was making it up as he went along. Just a man caught up between a rock and a hard place, as he saw it. It was all pretty amateur but Dunbar was winging it at that point. I think he was excited too, pumped up with adrenalin and the thrill of being clever. Cleverer than you. And he was a bit feverish about everything going belly up, and in a real fury with you.

'He parked in a street parallel to yours. On the way to your house, Ben said he wanted chocolate and nipped into a corner shop. Dunbar told him he'd see him at the house. He walked on and spotted Vlad going next door and leaving your front door open. He entered your place, did a quick recce and found that the top flat was open. He waited at the top of the stairs and called to Ben when he arrived. Ben went up. Dunbar hit him with the stone and taped the bag around his head. He's a strong bloke despite his droopy appearance, used to hefting stuff at the garden centre, so it didn't take him long to shove Ben in the wardrobe and leave. He chucked the bike into a hedgerow just north of London on his way back.'

'Did Adela know about any of this?'

'No. Well, Dunbar says not and she claimed she didn't. I believed her. She looked genuinely shocked. She said Dunbar had told her he had to find the right time to leave Elaine as she could be very vindictive and he didn't want Adela exposed to that. Amazing how intelligent people swallow lies they want to hear.' Baptiste chuckled. 'He's a curiously old-fashioned man at times. Likes to see himself as Adela's knight in shining armour. Said something along the lines of wanting to shield her from any unpleasantness. As if murder was nothing more than a disagreeable episode.'

'Ben didn't die directly because of Kim, then.'

'No, he stumbled over something different. Different but linked. It was the connection to the money and the stolen artefacts that killed him. It's his funeral next week. Are you going?'

'I don't think the family would appreciate my attendance.'

She chuckled. 'No, I suppose you're right. All the poisonous stares might kill you.'

'Or Sadie Stanley might stick one of her hair grips in me.'

'Painful. I'll get our tape removed from your house sometime this week so you can have your home back. Look after your crypto thing.'

The courier van arrived as the call ended. Swift handed the parcel over and watched it depart. His phone pinged with a text from Bella.

Last night was lovely. Hope you're feeling okay after your exertions. You did well for a man who's been bashed about. I've got a spring in my step. Come to mine for dinner Saturday, about 8. I'll make something light. Jack's going to see friends in Liverpool for a couple of days so we'll have the place to ourselves x

He texted back.

It was lovely. And I don't think I told you any of my woes this time around. That was a relief for you. See you Saturday x

He locked the garage and walked down to the river. The waters were black and full under a muddy sky. He leaned on the parapet, watching them glide, then took his solicitor's letter from his pocket and opened it. The breeze caught at it as he read. A date had been set in January for a hearing about Cedric's will. Something to look forward to in the New Year. He shoved it back in his jacket.

It occurred to him that if Kim had died intestate, her property and any money she had might go to her mother as next of kin. The courts might try to retrieve some of it but that would be a difficult process and they probably wouldn't bother. He could only smile at the irony of Paula moving in to Little Venice, thrilled at having a posh flat and a plump bank account. If the dead could have seizures, Kim would succumb to one. Gill would be furious and Sadie would have plenty to say about ill-gotten gains.

In the end, he thought, it had all come down to greed and money.

He sniffed the breeze and suddenly remembered that he hadn't yet returned Joyce's call. He groaned. It would mean explaining about Nora and why she wouldn't be coming to dinner. Maybe if he left it long enough, Joyce would be away on a cruise again. She'd mentioned going to the subantarctic islands. He'd wing it for another couple of days.

Right now, he was hungry and needed a beer. Milo might be in the Silver Mermaid. He'd go there and raise a glass or two to Ben and Cedric.

THE END

Thank you for reading this book. If you enjoyed it please leave feedback on Amazon, and if there is anything we missed or you have a question about then please get in touch. The author and publishing team appreciate your feedback and time reading this book.

Our email is office@joffebooks.com

www.joffebooks.com

ALSO BY GRETTA MULROONEY

ARABY
MARBLE HEART
OUT OF THE BLUE
COMING OF AGE
LOST CHILD

TYRONE SWIFT BOOKS
THE LADY VANISHED
BLOOD SECRETS
TWO LOVERS, SIX DEATHS
WATCHING YOU
LOW LAKE

46562730R00204